Winds

of Change

CAROLE EGLASH-KOSOFF

WINDS OF CHANGE

by

Carole Eglash-Kosoff

Published by:

Valley Village Publishing

www.ValleyVillagePublishing.com

Cover Design and Illustration by:
Barbara Kosoff • BarbaraKosoff.com

10-Digit ISBN: 0-9839601-0-0
13-Digit ISBN: 978-0-9839601-0-2

Printed in the United States of America

I found **Winds of Change** to be very adventurous as well as a wonderfully accurate historical novel. This book is truly a masterpiece. The language used is exquisite, the characters well drawn and believable. Carole Eglash-Kosoff kept me in suspense and involved me in the lives of the characters by using highly developed visual imagery in her writing style. This book displays how families from different cultures and values lived in the rural South, having diversities in people not generally accepted.

Winds of Change truly brings the terrors of the Spanish-American War, World War I and deathly activities to light as one can virtually feel the characters' pain. But the beauty of the writer's language pulls the reader on, no matter how horrific the circumstances became.

Carole Eglash-Kosoff makes it easy to understand and appreciate the generations of not-so-long-ago. I loved reading her book, allowing myself to step back in time to "savor" the home-cooked Southern meals and "hear" the heavily accented Southern folks talking to one another throughout her excellent descriptions.

Pacific Book Review, August 2011

Dedication

This book, like the other two I've written, deals with injustice. It may never disappear from the human condition but I dedicate this book to all those who devote their lives to eradicate it whenever it rears its ugliness.

Carole Eglash-Kosoff

The Civil War had ended, and for more than a decade a wave of equality spread across the states that had formed the Confederacy under the protection of 200,000 Union soldiers. Black legislators were elected and equitable laws passed. Children of all races were educated and minority businesses flourished.

In 1877 Rutherford B. Hayes withdrew all troops from Confederate soil, as he had promised Southern White democrats he would do, to secure his Presidency and resolve the election impasse between him and Samuel Tilden, the Democratic nominee. Old attitudes resurfaced as Rebel flags were raised once again, not in battle, but heralding the return of White superiority. New and expanded Jim Crow laws were passed, Ku Klux Klan membership increased, and racial blockades that prohibited Black families from leaving the south followed. Thousands of Blacks were beaten or lynched without trials, and the states that had abandoned the Union now successfully deprived Negros of their civil rights

The decades that followed were filled with a unique American energy. Railroads continued to expand westward. The Patent Office was busy registering new inventions that fueled the industrial revolution. America was becoming increasingly urbanized and moving vast resources from the land to the factory.

The 14th, 15th and 16th Amendments, which had been passed during the Civil War to guarantee equal protection to people of all races, were being successfully challenged in state courts throughout the old Confederacy. Racial mixing would not be permitted. Separate schools and churches were becoming obligatory and separate train cars and eating facilities were becoming mandatory for Blacks and Whites.

Hayes was succeeded in 1880 by James Garfield but four months after taking office the new President was assassinated by a crazed and frustrated office seeker who thought he'd been wronged. His Vice-President, Chester A. Arthur took over the reins. Arthur, a Union Army General, was more interested in reforming the Civil Service system of the Federal Government than in taking any action to defend the new Amendments against the South's Jim Crow laws. In the nation's new racial consciousness he also signed a Bill making it impossible for any Chinese immigrants to become citizens.

Another blow to racial equality in the south came in 1883 when the Ku Klux Klan Act, that had been passed in 1871 to fight the organized *violence of whites against blacks, was overturned by the Supreme Court decision averring that the Federal Government had no right to interfere with state activities. Racial policies, henceforth, would be matters for states to deal with and of no interest to the Federal government. 'Separate but Equal' became a government mantra in facilities that were rarely equal.*

A new century dawned and the United States, now one hundred million souls spanning the continent, embarked on a time of great changes. It was the era of Andrew Carnegie, John D. Rockefeller, William Randolph Hearst, Thomas Edison and the Wright brothers. It was the time of Emily Dickenson, Scott Joplin and nickelodeons. It was the time of one of the worst economic depressions in the country's history. It was not a time of racial harmony.

Within a decade war spread across Europe as countries found new ways to kill. Arsenals now included tanks, airplanes and gas warfare. Americans were called on to enlist in the struggle but a racist mind set continued to separate white from black.

Prologue

There is a dance that accompanies the rhythm of our lives. It has a logic...a pattern...a beat. Different sections of the orchestra blending into a single melody that defines who we are. I'm a man; you're a woman. I'm white. I'm tall. I'm a Christian. And then... wait a minute. It seems I'm not white. I have some Negro blood coursing through my veins that I'd never known about. The beat of the music suddenly changes as one section, maybe the woodwinds, puts their instruments away. The new rhythm is discordant...a rhythm with which I'm unfamiliar. It's a different tune, a genre I don't know how to play. I've lost the beat. The other orchestra members are staring at me in a different way.

I'm not sure what it all means. This isn't the South. It's already 1883. Slavery's been gone for nearly twenty years and the country has moved forward. I had a baby sister who was born colored. I'd never known and it's interesting, but it happened too long ago for me to feel sad. She died, my parents are both dead, and I'm still me. But that's the problem. In my head I suddenly feel like a different me.

My name is Josiah Rogers. My father and two generations before him grew cotton and got quite wealthy off the back-breaking work of the slaves they owned. Apparently my grandmother, my father's mother, had a black parent and no one knew it until a sister of mine, who I'd never been told about, was born chocolate brown. Amy, my aunt, and the woman who raised me after my parents died, understood that I could spawn such a child and I deserved to know that I had black blood in me. I had so many questions that evening she told me and yet there was nothing I could ask. I kissed her on the cheek, grabbed my jacket and my trumpet, and walked out of the apartment. Nothing was very clear those next hours. I remember sitting on the wharf and watching the last of the sun fall into the Pacific and a few remaining fishing boats pull into San Francisco's harbor. I remember walking through a cloak of evening fog, seeing buildings and people come into view like unearthly spirits and then vanish again. I found an array of tiny North Beach bars, picked one at random, and took a seat with a few tired musicians still blowing their horns. I pulled out my trumpet. I have no idea what I played or where I was.

We were a family of four. Amy held us together. Her daughter, Bess, was a few years younger than me. She had her mother's beautiful red hair and a face full of freckles set atop two deep dimples. Bess' father had been a career Union Army officer until he was killed in some battle with rebellious Indians. She had her father's height and gentle nature, which was good, because Amy was definitely not a laid back soul.

The last of our quartet was Stephen, my sort-of brother. He was the son of Amy's closest friends, the Carmodys, from when she lived near Baton Rouge. They had been slaughtered by Klan members in the same race riot that killed my father. Stephen and I are the same age. He's colored…really light-skinned, handsome, with blue-green eyes that always sparkle, but definitely colored. Girls, white and black, hover around him like lemmings. His color never made any difference to us but he occasionally felt the sting of some ignorant bigot and I know their slurs hurt him. He and Bess are in love. We all know it. Amy knows it as well and while she never speaks against it, it's clear that the intensity of their feelings make her very nervous. She does everything reasonable, and sometimes unreasonable, to keep them apart. Her efforts have only succeeded in bringing them closer together. Their young raging hormones have not only connected, they've intertwined.

We received a phone call from San Francisco General, the hospital where Amy worked as a nurse. She was dead. She had caught an infection from one of her patients and before anyone even knew she was ill, she was gone.

Our anchor, the glue that held us together, had died.

Chapter One

The three of them sat, stunned and inert, in their small San Francisco apartment around the corner from Kearny Street. The city's omnipresent summer fog blanketed everything outside their window in an eerie epitaph. Stephen called in sick to the Examiner, the newspaper where he worked. Bess called in sick to Granger's bank where she was a teller. Josiah didn't need to call in anywhere. He wasn't working regularly. He was a pretty fair trumpet player but jobs for pretty fair trumpet players were scarce these days.

They laughed a little as they struggled to lift their spirits by recalling some of the silly things that had happened through the years.

"I remember leaving Louisiana and all of us traipsing half way across the country to San Francisco because Amy told us we should," Josiah recalled. "She was our aunt, our mother, and our Pied Piper."

Bess' tears flowed openly while Stephen and Josiah struggled to maintain a minimal masculine grace. Stephen sat down next to Bess and put his arms tightly around her. She nestled in the crook of his arm and bawled…deep sobs. For a long while her sobs were the only sounds in the room.

"My mother can't be gone. Stephen, it must be a mistake. Let's call the hospital again."

"It's not a mistake, Bess. It was Susan who called me…Amy's best friend. No one knew she was sick and then they found her, collapsed. They couldn't revive her. My heart is as torn as yours, darling. We'll get through this. Together the three of us will be there for one another. We all loved her."

By the third bottle of wine they were trying to decide what to do next. What does one do when your compass falls overboard or fails to point to magnetic north? They were adults but they weren't used to making decisions without Amy to counsel them. They finally fell asleep on the couch, Stephen's arm still wrapped tightly around Bess.

The next morning, their three heads pounding and their bodies stiff from sleeping in uncomfortable positions, Josiah fixed coffee while Bess started to go through her mother's personal belongings. There, hidden where it would clearly be found, was a letter she'd written. It was undated but the paper was so yellowed on the corners it was easy to conclude that it had been written some time ago.

> *My dear loved ones,*
>
> *If you're reading this you have either been digging through my personal belongings or I've passed on. It's not fair of me to do this to you and I hope that you will forgive me. I would like to be buried at Moss Grove. There is a particular magnolia tree near the river that has a great deal of significance for me. I know the trip will inconvenience you but it will give you an opportunity to meet the people who meant so much to me during my life.*
>
> *It will be a return to where each of you spent your younger childhood. Eli Fineman, his wife, Ruth, and their children, still call the plantation, Moss Grove, their home. Contact them…they will know what to do.*
>
> *I leave you in the hands of God and one another. They will all serve you well during your life.*
>
> *Your Amy*

It was Amy's last request and they couldn't deny the woman who had dedicated so much of her life to them. It took nearly two weeks to make all the necessary arrangements. Bess and Stephen both got condolences on their loss from people they worked with and were given leaves of absence. Josiah had no one who cared.

They closed up the apartment and climbed aboard a train heading east. It was far more comfortable than the one that had brought them west more than a decade earlier. No one spoke much during the trip. They were still overwhelmed by the sudden change in their lives. Stephen and Bess held tight to one another and now that Amy was gone, the impediment to their getting married was gone.

You could still see the last of the snows melting into the Truckee River as the train chugged its way from the heights of California down into Nevada and beyond. From the train's grime covered windows they watched horses carrying men and goods moving toward Carson City and the silver mines that lay scattered like gopher holes across the land.

After several days, and numerous train connections, they reached Natchez where they rented a wagon and headed south. They passed the first cotton plantations they'd seen since Amy had carted three children out west more than a decade earlier.

There were new unfamiliar types of equipment plowing the dark brown earth but the bent over sweaty black backs toting long bags hadn't changed. Smoke wafted from the tiny cabins and small dark-skinned children ran in and out of the jeans and cotton dresses hanging from the clotheslines. The war had allowed blacks and coloreds to be free men but, in fact, their lives had scarcely changed.

They swung their wagon up the long well-tended pathway protected by towering oak trees. Josiah's grandfather had planted them all a half-century earlier, building a cotton plantation from scrub and marsh land. They approached Moss Grove's main house and a shiver ran through Josiah's body as memories of his childhood overwhelmed his body. Bess sensed it and clasped his hand. Stephen held her other hand. It was an uneasy step into the past for each of them.

Eli and Ruth Fineman were waiting at Moss Grove's front portico as their wagon pulled to a stop. Two handsome young adults stood next to their parents, the entire Fineman family smiling warmly at their arrival. Mr. and Mrs. Fineman looked older, grayer hair… less tone in their demeanor. Stuart, their son, was barely recognizable. The lanky boy they'd played with had grown into a tall oak, his near black hair flowing while he sported a carefully trimmed mustache. Stuart's eyes twinkled as he clasped Josiah's shoulder affectionately. They had been close boyhood playmates getting into all sorts of trouble. But it was his sister, Rachel, who took Josiah's breath away. Stuart saw his eyes lock on her and laughed.

"She's too old to have her hair pulled, I think," Stuart laughed.

"Rachel, hello," Josiah stammered.

"Hello, Josiah," she said, in a soft voice that matched the sultriness of her purple eyes. Her cream complexion and full lips were framed by dark hair formed into long loose curls that cascaded down around her bare shoulders.

"Bess! How good to see you all again. You have your mother's beauty," Rachel said, sliding easily across the porch and extending her arms in greeting.

"And Stephen, you are quite dashing. I would venture you have left a trail of broken hearts in San Francisco."

"We are so shocked to hear of Amy's death. She was a unique woman and we all loved her very much. But your journey has been a long one. We will all have time to reacquaint ourselves. Take some time to settle in your rooms and get comfortable," Ruth Fineman interjected.

Moss Grove lies just north of Baton Rouge in Louisiana's lush fertile cotton growing area. Josiah's father, Henry Rogers, like his father and grandfather before him, oversaw the plantation along the Mississippi river where his cotton could be easily shipped and black slave labor was plentiful. The Civil War brought an end to men being able to own other men but the economic realities of life returned many freed slaves to the same harsh work and similar poverty, now as share croppers.

Josiah found himself wandering the rooms he'd haunted as a young child. He imagined hearing the voice of his father shouting instructions to his overseer, or the thinness of his mother's voice, overwhelmed with the task of organizing the kitchen or managing the household staff. She always seemed to speak in a high pitched beseeching fashion, he recalled.

He walked outside to the small family cemetery and stood in front of the marble headstones that marked the graves of his mother, Elizabeth, and his father, Henry. Josiah was a young boy when his mother died and his only recollection of her was as someone who always sublimated herself to her husband. It eventually drove her to overdose on laudanum, and when she died, he remembered being sent away to a boarding school. His father's personality, on the other hand, dominated everyone who crossed his path.

Henry Rogers, 1835 - 1873
Soldier, Husband, & Father

The brevity of an inscription doesn't tell very much about a man's life, does it? So many memories! Josiah knew that his father had been a Captain in the Confederate Army. An artillery shell had taken off his arm and nearly cost him his eyesight as southern forces vainly made their last stand against a Union flotilla moving up the Mississippi River, making it impossible for the Confederacy to move supplies or sell its cotton. Thaddeus, then a young runaway slave from Moss Grove and who, coincidentally, was fighting in that same battle, saved his father's life and brought him back through enemy lines here to Moss Grove.

Years earlier, when Henry Rogers was in his teens, he'd raped a young slave girl who was picking cotton in the fields. Nine months later she gave birth to Thaddeus, a mixed race infant. Josiah's father always hated seeing the boy, a reminder of his youthful impropriety, but there he was, a colored son, sharing the same icy blue eyes as the father who sired him and his legitimate son.

Thaddeus and his son, Robert, had come to Moss Grove for Amy's funeral, as well, traveling from their home just outside Washington D.C. Thaddeus was older, his hair more than a little speckled with grey, but his electric blue eyes shined as bright as they had when we'd first met nearly twenty years earlier. Josiah was a sad young toddler before he understood that he and Thaddeus were half-brothers, but it wasn't until Amy's revelation that he understood that they both had colored blood in their veins as well.

A light breeze began to rise off the Mississippi River, not too far away, tiny white caps breaking the surface. The late afternoon sun was drifting lazily down toward the western river banks and the voices of the early evening birds broke the silence. A horned owl picked up the rhythm and one could feel a chill from the approaching evening. Josiah couldn't move. He remained frozen in front of his father's headstone, his thoughts locked in the past.

Amy's funeral was the next day. The sun came out and cast its glow on Amy's special magnolia tree as the Reverend spoke. The cicadas sang a soft dirge, accented by the occasional whistle from a paddle wheeler moving north or south on the nearby Mississippi. Josiah took out his trumpet when the service was finished and played some of the songs she'd love most to hear, including 'Everyday 'll be Sunday By and By.' Their hearts were empty as four strong Negro sharecroppers eased the casket bearing this woman they loved, slowly into the ground. Tears flowed freely as they hugged one another but there was nothing to say. Eventually all they could do was remember what Amy had meant to each of them. They drifted toward the house, each carrying heavy burdens of their personal sadness. Everyone except Thaddeus! He sat down under the same magnolia tree, Amy's special tree, his blue eyes red with sadness, lost in his thoughts. They left him there to his solitude and all the personal things that had passed between him and Amy so many years earlier.

The rest of the family wandered through the house recalling moments long forgotten, their conversations brief and in hushed tones until they sat down for dinner. Thaddeus' chair was empty. Everyone assumed he'd returned to his room, exhausted from the trip, and the emotion of the funeral. Eli and Ruth kept looking over at Bess and Stephen. It was impossible not to notice their hand holding, secret looks, and knowing smiles. They were clearly two young people in love. As dinner ended Eli took Stephen and Josiah aside.

"May I speak to you privately?" he asked, ushering them into the library and closing the door.

"Ruth and I have come to the realization that there is a part of your history that was never explained to you."

"If you mean my having colored blood in me," Josiah responded, "that bombshell has already been dropped."

"No, Josiah, although I'm sure that was quite a shock. I'm referring to you, Stephen," he continued.

"I know I'm colored, Mr. Fineman. That's never been a secret; both of my parents were mulatto."

"Let me just blurt it out," Eli said, uncomfortable with the task he'd taken on. "Your parents were not who you were told. The Carmodys agreed to claim you as their son and raise you out of the love they felt for your real parents."

"You're telling me that Rufus and Melanie Carmody were not my parents," Stephen stammered. "That's ridiculous. I know I was pretty young when they were killed but no one ever said anything. And why would Amy drop one bombshell and withhold something so critical?"

"I'm sure she never assumed she would die suddenly, Stephen. She loved you so much, but she kept the secret of your birth out of her love for your birth father," Eli stopped and took a deep breath. He, too, had always been bound to keep their secret. But now, the blatant love Stephen and Bess were displaying left him no option.

"Amy was your mother…Thaddeus is your father! You and Bess are half-siblings."

"Holy shit!" Josiah cried as he and Stephen both sank into deep chairs.

There was silence for a few minutes. Eli wanted to give both of them time to absorb what they'd just been told, particularly Stephen.

"Thaddeus and Amy were emotionally connected from the moment they met as children here at Moss Grove. Amy's family moved here when Baton Rouge was occupied by Union troops early in the Civil War. It would have been too dangerous for them to remain there.

"Thaddeus was being reared as a house slave, the property of the Rogers family. Each of them felt different, and quite alone, until they met. They were drawn to one another and became immediate soul mates. Their feelings never diminished and by the time Thaddeus returned from the Civil War as a Union soldier, no longer a slave, their affections had fully blossomed. They both understood that their sort of a mixed race relationship had no chance, especially here in the south. At some point love overcame caution and Amy became pregnant. She kept it a secret from everyone but her closest friends, Rufus and Melanie Carmody. Thaddeus was never told that he and Amy had conceived a child together."

"And Bess' father, Amy's husband, John Shipley, what did he know?"

"She told John, when he first proposed, that she'd always loved Thaddeus. Obviously he loved her enough to marry her anyway and they had their own special love between them. The same is true of Thaddeus and his wife, Sarah."

"So not only is Bess my half-sister but Robert is my half-brother," Stephen blanched.

"Holy shit," Josiah interjected. "That means we're blood relatives as well."

Stephen looked confused until Eli spoke up.

"He's right. I never made that connection. Josiah's father, Henry, was also Thaddeus' father. It resulted from the bastard's rape of a young slave, Thaddeus' mother."

"Uncle Josiah…I don't think so," Stephen said angrily. "I don't want to believe any of this. I love Bess and she loves me. You have no proof of any of this."

"Perhaps not, but it's true nevertheless. That's why I felt I had to tell you. Marrying Bess would be a sin before God."

"Your God, Eli? Your God isn't my God. You've suddenly decided to reveal a lot of information that's been kept from a lot of people for a long time. Do you think that was fair?" Stephen asked, unsure what type of answer he expected.

"I'm sorry. You have a right to be angry but everything was done out of love. Each of you was loved by both the people who raised you and the people who bore you. Violence interrupted everyone's plans. Rufus and Melanie Carmody were killed. Henry Rogers was killed. John Shipley was killed. And now our Amy is dead. That leaves a lot of ache and sorrow scarring our emotions. I'm sorry but it was their choices to make, not mine."

"Bess, I've just been told we are half-siblings," Stephen said angrily, storming into her room. "It seems that Amy was my mother as well as yours...and Thaddeus was my father. The Carmodys were close friends but they weren't my parents. I don't believe it. People can't keep this kind of information hidden for so long. I don't want to change our lives because of bull shit stories of events that may or may not have happened two decades ago. Marry me! We love one another. Let's complete the formalities."

"I want to. I've always wanted to. But I'm confused. Ruth Fineman spent an hour explaining how terrible it would be if we married...deformed children and such things. I don't know what's right. The only person who can tell us is Thaddeus. He should be able to clarify everything."

Everyone waited with anticipation the next morning at breakfast to see Thaddeus and Robert. There was so much to say, so many questions to ask, so many feelings to unravel. Stephen made it a point to sit as close to Bess as possible. Their hands clasped with one another, their body language shouted that they were in love, consequences be damned. But her eyes were red and it was clear that her outward bravado masked her inner uncertainties.

Robert walked in, but he was alone.

"Where's your father?" Stephen asked.

"Still asleep, I guess. I never saw him last evening. I'm going to check his room. I don't ever remember him sleeping this late."

A few minutes later Robert returned.

"He's not there and his bed hasn't been slept in."

Without a word they all rose and walked toward the river and the magnolia tree under which Amy had been buried. Thaddeus was still sitting on the ground, his head tilted. His eyes were closed and he looked to be asleep…but he wasn't! Sometime during the night he passed on, a serene look on his face. In his hand he was grasping a tiny scribbled note.

Our stars are finally aligned!

"I don't understand," Robert asked as he embraced his father, laying still, a look of serenity on his face.

"Let's bring him in the house. There are things you need to understand," Eli said.

Stephen, Bess and Josiah sat silently as Eli tried, once again, to explain to Robert that his father had another child that no one had known about. Bess listened intently, hoping that hearing the story again would make it easier to understand how her mother, whom she idolized, had a child who she had never been able to openly acknowledge. And that child was the man she'd loved since childhood.

They buried Thaddeus the next day in a plot adjoining Amy's, the woman he loved. A love neither of them was ever able to acknowledge during their lifetime. Bess stayed in her room, emotionally crushed and confused by the revelations that unraveled so much of what she knew about herself. And the man she loved and planned on spending the rest of her life with would never hold her with the intensity she needed…never lie next to her in bed…never make love to her.

Chapter Two

Robert came down to breakfast early. The rays of the morning sun streamed into his room telling him it was morning but he had just tossed most of the night, unable to sleep. Eli had stayed with him into the morning hours relating so much about his father's early years that always been glossed over. Now, his eyes red, he was still struggling to understand the earlier life of a father he thought he'd known. It was so different from anything he and his brother could ever have imagined. His coffee turned cold and he rebuffed the servant's offer to bring him a fresh cup. Tears dried on his cheeks. Stephen walked in and Robert just stared, angry without understanding why, trying to see if he could detect any physical traits that connected them. Stephen was much lighter, a color that might pass easily in the north or the west where people were inclined to be less race sensitive. He did have his father's blue eyes, not quite as intense as his father's or Josiah's but still distinctive.

"I guess we're related," Robert said as Stephen examined the food on the side board.

"I guess we are. With all these revelations I feel like I must be related to half of the state of Louisiana. I don't know how it feels to you but I'm more than a little stunned by these disclosures that deny everything I thought I knew about myself."

"I'm sure. I picked up a brother but you picked up new parents as well."

"I think I also lost the woman I love" Stephen remarked. "I'm told that she's my half-sister but I'm going to need more than an old man's memory of ancient events to convince me. If they're true I've got a father in common with you and a mother in common with her. If it isn't true then someone is playing a very sick joke."

"Bess is very attractive but I don't know if she's related by blood. I do know that the two of you make a stunning couple."

"Thank you," a soft feminine voice remarked.

Both men turned to see Bess enter the dining room.

"It's always a little unsettling when I find two men talking about me."

"We were only saying nice things," Stephen smiled as he walked over, took her hand and planted a kiss on her cheek.

"Well, that's OK then," she said, looking into his eyes. "We'll work it out." She put her hand on his cheek and smiled.

"You need a shave."

He smiled. "It wasn't an important priority since we arrived."

"So, Robert, was all of this a surprise to you, too?" she asked as she poured herself a cup of coffee.

"You need to have known my father in recent years" he said, rising and pouring himself more coffee this time, trying to make sense of his feelings.

"He was an aide to Congressmen and Senators, at least the few Negro ones that could still get elected. He was held in high esteem by many influential people for everything he'd accomplished in his life. And, we always knew him to be completely devoted to our mother. Having another woman in his life…a white woman, casts an entirely new light on this man we all admired."

"Would it have been alright if she had been a black woman?" Bess asked, unsettled by the distinction.

"Let's just say it would have been one less shock. We're talking about a man who was born and grew up as a slave on a cotton plantation where it was common practice to lynch 'niggers' for even looking at a white girl. Maybe it doesn't rise to jail or lynching in California but I assure you that this side of the Mason-Dixon Line such things are treated pretty much the way they were a hundred years ago."

"So, what now?" Stephen asked. "We're told a story that our parents had relations before they got married. He tells me I'm not all mulatto...I'm half mulatto. I don't think that it's going to change the situation that I'm not all white. I wasn't yesterday and I'm not this morning. What I am this morning, however, is a man in love with a woman who could be his half-sister and no way to validate it."

"How about being that woman in love with a man who could be her half-brother?" Bess interjected.

Each of them returned to their own thoughts as a nattily attired servant served them breakfast.

"Are you two returning to San Francisco?" Robert asked, trying to reduce the tension wafting through the room. They had all been snared in a tale of events that were startling to believe.

"I work at a newspaper and Bess works at a bank," Stephen replied. "I suppose we'll continue doing that until we're better able to absorb all these emotional shocks. Thanks to Amy's prudence, at least we're OK financially. I'm not sure what Josiah will decide to do. I don't think his familial relations changed the way ours did, although given what we know about his father, Henry, who I'm now told is my grandfather, there was some real ugliness in those loins."

"Come to Washington. See the country. Meet my brother, Noah. After all, he's also your stepbrother."

"What's he like?" Bess asked.

"He's a few years younger, tall, dark skinned and a talented artist. At least I think so! I'm definitely better looking," Robert laughed easily. My God, he thought, Noah is going to be shocked. He loved our parents as much I did.

"Well, well, a family reunion," Josiah smiled as he entered the room. "How quaint! Trading stories of the family tree, are we? Lots of skeletons?"

"There are a lot of connections, it seems," Robert said, uncomfortable with the acerbic undercurrent of Josiah's tone.

"Let's all hope the Finemans have no more family skeletons to reveal. Our Amy turned out to be quite a vixen. Still waters run deep, I'm told," he said.

"Be a little more sensitive, Josiah. She loved us and cared for us."

"She could have been more forthright, don't you think? You two were her offspring. Aren't you angry she never told you? I'm grateful she cared for me but whatever reasons she had, she's taken them to her grave.

"Anyway, I've decided to remain at Moss Grove, assuming Mr. and Mrs. Fineman don't mind a houseguest for awhile longer. I have nothing waiting for me in San Francisco and there are memories here that I need to sort out. Seeing my parent's graves; remembering my childhood. It's all very unsettling."

"Come back to San Francisco with us for awhile. The three of us have been a family for the past decade. We've lost Amy. I don't want to lose you too," Bess said.

"You two have jobs waiting, I don't. This was my family's home. Moss Grove had always been owned by Rogers. I know it sounds crazy but there is something pulling at me to remain here. I need to figure out what it is."

"I've invited Bess and Stephen to come to Washington. You're welcome, as well," Robert said, sipping his now cold coffee and hoping, for no discernible reason that Josiah wouldn't accept.

"And, are you both going to Washington?" Josiah asked. "We could all leave San Francisco behind. You could start fresh with your new identities."

"We'll see." Stephen said. "Bess and I need to think long and hard about what we've been told and we need to do that away from here. And, my editor at the Examiner has finally allowed me to write a story. It wasn't much but it was a start. I'll try it a little longer. And your teller job, Bess...you can do that anywhere."

"We left too much unresolved in San Francisco to not go back. I may not return to my job but I'm not ready to leave it all behind, not just yet!"

"Eli...Mr. Fineman. I'd like to stay here at Moss Grove a while longer, if you'll allow me," Josiah said, in a voice not quite a statement, not quite a question.

"Ruth and I would be delighted. And I'm sure Stuart and Rachel will be equally pleased. This was your home once; stay as long as you like."

"So much has happened. I'm feeling things about myself I'd never known. I lost Aunt Amy. Thaddeus died. I'd like some time to think through my life."

"I understand. Take your time."

"Stephen and I are leaving tomorrow," Bess said as she and Josiah walked through the flower gardens adjoining the veranda. The roses had not yet bloomed but the scent of the small buds gave a hint of the beauty to come.

"I love this time of year," he mused. "I remember the smells from when I lived here. The cotton blossoms were just getting ready to turn brown and the days were getting longer. I had a hound dog named Whisper. He and I would run between the rows of plants that were beginning to pop fluffy white bolls, trying to avoid their sharp thorns."

Bess watched her friend and listened to him drift back into his childhood days. He'd never spoken much about that time.

"Are you ready to move forward?" Josiah asked, brushing his blond hair from his forehead and bringing himself out of his reverie.

"Probably not, but I'm not ready to stay here any longer, either. This may have been your home but it wasn't mine. And, except for her love for Thaddeus, I don't think my mother ever thought of Moss Grove as her home. Remember, both her parents and her sister died in this house."

Josiah nodded, memories of those events flooding back all too vividly.

"How's your head?" he asked. "You took a pretty good emotional beating this week."

"Yes! Discovering my mother wasn't a saint still roils me. Why do you suppose she never told us?"

"I don't know. I guess we never really know our parents. We always see them as these older authoritarian figures and forget they struggled with their feelings when they were younger, just as we are. She certainly flaunted convention didn't she?"

"I never knew Thaddeus very well and poor Stephen never got to know him at all. They hadn't even met until we all arrived here for Amy's funeral."

"He was a good man, I do remember that much. He and Amy even brought me a dog when my father sent me to Boarding school and wouldn't let me bring Whisper from Moss Grove."

"Will you ever come back to San Francisco?"

"I'm not sure what will happen. I'm just going to take each day. My head is too unsettled to think of the future."

"I wish you'd stay a little longer, Bess," Stuart said as he stood in the open doorway watching her pack.

"You startled me. Come in. I'm just getting a few things organized."

"It's rather strange to see the little girl I threw in the mud so grown and so beautiful."

"I'll bet you say that to all the little girls you threw in the mud," she laughed. "And if I recall correctly, it wasn't just the mud, it was where the pigs laid around."

"You're probably right. I'm surprised that you're still willing to speak to me. I was a terror."

"The plantation looks wonderful, Stuart. You and your family have maintained it as lovely as I remember from years ago."

"Yes, it's done well, mostly due to my father's business skills. Are you going to be alright?" he asked solicitously. "I wanted to hold you close when my father told you all that history about your mother and Thaddeus and learning that Stephen was your half-brother. It's pretty obvious that the two of you are very close."

"Yes! Yes, we were…I mean, we are," she stumbled. "How sure are you of what your father told us?

"He and my mother would have no reason to concoct such a story, Bess. Their memories are quite clear on the subject."

"But Melanie and Rufus were expecting a child. Amy always said so. Then she said they had twins and one of those got killed in that Klan raid. What if that was true and not what your father is telling us now? Then Stephen and I could remain together."

"It isn't true and you'll find someone else. Maybe it's someone you've also known for a long time," Stuart smiled. It was a soft, tender smile.

Bess looked at him and the sadness in her face seemed to ease as she stared into Stuart's face, seeing the man that was no longer the boy with whom she'd frolicked.

"Stuart, are you flirting with me?"

"Absolutely! I didn't want to be too subtle. After all, you are leaving soon unless I'm able to convince you that I can offer you more by staying."

"You are a rogue. A handsome one, I'll admit, but still the troublesome boy I remember."

"Does that mean you'll stay, at least for awhile?"

"No, but I am flattered. I have to return to San Francisco and see if I can sort out the pieces of my life. Stephen and I need to work out how we move forward. Perhaps you'll come visit us?"

"I don't think I want you out of my life again, Bess," he said, more seriously than he intended. "You and I may have unfinished business."

She came close, lifted her head and placed a warm kiss on his cheek. Gently, he turned his head toward hers, looked into her green eyes and put his arms around her. He kissed her, softly, caressingly, as he stroked her hair and their eyes saw one another as man and woman for the first time.

"I'll see you in San Francisco."

Everyone said their goodbyes the next day and Moss Grove returned to its primary task of growing and harvesting cotton.

Josiah wandered those next weeks, watching the men work the fields as the first of the unique hibiscus flowers that would yield cotton began to turn brown and the long days of summer loomed ahead. This year's harvest would be excellent and with cotton prices stable, Moss Grove's profits would be substantial.

Usually Josiah walked but occasionally he borrowed a horse from the many always available at Moss Grove. His memories of being on his father's horse and riding through the fields were the good memories but it was the other recollections that haunted him, the memories of death and abandonment. He grew increasingly angry. He had been cheated of the happy childhood that should have been his.

"You're spending a great deal of time alone," Rachel said, bringing her horse alongside his, early one morning, the trees surrounding them still dripping intermittently from their overnight cache of dew.

"We all thought we'd see a great deal more of you."

"Yes, I'm sorry. I know that Stuart has gone to Chicago on business and I didn't want to be a bother to the rest of you."

"Come, let's ride for awhile. The air isn't always this cool," she said as she kicked her horse into a gallop.

Josiah smiled and followed her. They galloped though the brush and trees for several minutes before she stopped by a small brook and climbed down.

"You ride quite well. I'm not used to seeing women straddle a horse. It seems a little indecent."

"Perhaps I am," she chided.

He sat down next to her and they both remained quiet, watching fish break the surface of the water to snatch a quick meal from the occasional passing fly or gnat.

"How do you feel about younger men?" he asked.

"In general, or did you have someone particular in mind?" she bantered.

"Don't play with me, Rachel. I'm not your kid brother's playmate."

"I know you aren't, Josiah, but we've known each other a long time and my feelings aren't able to transition overnight."

"Fair enough! I find you quite desirable but I don't think I can court you as a southern gentleman might. I'd feel ridiculous."

Rachel started to rise when Josiah grabbed her, brought her back to the ground and took her in a full embrace. He kissed her and found no resistance. When he finally released her they just stared into one another's eyes. She stood, straightened her dress, mounted her horse, and rode off, not looking back.

Josiah smiled at the retreating horse and sat back down. A few minutes later he pulled his trumpet from its ties on the back of the horse and returned to the banks of the brook. He began playing, no song in particular…just playing. He relaxed when he played.

He closed his eyes and thought that it wasn't the mouthpiece of his instrument but Rachel's lips. Makes the notes sweeter, he thought.

On his return he found himself passing near some of the share cropper cottages. He heard the strains of a banjo and stopped. The player was talented…good chords, quick fingering. Josiah didn't want to scare whoever it was. Still on his horse he pulled out his trumpet once again and began to play harmony to the banjo's melody. The playing stopped briefly, as if unsure about the sudden accompaniment, then it began again and the pace of the music quickened. Each man began testing the other. It went on for several minutes before they both stopped. Josiah dismounted, walked around the corner and there he was, a smiling, black, teenage boy the size of a small oak tree.

"Josiah," he said, holding out his hand.

"Edgar," the banjo playing boy responded, his huge paw-like hand swallowing Josiah's.

"How do you play that thing with such big hands? Edgar laughed. "Carefully! I pretend it's a young girl that needs caressing."

"I guess that'll do it."

He began plunking a tune on his banjo that brought a smile to Josiah's face.

"I haven't heard that in years," Josiah said, hitting a few false notes before picking up the melody. The two played enthusiastically, laughing between songs, each one giving the other the courtesy of long riffs. Some of the other sharecroppers gathered around clapping happily to the beat. They didn't stop until it was dark and the crowd began to thin as their evening meals were on the table.

"You're welcome to join me and my folks for a small dinner, Ma always makes extra."

Edgar's parents didn't talk much over the meal. It was clear they were uncomfortable having some white musician chatting with their son and sitting in their small one room cabin.

Stuart Fineman, Eli's son, took Josiah aside a few days later.

"How was Chicago?" Josiah said, lazing around in the early afternoon.

"Chicago was fine. It keeps growing and the acrid smell of the cattle yards fills the air all the way to Lake Michigan. Sometimes we ship cotton up there and it's getting a little more difficult for my father to make the trip, so I go in his stead. You've been OK here it seems. I understand you and one of the young share croppers have been spending a lot of time together. Blacks and whites socializing together, playing music, can cause trouble around here, Josiah."

"Edgar is a good kid, Stuart. We just do it for ourselves."

"He is a nice young man, his parents have been with us a long time, and we want to keep him out of trouble. We'd appreciate it if you didn't do it anymore. White patrols visit the plantations a couple of times a month, without a schedule. Their job is to make sure blacks don't get too uppity."

"Uppity? What does that mean? Slavery is over."

"You've grown up in California. I don't know how things are there but here segregation is the rule, not the exception. Your father was shot when they found out he had a little black blood in him and that was years after the war had ended. You could be endangering both Edgar and yourself."

Josiah decided to leave Moss Grove and visit the school near Baton Rouge that he'd called home for nearly two years after his mother died of an overdose of sadness. He found the building still standing but the shiny dark wood and crisp curtains he remembered were gone, victims of a decade of neglect. Children ran through the halls of this now, rundown, school but no one lived there anymore and the memories of the people and his time there were badly tarnished.

He continued on to New Orleans. He'd never visited the city but as he approached it he could feel the same sense of charming immorality he'd always associated with his own city of San Francisco, a combination of attractive women, a bevy of saloons and restaurants, and a cacophony of languages from visiting ship's crews. It was a city of smells as well as sights, dark coffees, beignets, and the scent of spices from the ports of the world.

He checked into a small hotel on Dauphine Street and just started walking, feeling, as well as seeing, the city. As many people ignored him as looked at him in passing. He saw more mulattos, men, women, and particularly children, than he'd seen in his entire lifetime. Despite what Stuart said about race at Moss Grove, the New Orleans attitude was clearly laissez faire, live and let live. There was music blaring from behind doors, beckoning you in. Several times he tried to join the small groups playing within but to them this young trumpet player was white and they were black. The thought of a white trumpet player sitting in made both the owners and the musicians nervous. It might have been acceptable in California but not here. Each time he'd put his instrument away, finish his drink, salute the band, and leave.

Riding back from New Orleans, Josiah had reached a decision that he would like to remain at Moss Grove. San Francisco was great but it had never been his home, he thought. For good or evil, this was where he belonged.

"Mr. Fineman, I'd like to purchase Moss Grove and return it to the Rogers family. I think I can put together enough money to satisfy you."

"It wouldn't be the money, Josiah, but perhaps I should explain the background on how we got here. When your father was killed, you and Thaddeus, as his two blood children, became the immediate heirs of Moss Grove because neither Elizabeth nor Henry had prepared a Will. Thaddeus decided it shouldn't rightfully be his and he relinquished his ownership. Amy picked you up from your Baton Rouge boarding school and brought you here along with Bess and Stephen. Ruth and I offered to help her manage the plantation. We all lived here together as one large family.

"Amy grew increasingly concerned that someone, someday, would discover you and Stephen had black blood in you and cause trouble. She decided you would all have a better future in California. We purchased Moss Grove from her for a fair price. Now she's dead, Thaddeus is dead, and you have returned. You tell me that you are interested in remaining here. But let me be blunt. Moss Grove's neighbors are not pleased about having a Jewish family owning a significant plantation here along the Mississippi. They would be even less pleased having a person owning it who had colored blood in his veins. They killed your father when they learned he had a black strain and you could face the same risk."

"I can change my name. I wouldn't need to remain a Rogers. I can as easily be a Williams, my mother's maiden name."

"And what would you have me and my family do?"

"Stay for two years. Teach me the intricacies of growing cotton and then retire. Enjoy the rest of your life. You've earned it."

Eli Fineman stared at the young blonde man with the intense blue eyes that pierced into your soul. It was hard to look at him and not see his father, a white bigot who was an evil man. He hoped that Henry Roger's offspring hadn't inherited similar traits.

"I will think on it. I may even ask God's guidance."

A sliver of the moon reflected off the river as eight riders quietly moved through the trees toward the row of shacks lined up forty yards away. As they walked their horses, they neither smoked nor talked. Ten yards from the second shack from the end they stopped and reached into their jackets. One by one they pulled out a large white cloth, stuffed their hats inside the bedroll tied on the back of the horse and donned the cloth that had been shaped into a conical mask with large cutouts for eyes and mouth.

The man in the center looked to both sides and, satisfied that all masks were in place, pulled his horse two paces forward.

"Edgar! Edgar, wake up! We want to talk to you."

For a moment there was no sound, and then the silence was broken by sounds inside several of the cabins that were nestled close together.

"Edgar! You hear me! Unless you want us to light fires to everything around here, and hurt your parents, you need to come out."

As he spoke another man passed a short blazing torch to each rider and the night took on a rich orange glow.

"What you want?" a disembodied voice shouted. "Edgar's not here."

"Who are you, old man?"

"I his daddy and you can come inside and look. He be gone for three days now and we no idea where he go."

"Charlie, get down and see if the old man is lying. Then check a few of the other cabins."

"If you lying old man, we'll string your black ass up to the nearest tree."

"He ain't here."

"What's going on here?" Stuart and Eli Fineman had heard the commotion, seen the lit torches and understood instantly what had happened. The Ku Klux Klan night riders had ridden in to cause more fear among the black share croppers.

"Get back to your house, Jew boys," the leader seethed. "We know how to take care of you Christ killers.

"Leave our people alone. They're just plain hard working folks."

"Edgar ain't!" another rider injected. "He been playin' music with a white visitor you had from California." His words came out sounding like Cal-ee-fon-ya.

"That white boy's family used to own this place," Edgar's father shouted. "He the Roger's boy, all growed up."

"The Roger's boy? Henry Roger's son? Well, don't that beat all?

"Boys," he said to his men, his voice laughing. "You remember my story about riding with the White Camellias after the war. That night I rode with Colonel De Blanc. Henry Rogers was with us and we discovered he had colored blood in him. I was the one who shot him.

"Well," the man said, turning to Eli, "Get his ass out here too. We can have us a really special evening."

"He's not here either. Hasn't been here for days," Stuart added. "Now will you men leave?"

"Listen Fineman...both of you Jew boys. We tolerate you around here. We don't like you but we do tolerate you. Just make sure you keep these blacks to they selves, you hear, or we may just light up this whole place. And you tell Edgar and that Roger's boy neither of them is wanted around here.

"Let's go, men. I can't take any more of the stink from these niggers and Christ-killers."

He turned and his men followed, shouting epithets as they kicked their horses into a gallop.

No one got much sleep that night. Ruth and Rachel brewed some tea and the Finemans sat there, trying to calm their nerves.

"So much hatred," Ruth said, her voice breaking.

"It's always there," Eli added. "Sometimes it's below the surface and we all get along. But their anti-semitism is like a volcano. When it erupts, it spews misery and ugliness everywhere. That music between Edgar and Josiah! That's what started all of this. Somehow those night rider bastards learned about it."

"I warned Josiah but he has no idea how things are here," Stuart added. "And how did the blacks learn about Josiah being Henry's son?"

"They know?" Rachel asked.

"Edgar's father knew...he blurted it out."

"We need to find Josiah and warn him."

Chapter Three

"Mr. Plunkett, I'm here on legal business, personal business that I wish to be kept in complete confidence."

"You can be assured of my total discretion, Mr....? I'm sorry; please give me your name again. My secretary wasn't very clear."

"In due course, Mr. Plunkett. I have two matters that will require your attention and I will be happy to pay your fee if you are able to assist me. One of the things I wish to do is legally change my name to Josiah Williams. The other is to secure financial information on a certain individual and the property he owns."

"Unless you have a criminal record, sir, changing your name will not be a problem. What is your current legal name?"

"Josiah Rogers."

"And may I ask the reason for the change?"

"Is that a legal requirement?"

"No, it is not."

"Then the reason is of no concern to you. As to the second matter, a Mr. Eli Fineman, a Jew incidentally, owns title to a plantation north of Baton Rouge called Moss Grove. I want to find out if he is indebted to any bank, how much he owes, and the terms of such loans. Can you find out that information?"

"Mr. Rogers...sorry, Mr. Williams! With a few well placed dollars I can find out the last time Mr. Fineman took a shit, if you'll pardon my bluntness."

"Josiah, you can't remain here. At some point the Klansmen will return and your life will be at risk."

"I've changed my name, Mr. Fineman. I'm now legally Josiah Williams and I wish to purchase Moss Grove."

"A name change won't work, Josiah. The sharecroppers know your background."

"Then I'll get rid of them and get new ones. Plenty of black families looking for work these days."

"We're not going to sell Moss Grove, Josiah. Not today and not tomorrow. Stuart will inherit this plantation when I die and he will care for his mother and Rachel as long as it's necessary." Eli Fineman's tone made it clear his decision was final.

Josiah's steel blue eyes glared and then softened.

"I accept that you have no interest in selling me Moss Grove at this time. I am disappointed, of course, but your family comes first. Will you permit me to remain here for awhile, however, and learn a little of what you know of the cotton business and running a large plantation?"

Josiah's voice literally dripped with molasses but the sarcasm hidden within was undeniable.

Eli Fineman was not a stupid man. He had risen to the rank of Captain in the Union Army despite its antipathy toward Jews. His business acumen was undeniable. He had taken a deteriorated plantation and the new economics of share cropping and turned it into a success. Reading Josiah's body language came much easier.

"Josiah, I know this was your home and that your parents are buried here. And, you will always be welcome. But Ruth and I think it is time for you to move forward with your life, not look back. I'm told you have great musical skills. Perhaps that is a better calling for you. Stay another few days, if you like, but then we all need to get on with our lives."

Josiah left at the end of the week. He tried to see Rachel but she had successfully avoided him. As their visitor rode down the path through the copse of oak trees that had been planted by Josiah's grandfather, Eli and Stuart watched from the front portico.

"He's trouble, just as you described his father. I'm glad he's leaving."

"Unfortunately, I don't think we've seen the last of that young man," Eli said.

Josiah rode slowly away from Moss Grove. Stuart had given him the horse as a gift. A small saddle bag with his few belongings was tied to its rump. The young trumpet player hadn't brought a lot of clothes on the trip. In truth he'd never owned a lot of clothes. How he played was always more important than how he looked. At one point he thought of inviting Stuart or Edgar to join him but the relationship with his old friend had turned chilly after he indicated his desire to purchase Moss Grove and his relationship with his new friend was cooled by Stuart's warnings about mixing with a black man. He realized he hadn't even seen Edgar during this last visit.

Josiah moved back into the hotel on Dauphine Street and laid out his meager possessions in the small room. He lay down on the bed and stared at the ceiling while the noises of the French Quarter and the traffic on the Mississippi mixed in arrhythmic tones. He certainly had enough money to live better and it would soon be time to decide what impression he wanted to leave if he chose to remain in New Orleans and not return to San Francisco.

When he woke it was dark and he realized he hadn't eaten all day. He walked to Claudette's, a savory-smelling bistro with only eight tables a few doors away, and sat in a corner watching a variety of the locals come and go. He ordered a beer and relaxed. In truth there was nothing in the world he needed to do nor was there anyone who knew where he was. He also realized that very likely no one even cared. He decided that he would put his new isolation to good use.

Steam and strong smells emanated from the kitchen and a board in the corner announced today's specials. There was nothing listed that he recognized from his years in San Francisco. It was Creole this and Cajun that.

"Give me something with shrimp in it that isn't too spicy," he said to the colored waitress who came over to take his order. "And another beer! A large one!" he added.

A half hour later, his appetite quenched by a delicious shrimp concoction with okra and vegetables that was much hotter than his taste buds considered acceptable, Josiah walked out and faced the humidity of a summer New Orleans evening.

Around the corner the traffic was heavier. Elaborate coaches dropped well dressed passengers in front of restaurants where they were greeted by liveried footmen. Josiah stood as two elderly men, French and well-to-do, escorted two mulatto women attired in beautiful gowns for an evening that might begin with oysters and champagne but would, more often than not, end with a romp in bed. San Francisco wasn't much different, he recalled, except the women would more likely have been sultry Chinese.

He continued walking. Four doors away a minstrel show was in process. He entered through a beaded curtain and saw a dwarf on the stage...a black dwarf. With the accompaniment of a five piece orchestra, and bedecked in a tuxedo, the man was singing and dancing for the entertainment of the audience, who threw one coin after another onto the stage.

"Who is he?" asked Josiah of the bartender.

"Name is Thomas Dilward...first time in New Orleans. Big name out east...like New York."

"You put darkeys on stage here in front of white customers."

The bartender stared at this upstart.

"This is New Orleans, mister. We don't put white and black on the same stage but we get all kinds in the audience. If they pay, we let 'em in, but we don't seat 'em together. We did once or twice but a few of the Klan threatened my boss and since he don't want any kind of trouble, he stopped."

Josiah watched the rest of Dilward's performance. Then he watched a full minstrel show...blacks doing blackface.

"That's the craziest thing I've ever seen, blacks putting on black makeup, what kind of joke is that?" he asked the bartender.

"I can't tell you what or why, but it sure is popular."

Josiah ended his evening there, now early morning, and walked unevenly back to his hotel. He had made at least one decision; he would remain in New Orleans.

Chapter Four

The train ride back to San Francisco seemed to take forever. Both Bess and Stephen struggled with the mystery of what their new relationship was supposed to be. Each time they touched, wanting to hold one another more tightly, they pulled back and meeting the other's eyes for more than an instant created an electrical mine field.

"Stephen, we have to work this out," Bess said, their third night out on the Southern Pacific moving out of Kansas City. "I love you and I know you love me. But we're going to destroy one another if we don't move decide what to do."

"I know! I know you're right, but I've wanted you so badly for so long," he said, depressed, his hands fidgeting nervously. "We always knew we were meant for one another…that we'd marry and raise a family. Why can't we do that? We don't even know if it's even true. Mr. Fineman could have confused the entire story. And, we don't need to have children. We can adopt," he pleaded.

"I want that as much as you do. The thought of you not holding me tears as my soul. Neither of us is religious but Ruth Fineman says it would be a sin, no matter how right it feels. If we made a mistake one evening out of passion and I got pregnant, what then. I want you to go back to work for the newspaper when we reach home and I'm going back to the bank. We'll try and find a doctor who can advise us. Meanwhile, we'll continue to live together… at a safe distance," she smiled.

Stephen could never resist her smile and when she reached for his hand, he responded, and he knew the two of them would always love one another. He just didn't know how he could change the way he felt...the way he'd always felt.

When people told me I looked like my mother, I felt proud, Bess mused as she sat and watched the train pass into Utah. She pushed a strand of her red hair from her face. It was early in the morning and Stephen was still asleep in the adjoining compartment. It was a cool clear day with small white cumulus clouds punctuating the sky and snow capped tips on the mountains all around them. The rocking of the train and the clicking of the wheels on the tracks were thrumming in a faint cacophony.

"There is rioting in the city," the conductor said, as the train pulled into Salt Lake. "You are all advised to stay on the train."

"What's happening?" several of the passengers shouted, rushing over to the window and pushing Bess aside.

"The Congress has passed some kind of a law that says they won't make Utah a state unless it makes polygamy illegal and the rioters are saying it's their business, not those of the busy bodies two thousand miles away."

The passengers began arguing for and against Utah's Mormon policies. Immoral! Their own business! Bess moved away from the crowd and the noise. She wanted to be alone with her thoughts. She loved these early mornings before the energy of the day sent everyone scurrying like ants. Two months ago she had a mother and two men in her life, one whom she loved and wanted to share the rest of her years. Now her mother is gone, one man remained in Louisiana and the other has now been revealed as a half-brother, someone with whom she can never share a bed...a lot to absorb.

But it was the revelations about her mother that affected her the most. Amy Williams wasn't just lovely on the outside with her striking red hair and green eyes sitting atop a cute pattern of dimples, she was a lovely and giving person on the inside.

Bess didn't remember much about her father except for what she'd been told growing up. Major John Shipley, her mother had explained, was a small town boy from a farm in Michigan. He grew tall, blonde, and handsome. He'd joined the Union Army but he'd never lost his boyishness. He was smitten the first time he'd seen her mother. They were married and soon thereafter she was born and named Elizabeth, after Amy's sister. But she was never an 'Elizabeth.' She was 'Bess' early on and remained Bess.

John Shipley had been responsible for the Freedman's Bureaus across Northern Louisiana that were meant to help slaves get farms of their own and some education for their children. After the war the government closed them and reassigned all its military personnel. When the Army reassigned her husband, Amy followed with a screaming Bess getting sick in the wagon. They traveled from Baton Rouge all the way to Fort Leavenworth, Kansas. John Shipley was on a scouting tour with General George Custer when their entire troupe was massacred and Amy was suddenly a widow.

The two women, mother and infant daughter, now alone, headed for San Francisco when Amy learned of a horrific massacre by white racist marauders near Moss Grove. They'd killed Henry Rogers and her closest friends, the Carmodys, to whom she'd entrusted raising Stephen as their own. He was the son she and Thaddeus had conceived but couldn't acknowledge.

As soon as Amy heard the news she stopped their trek westward and returned to Moss Grove to help raise Josiah, her nephew, Henry and Elizabeth's son, as well as her never acknowledged son, Stephen. Josiah inherited Moss Grove when his father died. Eli and Ruth Fineman, a Jewish family and close friends, helped run the plantation. Eli Fineman had served with John Shipley in the Union Army. With the addition of their two children and various sharecropper children that came and went, the plantation now had its own schoolroom filled with white, brown and black children from five to fifteen, all learning their lessons together.

Bess had listened as Eli and Ruth Fineman explained the conundrum Amy faced. Whatever the anguish, Stephen was her half-brother, and her mother was not the saintly, sacrificing woman she'd put up on that high pedestal. The shocking revelation had come after all the emotion of seeing her mother lowered into the ground and gone from her life.

They spoke in the gentlest tones of her mother's love for her father, and her separate, very different, love for Thaddeus, who had always been thought of as just a close friend. Ruth sat next to Bess, trying to comfort her as she explained how Amy had told John Shipley, before agreeing to marry him, that she had a long time relationship with her boyhood friend that could never go anywhere because he was colored, the offspring of a young Negro slave who had been raped by Henry Rogers, the teenage son of the owner of Moss Grove.

"At best, the two of them would have been ostracized, at worst Thaddeus would have been lynched," Ruth explained while Bess sat, awestruck at the revelations that her mother was not who she had always believed her to be.

Her eyes glazed over with tears and her hands moved with an unfamiliar nervousness as these strange words of love for another man poured forth seamlessly. Who was this different woman Ruth was describing? She had traveled twelve hundred miles to Louisiana with Stephen and Josiah, to fulfill Amy Shipley's last wish, to be buried under a specific magnolia tree near the banks of the Mississippi river...a tree where she'd first fallen in love, not with John Shipley, but with another man. The story is so incredible, it must be true, she thought. But if it is true, what does that mean for the love Stephen and I share for one another?

And lastly, Josiah! He changed after the first few days at Moss Grove, Bess thought. It was nothing she could put her finger on but he had definitely become more aloof. It was all very strange. She wished that he had returned with them to San Francisco rather than remain in Louisiana. She wasn't sure the coming together of Josiah and Moss Grove was a good thing.

I'll be glad to get back to San Francisco, Stephen mused, as he lay in his small train bed. He had awakened to thoughts of Bess and he could feel an erection pressing against the bed covers. They would need to find a doctor to assure them they could marry and raise a family without fear.

He'd felt the train pull into Salt Lake and he could see the crowd and hear the noise from the tumult at the railroad station. They were complaining about something. He propped his head on the pillow, ignored the crowd and began making notes about everything that had happened these past few weeks.

A month before Amy died I was still struggling with my desire to be a reporter, he recalled. He had done some writing in school but he knew he wasn't as good a student as Bess or that he had Josiah's ear for music.

The trained pulled slowly out of Salt Lake. Stephen closed his eyes and recalled landing a job at the Daily Examiner but it wasn't reporting….he was a copy runner. A gofer….go for this… go for that! The reporters would write up their stories and shout for the copy runner to come and get them. Stephen would rush their scribbled papers to the editors and when they were finished putting their pencil marks all over the story he'd rush them to the type setting department. Everything was a rush. Everyone wanted to see their stories in print and out on the street before the other newspapers. It was a perpetual race. The paper had brought in a new machine the previous year, it was called a typewriter but most reporters still preferred to write their stories in pencil.

Stephen was pretty sure that no one at the paper knew that he was colored. They had never asked and while he might occasionally get a few looks, he'd adopted a habit of returning the stare with an innocent smile. He was light enough to pass, his hair wasn't gnarly, and his accent was San Francisco, not Baton Rouge.

"Carmody…copy!" Reynolds shouted in Stephen's general direction.

"Get this downstairs, right away."

"Say please." It was a game they played. Stephen thought it was funny but it wasn't clear whether the older reporter thought it was cute or whether he was just tolerating the younger man's bullshit. 'Tip' Reynolds had been with the paper since it was started ten years earlier and had repeatedly proven himself to be a skillful writer with contacts throughout the city.

It was only those several minutes after the paper was put to bed, before they had to worry about the next edition that an easy camaraderie spread across the press room.

The Examiner wasn't the biggest paper in the Bay area but it was rapidly becoming the most aggressive. A few years ago the paper was purchased by some mining engineer who used his savvy to locate a rich vein of silver. George Hearst and his money had breathed life into its dormant staff. There were rumors he was going to turn the paper over to his son, Willie, but for now Stephen's immediate boss was Sam Russell, the Managing Editor. Russell was the antithesis of what he'd expected. The man didn't walk around with a cigar and rolled up sleeves. In fact he was never seen without wearing his waistcoat and rimless glasses. He never smiled but he knew the city and everyone in it. Sam Russell knew where every body was buried and who was on the take.

The city was booming. The hordes of people who had arrived from around the world for the gold strike and the building of the transcontinental railroad had changed this enclave with a large deep welcoming bay from a harbor to a metropolis. California was a state and San Francisco was its heart. Each day ships came and went, railroads brought more people, and corruption fed the local economy.

"Carmody," Russell shouted. He always shouted. "You want to be a reporter. I'm going to give you a chance."

"Yes, sir," Stephen answered, almost slavishly.

"They're having a baseball game at Recreation Grounds. You know what baseball is?"

"Sure," he nodded, although he hadn't a clue.

"You know where Recreation Grounds are...in the Mission District off Harrison?"

Another nod, although he only knew the general neighborhood.

"Get me five hundred words...not four hundred or six hundred. Understand?"

"Yes, sir!"

"Then go, the game starts in one hour."

The embryonic reporter grabbed some pencils and paper and someone's card that said he worked for the Examiner.

The trolley took him to within a mile of the park and he ran the rest of the way. He had never seen a baseball park or understood the game. He scanned the crowd outside the field, trying to find someone, quick, who could explain what was going on.

A young boy, his hair messy and his shirt untucked, was standing outside asking if anyone had a free ticket.

"Hey, kid! Do you know anything about baseball?" Stephen asked.

"Ask me anything? Go ahead!" he sassed back.

"Who's playing?"

"Oakland All-Stars against our San Francisco Acorns."

"Good enough. That's more than I know. Tell you what. I'll buy you a ticket if you'll explain the game to me."

"Will you throw in a drink?"

"A big one!"

"Good job, kid," Russell smiled. "I didn't even know you knew sports much less how to write."

It was Stephen Carmody's first story.

Chapter Five

"There is no way to prove that you are related by blood," the doctor had told them. "Is there any proof of what you were told… birth certificates…eye witnesses?"

"No," Bess said as she and Stephen sat nervously next to one another. This was the third doctor they'd visited. "Everyone involved is dead and the people who told us had been told of these events years earlier. They had no reason to make up the story."

"No reason that we're aware of," Stephen added obstinately.

"You'd be taking a chance having a child. Not a big chance but there is that risk and the religious tenet that siblings shouldn't marry."

"Thank you, doctor," they said, their shoulders bent, as they left his office.

They sat at a small café overlooking Montgomery Street, watching people moving quickly to and from California Street.

"You know it's true, don't you Stephen? I feel it. I don't want it to be but deep inside my heart I know that what Eli and Ruth told us was the truth."

Stephen sighed…a deep sigh that signaled a type of surrender. He nodded and tears filled his eyes.

They both sat, filled with despair and all the days that might have been.

"We may never be able to marry," he said, finally, "But I don't think we can ever stop loving one another."

"No, I will always love you as I know you love me."

"Good morning, Mr. Liu. How have you been?"

"Miss Shipley! It is nice to see you back here at the bank. You were gone and I missed your smile. Is everything now satisfactory with you?"

"I lost my mother. She died unexpectedly and we took her back to Louisiana to be buried."

"I am sorry. I will light a candle for her and I will ask Buddha to watch over her."

"Thank you, Mr. Liu. Is the business at your restaurant good? I missed your wife's special won-tons. Stephen and I will have to come for dinner soon."

"We enjoyed serving the four of you. Your mother always made my wife laugh."

"Well, now we are down to just me and Stephen. Josiah decided to remain in Louisiana for a spell."

"Xie....xie. *(Thank you)*. I will see you soon then."

"Good morning! I wondered if you could cash this out of state check for me," the man said as Bess continued to look down, completing Mr. Liu's transaction.

"I'll be right with you."

Moments later, she looked up, dropped her pencil, and blushed.

"Stuart? Stuart! My goodness! What are you doing here?" she stammered.

"I decided to visit California. I hope you're glad to see me," he grinned. It was a smile that lit up his entire face.

"I'm stunned. It's only been a few months but it seems much longer."

"I know I've interrupted your work. Could we have lunch, perhaps?" he asked, dropping his voice in a conspiratorial tone.

A few minutes later, Bess donned her short red satin cape. It was a small concession to current fashion that she'd bought for herself in the hope that it would lift her spirits. They stepped onto Market Street and a day that was unusually sunny. It was late summer and a breeze from the Embarcadero had blown away the fog that normally blanketed the city this time of the year.

"I know a nice café on the next street if you don't mind walking," Bess said as she took Stuart's offered arm.

"Stop! Please stop!"

Bess recognized Mr. Liu's voice and saw three men scuffling over his prone figure up ahead.

"Fucking chink. Stay in your own part of town," one man shouted, leveling a foot at the elder man's groin.

"Hey, stop that!" Stuart shouted. "Stop kicking him!"

"Stay out of this," another of the attacker's shouted. "Ain't none of your business!"

"Bess, find a Policeman," Stuart said, moving forward and grabbing the arm of the closest attacker. He turned the man and swung hard, dropping the man to the ground.

The groin kicker turned toward Stuart, furious at the interruption.

"Faggot, you're going to be very sorry you mixed in." The man grabbed Stuart with his left hand and cocked his right hand, now gripped into a fist.

Stuart heard a Police whistle and felt the impact on his cheek at the same time. He collapsed to the ground as the man hesitated and then ran off. Stuart had fallen next to the middle age Chinese restaurant owner as Bess knelt to help them both. Stuart's nose was bleeding and a welt was already beginning to form on his cheek. Mr. Liu was trying to sit up but he, too, was unsteady.

"Nice welcome to your city," Stuart said, leaning on the Policeman's arm to stand.

"Either of you want to file a report?" the uniformed officer asked.

"Would it do any good?" Stuart asked.

"Probably not!"

"Please, come to my restaurant. You can get cleaned up and eat something," the elderly Chinese said. "Thank you for coming to my rescue. My name is Lee Liu. It really isn't but it is easier for Americans to pronounce. You are obviously a friend of Miss Shipley and you are now forevermore my friend."

They walked slowly, the two men hurting and unsteady while Bess tried to help cushion their steps. Another block and around the corner they encountered throngs of Chinese moving hurriedly in and out of small buildings. Most of these old buildings housed laundries and the smell of lye mixed with steam spewed from their doorways onto the narrow streets.

"Oh, my God! What happened? Are you alright?" seemed to be what Mrs. Liu was shouting when she saw her husband, bent over, walk painfully through the door into their small restaurant of eight tables. The Chinese sounds were guttural and could have been anything. Mrs. Liu spoke very little English and rarely left the Chinatown enclave that abutted Portsmouth Park.

"They'll be fine, Mrs. Liu," Bess said. "Let's get some soap and water and we'll clean them up."

By the time their scrapes and bruises had been cleansed and Stuart's cheek bandaged, they were all happy to sit quietly and sip tea. Mrs. Liu kept bringing more dishes to the table but most remained untouched.

"I like the way you use those chopsticks," Stuart laughed, immediately regretting the hurt to his face from trying to smile.

"Shhh," Amy suggested. "Just sip your tea. And, tell me, are you always the Lochinvar coming to the rescue?"

"What was that all about, anyway? Mr. Liu seems like just a nice old Chinese gentleman."

"He is but there is a lot of anger against all the Chinese here in the city at this time. All the laundries are owned by the Chinese but none of the buildings. The city won't give permits to any Chinese to own a building and there is a lot of pressure to send them back to China now that we don't need them to build the railroad. It even applies to the young ones who were born here. At the moment no Chinese person can become an American citizen."

"Shit, it's as bad as the south, only a different color."

"You were going to tell me what you're doing here in San Francisco when you got distracted."

"You're the reason, plain and simple."

Bess stared and her green eyes met Stuart's dark brown eyes. And while she would never be able to explain it and it defied all logic, the cloud that had been hovering over her life lifted just a little.

His hand reached across the table and his fingers intertwined with hers. He smiled and then winced in pain.

Bess smiled, leaned forward, and kissed his injured cheek.

"Stephen, we have a guest," Bess declared, opening the door to their apartment, Stuart following her slowly in tow.

"Stuart! This is rather unexpected. Did Bess give you that bruise? Your eye is going to be a lovely bright purple by tomorrow morning."

"Hello, Stephen. I think it was meant as a 'welcome to our city' gift."

"He stepped in to stop three hooligans beating on Mr. Liu. He did so well that Mr. Liu has now bestowed on him an informal adoption."

The three of them began to relax. Stephen felt a twinge of jealousy. He was sure that Stuart's visit was not accidental. His boyhood friend from Louisiana was interested in Bess…his Bess, and he'd traveled two thousand miles to stake his claim. No one was hungry so they sat, drank wine and talked about various nothings.

"What brings you here?" Stephen asked nonchalantly.

"Just curiosity! I wanted to see all the gold they talk about. You could easily get the impression where I come from that all of the buildings in San Francisco are made of gold. Anyway, Moss Grove will be quiet for a few months now that all the cotton has been harvested and shipped."

Stephen watched Stuart's eyes repeatedly settle on Bess and, when she didn't think anyone was looking, her eyes fixed on Stuart. His heart jumped. He dreaded what he instinctively knew to be true. His love, now an unavailable half-sister, had a suitor.

"What do you hear from Josiah?" Stephen asked, eager to break the unspoken emotional connection that was so evident.

"Nothing, actually! He's living in New Orleans. A problem arose before he left that could have had serious consequences."

Stuart described the episode with the Klan's night riders learning about the music Josiah and one of the workers had been playing together.

"They knew about his bloodline?" Amy asked.

"One of the tenant farmers had heard the rumor and blurted it out. That and the fact they didn't like Jews either. Anyway, we haven't heard from him since then."

"Stephen," Bess said, "You should get your paper to write an article about the treatment of the Chinese. It's really terrible how our city treats them."

"I doubt Sam Russell, the editor, cares much about foreigners."

"What if you write it first? Would that make it easier for him to say yes?" Stuart asked.

"It might. It might prove to them I was a good reporter and if they did like the idea it might get me the assignment instead of one of the older men. We can go see Mr. Liu in the morning."

The next morning Stuart and Stephen headed for Mr. Liu's restaurant and explained to him what they wanted to do. For the next two days he was pleased to be their guide, introducing them to the owners of several laundries and small businesses. He explained that even those Chinese who had been born in California were not permitted to become citizens or own property under The Chinese Exclusion Act that the Congress had passed the previous year. The three men stopped for a few minutes to admire the Old St. Mary's Church, the first Asian church in the country. Stephen's mood was somber. He was sure he had an important story. That evening, after dinner, he gathered his notes and began writing.

"You write well," Stuart said, studying the two page article.

"Stop wasting your time, and mine," Russell said, throwing Stephen's papers back at him.

"But these people aren't being treated fairly."

"No, they're not, but let me give you some basic facts. No one who buys our paper cares. The Chinese don't buy The Examiner nor do they advertise in it. If we printed your story, which I admit, is well written, we'd piss off city officials and advertisers. So, if you want to preach righteousness, you're going to need to find a different forum."

Stuart stayed for three weeks. He consciously avoided asking either of his hosts whether they'd resolved their dilemma. It was clear from their behavior that they had accepted their new relationship. It was equally clear they were still in love and he'd have to tread lightly if he had any hope with Bess.

They alternated days off during the week to show him the city but during the evening Stephen alternately forced himself to allow them time alone and then ungallantly intruded. He actually liked Stuart although the idea of anyone else being with Bess nettled him.

"Will you come to Moss Grove next spring?" Stuart asked her as he prepared to board his train.

"I'll try…I really will," she promised.

"You know we're meant to be together."

"I know I feel strongly about you, Stuart. My heart tells me how much I'll miss you but my mind says I'm not ready to make such a commitment and I know I still love Stephen. If you care for me, I need you to be patient."

Chapter Six

"I'm sorry that you weren't there with me to bury our father, Noah, but his death came so suddenly there was no time to notify you. I went to find him the morning after Aunt Amy's funeral but he wasn't anywhere in the house. We all trekked down to the river where we'd last seen him and there he was, just lying there. He looked strangely serene. We buried Aunt Amy one day and then we needed to bury our father the next," Robert said as he and his younger brother sat alone in the kitchen of their Georgetown home. "The Finemans revelation of our father's life-long love for Amy was a shock."

"I'm still having trouble absorbing the fact of having a half-brother we never knew about," Noah said, his shoulders drooping, his eyes red. "I've been trying to finish a picture of father and mother from a fading tintype photo he had on his dresser. I worked on it after you left and I was saving it to give him as a gift this Christmas. Now maybe I should just throw it away or paint a white woman in and make it a threesome."

"It won't do any good to be bitter. Apparently our father didn't know he had a son. Amy never told anyone she was pregnant. She would never have been able to explain raising a colored child so he was given to friends to rear. Eli Fineman explained that our father and Amy had loved one another since childhood but because she was white and he wasn't, it was impossible for them to be together. Remember, this was even before the Civil War and dad was born a slave."

"I'm not sure it's very different today with all the states that have passed miscegenation laws."

"Our father told mother that he'd loved Amy but neither of them knew of the child, though I'm not sure he ever admitted to her that he and Amy had slept together. Knowing our mother, that might have been a little too much for her to accept, her father having been a church person."

"Thaddeus Williams, our father, was a far different person than we ever knew, wasn't he?"

"I don't know whether to admire him more for what he accomplished or whether to be angry for everything he hid from us."

"Let's not be angry, Robert. It will serve no purpose. I'm sure he loved our mother and he certainly loved us. I think we need to leave it at that."

"You're the artist and the poet, Noah. Either way, it's just you and me now. Let's go get some dinner. I definitely need a drink!"

A memorial for their father was held the following week and more than a hundred well wishers attended to show their respect.

Reverend William Patton, President of Howard University, recited a prayer and read from his most famous work, John Brown's Body. Even John Mercer Langston, Virginia's only remaining black Congressman stayed for the entire service. He and Thaddeus had met weeks earlier and he had offered Thaddeus a job as a Congressional aide. News of Amy's death interrupted his decision making and now no decision was be necessary.

"I'd like you boys to come by and see me when you feel up to it. I was a great admirer of your father," Congressman Langston said as he shook the boys' hands. He was a tall, distinguished man and it was easy to understand why voters supported him despite his color.

It was early fall before Noah and Robert decided to accept the invitation to visit Mr. Langston.

"My brother, Charles Langston Hughes, has set up a black college in Kansas. He's using one of the many abandoned Freedman

Clinic buildings. And a few years ago, a fellow by the name of Booker T. Washington got the government to set up a black college in the middle of Alabama, a place called Tuskegee. They're in sore need of people with an education to teach. We have plenty of anxious students, mostly the children of ex-slaves. What we don't have is enough teachers and I want to invite the two of you to go down there and be teachers."

"Leaving Washington isn't an easy decision, Congressman," Noah said. "We've never lived in the deep south. Prejudice in Washington, D.C. is bad enough but down there they lynch black folks for sneezing. Please give us time to think seriously about it. Georgetown has always been our home."

"It needn't be a permanent decision. Think of it as a temporary adventure."

In the end they decided that they owed it to their father's memory to share some of the benefits they'd gained from their father's efforts. Two weeks later they gave up their Georgetown apartment and headed south to Alabama.

"The meeting will come to order," the young man shouted as he banged his gavel to quiet the large empty warehouse that was filled with more than a hundred people, all white and male. Some were young, most had fought for the Confederacy, and all of them were convinced they needed to defend their racial superiority.

"This meeting of the Knights of the Ku Klux Klan will come to order," he declared with unnecessary formality.

Albert Pike smiled and stroked his beard. He licked the palm of his hand and slicked down a few obstinate stray graying hairs on his head. He loved attending any meeting where he was the guest of honor and being invited to this huge New Orleans Klan meeting was special. He loved the city, especially the food and the music. The Klan had agreed to pay his travel and lodging expenses and he had already gorged himself by devouring all the oysters in his hotel's kitchen.

"We are pleased to have the Grand Wizard himself, Albert Pike, here to celebrate with us, The White League of the Klan in our great state of Louisiana," Roger Cadway shouted, his hands raised high as everyone stood in an enthusiastic response.

Cadway was the White League's new Louisiana President and he was young and eager. He had light brown hair and sported a neatly trimmed beard and mutton-chop sideburns. He wore glasses and could easily have been mistaken for a college professor but he was tall, lean and strong. He had a small dimple in each cheek and a well-defined cleft in his chin. He was a local builder and he took great pleasure in terrorizing every black, brown, or immigrant laborer who worked for him. He strode around his projects toting a riding crop, constantly smacking it against his leg. This new post as President of the local Klan made him special. He knew he had overspent the League's limited budget to get Pike as a speaker, but he felt it was worth it. He had every intention of making his city's Klan important.

Pike stood, pulled up his pants, straightened his jacket and moved slowly to the lectern. He was a practiced speaker and rabble-rouser. It was said he could charm a pig out of its squeal. He looked over the sea of intent faces, each of them eager to have their attitudes confirmed by someone more important. He waited until the overcrowded room grew quiet.

"Wops, kikes and niggers are not your enemies. Catholics are not your enemies. Republicans are not your enemies. They are the tools of Satan and Satan is your enemy. It is our job, yours and mine, to protect the values of a white, Christian America, an America our forefathers founded and built. And it is your God-given task to keep this land racially pure by whatever means is necessary."

For twenty minutes more he railed, his cheeks turned red, and the temperature of the room rose from the heat of his words. He intended to give these people their money's worth.

With the big meeting over, and his wrist sore from shaking hands, he, Cadway, and three other men retired to a nearby restaurant.

"Good speech, Mr. Pike," Roger Cadway, said, raising his glass of wine in a toast.

"Hear! Hear! A real boot thumper," another chorused. "Better than a good revival meetin'."

"Glad you liked it, boys. Always glad to please. Now, tell me. How are things down here in Louisiana?"

"Not as good as Mississippi. They've got the blacks pissin' in their pants over there and back sayin' 'yes sir' and 'no sir'. We do alright up in the northern part of our state but here in New Orleans things always been different."

"Maybe so but you've always had some of the best hot chocolate pussy in the country and I've tried it most everywhere," Pike bragged to the raucous laughter of his companions.

"Yes, we have some fine houses off Bourbon Street and they truly know how to treat a man. They've got French brandies that even the best restaurants can't get, the best Cuban cigars, and the women. They can do tricks even Ringling Bros. shows can't duplicate."

"I'm getting an erection just thinking about it," Pike smiled.

Josiah watched the men from a nearby table. The tall brown haired man reminded him of his father, brash and a little loud. He found that he continued to dislike the man he had met once before.

"Josiah, you are ignoring me," his beautifully gowned dinner companion whined. His date, a girl with delicate skin the color of milk chocolate, claimed to be nineteen but Josiah doubted she had even celebrated her sixteenth birthday. He didn't care. He had met her at one of the Gentlemen's Clubs, she looked good sitting next to him at a dinner table with her very ample breasts overflowing her lavish teal satin gown, and she could fuck all night.

His trumpet sat in a corner of his hotel suite. He hadn't played it in months. It had been pushed aside by the acquisition of a new wardrobe and a larger suite. He was pleased that he'd decided to remain in New Orleans for awhile. He had capital; he was a mysterious newcomer, and he was good looking. It was impossible not to notice a tall, blonde-haired man with steel blue eyes. Something appropriate would reveal itself soon, he was convinced.

As Roger Cadway, Albert Pike, and the others left the restaurant, they passed by Josiah's table.

"Mr. Williams, I believe. How nice to see you," Cadway gushed. The two men first met and shared an afternoon sherry after Josiah had watched one of Cadway's buildings being erected.

"Mr. Cadway, a pleasure. I didn't recognize you without your riding crop."

"It does keep my workers in line," he laughed easily. "They never know when it might lash out. Let me introduce you to Mr. Albert Pike, Grand Dragon of the Ku Klux Klan, and two of his associates."

Josiah's mulatto date blanched at the mention of the Klan but her young smile remained unchanged. Good girl, Josiah thought.

"Gentlemen!" was all he said, obviously reluctant to introduce his lady friend.

"Perhaps we could entice you to come to one of our meetings. We are certainly eager to get as many proper thinking gentlemen as possible into our organization and Mr. Cadway is putting together an impressive agenda of activities that might interest you," Pike said.

"I will consider it. Thank you for the invitation."

As the men left, Josiah's young date leaned over and whispered, "I don't like those men."

"I'm sure you don't. Come, let's go. Their presence has made me horny."

"Watch those walls. Make sure they're straight. And hit those nails straight. Every bent nail I find will be deducted from your pay," Roger Cadway shouted as men scurried to finish the second story wall on a new building. He was pleased that he was one week ahead of schedule. This was such a growing, upscale neighborhood he expected to turn a substantial profit. As he looked down he saw Josiah Williams on the street in front, staring up at him.

"I'll be back…keep working," he shouted as he climbed down the ladder.

"Josiah, how nice to see you again! Apartments upstairs, shops below…should do quite well."

"Looks good, Roger. You do nice work. Is there somewhere we can talk?"

Cadway led him to a small shed that he'd set up as an office.

"I'm afraid we need to leave the door open or this place will get terribly hot."

"This will do fine," Josiah said as he relaxed in the frail chair across from the builder. "I have some money to invest but I'm relatively new to the city and I need to associate myself with someone who has experience…someone who knows how to build and where to build."

"You've come to the right person, Josiah," Cadway said with a glint in his eyes that he was unable to hide. He was overextended at the bank and they were threatening to call his loans. He'd hit New Orleans God-damn fickle water table on two of his buildings when he went to lay the foundation. Fucking low-lying city, water could be anywhere.

"I have three buildings under construction and three more ready to go," he continued. "I can always use an astute investor. New Orleans hasn't begun to see its future. This city might even surpass New York in size one day."

"I'm sure you're right," Josiah agreed in a voice that bespoke naiveté. He figured if he gave this ass enough line he'd eventually strangle himself on it.

Plunkett, Josiah's attorney, had proven himself to be invaluable. He'd learned that Cadway had too many projects going at the same time and his bankers were getting very nervous. Plunkett, acting on Josiah's behalf, and spreading a little extra encouragement around, convinced the banks to sell their loans to him for $.50 on the dollar.

"I'm convinced you're a good risk, Roger, so how about this? I'll loan you $50,000 at 2% interest to finish these buildings. But if your bank loans are called, you'll repay my loan by giving me title to your other three properties. I know that won't happen, but it's just a little precaution, you see."

Cadway's eyes lit up. 2% interest was one quarter what the bank was charging him and with $50,000 he could clear up this water foundation nonsense in less than two months.

"I don't know, Josiah. Those other plots are worth close to a couple of hundred thousand combined in this market."

"Of course, Roger. I'm sure that part of the transaction will never occur and that you'll be repaying my $50,000.00 quite easily. I really just think of it as a way to get my feet wet and help a friend. Meanwhile, I'd like to join you at your next Klan meeting. You boys have the right slant on things."

Mention of the Klan sealed the arrangement. Roger Cadway had a new Klan member with credentials, a loan to tide him over, and, perhaps even, a new friend. They shook hands and the next day Samuel Plunkett brought over the Note, the Agreement, and the $50,000.00.

Three weeks later, acting on behalf of his anonymous client, Plunkett served notice that the notes were being called and the three properties under construction and the three empty lots were to be transferred to a new owner.

Two days later Cadway's body was discovered by his wife, sitting at his desk,one bullet hole through his right temple. He left no note.

Josiah walked into the bank and headed directly for the President's desk in the rear. He liked Merchant's Bank. It was serious and they didn't ask unnecessary questions. Josiah had transferred all the money Amy had kept for him, quietly invested with nothing being drawn out. Being the sole heir of Moss Grove had made him wealthy and he had every intention of making good use of the money.

Cadway's three buildings had been completed. Two were already sold at a handsome profit. Construction was underway on the other three parcels. Plunkett found him a most competent foreman, Rene Boudreaux, a Cajun tree trunk of a man with an abominable accent. The man didn't waste much time on words but he could scamper around a construction site like a twenty year old.

"Josiah? Oh, my goodness, it is you," a soft voice said, turning away from the counter.

"Rachel? For goodness sakes, you are probably the last person I expected to see in a New Orleans bank."

"And you look so different. What happened to the trumpet playing nomad from San Francisco?"

"Well, if you'll dine with me, I'd be delighted to enlighten you. Are you free this evening?"

"I wasn't, but seeing you is too delicious. I'm staying at the Clarion."

"Wonderful. I'll come for you at 8 o'clock."

"Do you come to New Orleans often?" he asked over the lemon sorbet. He had taken her to Lafitte's, one of the city's most exclusive restaurants, and made certain they had the best table. Their food and wine delighted Rachel's palette and it was difficult for her not to be impressed by the elegance of the evening and her suave companion.

"Do you always ask questions in such a seductive tone?" she laughed. "I still am not sure I know this Josiah sitting before me. You look more handsome, and certainly more confident, but you seem to have a haughtiness I'm not sure I'm comfortable with."

"Then I will try and recapture my old charm. Tell me, how are Stuart and your parents?"

"My parents are fine but Stuart remains a love sick puppy ever since he returned from visiting Bess and Stephen in San Francisco last year."

"Bess and Stuart? Interesting! But why not? If she and Stephen can't couple there is nothing to keep your brother from pursuing her. He always chased her when she was a child. Are there marriage bells in their future?"

"I don't know. I guess it's possible. And you! Why have you not visited us again at Moss Grove?"

"I'm not sure I'm welcome. There was quite a chill after I offered to buy Moss Grove and your father declined my offer. Even your brother became less than amicable. You absented yourself as well. I assumed my kiss had offended you."

"Yes, you were rude, definitely rude," she said, before changing her scowl to a smile. "But I forgive you. Actually I missed you. I tried to find out where you were living, but without success. No one seemed to have heard of Josiah Rogers."

"Not so curious. I changed my name to Josiah Williams and with it I thought I'd change my life style. May I invite you to my suite of rooms for a nightcap?"

"Your dress is lovely. The satin is as soft as your skin."

"It didn't take long for you to get my dress off," she laughed, sinking under the down covers and feeling Josiah's erection press against her."

He cupped her breasts in his hand and took one into his mouth as he squeezed the other, her dark brown nipple protruding toward him provocatively. He felt her body arch as he moved his mouth down her body, his tongue dancing over her skin. Then he stopped.

"Don't stop," she begged. But he paused and looked down into her face, drops of perspiration on her cheeks. He kissed them and smiled.

She opened her eyes and found herself staring into his blue eyes.

"Why did you stop? I was ready to climax."

"We'll get back to it," he said, his face grinning, but, she thought, not in a loving way.

"I just realized, I've never fucked a Jew. I mean, perhaps, figuratively, but never literally."

"That's a pretty tactless thing to say," she said.

"I thought you'd figured out by this time that I'm not a gentleman."

"You certainly give every appearance of having become one."

"A façade…purely a façade! Now, where was I?"

They spent two days together, visiting cafes for latte and beignet, and then returning to Josiah's suite. Their encounters became more physical and more gymnastic. Each time their bodies glistened with sweat and they laughed.

"Is this love?" Rachel asked.

"I'm not sure whether it's love or not, but it is certainly lust," Josiah laughed as he used his towel to wipe her brow. "You are truly insatiable. I am exhausted."

"And I thought you had unlimited stamina…tsk…tsk," she teased.

"Give me twenty minutes and we'll see whether my stamina is diminished."

"Twenty minutes…not a minute more. Then I shall have to get myself together. I need to return to Moss Grove before my parents think I've been kidnapped. I shall be back in three months, sooner if I can. That should give you plenty of time to restore your stamina. That is, if you don't exhaust it elsewhere in my absence."

"Best oysters in the world here in New Orleans," Albert Pike said as he and Josiah attacked their third platter. "We would like you to consider becoming the head of the Klan here in New Orleans.

"Why me? I'm just a new member," Josiah asked as he sipped his French Chardonnay.

"Why not? Cadway is dead. The weak bastard shot himself. Someone took him for a financial ride. It was probably you but I don't care and you have no reason to acknowledge it one way or the other. You're successful, white and, I suppose, to women you'd be considered good looking. We want someone who can mix in all circles. What do you say?"

"I need to think on it. I have an increasing number of business obligations and I've never been a joiner."

"The Klan could certainly help your business. Our members go out of their way to work with their own. We know we can trust one another."

As they left the restaurant, the sun was beginning to set. The sounds of a piano playing at a club nearby carried in the quiet air.

"You killed my father, you son of a bitch," a disembodied voice shouted and a single shot was fired.

Josiah felt the bullet enter his left shoulder and the impact pushed him to the ground. A second later he heard a second bullet explode nearby and then there was silence.

"What the hell just happened?" Josiah said, his breathing labored, as Pike tried to stop the bleeding.

"Don't talk. Cadway's son tried to kill you and you're lucky it only caught your shoulder. If we hadn't been walking, his shot would probably have gone through your heart and you'd be lying here dead."

"And what was the second shot?"

"Someone killed him."

"Who?"

"It was me, Monsieur," Rene Boudreaux said as he approached, holding his pistol at his side. "Monsieur Plunkett is dead. This young man shot him and then came after you. I saw you and your friend exit the restaurant but he fired before I could get close."

"Plunkett dead? This is all so crazy."

"Not so crazy, Mr. Williams. When you fuck with a man's livelihood someone is going to want revenge," Pike said knowingly.

Josiah stared at Albert Pike and Rene Boudreaux as he collapsed into unconsciousness.

Chapter Seven

"I've been offered a chance to go to the Republican convention in Chicago," Stephen said. He had finally been accepted as a reporter with the Daily Examiner and now that George Hearst had transferred the paper to his son, William Randolph, and hired well-known writers, its circulation had soared.

The new owner had no qualms about tweaking the noses of the politicians, or the public, and they couldn't get enough. His new style of sensationalism was catapulting the paper into widespread popularity.

"The Republicans may win the White House back in '88 and I want someone young and hungry to be at both conventions. Send that young kid, Carmody. Send him to St. Louis first. We need to see whether the Democrats do anything besides renominate Grover Cleveland, since he got them back into the White House for the first time since before the Civil War. Then he can take a train up to Chicago. It'll be interesting to see what the Republicans do. They're never predictable." Hearst's shouts into the telephone could be heard well beyond Sam Russell's office.

"Once the Conventions are over I want Carmody to remain in Chicago," he continued. "I hope to buy the Chicago American and I'd like someone we've got experience with on the inside."

"And," Stephen explained to Bess, "When Mr. Hearst makes a request it's wise to say 'yes, sir' if you want to keep your job."

"Stephen, that's so exciting. I think I shall travel with you part way," Bess laughed. "Stuart keeps asking me to come to Moss Grove and I've been hesitating."

They hadn't discussed Stuart since he'd left nor had they learned any more about their origins. Stephen wanted to take the gamble and marry but he knew Bess was afraid of getting pregnant and bearing a malformed child. They continued to be at an impasse.

"We haven't been away from one another since we were kids. Is this how things are going to be? Is this the first step toward moving off in separate directions? I'm not comfortable with that."

"Stephen, I love you. I'll always love you. But what are we to do? I'm trying to move forward. It isn't easy. Whatever I do… whoever I look at…wherever I go, I want to share with you. Stuart knows how we feel about one another. He hopes that his feelings for me will eventually be reciprocated and he is a wonderful man. I know you like him too."

Stephen could only nod…a reluctant recognition of the futility of his love.

"I'm going to visit Moss Grove. It's time I accepted his offer and you and I can travel as far as St. Louis together. Please understand. We shan't stop loving one another…ever, but we both know Mr. Finemans revelations are probably true, and if they are, we both need to find someone other than one another to love."

They shared adjoining compartments as far as St. Louis. Stephen helped Bess change trains for New Orleans. There seemed to be a great deal of anger and frustration on the platform as the two of them struggled through the crowd. They seemed to be in the midst of a storm as dozens of blacks with their children and luggage moved along the tracks.

"This place has the energy of an ant hill. Where are they all going?" Bess wondered, stopping a Conductor to inquire.

"Your train is heading into Louisiana and the Railroad Company has been asked to separate blacks from whites and make the blacks ride in the cars in the rear," the uniformed railroad employee said. "Better for both races, I think. It certainly avoids possible trouble."

"Welcome to the south," Stephen jibed. "The Confederacy lives on. You sure you want to visit Stuart?"

Stephen took a carriage from the rail station and was soon drenched from the heat and humidity. He had rooms at the Planter House, a St. Louis landmark that had become threadbare. It was old and slated to be completely remodeled once the convention was over. The political circus lasted for three days and outside of a small tiff on who would be the Vice-Presidential nominee on the ticket, the speeches were too long and too dull. Stephen dutifully sent back dispatches to his newspaper trying to engender some excitement where there was none. How many ways can these men say we did a good job for four years so reelect us? He was glad when it was over and he could climb aboard a train for Chicago.

The Republican convention had to be more interesting. Would Governor Blaine run again? They would certainly lambaste Cleveland's administration. But summer in Chicago does not incline one to be patient. The heat and humidity made everyone grumpy and the cool breezes one hoped for from Lake Michigan never materialized. Benjamin Harrison, another not-to-well known Union General, who could enunciate thoughts clearly, was nominated, but not quickly enough to avoid his listeners dozing off from boredom.

Several black groups picketed the convention and he thought there was a good story there. Placards held pictures of blacks who had been lynched across the south, nearly eighty in the past year. He had pictures taken, wrote stories, and sent them to Hearst, who replied with a terse telegram:

> *No one gives a shit. Stop. Blacks don't buy papers.*
> *Stop. The only black thing I care about is the price of ink.*
> *Hearst*

Stephen began inventing interviews with 'undisclosed sources'. Most of it was fabricated but it was all amusing and Hearst never really cared if it was true. The young reporter had adopted his boss' mantra. True or not, make it interesting.

There were now thirty-eight states in the Union and more than ten million voters. Telegraphs were sending news constantly and the public's thirst for the latest gossip kept newspapers filled with the latest dirt.

Ultimately the fall election was closer than any of the pundits predicated. Cleveland won the popular vote but Harrison carried twenty states and a solid majority of the electoral votes. The Republicans had regained the White House.

The train pulled into New Orleans and Bess climbed down the two stairs to the platform. As she started to turn she was startled by an embrace and intense kiss. She recognized the lips and the smell of the dark haired man kissing her. Stuart had wasted no time in saying hello.

"Let me catch my breath," she laughed.

"I'll think about it." His eyes lit up and, as they turned to leave, they bumped into the other passengers alighting from the train.

"Excuse me! Excuse me!"

They both laughed and held hands as they walked up the platform, a porter following with her luggage.

"Are we going on to Moss Grove this afternoon?"

"No. I want you all to myself for a few days before I share you with the family. I've booked us rooms at a nice hotel here in the city. Separate rooms, of course, but quite close together."

"How close?" she grinned.

"Across the hall…a very narrow hall."

They left her luggage at the hotel and walked past Bourbon Street to the quay and a small café.

"We've been apart far too long, you know," he said.

Bess stared into his eyes, forcing herself to remain noncommittal, her loyalty to Stephen churning within her. She needed to move on and she liked Stuart. She wasn't sure whether she was ready to abandon everything she'd felt. It would take time.

"Are you over Stephen?" he asked nervously, seeming to read her thoughts.

"Yes and no! What he and I had was always so special. He'd get something for me before I'd asked. We'd complete one another's sentences. We're both struggling. We know that what your father told us is likely true but there is that small possibility that it isn't and we are being forced to lead our lives never knowing for sure. We do have to move on. It hasn't been easy and I appreciate your being so patient."

"It's because I have feelings for you…serious feelings. I guess I've always cared, even when I was pushing you into the mud. And, while you're pondering your issues with Stephen, you are also going to have to consider the possibility of falling in love with a Jew? Is that going to be a problem? I have to ask."

"It isn't something I've ever thought about it. I rarely think about such things. I mean…we were all raised together. We celebrated Christmas and Easter as well as Hanukah and Passover. It may be more likely that your parents could have a problem with you being involved with a woman who isn't Jewish?"

"That's also a possibility! I'm like you…not really caring, but my parents don't really know about us. I know they adore you. We'll just have to convince them. Rachel certainly won't care, although she isn't around much anymore. We're not sure where she goes. She's become very secretive."

"Do you see Josiah? He hasn't written in several months."

"No. He never returned after my father told him the Fineman's had no interest in selling Moss Grove."

For the next few days the young couple traversed the city. Their rooms at the hotel were close to one another but Bess had asked Stuart to not push their relationship and he reluctantly agreed.

They enjoyed the sites of New Orleans. They took a small boat through the harbor where ships from around the world came and went. They shopped the stores and marveled at the variety of goods. They walked the markets and smelled spices with strange names…cardamom, saffron, and sage from India.

The affection between them grew. Bess' hadn't yet reached the stage where she could admit she loved him but her feelings were strong and the sexual intensity between them had become difficult to ignore. When they kissed good night at their respective doors after another enjoyable day together, they could barely contain their laughter at the farcical situation in which they found themselves. Stuart waited until Bess closed her door, went inside his own room, took off his jacket, opened his door quietly, and peeked down the corridor. It was deserted and the lights were dim. He crossed the two paces and tapped on the door. It opened quickly and he stepped in. The room was dark and a figure was jumping sprightly into the large feather bed, the only light reflecting from the street below. A soft breeze cooled the room from the open window.

"I love you, Bess, and the time without you has been a torment I don't ever want to repeat."

She wanted to reciprocate her words of love but Stephen's face appeared before her and she could only remain silent. They embraced. Stuart helped her remove her nightgown. He removed his robe and they looked at one another for the first time.

"You are so lovely. You are more than I ever imagined, and I've had too many lonely nights to imagine." He kissed first one breast, then another. His mouth circled her breasts and she laughed.

"Your mustache tickles." It was her last decipherable words as she felt his penis harden against her and her back arch toward him, her breathing quickened and her eyes closed as her other senses took over. His hand caressed the mound between her legs and they spread in encouragement. Their bodies twisted as she gathered his joint in both her hands and caressed the smooth shaft. She felt the uniqueness of his circumcision and smiled. She had seen Josiah and Stephen growing up close together and the male member always held a curiosity but neither of her family had ever been circumcised.

"Are you alright if I go inside?" he asked tenderly. "I mean we aren't married."

She paused before responding. "Yes, I'm ready."

She felt a sudden pressure for her first penetration but then all she could feel was a oneness with this man. She bit her lip as she almost shouted out Stephen's name. She grabbed Stuart and kissed him intently, muffling any outbursts that might come out unexpectedly.

It was morning before Stuart returned to his room.

Their last night in the city, they dined at Antoine's. It was one of New Orleans' finest restaurants. Antoine Alciatore had opened his establishment a half-century earlier and walking through the wrought iron façade was like stepping back to an antebellum era. Now his sons ran the restaurant but the quality of the food had never suffered.

As the maître'd led them to their table, Bess bumped a chair.

"Excuse me," she said, and then stopped as her eyes connected with the handsome, exquisitely dressed man sitting there.

"Oh, my god! Josiah!" she gasped.

"Bess?" he jumped up and grabbed her, brushing other tables on both sides.

Their reunion was genuine as they hugged, kissed, and stared at one another.

"Please, you must join us. Bess, Stuart, this is Miss.....I'm sorry Beatrice, I don't know your last name."

"Fontineau," the beautiful woman said, extending her hand to Stuart.

"Beatrice is the star of the show at the Galaxy Theatre. They're touring from New York. Please, everyone sit. Beatrice," he said, continuing to smile, "These are very close friends. Bess, Stuart, and I grew up together. Now tell me, Bess, what are you doing here in New Orleans?"

For the next two hours the wine flowed and the conversation was lively. Bess managed to avoid explaining about her and Stuart but Josiah's experienced eye knew instantly what the two of them were up to. He was more concerned about keeping his activities private and he certainly had no desire to share any tales of intimacy regarding him and Rachel. Stuart would probably have him shot if he knew.

Stuart remained quiet. He didn't like the man Josiah had become. He may dress like a dilettante but he still possessed an icy blue eyed stare that was always most troubling. He doubted that Bess noticed the difference. She was just so happy she had found him before they left in the morning for Moss Grove. Then his reverie was broken.

"Josiah, congratulate us. Stuart and I are going to get engaged," she blurted out, clutching Stuart's hand in partnership, while the two men gaped at the unexpected confession.

"How wonderful! Bess, Stuart, we must celebrate. Waiter, a bottle of your best champagne", he said, waving his hand at the mulatto sommelier standing nearby.

It was a peculiar twist of fate, Josiah mused. His plan to call all the loans on the Fineman's property was still waiting for the right moment and now Bess would be living there. He'd have to give this conundrum a great deal more thought.

"We haven't seen you in quite a while," Stuart said, anxious to change the subject. "Are you still playing the trumpet?"

The question didn't register for a moment. Josiah was still trying to absorb the news about Bess and Stuart and wondering how much of her brother's relationship Rachel was aware of.

"Not much. Other things are keeping me occupied. Things like Beatrice here. She's far more intriguing than blowing air through a brass pipe. Actually, I now own some property and I'm involved doing some construction. New Orleans is growing and there seems to be endless opportunities."

"You have settled down. I hope you'll have time to visit us at Moss Grove. You, too, Miss Fontineau, if you can arrange it the next time you are in New Orleans."

They kissed and parted, Bess ebullient, but Stuart and Josiah each deep in his own thoughts, knowing their paths would cross again all too soon.

Chapter Eight

Eli and Ruth were ecstatic to see their son and Bess. Their embraces and smiles were heartfelt. Having their son close to them was important. Rachel joined the small throng, kissing her brother and embracing this red-haired girl she'd grown up with...it was always the two of them against the boys.

It was soon clear to all that this wasn't going to be just a casual visit. The secretive glances between the recent arrivals didn't go unnoticed, but without realizing that it was apparent to the others, each decided to bide his time until their son was ready to disclose his feelings to the rest of the family. At dinner that evening they chatted casually about the pleasantness of the train ride, Stephen's recent successes as a political reporter, and the weather. Bess was sure the Finemans would be reluctant to accept her as a wife for Stuart since she wasn't Jewish. The thoughts made her uncommonly nervous and she realized she was chattering way too much.

As dessert was being served, Bess, still searching for innocent small talk to cover her uneasiness, casually mentioned that she and Stuart ran into Josiah and shared a lovely dinner their last evening together in New Orleans. She didn't notice how the mention of Josiah's name altered the temperature in the room. Rachel wanted to disappear when Bess described Josiah's very attractive companion for the evening, the star of a traveling show. She'd make him pay for that indiscretion, Rachel promised herself.

"Bess and I want to become engaged. I'm hoping that she will eventually agree to marry me," Stuart said as he sat alone with his parents while the girls took themselves out on the veranda. Eli and Ruth looked at one another, their response less than enthusiastic.

"Stuart, Bess is a lovely girl and your feelings for one another have been obvious since you returned," Ruth said, holding her husband's hand. "We adored her mother and we've known Bess since she was an infant."

"But? I know there is a 'but' somewhere in there," Stuart replied, already dismayed at their reaction.

"She's not Jewish. You'd be marrying out of our faith," Eli added somberly.

"That's not important to me, and I doubt it's important to Bess. We love one another. We've never even discussed religion."

"'Love conquers all' is for books," Eli added. "This is life. You'd be subjecting her to criticism and even anger from all the Jew-haters that are out there. Have you forgotten our recent visit from the Klan when they came looking for Edgar?"

"And children? How would you raise your children?" Ruth asked.

"I don't have answers to any of this. I know we love one another and I've never met anyone else I want to share my life with. But," he acquiesced, "She and I will discuss it."

"My parents are worried you'd be making yourself terribly vulnerable by marrying a Jew," Stuart said as he and Bess sat on the veranda that evening after Rachel excused herself. The scent of the nearby roses blended with the kitchen odors emanating from the cabins fifty yards away and tickled her nose. The stars twinkled through the umbrella of tall trees that kept the back of the house cooler during the summer's hot days.

"I'm sure they're worried about your making a mistake as well. You're their son and they take great pride in what you've become. Stuart, we were all a family for my entire childhood. I'd never want to hurt them," Bess confessed. "I reluctantly agreed that you could ask your parents if we get engaged. You know I'm not ready to say 'yes' to marriage. What do you want to do?"

"I want us to marry and live here at Moss Grove. Whatever happens we'll face together."

"If and when we marry, I'm willing to have our children raised in the Jewish faith but would you be upset if I didn't convert? I don't have enough religion in me of any faith to make such an effort, and whatever I did would lack sincerity. I've seen so much needless death that I'm not even sure what I believe about the existence of a righteous God."

"Agreeing to raise our children in the Jewish faith will make my parents happy. As for getting married, I'll be patient…at least I'll try."

"You bastard!" Rachel said quietly. "You're fucking showgirls? Really, Josiah, I thought you'd be more discrete."

"You're jealous. How delicious. You weren't here and I thought it would be fun. Bumping into your brother and Bess was completely unexpected."

"They're planning their wedding. Did you know they were in love?

"I suspected. When do I get my invitation?"

"Oh, you'll get one, but please don't come. I have no idea how I'd react."

"Perhaps we should get married. We could even make it a double ceremony," he laughed.

"My parents would both have heart attacks if they even knew we were seeing one another. And marriage? I never thought you were the marrying type."

"I'm ready to settle down, Rachel. You are the only woman I've ever been with that's kept my interest. And you certainly do energize my libido. When you aren't here, I actually miss you. Most women I meet are vapid. If you like, I'll go down on one knee and propose."

"I think that if you go down on one knee we can find a more interesting activity," she said with a wicked smile on her face. "I don't know, Josiah…I really don't know. My parents mistrust you."

"Is it because they know I have Negro blood somewhere way back? I mean, you're all Jewish and I'm not complaining."

"No, I don't think so but having a Jewish colored baby here in the south would certainly stir things up," she smiled and they both laughed at the possibility.

Their sex that evening was better than ever.

A well turned out carriage, led by two prancing black horses, containing four men came up Moss Grove's long entranceway shaded by aging oaks trees, and stopped. The men climbed down and slapped their hands against their jackets, trying to rid themselves from the dust of the long trip. The front door opened and a grey haired black servant faced them.

"Gentlemen, please come in," he said, holding the door as another servant offered to water the horses.

"Mr. Fineman, thank you for seeing us," Louisiana's ex-Governor P.B. Pinchbeck said, as he and three other men were greeted by the plantation's owner and settled in Moss Grove's spacious living room. Pinchbeck was the first nonwhite elected as Governor of a state and although he served only briefly, it provided him a unique stature. Drinks were served but there was little small talk.

"You've ridden a long way. How can I help you?" Eli Fineman asked.

"As you may have heard, the Louisiana legislature has passed a law similar to those being passed in other Confederate states mandating separate railroad cars for blacks. It is an affront to free men and we believe it violates the Fourteenth Amendment which, as you well know, was enacted to provide equal opportunity and rights for people of all races."

"That's all very good, and I support your efforts, but what do you want of me?"

Stuart and Bess entered the room and stood in the back.

"Gentlemen, this is my son, Stuart, and his fiancée, Miss Elizabeth Shipley. My son manages much of our plantation and I hope you won't object to their being present."

They nodded their assent and Pinchbeck continued.

"We're mounting a legal defense to take this egregious law all the way to the Supreme Court and we need to raise money to fund our efforts. We are hoping you will make a contribution of $500.00 toward our cause."

"How do you plan to proceed?" Stuart asked now that he had a very personal interest, given the mixed color status of Josiah and Stephen.

"Let me first introduce these men who have come with me. This is Mr. Homer Plessy. He is an octoroon. Mr. Plessy lives in New Orleans and he has agreed to purchase a first class ticket on the commuter train between New Orleans and Covington. Once the train leaves the station, he will announce to everyone that he is one-eighth colored. He knows he will be arrested when he refuses to move to the car in the rear designated for coloreds. We will hire white citizens to be on the same car who will attest to the circumstances so that some stranger doesn't come forward to misstate the facts and simply claim that Homer was just a vagrant. The railroads are on our side. This new law forces them to add extra cars they really don't need.

"These other gentlemen are Mr. Albion Tourgee and his associate. They have agreed to represent our group, the Committee to Test the Separate Car Act. In addition, we have enlisted many influential white and colored gentlemen to support our efforts."

"Mr. Tourgee! Your reputation as a rabid advocate precedes you," Eli laughed. "Stuart, I don't know if you know who this gentleman is, but as a judge he made sure that in every Klan case he heard the bigot got the maximum sentence. The KKK has a bounty on his head. The man has been tireless in his battles for equal rights. He wants a country that is color-blind. It's a phrase he used in one of his more contentious decisions that has captivated people's imaginations."

"I'm pleasantly surprised, Mr. Fineman. You seem to know a great deal about my meager efforts toward our struggles," Tourgee bowed his head graciously.

"And you, Mr. Plessy, would you tell us something about yourself?" Bess asked.

"My grandfather was white, a Frenchman born in Bordeaux. His grandmother came over from Haiti with thousands of other people trying to escape the bloodshed of the slave rebellion. I don't pretend to understand the arithmetic but somehow the government classifies me as 7/8's white or, for our purposes, 1/8 black."

"Gentlemen, I don't know how much a small financial contribution will help your cause but most Jews understand persecution. Our family will be pleased to help finance your legal battle."

The next two months passed and Bess' return to San Francisco never happened. She and Stuart settled into a comfortable phase. They'd ride early in the morning before the days turned hot and sticky. They had discovered a small inlet off the river where they could make love discreetly. It was clear to Ruth Fineman, as she joined them for morning coffee, that Bess' cheeks flush from more than her morning's canter.

"Stuart, I'll marry you. I do love you but I need to be truthful. I don't think I can ever stop loving Stephen. I will never act to that love and I don't quite understand how I can love two men in the same, yet very different, way. If that's acceptable I'm more than happy to be your wife."

"Bess, I love you. I'll even promise to continue to be fond of Stephen. Let's go tell my parents."

An old ornate lace chuppah was set up in the garden. It had belonged to Ruth's parents and came with them across the ocean from their small Eastern European shtetl. The small canopy under which the couple would be married was held in place by four posts. The Rabbi from Baton Rouge would perform the ceremony. He had traveled up earlier that day with two families from his small Congregation. There were nearly fifty guests, but most important, Stephen had arrived from Chicago and Noah and Robert were traveling all the way from Alabama, where they had begun teaching at Tuskegee Institute.

Bess had taken Stephen by the hand shortly after he arrived and the two walked down to the river where their mother was buried. They could hear frogs croaking at the edge of the river. One large toad sat arrogantly on a piece of flotsam, his long tongue flicking to catch an errant mosquito.

"I'm happy for you, Bess," he said, a catch in his voice. "I still love you, you know, but Stuart is a good man."

"I've told him that I still love you and that I was sure I always would."

"Not a good way to go into a marriage."

"Maybe not, but I didn't want to deceive him. I'll work hard to make my marriage work, Stephen, but please don't ever go out of my life. I need to know that you're out there, somewhere, leading your own life but remembering what we had."

They sat until the moon rose, stood, and looked at one another. Bess kissed the tips of her fingers and touched them gently onto the two headstones.

"Come," she said. "It's time to face the realities of life."

Josiah had been invited but he hadn't responded and no one knew whether he planned on being present. Bess hoped that he would be at Moss Grove so that he could walk her down the aisle since Stephen had agreed to be Stuart's best man. Eli Fineman offered to walk her down the aisle if Josiah didn't come and both he and Ruth hoped the happiness of the day wouldn't be marred with Josiah's presence.

The elder members of Baton Rouge's Conservative Jewish congregation had openly said very little about Stuart marrying a girl who wasn't Jewish, but it was clear that there had been a great deal of discussion when the Finemans weren't present. It was a 'shanda', a shame, they thought, especially when there were other nice Jewish girls that Stuart could have married.

Bess wore the dress her mother had worn when she married John Shipley. It had been carefully packed and stored at Moss Grove when Amy was unable to take it with her to Fort Leavenworth. Her red hair was fashioned into a chignon with yellow rose buds intertwined. Her green eyes glistened like emeralds. She couldn't have been happier. Now if only Josiah would make an appearance.

"You look beautiful, Bess," Ruth Fineman said, a tear in her eye. "I was at your mother's wedding and she would be very proud to see you today. You look so much like her."

The two women hugged.

"I'll try and make Stuart a good wife, Ruth. I really will."

An hour before the wedding was scheduled to begin, a palomino stallion rode up and a tall, blonde man attired in the latest fashion, alit. Josiah carried a box under his arm, which he set down as he brushed the dust from his coat.

The first person he recognized was Stephen, who came running toward him.

"The prodigal arrives! Nice that you let everyone know you'd be coming," he said sarcastically. "I hope you brought your trumpet."

"Actually, I did, although I haven't played it in months. How are you, Stephen? You look quite grand. A little older, perhaps, but still dashing! Have you deflowered any of the young ladies here yet?"

"No, but there are some lovely candidates. Come, Bess will be anxious to know you've arrived."

Rachel's eyes glared as she watched Josiah walk Bess down the aisle. Stuart and Stephen stood next to the chuppah. Ruth's grip on her husband's hand tightened as they watched from the front row. Bess was a picture of beauty. Those who had known Amy thought she had been resurrected, the same red hair, the same green eyes, perhaps a few less freckles. Everything was as the new bride had hoped. All the men in her life were there to share her happiness.

"Mazel tov!" the gathering shouted as Stuart's foot came down on the wine glass wrapped in a white cloth at the end of the ceremony. Mr. and Mrs. Stuart and Elizabeth Fineman were husband and wife.

"You had to make an appearance?" Rachel asked in a soft whisper, once Josiah and several guests shook hands.

"You are almost as beautiful as the bride," he said, kissing her on the cheek.

"Shall we get refreshments?"

Josiah grabbed her arm firmly and walked her away from the crowd.

"I want to ask your father for your hand in marriage," he said quite seriously, his steel blue eyes glistening in that way that always excited and challenged her.

Rachel stared. She loved the heat and energy when the two of them were together but she doubted that he'd make a very reliable husband. And her parents, they might even disown her. They'd certainly disapprove.

"I don't know, Josiah. I just don't know."

"I love you, Rachel, and I think you love me. Let's at least tell them we've been seeing one another and I'll try and ease their concerns about me. I'm really a most charming fellow," he teased.

Josiah pulled the trumpet from his case and joined the small group of musicians that were hired for the affair. The addition of a trumpet's sweet tones brought a new awareness of the music to the guests. Bess grabbed Stuart away from a group of well-wishers. She apologized, and led the two of them closer to the front. Her dear friend was in his own element. He was feeling the music. It was a condition that Bess recognized. When he played like that he escaped into his own dimension. The sounds thrummed all the way to the river and Bess was sure that her mother could hear it from wherever she had gone. Stephen and Rachel stood nearby. Noah and Robert were next to them. It wasn't a melody that anyone recognized and all the musicians could do was play softly behind him.

"It was for you, Bess. Congratulations," Josiah said. "I even wrote it down and you know I rarely do that."

"Josiah, I was so worried you wouldn't come. It wouldn't have been the same if my guys weren't here. Thank you."

Many of the guests left before night fell but a few, who preferred to travel unfamiliar roads during the day, were made comfortable.

"How do you like teaching at Tuskegee?" Stephen asked, sipping a warm glass of tea, trying to clear his head after imbibing too much wine during the afternoon. The house had gotten quiet except for servants still trying to clean the debris from the afternoon's celebration.

"Nothing like we expected," Robert admitted. "We assumed it was a functioning university, much like Howard University in Washington, where our father taught.

"Initially it was one building, an old church, until they got all of us busy erecting more buildings. More students showed up and we'd put up another building to house them."

"When we were all too tired from carrying boards or pounding nails, or it got late, we'd teach. The next morning, more hammer and nails followed by more classes," Noah added. "But the students are so enthusiastic, so eager to learn, that it makes us happy to teach them."

"Where do they all come from?"

"Most are ex-slaves or the children of slaves. They come from all over the south although most are from Alabama or Mississippi."

"Do you get much trouble from the whites in the area?"

"Of course! It's Alabama, remember. Two of our students were lynched one week after they arrived. They'd come all the way from Kentucky and must have been pretty naïve. The Sheriff said they'd insulted some white woman. They hadn't. They'd only asked her for directions but it was her word against theirs, so a white mob assembled and hung them."

"What did you do?" Stephen asked, awestruck at the story.

"We complained and tried to stop it. When we couldn't, we had all we could do just keeping our students from rioting. If they had we would have had a real blood bath," Noah said.

"Then we had the pleasure of taking a train through Mississippi. We can't sit where we want anymore. Blacks, and any one they think might be black, are relegated to the cars in the back. Anyone who tries to complain faces angry white men pacing the tracks with billy clubs. I had to restrain Robert. He was ready to hit one of the men," Noah said.

"You look like you could have handled them, Robert," Stephen said.

"Probably, but then Noah wouldn't have had anyone to take care of him."

"Always the protective older brother," Noah said, smiling.

Josiah had entered the room but he stood aside as the two brothers described their journey. These were Thaddeus' sons and he knew they were all related but they were much darker skinned and didn't share the cold blue eyes that Henry Rogers had bequeathed to him, Thaddeus, and, ultimately to Stephen.

"Why not consider moving here to New Orleans? It's certainly a lot more civilized than Alabama or Mississippi and there are countless opportunities for you in a growing city," Josiah interjected.

"That's a nice offer, Josiah," Noah said. "I think we both feel we're accomplishing something teaching black people who were deprived for so long."

"Your father would have been very proud," Eli Fineman said, joining the small group. "It's the sort of thing he would have undertaken. I'm so glad you could both join us for Bess and Stuart's wedding."

The sun came up hot and bright the next morning. The newlyweds were sleeping in, but the other visitors who had remained straggled in to the dining room one at a time.

"Do you have a moment, Eli? I'd appreciate a private chat with you," Josiah asked.

"If it's about purchasing Moss Grove, I'd rather not. I thought we had closed that subject the last time you were here," Eli said, the chilled tone in his voice something he was unable to hide.

"No, something else! Truly!"

Eli closed the door to his small library and lit a tiny cigar.

"I didn't know you smoked, Eli. I would have brought you some wonderful Cubans I was able to acquire."

"Thank you, but it's a limited transgression that I hide from Ruth. Now, what is this important matter we need to discuss in private?"

"Rachel and I are contemplating marriage and I am asking your permission to continue to see her," he said, a rare tone of insecurity in his voice. He had become increasingly uneasy asking anyone's permission for anything.

"You're not serious," Eli said, trying to stifle a laugh. "Did you not think that I might learn of your inquiries into my finances? Whoever you hired wasn't very discreet. You intended to acquire Moss Grove through your devious machinations when I wouldn't agree to sell and now you think you can acquire it through marriage. Josiah, you're more of a villain than I would have believed. I regret that it brings to mind unhappy memories of your father, Henry. This is the type of thing I would have more expected of him."

"I am not my father, Eli. I admit that originally it was my intention to possess Moss Grove in any way possible but you must also know I've taken no action in that direction, nor will I. Meanwhile Rachel and I are in love and we would both like your blessing."

"I will speak with Ruth, and with Rachel, but at this moment I am disinclined to grant your request."

Chapter Nine

"Well, Mr. Josiah Rogers…excuse me, Josiah Williams, now that my father has indicated he has no interest in making you his son-in-law where does that leave us?" Rachel asked, removing the green silk shawl that covered her bare shoulders.

They had taken off their shoes and let the waters of Lake Ponchartrain wash over them. Close by a blanket covered the ground and a picnic basket sat, unopened. Rachel had ridden her horse down from Moss Grove while Josiah had brought his small carriage up from New Orleans.

He was still angry about Eli Fineman's reaction. It made him more intent than ever to wed Rachel.

"We could elope," he said, almost to himself. "He'd have to accept me then."

"Were you really going to try and steal Moss Grove from our family?" It was a question she'd avoided asking ever since her father had explained why he detested the man she loved.

"Steal is an ugly word. Moss Grove was built by my forbearers and I want to regain ownership as a legitimate descendent. I tried to buy it from him but he refused. We never even got as far as a discussion of price.

"Your father owes a great deal of money against all that land. He likely needed it when cotton prices collapsed for three years. Now he owes that money to me and a few friends of mine. I thought I'd eventually be able to make him see reason. But all of that was before us. Things changed after you and I…."

He hesitated in the middle of the sentence and he looked at this woman with whom he had unexpectedly fallen in love, her raven black hair and dark eyes, her total sexuality that drove him wild in every encounter. He loved her breasts, the smell of the dark mound between her legs that held such mystery and such fury, and even thinking about it brought a pressure in his pants as he got aroused.

They didn't bother to eat their picnic lunch nor did they speak. Josiah kissed her bare shoulders and, as she stroked his hair, their passion erupted, not caring whether others might have also stopped to enjoy the coolness of the blue lake. An hour later they resumed their journey. Rachel's horse was tied to the back of Josiah's carriage and he pushed the horses into a gallop as the two of them laughed with abandon, anxious to reach New Orleans.

They coupled again with a hunger, their clothing strewn around the room, each touch matched with sighs and laughter. Neither of them was a gentle lover. Their love was physical but they both understood it had become a great deal more than lust. It was true passion and regardless of who they were or how they lived their lives, they needed to be together… to consume one another.

The telegram Eli and Ruth Fineman received was terse.

> *Josiah and I are married. Stop! Please don't be upset. We love one another. Stop! We have taken a ship to New York and Boston for our honeymoon. Please accept us when we return. Stop! Your loving daughter,*
>
> > *Rachel*

Stuart and Bess were in the room when the telegram was read.

"Oh, that's wonderful," Bess said, excited for these two people whom she had always loved.

Neither Stuart nor his parents were able to share her enthusiasm and they could barely eke out a token smile.

The ship out of New Orleans made a stop at Key West before rounding the Southern coast of Florida and heading up the Atlantic seaboard. The young married couple rarely left their room to the salacious grins and suggestive comments of the crew and the other guests on board.

Heavy ocean winds began to batter the ship. The Captain ordered her sails hauled and slowly plowed forward on her steam engine. As they approached Cape Hatteras and Carolina's outer banks they could barely make out the 200 foot lighthouse rising staidly as a guardian warning ships of the treacherous sandbanks nearby. The ship turned into the wind and dropped anchor, finding it more prudent to stop than continue to struggle against the heavy surf.

When Josiah and Rachel awoke in the morning from a night of the ship's heavy rolling, the sky was clear and the air was clean. Looking heavenward, blue was visible only through flared wings of the thousands of gulls and other birds that filled the sky. It was a breathtaking morning and the young couple walked the deck, arm in arm, greeting the crew with smiles.

Josiah and Rachel opted to leave the ship in New York. Neither of them had ever visited the city and they were overwhelmed with the sheer throngs of people, horses, and streetcars. They stayed at the Waldorf in a suite occupied days earlier by a Pasha from somewhere in India. They walked out the front door and stared at the crowds of well-dressed people hurrying somewhere. Hansom cabs were lined up in front waiting for their next fare. Mr. and Mrs. Williams climbed in, threw a waiting blanket over their legs and enjoyed passing the lavish shops along 5th Avenue…so many people and so many stores.

"I always thought New Orleans was big and vibrant," Rachel said as she gathered the boxes of new clothing around her. Josiah just smiled, glad that they had chosen to elope and not face the wrath of Rachel's parents.

"Driver, we'd like to see those slums we've heard about where new immigrants live in shacks stacked ten deep."

"Not in the evenin', no sir…it isn't safe," he said, shaking his head. "It's likely we'd all be robbed. Tomorrow, early, if you're willing."

The cabbie picked them up the next morning and they rode through the already busy streets down to the lower east side where more than three hundred thousand immigrants crowded into a few square blocks. The rancid smell of fish and sewage filled the air as children ran through the streets and hawkers shouted their wares.

"And our coloreds think they've got it bad," Josiah remarked.

"I wonder if these people are still glad they came from Europe to live like this. It's hard to believe that what they had in the old world could have been worse."

"Got a coin, Mister," a disheveled man said, extending his dirty palm as he walked to keep up with the carriage. "I was in the war, I was…Bull Run."

"Get away," the driver said, cracking his whip within inches of the man's head.

"Here, fellow, I'm feeling good today. Enjoy a hot meal," Josiah smiled, passing a bill to the man.

"Josiah, that was very sweet of you. I'm beginning to really like you," his new wife blushed.

For a week they enjoyed theatre, dining, and horse racing. They noticed that Beatrice Fontineau had returned to New York and was appearing in a theatre on 46th St. Rachel wanted to go but Josiah thought that having his wife see another woman with whom he had a dalliance might not be a good idea.

It was time to return to New Orleans. They enjoyed the luxury of a Pullman car, complete with beds and dining car for the entire trip. Mostly they enjoyed having sex to the sound of the wheels click-clacking over the train tracks.

The newly married Williams settled into a two story home in a fashionable part of the city and Rachel sent word to Moss Grove that they had returned. A week went by and she still hadn't received a reply. Meanwhile, she was feeling ill and she'd awaken in the morning with her stomach upset and the color drained from her face.

The doctor smiled as he put his stethoscope back in his bag.

"It looks as if you're pregnant, Mrs. Williams. You'll be just fine. Congratulations."

"Pregnant, that's marvelous," Josiah beamed. "Me, a father! Can you really know you're pregnant so soon?"

"Well, I missed my second period," Rachel said. "But I've always been irregular so I didn't think much about it."

"Does that mean no more fucking for the next seven months?" he frowned. "I don't think I'd like that."

"Come close and let me whisper something in your ear," she teased.

As Josiah bent over the bed she grabbed his crotch and began massaging.

"I'm told sex is better when you're pregnant, bigger nipples, no worry about your next period, and, best of all, lots of moisture. Shall we test the rumors?"

It took Josiah less than a minute to disrobe and join Rachel in bed. Neither of them left before the next morning.

"Rachel is pregnant. She's in her third month. What do you wish us to do now, Eli?" Ruth asked. "It will be our first grandchild and whether you approve of her husband or not, I will be there for her."

The following week Ruth and Bess had their carriage man drive them to New Orleans.

"Rachel, you look wonderful," Bess chimed. "I'm sorry Stuart couldn't make it but some piece of equipment broke and it seems he might be the only one who can fix it. He sends his love. He'll try and come down in a few days.

"Josiah, you are a rogue. I don't know how you convinced Rachel that you are a gentleman instead of a horn blower but I am so proud of you. Your home is lovely and the two of you look very happy."

"And how are you and Stuart doing?" Rachel asked. "I haven't seen my happily married brother for awhile."

"He and Eli will likely come to New Orleans together, but not for a week or more. The plantation is quite busy at the moment."

"Will there be a bris if it's a boy?" Ruth asked, not sure she should address the question to her daughter or to Josiah. The issue had occupied her and Eli since they learned their daughter was expecting.

Her son-in-law laughed.

"Ah, yes, the Jews like to cut off the tip of the boy's pecker. I don't think so," he said, moving to the sideboard and pouring himself a drink.

"We haven't discussed it," Rachel hurried to take the sting from her husband's comments. "And we don't have to make the decision for several months, if at all."

That evening they all went to dinner at Chez Francois, a small, pleasant eatery in the old Quarter where Josiah knew the owner.

"Francois, it's good to see you again. I hope you have a table for me and three lovely ladies."

"Of course, Monsieur Williams, and, we have some lovely escargot I'm sure you'll enjoy. They aren't on the menu... I save them for my special customers," he said conspiratorially.

There was an eclectic group of men at a nearby table. Josiah recognized the ex-governor, Pinchbeck, as well as several well-dressed colored and black. One man, tall, very light-complexioned excused himself from his friends and came over.

"Excuse me, but aren't you Mrs. Fineman," he asked. "You may not remember but the Governor and I visited your father-in-law and your husband last month. We were introduced as we were leaving. I'm Homer Plessy."

"Of course, Mr. Plessy. Now I remember," she said as her eyes lit up with the recollection. "Mr. Plessy and his associates are going to challenge the new law that requires blacks to travel in separate railcars," she explained to the others.

"We all think it's a terrible law and since Mr. Plessy looks white but is technically an octoroon, he will be the one on the train that gets arrested. It's all quite exciting."

Josiah blanched. He always felt uncomfortable around such light colored blacks. He was certain they knew he was one of them and even the unlikely possibility of his being revealed was enough to send a chill through him. He felt as though Plessy was looking at him with the unspoken awareness of a kindred soul.

Introductions were made and Plessy returned to his table.

"What did they all want with Eli?" Josiah asked.

"They wanted a small amount of financial support to launch their case."

"Why would he want to get embroiled? It's very likely to stir up some very distasteful people."

"Like the Klan," Bess interjected. "I hope it does stir up something. Those people have to be stopped. They'd return Louisiana to slavery if they could."

Neither Rachel nor the others knew that Josiah had accepted the offer to become President of the New Orleans Klan and it was clear that this extra-curricular activity was something he'd never be able to share with Rachel, Bess or anyone else from that portion of his life.

Chapter Ten

Stephen left Moss Grove after the wedding, wounded and tearful. Bess looked so beautiful coming down the aisle, he mused. The only damn problem was that she wasn't walking toward me. He knew he should be happy for her but those thoughts came from his intellect, not his heart. He had to stop and dry his eyes.

He forced his thoughts to Josiah. He hadn't been aware of the depth of the feelings Josiah and Rachel had toward one another. He had grown up with Josiah and this certainly wasn't the type of symbiosis he would have expected. He had never known his friend to have a serious relationship. Josiah was, indeed, a changed personality. There is an ugly sharpness to him now. He projects an acerbic anger that hadn't been there before. But he certainly can do magic with that trumpet.

Stephen needed to get back to work and onto Memphis, Tennessee. Mr. Hearst would be expecting him to be telegraphing back stories by this time.

Having had enough of trains, he opted to travel there on horseback. It would be slower, of course, but it would allow him to see parts of the country that have never seen railroad tracks. His paper's new owner, the young Willie Hearst, had wired him suggesting that since he was already in the area, he remain and write a series of stories about the increase in public lynching in the south. Hearst made it clear that he had no desire to generate support for the blacks. It was the violence and public's appetite for the blood and the spectacle that intrigued him. He wanted stories and graphic pictures or illustrations to put on the front page of all the newspapers he was acquiring. Violence was a great circulation booster, he contended.

Memphis had already played host to several spontaneous public lynchings. The city was nearly bankrupt from the yellow fever epidemic that had taken the lives of more than half the city's population but the decline in the size of the city hadn't stopped nor even slowed the Klan's efforts. That city's desire for racial violence was unabated.

> *The People's Grocery Company was a small business owned by Herman and Clarence Cutler, brothers, and Abel Jefferson. All three had been slaves less than a decade earlier. Now they were attacked by a white mob shouting epithets that these 'niggers' were taking business from a white-owned business across the street. Three white men were shot during the melee and others were injured. The three black men who owned the People's Grocery were arrested and put in jail. Early the next morning the jail was stormed by a large white mob. The innocent black owners were publicly lynched as more than a hundred white men, women, and children looked on and cheered, while others hawked drinks and souvenirs to the crowd as the ropes tightened and the men dangled like stuffed dolls. They were left hanging for two days before several blacks found enough courage to take them down and give them decent burials.*

It was difficult for Stephen to understand such callousness. He needed to find someone who could better explain these local attitudes and blood lust. He searched out the woman who had written about these events in a small colored paper. Her name was Ida B. Wells, a local black reporter and activist. Ida had been arrested in 1884 for refusing to give up her seat on a Chesapeake and Ohio Railroad car. Two conductors hauled her out and tossed her into a rail car at the back set aside for blacks. She sued but lost when the Tennessee Supreme Court threw out her case and demanded she pay all court costs. They contended her suit was frivolous and that she was just being a troublemaker.

Stephen was most intrigued with the last paragraph of the article she had written after the People's Grocery lynchings:

> 'There is, therefore, only one thing left to do; save our money and leave a town which will neither protect our lives and property, nor give us a fair trial in the courts, but takes us out and murders us in cold blood when accused by white persons.'

"Mrs. Wells, my name is Stephen Carmody, and I'm a reporter for the San Francisco Examiner. My paper wants to do some articles on these public lynchings that seem to be so popular here in Tennessee and I wondered if you could help me?"

She stared at the handsome café-au-lait man standing in front of her. He was a full head taller than she was and his eyes, so blue, emanated a sense of trust and a kind of energy. If only she were ten years younger, she thought as her mind drifted. Embarrassed, she returned to the question he'd asked.

"I have to ask you, Mr. Carmody, are you white or colored?"

"Does it make a difference on whether you'll help me?" he asked, shocked and visibly uncomfortable with the question.

"Maybe not in San Francisco, but it definitely matters in Tennessee. What do your managers think at your newspaper, white or non-white?"

"To tell you the truth, they've never asked."

"Which tells me you've got some colored blood in you from somewhere, or else you'd have really been insulted by my question. You'd probably have searched out a white person to talk to you about the lynchings instead."

"Can it be our secret?" Stephen asked, a little contritely.

"I'm happy to keep it between us but I'd be a little careful about where I ate my meals in Memphis, racial tensions being what they are."

Ida Wells agreed to give Stephen a spare bedroom in her home to avoid having him stay in any hotel where his race might be questioned. They talked long into the night. It was one of the rare occasions Stephen was willing to explain his background. Ida was a good listener.

They managed only a few hours sleep before heading out the next morning. They rode an hour north of the city in her tiny one horse shay to a small farm. As they approached they could smell the stench of a burned out building, charred smoking timbers all that remained. A tiny fresh grave with a hastily made cross pushed into the fresh dirt sat twenty feet from a small porch.

The black scrub farmer stopped swinging his hoe. There hadn't been much energy in his effort. His eyes were red and carried a look of fear mixed with anger.

"Charlie, this is Stephen Carmody from San Francisco. He's a reporter come to do some reportin' about the Klan's maiming and killing.

"Stephen, this is Charlie Culpepper. Charlie, tell him what happened to you."

"Four riders wearin' white hoods came ridin' up 'bout midnight. They began shouting for me to come out. They said if I didn't they'd burn the house down with me in it. My little girl, Dora, was sleepin', she's not even five 'til next August.

"I went outside and asked 'em why was they there. They said one of my fences was over on my white neighbor's land and I needed to move it twenty feet. I told 'em it had always been this way and no one had ever complained. That's when the ruckus started.

"Two of the men got down and smacked me in the head, accusin' me of sassin' them. They grabbed an axe that I used for makin' kindling and jus' chopped off two fingers from my left hand. My little girl heard the noise and ran out to see if I was alright. One of them white men panicked and shot her. Killed her! I grabbed a rag to stop the bleeding and ran to her but it was too late.

"The men musta' got scared. The four of them rode off but as they left one of them tossed some lit branches into my barn and all I could do was watch it burn, my hand bloody and my little girl nestled in my arms, not moving, like she was still sleeping."

"Where was your wife, Mr. Culpepper?" Stephen said, suppressing a need to vomit, fully traumatized at what he was hearing. It took him a few minutes to regain his composure. He was riveted by the tragedy he'd just been told.

"She died of the yellow fever last year. It was just Dora and me."

"Were the men who did this arrested? Did you tell the Sheriff what happened?"

"Charlie, you tell him. I'm not sure he'd believe me," Ida said.

"One of them four men was the Sheriff," Charlie nodded, tears in his eyes, as he relived the horror of that night.

"How do you know?" Stephen asked, continuing to write down everything Charlie Culpepper was telling him.

"I recognized his roan colored horse. The Sheriff and another man came out to see me the next day when I was burying Dora. He seemed downright sorry and all my black neighbors were impressed that he was there. Then I recognized his horse and he musta' seen in my eyes that I knew he'd been there. He hadn't done the shootin' or the cutting off of my fingers but he'd been there and we both knew it. We also both knew I couldn't say anything without risking the lives of all the black folk that had come to pray over Dora's grave.

"You tell my story, Mr. Carmody. Sheriff's name is Bascom, Wilbur Bascom. You tell your readers about my beautiful Dora. I don't care anymore. I'm leaving. Not sure where, but hell couldn't be any worse than stayin' around here."

Ida introduced Stephen to six other victims of lynchings and terror. A frail black woman, her voice barely a whisper told about her son, the only one of her seven children to survive into adulthood. He was known to have had sex with a white woman. They both swore that it was consensual and they loved one another but the mob didn't care. They tied the man's arms to one mule and his legs to another in front of a crowd of both adults and children. The black man begged for his life before the mules were whipped to push off in opposite directions. There was very little left for his mother to bury and now there was no one to care for her in her remaining years.

The white woman he loved was tarred and feathered and left naked at the city limits. She died two days later of exposure when no one would help her. Ida had ensured that there were pictures taken of such traumatic violence. She didn't ever want anyone to claim she had fabricated these horrors. The grim and graphic details made Stephen sick but he knew that Hearst would love them.

Stephen felt his stomach twist in discomfort at the story of the murdered lovers and for the first time he fully understood the conundrum that his parents would have faced. Thaddeus and Amy would never have been permitted to share their lives together, not in this hate-filled environment.

The articles and pictures were front page in twelve papers in the north and the west and Stephen's byline was prominent. It didn't take more than a few days for copies to arrive in Memphis. It was time Ida and Stephen left. The Klan would be looking for them both and the results, if they found them, wouldn't be pleasant.

"You're coming with me to Chicago," Ida ordered. "Some of the good old white boys…you know, the ones who like to dress up with white hoods, are looking for you. We're going to the Columbian Exposition in Chicago and tell your stories to the world."

The Chicago World's Fair of 1893 was held to honor the 400th Anniversary of Christopher Columbus' discovery of the Americas. The city won the competition over vigorous political opposition from New York, Washington D.C. and St. Louis. The exposition boasted the city's resurgence from the famous Chicago fire twenty years earlier that had destroyed the city. Twenty-seven million people would attend, more than half the country's total population at the census of 1890. Exotic building designs would excite a young L.Frank Baum into later creating the Emerald City of the Wizard of Oz and a young Walt Disney into envisioning Cinderella's castle. Forty-six nations would have pavilions or exhibits but there would be nothing to denote the deplorable condition of blacks or immigrants in America.

"Stephen, this is Mr. Albion Tourgee. He has taken a break from his work on Homer Plessy's appeal to work with Frederick Douglass, and a few of us who are likeminded, to encourage Negros to boycott the fair. We've prepared a pamphlet, '*Reasons*

Why the Colored American is Not in the World's Columbian Exposition.' Much of the information came from the stories you wrote for your newspaper. Those articles did a great deal to shed some light on these tragedies. With the help of Hearst's Chicago paper and The Chicago Conservator, the oldest black owned paper in the city, we plan on printing and distributing more than 20,000 pamphlets. We have no pavilion. These writings will have to be our voice."

"Mr. Carmody, you write a powerful story," Tourgee said, extending his hand and smiling. "We are very grateful."

"Thank you Mr. Tourgee. You can thank Mrs. Wells. These people would never have trusted me nor spoken to me without her assistance."

"Yes, none of us wants to get in Mrs. Wells path. She can be like a runaway train in defense of justice. That's why we all love her.

"We are struggling, Mr. Carmody, and we are losing," he continued. "Mississippi has disenfranchised nearly 200,000 voters, mostly Black. And the new laws being proposed in Louisiana will do the same. We have nearly 150,000 Black voters in Louisiana. The new laws that have been proposed by the now-White legislature will reduce it to less than 5,000. We need to educate Blacks and we need to fight these laws.

"Tell me, would your Mr. Hearst consider allowing you to come to Baton Rouge with me to get some national reporting on our efforts to stop this separate rail car issue and these new voting laws? I think that we have a good case on the separate rail cars with Mr. Homer Plessy as our plaintiff."

"I'll certainly ask. I actually grew up just north of there. Perhaps you know a plantation called Moss Grove."

Tourgee's eyes lit up. "The ways of the Lord never fail to amaze me. He truly moves in strange ways. You must know Eli Fineman and his son, Stuart."

"Quite well. I was just there for his marriage to my half-sister."

"They are helping finance our venture. You'll have an opportunity to see them sooner than you expected."

"Are you going to allow our child to be circumcised if it's a boy?" Rachel asked.

"I said that we'd consider it when and if it was necessary," Josiah responded, clearly not interested in discussing what he considered a barbaric subject at such a delicate moment.

They were nestled under the down covers. The room had chilled. The heat from the fire place had diminished as the glow of the last embers faded. The night had turned unexpectedly chilly and as their naked bodies intertwined, Josiah had little interest in getting up to add kindling or in thinking about his unborn child.

"Oh, that hurts," he yelped as Rachel grabbed his scrotum and squeezed.

"What the hell are you doing?"

"Getting your attention," she said. "I want you to promise that we will have a bris if the baby is a boy or I will squeeze your nuts until you beg."

"You are a vicious bitch," he writhed.

"How about if I threaten to bite off your beloved dick? Would that convince you to let me have my way on this matter?" Her tone softened and her grip turned to a caress.

"Is that better?"

"Your arguments do have a persuasive tone," he said as he moved to her touch. "I'm persuaded," he laughed.

"Thank you, darling," she giggled as she snuggled down the covers to the pleasure of them both.

Samuel Rogers Williams came into the world a month later at the comfortable weight of 7 lb 2 oz. Rachel bled a great deal and her life hung in the balance for several hours. Josiah, Ruth, and Bess hovered close by, tending to the boiling water, bringing clean linen, and urging the mother-to-be to push and breathe at the appropriate times. The doctor remained longer than normal, easily coerced by Josiah's enhanced financial incentive. Eventually they were able to stem the bleeding, and with the help of a small dose of laudanum, the new mother fell into a deep sleep.

The bris was held a week later and the house was filled with guests. The only one Josiah thought to invite was his foreman and savior, Rene Boudreaux. Rene brought his wife, Charlotte, a short, swarthy, but most attractive Creole woman, and their teenage daughter, Cerise. It was easy to see that she was rapidly acquiring her mother's beauty. It seemed that every Jew within a hundred mile radius had come to share the 'mitzvah' of a new male child. Stephen had arrived the evening before and, even Josiah had to admit, it was a grand reunion. The rooms were radiant with good wishes and many of the guests brought gifts. Stephen brought a bright brass trumpet, made smaller for a child's hands.

'May he accompany his father in all good things,' the card read.

He hadn't been able to get time alone with Bess. She looked drawn. Outwardly she was bubbly but he knew her and he knew something deep was troubling her. They had hugged when he'd entered like two celibates careful of their bodily contact. He shook hands with Stuart and recognized their shared discomfort.

Eli Fineman looked tired and ill on an occasion which should have thrilled him. Stuart looked equally glum. Once the Moyle performed the ritualistic rite and the guests shouted Mazel Tov, the celebration began in earnest.

"Josiah, father and I need to talk to you away from your guests," Stuart said as he grabbed Josiah's arm and pulled him to the side.

Josiah bridled at Stuart's heavy handed attitude but his brother-in-law looked sad, not arrogant. His brow was furrowed and his shoulders were bowed as if he was carrying the burdens of the world. Josiah nodded and led the Finemans into his study and closed the doors.

"First, Josiah, this is an occasion of great celebration and I wanted to thank you for agreeing to have Samuel circumcised. I know you have made Ruth very happy," Eli said quietly, sitting, obviously under strains that were both physical and emotional.

"Your daughter is most convincing, Eli. And despite your antipathy toward me, I love her as I will love my new son."

"I'm sure, but that's not why we need to talk. You are as aware as we are that the country seems to have entered a serious economic depression and no one really knows how long it will last. Cotton prices have fallen by a third in the past four months. Nearly every railroad in the country is in bankruptcy or struggling to avoid it. You own the mortgages on Moss Grove. If this situation continues we won't be able to make our payments and you are in a position to foreclose. We want to know what you intend to do."

"You are not the only ones in difficulty," Josiah nodded as he poured drinks for himself and his guests. "Housing prices in New Orleans have collapsed and I have loans I must contend with. Reluctant as I am to share my problems, Eli, we are in this sinking boat together. I may need to sell the paper I hold on Moss Grove just to generate enough cash to salvage my other obligations and what those buyers might do is something I have no way of knowing."

There was a knock on the door and Bess entered.

"I know what you are talking about and I want to be here," Bess asserted firmly, sitting down before any of the men could object.

"Bess," Stuart pleaded. "I know you and I have discussed this situation but my answer is still 'no.' Please, leave so we can continue."

"No, I won't leave," she said in a voice and tone that reminded Josiah of Amy's firmness when confronting a problem.

"You are your mother's daughter," Josiah laughed. "Can we all be privy to this marital disagreement of yours?"

"I want to make the money Amy left me available to help save Moss Grove. I am aware of what's happening to the economy and to have my money sit idle when it could be helping alleviate this problem is silly."

"But that's your money, Bess. It is your personal nest egg," Stuart pleaded.

"If it's mine then I should be able to do with it as I please and I please to invest it in Moss Grove."

"If you knew Amy better," Josiah repeated, "You'd know it's futile to argue with her or haven't you two been married long enough for that to be apparent."

"I'm not comfortable having you continue to hold our mortgages, Josiah," Eli said angrily. "You may be married to Rachel but you continue to make Ruth and me very uncomfortable."

"Yes, I know. You think I might turn out to be like my father. I'll make you an offer. I want my son, and your new grandson, Samuel, to eventually own Moss Grove. I want him to inherit it either from you or, if Stuart intends to remain there, then when he dies."

"What about any children Stuart and Bess hope to have? They should have the first right of inheritance," Eli said, happy that, at least, the ownership of his plantation was finally an open conversation.

"No, I am firm on this. I want to return Moss Grove to the Rogers male line that built it. In exchange I will cease any action to call your loans and I will put those notes in Samuel's name subject to your agreement. Face it, Eli, with cotton prices down and not expected to rise for at least three years, Moss Grove is technically bankrupt. You'll be lucky to generate enough cash to keep your sharecroppers from running off. You'll need Bess' money to keep you afloat and since Stuart and Bess should have a nice long life, they'll have plenty of time to finance a new direction for their children."

Bess sat there staring at the man she had grown up with, a lackadaisical trumpet player without any interest in business or finance. He had now become resolute in a way she'd never seen. This man she'd grown up with and adored now seemed like a total stranger. In quick succession she'd lost her mother, the love of her life and a cousin she'd adored since childhood. It was all a lot to absorb. This was not the Josiah she'd always known.

"Thank you for the mitzvah today. Ruth and I will be leaving," Eli said, fury in his eyes, his hands shaking, the matter far from resolved.

The economic expansion of the past twenty years had fueled exorbitant speculation in gold and silver, overbuilt the railroads, and allowed the nation's banks to undertake questionable lending practices that depleted their financial reserves. Stock prices plummeted, and railroads, which had already been reducing their prices to fill their empty cars, found themselves unable to pay their debtors. Just as Grover Cleveland took office for his second term as President, people panicked and made a run on the banks to withdraw their savings. Bank loans were called, the stock market plunged to new lows and businesses closed their doors in financial ruin. Populists across the country blamed the economic morass on the Jew. Anti-semitism spread amidst false claims that international banking firms such as J.P. Morgan, the Rothschild banking giants in England and France, and other Jewish investment bankers were leaders of a financial cabal and responsible for bringing the country to ruin. Fear was endemic. 'Their ilk had killed Jesus and now they are trying to kill the American dream' was not a majority view but it gained new adherents caught up in the economic malaise. Jews everywhere suffered new insults from their Christian neighbors and the national economy sank further into stagnation.

Josiah had no intention of calling the Moss Grove notes. Doing so would take what liquidity he had and he was not prepared to run a plantation. Having Bess offer to step in solved two problems. It allowed the Finemans to continue to run Moss Grove for several years while the economy got on its feet again and it guaranteed a future for his new son. He was sure they'd eventually accept. They had few options. All in all it would be a successful arrangement.

Another problem that remained was the three buildings he had under construction. One of them abutted a building being erected by a colored builder using black labor. They worked cheaper than the men Rene was able to hire. Perhaps it was time to use his Klan influence.

"Why did Eli and Ruth leave so abruptly?" Stephen asked Stuart as he returned from putting his parents in their carriage.

"You'll have to ask your host. I need another drink. It's nice to see you, Stephen. We've been reading your articles. You're becoming quite well known. Is that what brought you to New Orleans? Are you going to do more lynching stories? They're very moving but I'm sure they aren't popular reading among some groups in the city."

"No, I've come down with Ida Wells and Albion Tourgee to follow-up the Homer Plessy lawsuit. My boss, Mr. Hearst, thinks it has national implications."

"I know both Plessy and Tourgee."

"Yes, they'd mentioned you'd agreed to help them."

"They're a very impressive group but there are strong forces opposing them. Come visit us at Moss Grove. Bess and I are leaving."

"Why so soon?"

"You'll have to ask Josiah."

Stephen wasn't able to learn what had caused the rift. He and Bess hadn't been able to have a single moment alone. He needed to talk to her, to hold her hand…to hear her voice speak only to him. But as she and Stuart got ready to leave, she beseeched him with her eyes. She still loved him but this wasn't a good time for them. As the guests began to depart he said his goodbyes as well, kissed his newborn nephew and left.

He was depressed and tired of chasing stories. He was unsatisfied with achieving minor successes and having no one with whom to share them.

"My life is fucked," he said out loud, watching the small fishing boats bob in the water as a light rain began to fall. He had some free time coming to him but it held little pleasure for him. Maybe I'll just get drunk and stay drunk, he thought. He was staying at a small hotel near the waterfront that accepted boarders of all races. It was one of the few in the city that made no distinction. As long as you paid your rent up front and didn't cause any problems, they were satisfied. The hotel was owned by the same Italian mobsters who controlled the docks. They had fought and beaten another, larger, Italian family three years earlier and no cargo was loaded or unloaded without 'busta,' a proper payoff. Their hotel was simply a convenient cover.

Rene Boudreaux had no misconceptions about his boss. The man had married a wealthy and very attractive Jew but he was quite certain that her family knew nothing about his membership in the Klan. It was likely even Josiah didn't know his foreman was aware of his involvement…and secrets were particularly effective. It was always nice to have some form of leverage when you worked for someone. Rene didn't mind working for Josiah Williams. He could hire his own crew and purchase his own materials from whomever he wanted. There was always a little overbilling he could arrange that would buy a new dress for his wife or daughter.

Rene's great- grandfather had migrated a hundred years earlier with the Acadians who came all the way from Quebec when the British took over Canada from the French. The English were uncomfortable having a large nest of troubling Catholics in their midst, especially French ones. Most of the entire colony traveled south and settled in French owned Louisiana where they could practice their religion without harassment. What they hadn't anticipated was that France would sell the land to Spain, although they would later regain it. When Napoleon needed money to finance his European wars, he sold his country's huge swath of land in the middle of America and Rene's father suddenly found himself a citizen of the new United States. Now the Boudreaux's were American, an identity that everyone seemed to interpret differently.

Intermarriage was widespread as Creoles, Europeans, Acadians, Haitians and others spread across southern Louisiana while maintaining their own dialect, music and food.

His wife's family came from Haiti. Charlotte was the only one of five children to survive the many diseases that pervaded the Louisiana's low-lying land. She married Rene when she was sixteen and together they had four children, Cerise being the eldest. Rene was a good provider. He was bulky and strong and throughout his childhood he had fought against taller white bullies. It wasn't in his nature to shrink from a challenge and he learned early in his teens how to make the first blow count.

Rene didn't trust Josiah Williams. The man might turn on him if it was to his advantage but Rene gave no inkling of his feelings. He was outwardly respectful and, having saved his boss's life, he had demonstrated his loyalty. But he knew that there was trouble ahead. Many of his friends were out of work as a result of the nationwide financial crisis. Even his two grown sons who worked on the docks had been pushed aside for Italians who had a family connection. There was less cotton and sugar being shipped and fewer ships arriving at New Orleans harbor to unload their cargo.

Homer Plessy boarded one of the cars of the East Louisiana Railroad. He took a seat along with more than a dozen white passengers, all of whom removed their coats, stowed their packages, and were now trying to make themselves comfortable. He helped an elderly woman, traveling alone, store her case. The train whistle blew and the five-car train pulled out of the New Orleans station. It had traveled less than an hour when Plessy stood, walked to the end of the car and faced the other passengers.

"Excuse me, ladies and gentlemen. May I have your attention?

"I wish to announce that I am one-eighth black and I am disputing the Louisiana law that says I may not remain here with all of you."

There was an immediate hubbub and confusion. A few people smiled at the man's effrontery but the Conductor, standing at the opposite end of the car, was not amused. He pulled the signal to have the Engineer stop the train.

"You will move to the black-only car or we will have you arrested," the uniformed train conductor said.

"I will not move," Plessy said.

Moments later two men grabbed Plessy's arms, lifted him off his feet and removed him from the train. The other travelers strained at the windows to see what was happening. Three passengers followed Plessy off the train to make certain he wouldn't be harmed. They were to be his witnesses. They waited at the side for the closest of the Sheriff's men to make the formal arrest while the train barked its signal and continued on toward Clarington.

One night of debauchery was all Stephen could handle. Beginning the next morning he focused on attending each one of Homer Plessy's court hearings and wrote his stories for the national public. He was pleased that Mr. Hearst was allowing his full reporting to be printed rather than be cut to fit pages not consumed by advertising.

Plessy's lawyers argued that he had been deprived of civil rights under the 13th and 14th Amendments to the Constitution. Judge John Ferguson decided against Plessy on the grounds that the Federal government, and therefore, its laws, had no authority over railroads that operated solely within a state. The case would now begin its slow, tortuous way to the U.S. Supreme Court.

"How are you Albert?" Josiah asked over dinner. "We don't have the pleasure of your visits very often."

Albert Pike hadn't returned to New Orleans since the Roger Cadway murder and his back room manipulation that followed to help make Josiah the new head of the local Klan.

"This financial mess in the country is affecting everyone, even the Klan. A large number of our best people have packed up and moved out west, hoping they can find work or good land to farm. I've been busy recruiting but a lot of people only care about the blacks if niggers are working and they aren't. Right now lotsa' people all colors aren't working. Mines are shutting down; banks have closed and run off with people's hard earned savings. No one's getting anything decent for their crops or the animals they been slaughtering just to keep their farms. Are you surviving OK?"

"Not easily. I've got some properties I wish I didn't have but nothing is selling these days," Josiah answered. He was in better financial shape than he chose to admit but he didn't want Pike asking him for a loan.

"How's the Klan membership here in New Orleans?"

"We've lost a few but we're still strong," Josiah lied, not certain how much Pike had heard from other members.

"Well, that's good. Any exciting projects I should know about?"

"We raided some of the coloreds and blacks that have been vocal in support of this Homer Plessy fellow. You know, the one they've got who filed suit to stop the railroads from keeping whites and blacks in separate cars."

"Good, but why not just lynch Plessy?"

"Law suits already up in Baton Rouge. We thought of stringing him up but we were a little afraid of the backlash. Without supporters we figured he'd just go away."

"Keep me posted. We're getting those separate laws passed in Mississippi and Alabama soon and a lot of other states will follow. We're even working on laws so the blacks and coloreds can't vote. That'll affect those monkeys good and proper."

"I want those black construction workers put out of business and that building they're working on destroyed," he said softly at the end of the Klan meeting.

Josiah had taken Philippe Broussard aside and offered him $200.00 for the one night's work. They agreed that Broussard would take three men with him, the same proven men he'd used on other raids. Broussard wanted enough men to do the job right but not too many that he'd have to share the money with. He was Cajun and a frightening looking man with a scar on one cheek and only one eye, the other one lost by a ball from a Union musket in the battle of Chickamauga.

Three days later when Josiah and his foreman arrived at their site they could see a few blacks digging through the rubble of their burnt out construction site nearby.

"What happened, fellows?" he asked genially as he walked over.

"Klan burned us out," one man offered. "You don't happen to know something about this, do you?"

"Me? What would I know?" Josiah said innocently.

"Strange how my building getting burned up makes your building across the way a lot more valuable," the man said, angrily, as one of his workers tried to pull him back.

"Listen, nigger, if you're accusing me of something, you better have some facts or I'll beat your ass and have you thrown in jail for libel."

"He don't mean nothin', mister. He's just upset over losing everything he had," his friend said.

"Then he better keep his thoughts to himself and his mouth shut," Josiah said, walking away haughtily, grinning inside.

Chapter Eleven

Violence and labor strikes spread across the country while the economy continued to be increasingly dormant. More than 50,000 miles of railroad traffic had been silenced by the widespread bankruptcy of several of the nation's largest railroads. In response, the Pullman Palace Car Company that provided sleeping cars for all the railroads, was forced to reduce the wages of its employees at its Chicago factory. Three thousand of their workers staged a wildcat strike. Eugene Debs, President of the American Railway Union, the country's first national union, added his support by urging a boycott in which his members refused to work any trains that included Pullman cars.

Pullman reciprocated by locking out his employees. Trains across the country were idled as Debs' union members refused to cross picket lines. Within a few days more than 125,000 workers in cities across the country were actively protesting. Members of other unions stopped work in sympathy.

The courts issued injunctions prohibiting Debs and his people from supporting the strike but they were ignored. Nothing would assuage the situation. Desperate to end the stand-off, President Cleveland called out the Army...12,000 armed troops were dispatched. More violence ensued and before the matter was settled dozens of men were killed or injured.

The depression deepened, and in just three years,

unemployment increased from three million to fifteen million. In New York twelve thousand clothing workers, most of them recently arrived immigrants, went on strike against their working conditions. Negro miners in Alabama were killed by white miners who had staged a work stoppage.

Robert and Noah were enjoying their time at Tuskegee. Their wages were minimal but the enthusiasm of the students more than made up for it. A few years earlier Booker T. Washington had moved them from their sparse single building in the Butler AME Zion church to an abandoned plantation. With the help of volunteers, students, and staff, buildings were erected. Everyone was eager to share in this grand experiment. However, the white townsfolk of Mobile, the closest town of any size, were less than enthusiastic.

Robert was teaching math and reading. And, whenever he could find time, he'd encourage his students to join him outside for some rigorous physical exercises. The only equipment they had was what they could fashion from felled trees. Meanwhile, Noah was teaching English, and showing a few of his students how to paint and think creatively. As slaves, learning how to read or do numbers was strictly prohibited. Now that slavery had ended, most were like sponges eager to absorb what they had always been deprived of. Two students, a brother and sister from Chattanooga, showed some real talent. Noah delighted in showing them how to mix colors from things they found in their surroundings. He even taught them how to make their own brushes. It was their pictures that were decorating the bare walls of the school's new buildings.

The brother's rooms were considerably less comfortable than their home in Georgetown but as long as it didn't rain they could stay dry.

"Let's go visit Mobile," Robert said. "We need a break from here and it's less than a two hour ride."

"Maybe I can find an art book for my students," Noah agreed.

They saddled horses early Saturday and enjoyed a leisurely ride through Alabama's back country. It was midday when they reached the outskirts of Mobile. The ride had made them hungry but they had trouble finding a café that would feed blacks although one colored cook in a white-only cafe offered to hand them their food through the back door. It was all so different than Georgetown or the nation's capitol where they'd grown up. Robert tried to object at one stop but Noah grabbed his arm and pulled him away. They finally found a place on the last block of the city, near the railroad tracks.

"Well, hello. You two are certainly handsome young men and I'm happy to serve you. Welcome to Clarisse's café. I hope you're hungry because my vittles is real good. My name is Clarisse," the waitress-cook- owner smiled as she dried her hands on her apron. "You boys don't look like you from around these parts."

"No, ma'am, we aren't. We were from Washington but now we're teaching over at Tuskegee. We thought we'd see what a big city in these parts has to offer."

"Well, be careful where you wander here in Mobile. A lot of the rough looking white men walking around are out of work and they don't like to see black folks that look like they're better off. If I were you, I'd eat and head back. You look like nice boys and things ain't real good around here." She shook her head sadly and walked back into the kitchen.

The two men finished their meal, thanked Clarisse, and walked around the corner where they'd left their horses tied up. Three unshaven and unkempt white men were gathered around them, checking their saddles and packs.

"Excuse me," Noah said. "Those are our horses."

"Pretty nice horses for niggers, ain't they Frank?" One of the men said, not acknowledging the two black men approaching them.

"Must a' belonged to a decent white man," Frank, the largest of the three answered.

"Bet these nags been stolen. We should go get the sheriff."

"He took the day off. Must be tired from searching for whoever strung up nigger pig stealers that got caught a few days ago."

"Exhausting work! Good thing he's got decent white folk keepin' their eyes out for more thieveries."

"We didn't steal those horses," Robert said as he came up to the three men. Robert was well-built and at least a head taller than any of the three scroungy looking men he was standing next to.

"Don't you sass me," the largest man said, as he swung the butt of his rifle against Robert's knees, dropping the young black man to the ground.

"Robert," Noah cried, as another of the men hit him with the handle of an old Confederate pistol.

With the two brothers dropped to the ground, the three hooligans moved with greater confidence, continuing to kick and pistol whip them. Noah and Robert tried to cover themselves and Robert tried hard to protect his smaller brother. The last thing Robert remembered before losing consciousness was spreading his arms across Noah's prone, limp body.

"You get away from those boys. Right now, you hear!"

A shot rang out and the three bullies looked up. Coming from the direction of Clarisse's were a dozen armed Negros. The attackers weren't going to stay against those odds and they didn't see any whites coming to their defense. They jumped up on the brother's horses and rode off.

"Bring them boys into my place," Clarisse ordered. As soon as she saw the boys being accosted she knew there was trouble brewing and she ran for help.

Robert and Noah were gently laid on adjoining beds and several of the men and women tended their cuts and scrapes.

Robert fell into a deep sleep and didn't wake for a day and a night. Clarisse and the others took turns watching.

"Noah," Robert's weak voice groaned when he finally began to stir. "Noah? Is Noah alright?"

He opened his eyes slowly and looked around. His brother wasn't there.

"Where's my brother?"

"He didn't survive his injuries. The man with the pistol hit him so hard in the head that the blow killed him," one of the men said, his voice soft and sad. "We buried him nearby. We didn't know whether you'd make it but you're bigger and stronger. Those men hit you both real bad."

"We hadn't done anything," Robert said. "They were stealing things from our saddle bags."

"You don't need to do nothin' in these parts to have trouble find you. Those some angry white boys and you ain't the first niggers they picked on, although none of the others died. We're all sorry we couldn't get there to help no sooner."

Robert tried to sit up but he could feel the pain in his ribs and groin where they'd kicked him. Two of the men helped him.

"I can't believe my brother is dead. I loved him. I was supposed to protect him. After our parents died, we grew even closer, and coming to Tuskegee to teach was a real adventure we could share."

"I don't think you should stay around here," Clarisse said. "Those boys'll be back once they discover one of you survived. They don't want you to be able to tell anyone what they done. Ain't likely, but someone could listen. You got kin you can go to?"

Robert had to think. He really didn't know anyone from his mother's family that was still alive.

"Louisiana! Near Baton Rouge! I've got some family there."

"If you have a little money we can get you a horse. Rest another few days and then travel at night. Let us know when you're strong enough and we'll all say a prayer over your brother's grave."

A lone, tired, Negro rider rode up the long path to the main house at Moss Grove and asked to see Mr. Fineman.

"Can I help you?" Stuart asked. "My father isn't….Robert, is that you? What happened? Come in, sit down. You look exhausted."

"Hello, Stuart. I believe one my wounds opened yesterday and I'm worried it might be infected."

"Phoebe," he shouted to the girl who ran the house servants, "Get Bess. Tell her I need her right now."

Bess, four months pregnant, rushed down the stairs and before she could ask what her husband wanted, she saw Robert, hunched over, wet red stains streaked across his shirt.

"Oh, my God! Robert, take that shirt off and come into the kitchen where we've got hot water and clean rags."

An hour later, Robert's wounds had been cleaned and bandaged. He sat, sipping hot tea, his breathing less labored as he felt safe for the first time since he and his brother left Tuskegee for a casual weekend.

He explained that Noah had been killed by three white hooligans, just hanging out, looking for trouble. The people who helped him warned against returning to Tuskegee and he didn't know where else to go.

"We're glad you thought to come here. You're family," Bess said, reaching out her hand.

"I can't believe Noah is dead. He was my younger brother and I always protected him. This one time I couldn't and he's gone." Tears flowed down Robert's cheeks. For the first time since Noah had died, Robert could give vent to his feelings. He had lost his father unexpectedly and now he'd lost his brother and his entire being felt empty. He was devoid of anyone with whom to share his life.

For the next few weeks Robert rested and let his physical wounds heal but as he wandered around Moss Grove his emotional scars remained raw. He didn't talk very much but if he saw one of the workers repairing a building or a piece of equipment, he was there to help. He even grabbed a bag and began picking cotton. It was clear to Stuart and Bess than he needed to be busy and to clear his head.

"I'm leaving for a few weeks. I'd like to borrow a fresh horse but I'll bring it back."

"Don't you want to wait until you're fully healed?" Bess asked.

"No, I'm fine. You're a good nurse."

Neither Stuart nor Bess wanted to ask him where he was going. Somehow they knew that Robert had made up his mind about something and they wanted to respect their friend's privacy.

Frank sat by the small campfire near the river. He had caught himself a two pound catfish, a big fat old thing, and he was enjoying watching it sizzle in the frying pan. Catfish is good eatin', he thought.

Frank never heard the footsteps behind him. The man had approached stealthily, taken off his shoes and waited until the last rays of the sun had dipped behind the nearby hills.

"Frank," the man said softly.

Frank jumped at the sound. He turned and began to stand when a rifle butt cracked across his cheek and he stumbled into the campfire. His shirt caught on fire and he danced around, slapping at the flames. Whoever hit him covered him with a blanket to snuff out the last embers.

His face covered with soot, his clothes still smoking, Frank finally looked up at his attacker.

"Remember me, Frank," the big young Negro said, still holding his rifle like a bat.

"You one of the niggers back in Mobile. We heard you weren't dead. Me and my friends looked for you for awhile but we got bored. All you blacks look alike."

"You killed my brother, asshole. He never hurt anyone and you three bastards killed him."

"Listen, nigger. You better clear out of here before my friends come back," Frank said with a bravado he clearly didn't feel.

Robert just smiled. "Frank, you know it's just you and me."

Without hesitation, the smaller white man leapt forward, catching Robert by surprise, his rifle falling to the ground. Frank pulled a knife and thrust his arm forward, catching the bigger man on the arm. Robert grabbed his bleeding arm instinctively but his eyes never left his opponent.

"Nice move, Frank," he said. "You have more courage than I gave you credit for. I thought you were just an ignorant honky but it won't help you. You're going to pay for killing my brother."

Robert feinted right and moved left. In two quick moves he disarmed Frank and locked his arm around the smaller man's neck from behind. Frank couldn't get free. He thrashed around and tried to make Robert lose his balance. Robert kept the pressure on, his forearm locked like a vise against the white man's neck. Slowly Franks' thrashing lessened and finally stopped. His body went limp.

Robert held his arm in place and walked the motionless man to the edge of the river. He continued moving forward out until the water was waist high, then he just released his arm and let Frank's body drop.

"Now the catfish can have you for dinner."

It was two weeks before Robert returned to Moss Grove. He left Clarisse a note thanking her for her kindnesses and a small amount of money to care for Noah's grave, maybe put fresh flowers there on occasion. She knew he had come back. There were rumors but no one knew anything for certain. Neither Frank nor his two friends had been seen nor heard from for two weeks. The Negros who had helped held their collective breaths. Would there be retaliation from the whites in the community? But none was forthcoming. After a few weeks people found other things to occupy their curiosity and everyone moved on with their lives.

"I'm going to Moss Grove for a visit," Rachel said, breast feeding their small child. "Bess is well along in her pregnancy and my parents haven't seen baby Samuel for awhile. Why don't you join me? It would do you good to get away."

"No, you go. There are a good many things I can take care of when the two of you are gone," Josiah said, his mind already at work. He had been delinquent about his Klan duties and he knew his group was growing restless. This would be a good time to make it right.

The sun was shining bright the next morning when the Williams' carriage left New Orleans and headed north. It was a brand new style carriage with comfortable leaf springs and leather seats. There were even encased kerosene lights that would shine on the road ahead if one chose to travel at night. Their carriage man was nattily dressed. The entire affair bespoke wealth, and that was the image Josiah wanted to convey.

It was a pleasant trip. Their cook had packed a picnic hamper and the carriage stopped along the banks of Lake Ponchartrain. The baby gurgled as Rachel let him dangle his feet in the cool water.

It was late afternoon when they arrived at the plantation and Rachel immediately lost possession of her young son. Samuel became the exclusive possession of his grandparents.

"Bess, you look marvelous," Rachel said as her obviously very pregnant sister-in-law came into the room.

"I feel as if I've swallowed a bale of cotton."

"Hello, sister of mine," Stuart grinned as he grabbed his sibling in a huge bear hug. "It's a good thing you're my sister or I'd be obliged to ravish you right here in front of my wife."

"That's because I'm ugly and fat and no longer desirable," Bess pouted insincerely.

"I'm sure Stuart doesn't think you are either. He looks quite husbandly and content," she said as a tall handsome Negro entered the room.

"Robert? What a lovely surprise. What happened to your face?"

"It's a long and not terribly happy story," Robert replied.

"Rachel, go freshen up," Bess interjected. "You've plenty of time to hear about what Robert went through."

"It's time we made ourselves known and frightened a few black asses," Josiah shouted from the front of the room, his blue eyes icy with a contrived anger. Now that he was alone it was time to reassert his leadership of the local Klan. "We've been quiet too long and a lot of the niggers around here are getting uppity. We need to put everyone back in their place."

"I hear tell there are three families loading up and heading out west," one of the men said, filled with indignation. Josiah recognized him as a small cotton farmer who had never owned more than one or two slaves before the war.

"They've been share croppin' a place that grows mostly indigo, south of here, but with prices for everything so low they wanna' get out. We lose that labor and there won't be any blacks around to work the fields when prices go back up."

"If we aren't running away from our responsibilities, we don't want them running away either," Josiah agreed. "It might be time to convince them they should stay."

Wagons loaded with the meager belongings of the three black share cropper families slowly made their way along the dirt road out of Houma heading northwest. It was that last hour before dawn and the leaves from the oaks and the Spanish moss that draped the dirt road were covered with dew. The sun would be up soon and it promised to be another hot muggy day. The men and women on the wagons were nervous. It had taken hours and hours of talking for them to agree that there was no future share cropping in Louisiana. The lure of cheap land somewhere to the west that could be their own had drawn them. They were convinced that as long as they stayed in any part of the old Confederacy they'd be 'niggers.' Maybe out west their children would have a better chance to be just plain folks.

Eight men on horseback wearing white hoods massed in front of the wagons.

"You folks up mighty early," Josiah said in a commanding voice.

"Yes sir, but we is peaceable. We got our wives and children here and we don't want no trouble," one of the men in the lead wagon said as his wife retreated to protect their two children.

"Trouble? Shouldn't be no trouble. Where you folks headed?"

"Movin' out west. Can't survive here with prices on all the crops down so low."

"Well, we all understand that, don't we men?" he asked the others. They all nodded in agreement.

"Fact is," Josiah continued. "Prices will be going back up soon and if folks like you leave there won't be anyone left to work the fields. Now you all understand that, don't you?"

"Maybe so, but we done decided, so please, mister, let us just go on our way," he pleaded as a few of the blacks from the other two wagons came forward.

"I don't think that will work out for us," Josiah said in a smile that couldn't be seen beneath his hood as he and the other men drew their pistols. We're gonna need you to turn your wagons and head back to where you came from. You'll have to tough it out like the rest...."

"I know that voice," one of the young blacks blurted out, interrupting Josiah. "You the trumpet player...you..."

A single shot rang out and the black teenager fell. As one the riders stared at their leader, holding his pistol, curls of smoke from the gun's barrel were visible in the morning air.

"You killed Edgar," the black in charge shouted. "Why you kill that young boy? He didn't do nuthin'? Oh, lordy, he dead and you murdered him."

Josiah tried to gather his composure. Edgar? The young black share cropper's kid from Moss Grove who played the banjo? What the hell was he doing here? Had to shoot him! Some of those Moss Grove share croppers knew about my father and his drop of black blood. I had to shut him up. I had to. His thoughts ricocheted through his head.

"Tried to sass me," Josiah said, trying to reassert control. "I don't take sass from a nigger. Now you folks turn around. We're leaving but we'll know if you don't and we'll come after you. Let's go, men."

"Now that the Plessy trial is on the docket of the Supreme Court and won't be heard for a year or two, what are your plans?" Josiah asked, as he and Stephen walked the quay. Stephen was due to leave the city. He was just awaiting instructions as to his next assignment.

Josiah was pleased the men in his Klan group were now a little more in awe of him. It would allow him some breathing room. He wouldn't be obligated to do anything violent for a while and he could return to his other life. Seagulls squawked overhead as a few men, likely without jobs to occupy them, watched their fishing lines dangle in the water.

"I'm not really sure. I've been gone from the Examiner and San Francisco for enough years that they've probably forgotten me. I think I've become sort of a freelance rover for Mr. Hearst. He does pay me, though, so I can't really complain. How long do you expect Rachel to be gone?"

"She'll probably stay at Moss Grove another few weeks. She goes up there every month or two, then sends me notes every day or two...Samuel is crawling, Samuel is saying 'mama' or shitting or he's doing something really amazing. But I know she's enjoys being with Bess and Stuart and her parents. Eli and Ruth have really aged and she's worried about their health. Seems they both take ill quite often. Besides it gives me time for other enjoyments. Marriage can be a little stifling."

"I heard rumors that some kid, whose family are share croppers at Moss Grove, was shot last week by some of the Klan."

"I didn't see anything about it in the local newspaper," Josiah said, eager to avoid the subject.

"The local white newspaper prefers to avoid writing about Klan transgressions. I heard about it from another reporter who writes for a black paper."

"Kid was probably a troublemaker, Stephen. There's always a reason for these things."

"You've certainly changed since you were nothing more than a trumpet player missing half the notes," Stephen laughed nervously. Josiah would have never offered such a ridiculous explanation in the past, he was sure.

"You seem to be living the high life now, tailor made clothes, fancy carriage, a large home," Stephen noted, dodging crates of fish being carried from a nearby fishing trawler to a fishmonger, waiting with his wagon.

"But I have to ask you, don't you get a little nervous every now and then about you know what?"

"I never think about it," Josiah lied, his eyes turning to an icy blue. "It isn't me, it wasn't me, and it will never be me."

"Can you be that sure?"

"I refuse to consider that it will ever be an issue in my life. Therefore, it never will be."

"Well, I admire your certainty. I'm not that comfortable in my skin down here in Louisiana with all the new laws and the new restrictions on both blacks and people of color."

"Keep your nose clean and you shouldn't have any trouble."

"Easy for you to say! Everyone you know believes you to be 100% white. I….."

"I am white and I'd prefer that you never indicate otherwise," Josiah said, the anger in his voice rising to a strident pitch.

"Anyway you want, Josiah. Relax. C'mon, let's get some food. I'll even let you treat me. But just to be safe let's make sure it isn't a 'white only' place."

It was early evening when they left the Cajun restaurant, sated by plates of shrimp creole. They had decided to walk back to Josiah's house and have a nightcap before Stephen returned to his hotel. Josiah had plenty of extra rooms but had never invited Stephen to stay there. They both knew why. Stephen traveled in a multicolor world that Josiah would never acknowledge.

"Hey, don't go down that street," an onlooker shouted. "Rioting! Blacks and whites are fighting one another with clubs and knives."

"What about?" Stephen asked, thinking that there might be a possible story, but the man who had warned them was already out of earshot.

"We can hire a carriage," Josiah said, preferring to avoid the conflict. "Let's walk down this other street."

"You go, Josiah. I'll meet you at your house."

Stephen ran down the two blocks to where the noise was coming from. A few policemen were trying to separate the men but their billy clubs invariably connected with black heads rather than white. By the time calm was restored, six blacks were dead, a number of both whites and blacks were bleeding and trying to leave the scene, limping and scarred. Remaining anywhere near the melee likely meant getting arrested, and the New Orleans police had little tolerance for anyone who came into their custody. There were conflicting stories about how the ruckus began, each racial cluster blamed the other.

"Six blacks were killed," Stephen said to Josiah, as he sat and drank his bourbon after making notes and walking the several blocks to the house "Useless violence! No one even knows what started the fracas. Probably one man took offense at a look or a word and the others just joined in."

Stephen didn't stay long, upset with the casualness of Josiah's remarks. His friend no longer cared about things that Stephen felt were important. He wasn't ready to return to the solitude of his small hotel room. He walked a few blocks, finding himself passing restaurants and shuttered stores he had passed a few minutes earlier. He came upon a well-lit house, banjo and piano music coming at him through an open window. A small brass placard adorned the gate of a white picket fence, Madame Bovary. He laughed. It was doubtful that Flaubert ever thought to transfer his bawdy heroine from Paris to New Orleans to open a brothel.

"Good evening, Monsieur," a dark latte beauty said, as she stood to one side to allow Stephen to enter. "Welcome to Madame Bovary's."

Stephen was not an innocent but neither was he a man of considerable experience. Crystal chandeliers, velvet settees, nattily attired servants and girls of every hue moving effortlessly through the room as if on air.

"Yes, of course. I'd like some brandy…"

"And a girl for the evening," she said, finishing his sentence. "My name is Tatiana. You are….?"

"Stephen."

"Yes, of course, Monsieur Stephen. Please follow me."

He was seated, made comfortable, and handed a large crystal brandy snifter with a Napoleonic crest emblazoned in gold. Tatiana sat down next to him, nursing her own glass of Courvoisier.

Other couples sat nearby engrossed in their own conversation. Some listened to the music, some drank heavily and some actively touched and embraced their companion of the moment, anxious to get to a private room upstairs.

"I think, Stephen, that you haven't been with a woman for some time."

"The woman I love has just married another man," he admitted, breathing the deep scents exuding from his glass.

"Then let me help you forget her, at least for the evening," Tatiana whispered.

He let her lead him up the stairs and into a blue velvet furnished room, candles flickering seductively.

Tatiana took off her gown ever so slowly, watching her new friend's reaction. With only her lingerie remaining, she moved to the bed to help Stephen disrobe. As her hands moved to unbutton his pants, he gasped and climaxed.

"I am so sorry," he said, embarrassed. "It has been a long time."

"Do not worry. You will be erect again shortly. I promise you," she laughed.

Chapter Twelve

It wasn't until 1896 when the case of Homer Plessy v. Ferguson reached the U.S. Supreme Court. By a vote of 7-1, one Justice abstaining, the majority declared that the Louisiana law did not imply any inferiority of blacks, which would have violated the Fourteenth Amendment. The law, they said, simply separated the two races as a matter of public policy. 'Separate but Equal' would be the new paradigm. After the decision, southern states accelerated the passing of laws that separated the races without regard for either equal treatment or comparable facility.

An early winter had set in and the dirt road crackled from ice crystals as Stephen rode his horse north of Baton Rouge. He was determined to have some time alone with Bess. His time with Tatiana had been a pleasant diversion and he'd returned to Madame Bovary's several times, grateful that he was now able to control climaxing. She had even helped him to become a better lover. Now if he only had someone to share it with.

He took a route that followed the Mississippi River. It was a little longer, and the roads weren't as good, but he enjoyed watching the boats moving north and south, so many different types of cargo, their steam whistles announcing their passing. What an amazing world it's become, he mused.

The plantation was wearing its early winter blanket as he arrived. The fireplaces kept the rooms warm and steam from the large pots of hot water glistened on the walls of the kitchen. It was easy to smell the camphor from the bedding that had been stored during the long summer months and was now being aired.

Stephen could also smell the maple and hickory odors coming from the smoke house as he got nearer to the main house. Everything in sight seemed to exude signs of warmth and cordiality.

He saw Stuart first, exiting the small windowless smoke house.

"Whew, it's hot in there," he said. "Stephen, you're a welcome surprise. I hope you've come to stay awhile. Bess will be thrilled. The baby is due any day now, so your timing is superb."

The realization that his love was due to have a child that wouldn't be his, returned his depression. He was determined to sublimate these negative thoughts. Stuart and his parents are good people. They love Bess and she loves them. I wish I didn't feel like a distraction, he said to himself.

"Bess, you look spectacular," Stephen said, laughing as he tried to embrace her.

"Difficult embracing a small whale, isn't it?" she smiled, her dimples and freckles as bright as cascading stars. "I've gained way too much weight."

"Well, you do look different from the bride who walked down the aisle several months ago or the svelte woman I saw at the bris. But you look happy, and that's the important thing."

Their eyes connected. Stuart discreetly gave them time alone. Bess had asked, and Stuart had just nodded, unable to refuse his wife, and convinced the shadow of her feelings for Stephen would always hang over them.

The entire family gathered for dinner that evening, including the Finemans, Bess and Stuart, Rachel, and Robert, who Stephen hadn't seen since Amy's funeral. Stephen was stunned to learn of Noah's violent death.

"Would you like me to do a story on what happened?" he asked.

"No. Publicizing it wouldn't do any good and there are people who helped me who could face retribution. In less than a year, though, I've lost both my father and my brother," Robert said morosely. "I feel rudderless."

"I've shared similar losses," Stephen said. "Anyway, now that the Plessy trial isn't news anymore I've been given the choice of joining the gold strike in the Yukon Territory or joining the Cubans fighting for their independence," Stephen said as they were served courses of guinea hens and smoked pork.

"Mr. Hearst sent me one of his typical telegrams," he said, pulling a crumpled piece of paper from his pocket and read:

> *Gold discovered in Alaska. Stop. More rioting in Cuba, war inevitable. Stop. Your choice. Stop. Extra pay if you choose Cuba. Stop. War stories trump gold for building circulation.*
>
> *Hearst*

"Cubans who migrated to this country long ago, and particularly those who came to the South decades ago, are already heading back to join their island's fight for freedom from Spain. I'm probably going to join them…at Mr. Hearst's encouragement, but I haven't completely made up my mind. I'd likely be living with and reporting what the rebels are doing. We've certainly romanticized them. We liken them to our Revolutionary war heroes."

"You'll also need to keep yourself from getting killed by the Spanish, I'd imagine," Stuart chimed in. "Perhaps we should liken them to the British Redcoats. How do you say 'The Redcoats Are Coming' in Spanish?"

"I think I could find myself going to Cuba," Robert remarked. "My father was very active in Washington for more than a decade, encouraging our country to do something. The Spaniards have bled Cuba for more than a century and all they've left the Cubans is poverty. Ninety miles off shore and they're treated like crap."

"You mean like American blacks," Stephen added, to the stares of the others.

"Not all blacks are treated badly," Eli Fineman said, his voice weak from a wracking cough that he'd had ever since the cold spell had set in.

"Maybe not, but not all of them are able to live in peace either. I understand a young man whose family are share croppers here was murdered by some crazed Klansman."

"Yes, we heard. A boy named Edgar. He used to play the banjo a lot and at one point he wound up doing duets with Josiah playing his trumpet. Night riders came to frighten him but he'd already run off. Did Josiah know about it?" Stuart asked.

"We discussed a young teen being shot and that his family lived at Moss Grove but at that point I'm not sure either of us knew it was this Edgar you're mentioning."

"I'm sure he would have said something if he'd made the connection," Rachel said.

"If you go to Cuba, when would you leave?" Robert asked.

"Soon! Care to come along. Maybe I could tell them you're my photographer or my illustrator."

"That would have been an ideal task for Noah. He was the artist. He taught me a little, but he had the talent. You'd have to teach me. I've never been closer to a camera than a few feet, although we saw lots of them in Washington. Senators, and people like them always want to have their pictures taken. It probably makes them feel important."

"Oh! I think it's time," Bess cried as she tried to stand. "My water broke."

"Someone get the doctor. Get the midwife. C'mon, Bess, I'll carry you into bed," Stuart said as he took charge. He lifted up his wife, kissed her gently as another contraction came and he could see her wince. She tried to stifle her urge to yell out as Stuart took two steps at a time while the other family members got flustered, each in their own way.

As Bess was undressed and settled in her bed, the black midwife entered the room and carefully washed her hands. She was short, with wrinkles that made it difficult to discern her age but her smile and confidence were reassuring.

"My name is Olivia, chil', and I berthed lots of new babies. You'll be fine." She turned to Stuart. "We won't need you here, Mr. Fineman, but if we could get some real hot water for some herbal tea, I'd much appreciate it."

The men were shuttled out of the room while Rachel and Ruth Fineman huddled around, wiping Bess' forehead, encouraging her to take deep breaths. The clock rang midnight a few hours later and still the baby hadn't come. Bess seemed to fall asleep until the next contraction came, minutes later, jerking her awake.

Dr. Rivers arrived in the early morning hours. No one was getting any sleep. He examined Bess, touching her as gently as he could. Several probes brought a look of uncertainty to his face and further discomfort to the exhausted woman in the bed. He stood and rinsed his hands, a worried look on his face.

"The baby is breech. The umbilical cord is twisted. She should be in a hospital but there isn't time. We could lose both the mother and the child."

"Oh, my God," Rachel cried. "This can't be."

"I knows you is the doctor," Olivia said, coming forward. "But my hands are smaller than yours and I seen this sort of thing before. If you'll let me try, I might be able to coax that little thing out a' there."

Dr. Rivers knew that many of his associates considered these black midwifes to be nothing more than voodoo charlatans, but he had personally seen them succeed in performing some complex procedures. He knew the herbs they often used were questionable but Bess would die if something radical wasn't done.

"If it's acceptable to her husband, I have no objection. I don't think there is any way I can save her here at home."

"Olivia, I'll take care of Stuart," Rachel commanded. "You save Bess….and the baby, you hear."

Bess was given enough laudanum to keep her just conscious enough to be aware of what was going on around her. They would only want her to push when they told her.

The exhausted pregnant mother was fully dilated when Olivia began massaging and slowly moving her tiny fingers. She hummed softly, urging Bess to stay relaxed. The room filled with an eerie silence as each of them was transfixed by Olivia's voice and slow rhythmic movements. Ruth Fineman finally succumbed to a lack of sleep and rested soundly in an overstuffed chair in the corner. The air in the room, unmoving, carried a palpable sense of dread, a fear that they could lose this woman they all loved. Rachel and the doctor stood to one side, their attention glued to the black woman at the bedside, calm and quite still, except for her right hand, moving ever so slowly.

It was another hour before a small smile lit up Olivia's eyes and the legs of the baby appeared. Another minute and the rest of the tiny infant appeared and issued a small cry. It was a baby girl and she was alive. Olivia handed the child to Dr. Rivers and returned to Bess.

"You gonna make it, chile'. You a strong one and you got yourself a new baby girl. You done real well. Now you sleep."

Rachel began crying, sobbing, as she hugged Olivia. The vacuum of tension in the room vanished. Rachel walked tiredly through the door to Stuart, Robert, and Stephen huddled together on the landing.

"You've got a wonderful baby girl, Stuart, and your wife is sleeping."

"Thank god we got the doctor here on time," he said.

"He didn't do it, Stuart. It was Olivia's magic. Bess and the baby would both have died except for her skill. The doctor had done all he could."

By the time everyone celebrated, and finally slept, it was the following midday. Bess was still asleep. Olivia had fallen asleep at her side, holding the new mother's hand, her head on the bedcovers. The baby was cleaned and set into the same tiny crib that had housed Rachel and Stuart a generation earlier.

The men and the doctor shared three bottles of port and had fallen asleep in various uncomfortable positions.

A day later the early signs of winter passed and the worries and pain of the birth became memories, quickly fading from the effervescence cast by the gurgles and smell of a new baby. Both Olivia and the doctor tried to leave on several occasions but the new parents were so eager to share their gratitude that food, drink, and ebullience poured forth like an ever flowing gusher.

"Samantha Fineman," they toasted. "Welcome to the world. You are a mitzvah, a gift from God, and your mother has survived to share in the celebration of your birth."

"I have permission for you to go to Cuba with me, if you're still interested," Stephen said.

"I think I am. You can pass for a white, a Cuban, or just about anything else but there's no question that I'm black. Are you sure you want to be seen with me? It might limit what you can do," Robert admitted.

"I have no idea but, what the hell, we'll deal with it as we go. I'm more worried that neither of us speaks Spanish."

"What do you mean? I can say dinero, muchacho, and gracias. What more do we need?" Robert laughed.

"Works for me. Let's get ourselves down to New Orleans and make the necessary arrangements."

With Stephen gone and Rachel still at Moss Grove, Josiah breathed easier. He was still upset that he had to shoot Edgar but the risk of letting the boy live and blab about the thin thread of color that he'd inherited from his father was too great. And, after the initial shock of what he'd done, the Klan's men that he'd ridden with looked at him with a new respect. It was definitely time to find some relaxation.

Renoir's was one of the plushest Gentlemen's Clubs and brothels in New Orleans. Josiah had only been there once, right after meeting Albert Pike. Several city officials and bankers were lounging on settees as he entered, each man nestling a beautiful woman, as he sipped a Napoleon brandy from a snifter or smoked a Cuban cigar. The women were a panoply of color from ecru to a rich Jamaican chocolate, each elegantly attired and delicately doting on their escort of the moment.

For reasons even Josiah didn't quite understand, he had brought his trumpet. No matter how his life changed, the instrument had always been part of him, almost an appendage, and it took a super conscious effort to not have it at his side. Renoir's always had a piano player, and sometimes a drummer or banjo player, providing music for their guests. He could hear the soft ragtime from the next room. He was sure the musicians were either black or colored. He'd never heard of any white musician sitting in.

Madame Renoir greeted him in her extravagant manner and, after a hushed conversation, she settled her guest into the library and brought him a drink. Josiah followed the sound of music floating from the adjoining room. Three men were playing listlessly until a statuesque black woman with long, straightened black hair adorned with a huge red ostrich feather that matched a form fitting red satin gown, walked onto the small stage and began singing.

Sisseretta Jones had a body and a voice that reminded Josiah of a crystal champagne flute, long and pure. Her show, Black Patti's Troubadours, had sold out for a week in a New Orleans theatre. The musicians behind her were too vapid, always a half-beat off. Without giving it a thought Josiah pulled out his trumpet, blew the valves clear, and walked forward. Sisseretta was stunned for only a second and then smiled, motioning this blonde white young horn player forward.

With the addition of brass, the musicians became more alert and energized. Sisseretta's songs grew more confident and her selections bawdier. People came in from around the house and soon the room was overflowing as everyone tapped their feet in time to the musical beat. It went on for nearly an hour before the singer begged for a break and the room burst into applause.

The musicians all came over to shake Josiah's hand as he and this very attractive woman eyed one another.

Madame Renoir walked over, a gorgeous, large breasted, mulatto woman at her side, the girl she and Josiah had selected for his evening's entertainment.

"We've never had a white musician play here, it was quite a treat. Let me introduce you to Marie. Marie, this is Josiah." No last names were ever used at Renoir's.

"I'm afraid you must forgive me, Marie, Madame Renoir. I think I am already committed for the evening," he said, never taking his eyes off this lovely black vocalist who was an inch taller than he was. Her eyes said that she felt the same way.

"You play a mean trumpet for a white boy," Sisseretta said, playfully, once they were alone, finding their own quiet corner. "You have any other talents?"

"Things you've never imagined," he smiled, holding up his brandy in salute.

The upstairs room that had been set aside for Josiah and Marie was decorated in dark green satin and smelled of lilac, the scent of choice after each previous dalliance.

"You ever been with a black woman?" she asked seductively.

"You ever been with a white man?" he countered and they both laughed.

"At night we're all the same color," she said, sliding gracefully out of her dress and slipping under the covers, her black skin glistening in the reflection of the single lamp across the room.

"Yes, but I'll bet your pussy smells different."

"Better, I have no doubt," she laughed.

For the next hour they explored one another as the heat in the room rose several degrees. She grabbed his penis and stroked, stopping before he could climax.

"Not yet, white boy," she teased. She grabbed his genitals, squeezed slightly and began licking them, slowly, very slowly, as his legs locked, his back arched and his body drove his mind blank.

He kissed her lips and found the nipples on her dark breasts particularly sweet. By the time he climaxed she had already done so and the two of them lay, side by side, breathing deeply.

"So much for equal but separate," he laughed.

"You do fuck pretty good for a white boy. You clearly not from around here. Where you grow up?"

"San Francisco, but I was born around here, north of Baton Rouge."

"Me, too, Lake Charles, near the Texas border. My daddy was a cowboy and my mother was a saloon singer."

"I didn't ask you."

She looked at him. Some men get kinda' rude after sex. Never knew what to expect. She waited to see what he might say or do next. Maybe this whole thing was a bad idea.

"You've got a good voice," he said. "What are you doing here? You sold out your run in town."

"I owe Madame Renoir. She was good to me when I needed a leg up. This is the best way I know to repay her."

"Got time for one more," he asked.

"Glad you're up for it," she smiled, feeling his flaccid penis come to attention.

Chapter Thirteen

Slavery was abolished in Cuba in 1886. Radical and unexpected changes in the fabric of the country's society erupted as many of the landowners and factory owners lost much of their wealth and stature. American capital flooded into the country like air into a vacuum. Cigar workers and artisans formed Unions but nothing succeeded in throwing off the yoke of Spain's oppressive rule.

Jose Marti, a Cuban exile, urged independence for Cuba and Puerto Rico. He was outspoken in rejecting any consideration of American annexation of these Caribbean islands. Early in 1895 small rebel forces from the island's rural eastern provinces staged uprisings against Spain. Twenty thousand Spanish troops supported by sixty thousand 'volunteers,' swelled to more than one hundred fifty thousand men by year's end in order to stop the incursions. The island was bathed in blood.

The rebels were known as Mambises, after a Negro Spanish officer who had changed sides and fought with the insurgents in an earlier, futile, attempt. With limited weapons, all the campesinos, the rural Cubans, could do were to mount a guerilla style war, attacking patrols and retreating into the mountains. Cuban exiles, ex-slaves, and other men seeking adventure hurried to their support. The American newspapers heralded the rebel's infrequent, but heroic, successes, and likened their efforts to those of the Colonial patriots more than a hundred years earlier.

It took a month for Stephen and Robert to connect with the rebel leaders hiding in the mountains around Camaguey and even longer for his first articles to get back to the states and into publication. Only the Spanish government in Havana had teletype machines. But Hearst, always creative, hired three small boats to ferry his reporter's stories, picking them up in clandestine meetings along the coast. It was an exciting time, if the two Americans could stay alive and avoid being captured by Spanish soldiers.

Pablo, an eleven year old boy who accosted them, asking for food shortly after their arrival, became their guide and translator. They never did understand his last name. The boy, in his tattered clothes, spoke only broken English, but he knew every hill and path and how to avoid the government patrols that seemed to be everywhere.

The two men and their young guide slipped out of Havana on a moonless night and arrived in Jimaguayu two days later while the five Liberation Army Corps leaders were meeting. The rebels were eager to share their plans with Stephen and pose for pictures with Robert. There was always hope they could convince 'los Americanos' to send them the arms they so badly needed without making their country an American colony instead of a Spanish one.

"The Spanish forces are equipped with Mauser rifles that fire smokeless ammunition. That makes it *muy difícil* to see from where the shots are coming," one of the Colonels explained in broken English. "Our *paisanos* are armed with outdated single shot, black powder rifles you call 'the Trapdoor.' We are a poor match in any type of pitched battle. We need your government to send us weapons. Usted sabe?"

Stephen nodded.

The rebel forces consolidated their hold on the Eastern provinces and struggled westward toward Havana, capturing land one farm at a time. Many of their men were killed or maimed by booby traps set along the roads the Spanish were sure the guerillas would be traveling.

The rainy season had ended and reasonable travel was finally possible. Both sides had been forced to wait out the hurricane season when keeping old rifles and ammunition dry was a struggle. The Spanish soldiers were no better off but their offices were content to enjoy the luxuries of Havana.

"Over here, Robert. Keep down," Stephen shouted. The two Americans were traveling with two dozen rebel soldiers approaching Cienfuegos along the southern shore. It was night and all they had was the faint light of a quarter moon to mark the dirt path.

"Look to your left, out toward the sea," Robert whispered. "You can see a clear reflection of the moon and the stars. And the ocean looks so peaceful, not a ripple."

"Stop dreaming. There are men pointing rifles our way and they don't care whether we're campesinos or Americanos. Pablo, can you see anything?"

"*Nada, senor, pero hay mas de veinte soldados alli,*" he pointed.

"Pablo says there are more than twenty soldiers up ahead on our left. Let's stay here until we see what happens."

Moments later rifle fire erupted on all sides. Two of the rebels nearby were hit. One of them was Colonel Pineda, the one who had urged Stephen to get them better rifles. By the time Stephen reached him blood was gushing from his throat where a bullet had entered. Stephen reached over the closed the man's eyes. He removed the family pictures the Colonel carried next to his heart. His wife would want them and his children would want to know their father died bravely.

Close by other men could be heard moaning as they lay in the dirt, unsure whether death or capture by the Spanish would be the worst outcome. Shrill cries broke out in front of him and he could hear the sound of feet scurrying through the underbrush. It all got very confusing. Shouts in Spanish…more yelling…more shooting. Pablo disappeared. He and Robert found one another and took cover in the scanty underbrush when three Spanish soldiers discovered them.

"*Ah, Americanos. Bueno. Venga!*"

Stephen and Robert didn't need to know the literal translation of what the men were saying, the pointing of their rifles was translation enough. The two of them stood, put their hands up and, led by one soldier in front, the other two behind them, they were moved off, down the hillside, and straight into Cienfuegos.

"Dos Americanos," the Commanding officer said, mixing his Spanish with a few words of English, as they were marched to his office. "We love to shoot rebels, especially those of you who were misguided enough to come to Cuba, somewhere you don't belong. I am General Nicolau and you are prisoners of war or spies or whatever I say you are."

"General, this is a mistake. We are not combatants. We are reporters. Here is my Press card. I work for the Examiner," Stephen said.

"And this big black man with you, he is your slave?"

"No, my photographer! We don't have slaves in America anymore."

"This Press card could be forged."

"We have no guns. You would be killing people who aren't even armed and when my newspaper reads about it you will have more trouble with America than you want."

"Stupido! Threats!" he shouted. "Guard, take these men to a cell. I will deal with them when it suits me."

Sentries grabbed Stephen and Robert by the arms and led them away.

"We are fucked...royally fucked," Stephen said. Their makeshift jail looked to have only a few cells but each one was crowded with rebels who had been caught. There were no cots. There was a drain for urinating and a pail for the rest. There was a large bottle of water and even in the dim light one could see that it was home to more than a few floating creatures.

None of the guards spoke English. Press passes and camera were still in the General's office. An hour later a rubbery tortilla and a plate of watery beans were passed through to them.

The next morning they were awakened by a squad of Spanish soldiers marching into the cell block. One of the doors was opened and six Cubans, barefoot, were marched out.

"Where are they taking those men?" Robert shouted down the corridor.

"To be shot," a disembodied voice responded.

"For what?"

"The General needs no reason."

"You speak English. Who are you?"

"My name is Rodrigo. I was a teacher. Since all my students were fighting, I thought it fitting that I joined them."

"We're reporters. Do you think Nicolau will release us?"

"*Quien sabe.* No one knows."

Later that day Stephen was taken from the cell and questioned. How many rebels did he travel with? What were the names of their leaders? Each time he refused to answer, a lit candle singed his feet. It went on for three hours and he had to be dragged back to his cell. Robert was afraid the wounds would fester if he tried to clean it with fetid water. The next day Robert was forced to undergo a similar interrogation with the same results. On the third day the men were led back to the General's office.

"Can you take my picture?" he asked Robert, ignoring his guest's burned feet…

"Of course he can. We can even tell the Editor to put it on the front page. Robert, take the General's picture."

"Then I will let you live. But you must also tell them that Spain wants only good things for Cuba and we will soon rid our island of these misguided fools who fight us. Cuba belongs to Spain and America would be foolish to get involved. The Spanish empire is strong and quite capable of protecting her possessions."

The next morning, after having their wounds cleaned and bandaged, the General sent the Americans to Havana where they could post their story by teletype rather than fishing boat. It was one of the first stories printed from the direct words of a Spanish commander:

> *General Nicolau told this reporter that he has grown tired of fighting skirmishes with small groups of rebels. He has launched a program of mass removal of the campesinos and the burning of their crops and fields. All those who object are being executed. It is a campaign of terror meant to destroy the morale of anyone choosing to fight the Spanish empire. Nearly one-third of the island's rural population are dying from malnutrition, disease, or a bullet from a Spanish Mauser as the Spanish forces continue to move eastward forcing the rebels to retreat to the far end of the island.*

Thanks to Nicolau's largesse, Robert and Stephen were able to move freely around Havana but they were eager to rejoin the rebels who still held sway on the other side of the island. That's where the action was and that's where the stories were. Each evening the two of them sat, nursing warm rum and enjoying Cuban music, relieved they were no longer captives. Slowly their feet healed. The days were a bore and they had run out of things to report. They needed to find a way to rejoin the rebels in the mountains.

"Good morning, senors," Pablo said, walking into the café where they were having their breakfast.

"Well, Stephen, look who's decided to join us, our little runaway."

"I am sorry but I could not stay and allow myself to get captured. Buy my breakfast and I'll explain."

"*Tres huevos, jamon, leche y pan,*" the young boy ordered from the bored overaged waitress. "I am very hungry. I have come across half the island to find you."

By the time his three eggs and ham arrived Pablo explained that his two older brothers were leaders in the rebel forces and the Spanish soldiers would have made him reveal where they were hiding. Besides, he says, those bastards have a reputation for liking little boys.

"I would be their '*puta,*'" he said angrily, his mouth full of food.

They could see tears form in the young boy's eyes.

"Aren't you worried about being seen here in Havana?"

"Yes, but my brothers told me to find you. It is important you continue to write stories about how brave and gallant we campesinos are, so the Americans will send us more rifles and ammunition."

Stephen and Robert waited in their rooms until it was dark and the Spanish patrols had gotten careless. They grabbed their few belongings and skirted lit streets to meet Pablo on the outskirts of the city where he had horses waiting.

"Where did you get the horses?" Robert asked.

"From the Spanish, *por supuesto.* Of course! They are the only ones with horses. *Venga!* We have many hours of riding ahead of us. Until we move further east far from Havana we can travel only at night."

They reached Camaguey a few days later and were greeted with smiles by the comrades they had lived with for several months. It was New Year's Eve, a new year, 1898, and the rebels were prepared to continue their fight for independence.

"Maria, these are my Americano friends," Pablo said proudly as he dragged his older sister to the small shack that Robert and Stephen had been given.

Maria was a sultry peasant girl with a wicked smile and dark eyes that danced as if they knew a secret no one else knew. She had to be twenty but she could have been a few years more or less. Neither Robert nor Stephen had seen such a beauty in several months. Most of the women on the island were younger than Pablo or older wrinkled crones. Those in between were either living in comfort with Spanish officers or they were being hidden by their families concerned about protecting their daughter's virtue.

"Pablo, where have you been hiding your sister?" Robert asked, pushing Stephen to the side.

"Wait a minute," his light complexioned friend said, elbowing his way forward. "Let's see if she likes light meat or dark."

"Dark, of course, much juicier."

Maria laughed as the two men jostled for her hand and her attention.

"Senores, I am happy to meet you both." Her broken English was tinged with a sweet lilt. "You are Robert, *el negro, si*? And you are Stephen, *el café a lait, si*? Pablo has told me much about his new friends."

"Well, Stephen, I guess we've been given new names."

There was little fighting for the next few weeks. A cold spell had drifted across the island bringing unusually heavy rains that made moving groups of men very difficult. Ever so slowly Maria and Robert gravitated toward one another. It was nothing either of them consciously planned but within days she was bringing him a few extra rations and he was making sure she was dry and warm.

"I think I should sleep in a tent and let the two of you have the shack," Stephen smiled. "The last thing you need is a chaperone."

"White of you to say so, old man," Robert teased.

"Funny! Maybe you can get a job after the war doing vaudeville on the 'chitlin' circuit."

With Maria's help a corner of the floor was set aside for Stephen and Pablo. She joined Robert in the one flimsy bed as far away as it could be set. Biology and their growing affection took over from there. Stephen made sure Pablo and he stayed out of the house until they could hear their friends snoring.

"One makes accommodations para sus amigos," Stephen explained in the few words he'd learned.

The four of them were sitting listening to a guitar when a rider rushed in. Everything stopped as he began to shout.

"Que dice? What's he saying?" Stephen asked one of the rebels who spoke English.

"Spanish loyalists in Havana have rioted against the new government. The United States Navy sent a battleship to protect Americans living there and the ship was blown up. Their ship, the Maine, was sunk and 268 Americano sailors were killed. Everyone is in a panic."

"Who sunk the ship?"

"No one seems to know."

"I need to send a wire to Mr. Hearst for directions on what to do."

It took nearly a week to get a reply and, as usual, his wire was terse.

> *Continue reporting. Stop. War inevitable. Stop.*
> *I intend to make it inevitable.*
>
> *Hearst*

Robert's camera had long since broken and no spare parts were available but he pretended he was taking pictures. Stephen had requested a new camera, months earlier, but it had never arrived. Meanwhile other reporters from the mainland were beginning to arrive at both ends of the island.

One of the reporters, Tutt Philips, was from Joseph Pulitzer's *New York World*. Both Pulitzer and Hearst seemed to be having their own ongoing war over circulation.

"We might as well cover this war together," Tutt said. "Between your Mr. Hearst's *New York Journal* and my *World*, our editors are going to make sure the U.S. declares war."

"Why?" Robert asked naively.

"To build circulation, why else? The joke around the newsroom is that your boss, Hearst, sent Frederick Remington, the famous artist, into Havana to draw illustrations of the various battles and atrocities the Spanish were supposed to be committing. He gets here, looks around and can't find any. He sends Hearst a wire saying it's a waste of time. Hearst sends him back a immediate reply that says 'You furnish the pictures, I'll furnish the war.' Damn papers will force a war for their own good but at least you and I will have a front row seat."

Neither Stephen nor Robert opted to disclose their capture and punishment, they just looked at one another knowingly.

The rebels were now content to lay low and await help from across the channel. Perhaps los Americanos would win their freedom for them.

> *For three months American politicians debated what action to take, spurred on by larger and brasher newspaper headlines demanding war. It was late April before President McKinley and the Congress agreed on a resolution that stipulated 'the island of Cuba is, and by right, should be, free and independent.' The United States had committed itself to free Cuba of Spanish control with whatever military action was necessary.*

Word came through that the American forces intended to invade the far eastern end of the island near the harbor at Guantanamo. It was believed they would have greater support from the rebels and less resistance from Spanish troops in that locale. Robert and Stephen, joined by Tutt Philips, and guided by Pablo, headed off to meet them.

The summer hurricane season hampered movement. Ships bobbled in the water at Santiago and Guantanamo Bays. Supplies that eventually did get ashore were drenched, often caked with mud.

"General Miles, we're reporters from New York and we'd like to get on one of Commodore Schley's ships out in the Bay," Tutt Philips asked.

"We're not allowing any civilians on our Navy ships. You'll have to do your reporting from here. Besides, from the hilltop you already have a superb view of the harbor and the American forces as they arrive."

"We have it on good authority that you don't intend to allow any Cuban troops into Santiago," Robert injected. "How can you do that? According to international law and our Congressional declaration, this is their country."

"I don't know who you are, young man, but I'm in command and I don't want Cubans taking reprisals against Spanish troops. Now, I'd like you all to leave. I have work to do."

As the three men left the office Stephen overheard a remark from the General to his adjutant.

"You keep niggers out of my office, you understand?"

Chapter Fourteen

"Well, one thing is certain," Eli Fineman said. "The war has certainly stabilized cotton prices. Thank God the economy is moving again."

"Replacing wool uniforms with those made of khaki certainly doesn't hurt," Stuart added.

Moss Grove was energized once again as this year's harvest looked to be especially good. Renewed demand for cotton was forcing prices higher than they had been in four years. There had been a concern that the boll weevil would take its toll on the crop once again but the weather had changed and only a few acres had been savaged beyond saving.

There was a joyous spirit from the main house through the share cropper cottages and along all the plantations that fronted the Mississippi River. The coming of the war had given purpose to a country exhausted by a moribund economy. People were going back to work and the curtain of malaise had lifted. Railroads had reorganized and trains were whistling across the country. Miners had gone back to work. Banks were lending. It wasn't quite euphoria but optimism had definitely replaced the gloom of the recent past.

At Moss Grove, however, one dark cloud remained…the health of Ruth Fineman. She'd taken to her bed three months earlier and hadn't left it. She continued to lose weight. She didn't seem to be in pain but she was listless, completely devoid of energy. Doctors came, examined her, and shook their heads in dismay.

"I'm sorry, Mr. Fineman. I can give her drugs to keep her sedated but her body just seems to have worn down."

"She's four years younger than me," Eli protested. "I'm supposed to go before she does."

"It doesn't always work that way," the Doctor said, packing up his small satchel. "I'm sure she's lived a full life."

Ruth Fineman drifted for another month and finally succumbed, never waking up one morning.

All the mirrors in the house were draped in black. Husband and son tore the lapels on their suits. Ruth's funeral was a family affair with the exception of a few friends and the rabbi who came from Baton Rouge to perform the service. The previous occasion for his visit had been the wedding of Stuart and Bess, a much more joyous event. Some of the male guests stayed for a few days after the funeral, sitting shiva in honor of the loss of their friend and loved one. She was the first Fineman and the first Jew to be buried at Moss Grove. Stuart asked Bess whether interring his mother next to where the Rogers were buried might be improper.

"No one cares, Stuart," she said. "Josiah is the only one who could have voiced an opinion and he doesn't own Moss Grove, you do."

One of the guests brought copies of a recent Baton Rouge newspaper describing the war. There on page one was an article by Stephen Carmody, reporting from Cuba.

"How exciting for him," Bess exclaimed. "I think I'll start a scrapbook and give it to him when he returns. Oops," she stopped, "I think it's time to breastfeed Sam again."

"Can't we call her by her given name, Samantha?" Stuart asked.

"Of course, darling," Bess agreed, "But she smiles when I call her 'Sam'. We can let her decide when she's older."

After Stuart realized he still had not won his first argument with his lovely wife, he returned to his newspaper. One page three, without fanfare was a tragic article:

'Negro child killed by rioting soldiers,
Cleveland, Ohio, 7 June 1898.

On 6 June white Ohio military volunteers seized a black child away from her mother and precipitated a race riot among Negro and white troops awaiting embarkation orders for Cuba. The rioters burned cafés and other business establishments before the police arrived. Seven men were sent to the hospital but none of the injuries were reported serious.

Following her mother's funeral Rachel and young Samuel returned to New Orleans. The dinners at Moss Grove now were smaller and more informal. Eli often chose to dine in his room. This night, however, still dressed in his robe, he joined Stuart and Bess at the table.

"I'm not very hungry," Eli said, pushing his plate away, to the continued worry of his son and Bess.

"Can we fix you something else, Eli?" Bess asked solicitously.

"Thank you. I'm just happy to join you and see your smiling faces. Where is my lovely granddaughter?"

"She's in bed already but you should stop by and see her. She looks more like her grandmother every day," Bess said as she could see a tear form in the old man's eyes.

"I'm so glad Ruth had a chance to see two wonderful grandchildren come into the world. That's what we all live for."

"Father," Stuart interrupted, trying to get his father out of the doldrums. "I'm thinking of volunteering to fight with our army in Cuba."

Bess stared in amazement. Her husband had never said a word to her about such a thing. She wanted to shout out the myriad of objections she had, but she decided to hold her tongue until they were alone.

"Are you mishuga?" Eli asked, suddenly becoming more alert. "Your mother just died and the cotton will need to be picked in the next few months, not to mention your new baby. What could you possibly be thinking?"

"I don't know," he admitted. "I thought you could manage everything. I just think I want more in my life than overseeing Moss Grove. This is certain to be a short war. I hoped I could find something more…a little excitement."

"A baby and a plantation isn't enough for you?"

"You were in the war, father. You could have stayed in Vermont like your family wanted you to. You told me the story many times."

"It was different then and your mother was able to go with me."

"It's not that different. I need something more than cotton while I'm still young. Bess will understand, won't you?" he pleaded with both his voice and his eyes.

I will never understand men, truly I won't, she thought. Her father was killed at the Battle of the Little Big Horn with General Custer. It was a simple, never thought to be dangerous, scouting trip, but it made her mother an instant widow. Now, despite having a new baby, her husband was ready to run off. She couldn't answer Stuart. She excused herself and ran from the room. By the time Stuart came to bed she feigned being asleep. She had cried and said her nightly silent prayer that Stephen was still safe over in Cuba and now her lunatic husband was on his way to share an adventure. As she finally drifted off her last thought was that men were truly alien creatures.

A week later, with the admonition that she wouldn't stop him, Stuart volunteered and was accepted in a unit formed under General Leonard Wood and the Under Secretary of the Navy, Teddy Roosevelt, who had resigned his Cabinet position so he could fight. Officially the unit was the First United States Volunteer Cavalry but the odd assortment of men who were being gathered together was immediately nicknamed the 'Rough Riders.' Men from fourteen different countries volunteered. Among the Americans were cowboys, college athletes and a few, like Stuart, who just wanted an adventure. They gathered in San Antonio, Texas for their military training. The training, scheduled for six weeks, lasted less than two. Teddy Roosevelt was anxious to see combat. The unit boarded a train and set out for Tampa Bay, Florida where a boat would take them across the narrow waters.

"Your brother did what?" Josiah asked in laughing amazement.

"The fool is off to fight in Cuba. Some stupid unit nicknamed the Rough Riders," Rachel said, shaking her head.

"Who's going to bring in the cotton crop with your father not feeling well?"

"Apparently Bess has taken charge. She's taken to wearing pants, and riding the fields every day, straddling a horse, just like a man. The share croppers don't know what to make of it. They've never had a woman boss. It's all quite a shock. Clearly my brother has taken leave of his senses."

"I imagine it is quite strange, but I grew up with that girl and it doesn't really surprise me. It's what her mother would have done given the same situation."

"I don't know why she didn't stop Stuart from going."

"Not her. She does what needs to be done after others have made their decisions. Being a new mother has obviously not changed that about her.

"I'll see you this evening; perhaps we'll go find some entertainment this weekend. You could plan a small party, perhaps." He intended to kiss her gently on the lips and leave but each of them was reluctant to pull back and they could both sense the growing heat of the moment.

"I'll definitely see you this evening," he smiled and was rewarded by the glint in his wife's eyes. A new child in the house hadn't quelled their desire for one another.

Albert Pike looked as if he'd gained another ten pounds but the extra weight didn't seem to quell his appetite as the waiter brought a third plate of raw oysters.

"I'm celebrating today, Josiah, and I want you to celebrate with me."

"Always happy to celebrate, Albert. What's the occasion?"

"We just succeeded in having Louisiana adopt a new constitution with a 'grandfather clause' that restricts permanent voting registration to whites and only those Negros whose fathers and grandfathers were qualified to vote as of January 1, 1867. Of course, there weren't any blacks qualified to vote in 1867 so now the niggers won't be able to vote. At least here in the south us whites are back running things like we did before the war." He paused to down another oyster. "Did you hear what they're doing up north in New York?"

"No, what has you so worked up now?" Josiah asked, tired of this pompous, overweight asshole who he continued to need as a contact.

"The government went and built an army base on the far end of Long Island, Fort Wikoff out at Montauk Point."

"So?"

"They've got more than four regiments of blacks and coloreds in uniform training to fight alongside our brave white soldiers going over to Cuba to fight the Spaniards."

"The Union army has always had colored units, Albert, ever since the Civil war. And, after the war they kept a couple of them to fight Indians. You know that blacks can tolerate heat and diseases better than whites because of their dark skin."

"Makes me nervous when I think of niggers with guns, Josiah, that's all I'm saying."

"Well, my Jew brother-in-law has enlisted also. I wonder if they send Jews to train with the coloreds or the whites."

"You do have an interesting family, Josiah," Pike said, returning to his oysters.

"And you, Pike, are a scoundrel. How you managed to get a new state Constitution is amazing. It should take the wind out of their black sails," he said, eager to change the subject.

"Did you read Alex Manly's editorial last week in the *Daily Record*."

"What are you doing reading a black published rag?"

"I want to know what my adversaries are saying, Josiah. It's always good to know," he said, pulling a folded piece of paper from his pocket and putting his glasses on. He set down his fork and began to read,

> *'our experience among poor white people in the country teaches us that white women are not any more particular in the matter of clandestine meetings with colored men than white men with colored women and poor white men are careless in the matter of protecting their women.'*

"It's probably true, Albert. It's been my experience that pussy is pussy for men and I imagine dicks are dicks for women."

"But we are for purity, Josiah, at least publicly," he grinned. "Anyway, we need to take action. We can't let this black shit head continue to publish his garbage."

A week later five hundred masked Klan members and other irate whites gathered in the armory before storming the offices of Manly's newspaper. Pike and Josiah, wearing their hoods, helped light the crosses as they incited the men to protect the purity of white women against lecherous niggers.

The crowd grew to nearly two thousand as they marched toward the newspaper shouting epithets and feeding their anger. They torched several adjoining buildings as Alex Manly escaped ahead of the mob and left New Orleans for parts unknown, while other black men, women, and children were forced to flee the city and take refuge in nearby woods and swamps. More than a dozen blacks were caught and beaten to death.

Albert returned to his wife and four children in Mississippi, well satisfied with his successes. Josiah feigned a business meeting and returned to Renoir's for another evening with Sisseretta. He arrived as she finished the last verse of a popular song. He knew the tune by heart and had even taken out his trumpet at home and played it for his young son, Samuel. But this black woman had a special erotic quality to her voice and that captivated him:

> *I love you as **I** never loved before*
> *Since first I met you on the village green*
> *Come to me or my dream of love is **O**'er*
> *I love you as **I** loved you,*
> *When you were sweet*
> *When you were sweet sixteen*

"I love to listen to you sing," he said as he began to disrobe upstairs.

"Even more than you like to fuck?" she asked, sitting on the bed, watching him. It was a word she rarely used but she knew it aroused Josiah to hear her talk dirty. She had no idea why she kept coming back to this arrogant white boy. There was certainly no future, but they were drawn to one another. She worried about what might happen if she got pregnant. She had missed her period and she was beginning to feel bloated. One thing certain, she knew she'd never tell him. There was something about race that haunted him, of that she was sure, but white men had this love hate thing about black women, she supposed, and she knew she'd never really understand it.

"I'm pregnant again, Josiah. With all our healthy fucking, your little swimmers have become terribly athletic," Rachel smiled. "I hope you're pleased. Samuel will have a brother or sister."

"I am pleased, very pleased," he said. "Are you alright? Do we need to have a doctor come here?"

"No, I'm fine. I feel so much better than the first time. I'd ask Bess to visit and stay awhile but that won't work, not while Stuart's gone."

"We don't need Bess. I'll make certain you have the proper care. Imagine, a second child."

Chapter Fifteen

William Randolph Hearst was eager to enjoy 'his' war first hand. When both the Army and the Navy rejected his repeated requests to join one of the military expeditions, he simply anchored his private yacht in Havana Harbor. His newspapers blared at readers with large type headlines offering a $50,000 reward for information leading to the arrest of the perpetrator of the February 15 explosion of the U.S.S. Maine. Most experts had concluded it was an accident and not the work of the Spanish. But facts didn't deter Hearst or Pulitzer from exploiting the incident. Hearst's war headlines lifted circulation of the New York Journal over 1 ½ million and made it the most read daily newspaper in the world.

While Stuart and the Rough Riders were on the train heading toward Tampa, the 9th and 10th Cavalry, and the 24th and 25th Infantry units of black and colored soldiers, assembled just north of Lakeland, Florida. Many of these men had never been south of that forgotten point of demarcation, the Mason-Dixon Line, that separated north from south both geographically and ideologically.

Six black soldiers entered Forbes drugstore in the center of Lakeland and ordered sodas. The pharmacist told them to leave and go somewhere that sold drinks to 'niggers.' Another colored soldier from Syracuse went into a barbershop to get a shave and was told to leave. These and other despondent blacks assembled on the street, confused by the rejections, while white onlookers began to heckle them with obscenities. Joab Collins, a white farmer who had been turned down when he'd tried to enlist in the Army, pulled out a gun. A black sergeant reacted by pulling his, fired one shot, and Collins lay dead in a pool of his own blood. Within minutes the barbershop was on fire and whites and blacks began attacking one another.

South of Lakeland, the ship, to which the Rough Riders had been assigned, hadn't yet reached Tampa. Roosevelt, always impatient, commandeered a boat meant for another unit, the Yucatan, and hurried his battalion aboard. They jammed themselves together on the smaller craft, which had never been intended to handle even half as many passengers. The journey across the Caribbean was typically an easy overnight jaunt, but under the weight of so many men, arms, and horses, the ship was unable to maneuver in shallow water. Men were disembarked too far off Guantanamo's shore with their heavy equipment and several drowned. Horses were thrown over the side in hopes they could swim to shore. Some never made it.

The drenched men, now with fewer horses and supplies, finally gathered on shore and struck out to join with General Young and the Army's main force. Before they could reach him, however, they were ambushed by Spanish forces just outside of the small town of Las Guasimas.

"Take cover," General Wood ordered as rifle fire struck down three of his men, including Stuart's Company commander, Captain Elroy Capron. This had been the Captain's first combat experience. He had finished in the bottom 10% of his West Point class for suspicions of cheating and blamed his misfortune on the Catholics, the Irish, the Jews, and whoever wasn't a God-fearing Baptist.

Stuart hid behind a wagon looking for the source of the enemy fire. It was his first taste of battle and he struggled to fight the fear rising like bile in his throat. It was difficult to see the snipers hiding in the thickets ahead of them, but the sun had risen and Stuart noticed a tiny glint of metal on a hill up ahead. Each man in his company had been issued one of the Army's new Krag-Jorgensen rifles. It was lighter and easier to shoot. He aimed at where he'd seen the glint, pulled the trigger and less than a second later, a man sixty yards away pitched forward.

"They're up on that hill," he shouted. "Aim at ten o'clock."

The men around him responded by opening fire and within minutes the ambush was thwarted. One bullet grazed Roosevelt's head as it ricocheted off a tree nearby. He dried the tiny trickle of blood and gathered himself.

"We've lost Captain Capron and Sgt. Fish," he shouted as the men returned to formation. "Fineman, good shooting. I want you to take over Sgt. Fish's squad."

"Yes, sir."

The Rough Riders were ordered to support the Army regulars as they advanced up Kettle Hill. Other army units moved up nearby San Juan Hill from a different direction. The army had both black and white units moving forward side by side. Stephen and Robert had attached themselves to the black 10th Cavalry while Tutt Phillips joined Roosevelt's white unit. The three agreed to exchange their stories but make them different enough so that neither Hearst nor Pulitzer would suspect any collusion.

Roosevelt, brash and devoid of military discipline, led his men up the hill so quickly that they passed both the regular Army units and the black volunteer companies. As he lifted his saber to urge his troops forward a bullet pierced his forearm, the impact dropping him to the ground. Stuart and his men stopped, unsure how to proceed.

Roosevelt refused to give up the attack and, a hastily applied bandage on his arm, he gathered himself and urged his men forward, not even slowing to clean his smudged eyeglasses.

Phillips had become part of Stuart's squad and, together, his men slogged forward until they reached the summit. They were eager to rest when heavy rifle salvos and a fusillade of cannon fire engulfed them. They dove into trenches the Spanish had vacated and hunkered down, hoping the barrage would end quickly. They were under siege but the Spanish forces, too, were sandwiched between American forces that had divided as they climbed. Machine gun fire and artillery bursts filled the air in every direction. As Phillips raised his head to see what Roosevelt was doing, he caught the blast from a mortar shell landing nearby. It threw him back into the trench, blood oozing from a head wound, his arm hanging by a few tendons. He was unconscious, barely breathing. Stuart and another man threw themselves into the trench and began trying to stem the bleeding. They fashioned a small tourniquet.

"Medic…we need a medic," Stuart shouted as he worked.

The black 10th Cavalry was taking heavy fire from Spanish machine gun placements. Stephen and Robert pushed themselves deeper into the muddy trenches. Stephen paused to write as quickly as his pencil could record his thoughts. This soldier from New Jersey was shot; this one from Massachusetts asked me to give his love to his mother before his eyes closed for the last time. Robert, unable to sketch the battle while it was underway, tried to tend the wounded, while avoiding being hit by an errant enemy bullet. Both the black and white battalions refused to give ground but men from both units were falling despite the color of their skin. The Spanish troops were making no distinction.

Frank Knox, a white soldier from Chicago, separated from his unit, was firing, shoulder to shoulder with black soldiers, the color of their skins forgotten in the chaos of the battle. Robert knew that it was a scene he had to draw. He found chards of a sketchpad and began depicting the blood, the bodies of both black and white soldiers, dead, lying askew next to one another, and the mayhem of the fierce battle that was engulfing them.

Stephen, out of breath and hungry, tried to move uphill with the others. As he began to kneel forward he was struck in the chest by flying shrapnel. He fell and lay there, unmoving, while soldiers skirted past him. It took him a few minutes to realize he was still alive, although he knew he was bleeding badly and needed treatment.

"First Aid!" he screamed. "Someone!"

Frank Knox and the others had moved up the hill as the cacophony of cannon and rifle fire overwhelmed all other sounds. Robert was twenty yards away, however, and thought he recognized his friend's voice.

"Stephen, what in the hell are you doing on the ground?" he said as he followed the voice. "Come on. Let me help you up and get you to the doctors. You're bleeding but I'm pretty sure you aren't going to die."

"Easy for you to say. I get terribly injured and you make jokes."

"You'll be fine. I'm just doing more training for vaudeville," he said as his friend lapsed into unconsciousness, the color drained from his face.

Stuart and his squad could barely see the American forces across the way taking heavy fire but the action seemed to exist in the midst of an ethereal haze. Smoke from the guns clouded the sky and emitted an acrid odor of gun powder and death. He was still crouching in a trench when he heard Roosevelt stand, sword poised upward, and order a charge against the entrenched Spanish troops ensconced on San Juan Hill.

His men either couldn't see or hear him or they were convinced the man was daft and they weren't interested in exposing themselves to reckless danger. Only five men left their trenches to follow him. Three of them fell before they got half way up the hill. The two survivors continued to fire while an angry Roosevelt returned to the trenches and urged the rest of his battalion to support the attack.

"Up, men. Time to take this damn hill. Follow Teddy," Stuart shouted. This time, to a man, the Rough Riders left their cover and pushed forward up the steep hill against intense withering fire.

Their movement was slow, as they ground out yard after yard. The hillside was soon strewn in blood and broken bodies. Stuart lifted himself for an instant to see how his men were doing and a bullet pierced his right leg just above the knee. He went down and grabbed his leg. He could see that there was a great deal of blood but he couldn't tell if the shell had hit a bone. He tore his shirt, grabbed a nearby stick and made a tourniquet. He shook the fog from his brain and began to limp forward.

It took another hour of fierce fighting before the Spanish troops fled and the white Army forces and black volunteer units hailed one another atop of San Juan Hill. The Rough Riders had lost nearly twenty percent of their five hundred man force, ninety killed, and another thirty-five injured.

"You fight pretty good for a Jew, Fineman," Solinski said, as all the men in his squad foraged for something to eat. "I always thought you 'yids' were cowards and I was ready to shoot you myself, if you bolted."

"And you aren't bad for a Polack," Stuart countered.

"How's your leg?"

"I got lucky. It should be fine."

"Let's go find someone to take a look," Solinski said, grabbing Stuart's arm and balancing him to take the pressure off the wounded leg.

"Stuart," a voice shouted as he and Solinski walked toward the medical tent just being set up.

"Oh, my God," Stuart stopped. "Robert! Small world! Solinski, this is my friend and family, Robert Williams. Let me introduce my good fighting buddy and temporary crutch, Private Solinski. He's a dumb Polack, but a great guy. Where is Stephen? I thought you were traveling together."

"He's injured...pretty bad, actually. They're working on him now. I threatened the doctors with the wrath of all the Hearst papers if they didn't take care of him properly. I think it worked. Hearst is a more fearsome name than Roosevelt or the U.S. Army."

Solinski was looking at the huge black soldier standing next to his white Jewish soldier buddy. He wanted to ask questions but they wouldn't come out.

"My first name is Jesus," he said. "With a 'J', not an 'H' like the fucking Spanish. Jesus Solinski! My mother was a really devout Catholic. That's why everyone calls me Solinski. I wouldn't want my buddies to think I walk on water. Hey, why are you writing that all down?"

"Stephen is a reporter for the *New York Journal* and you'll make a good story."

It was another two hours before the doctor came to tell them their friend would be alright but he'd sleep through the night. Meanwhile Stuart's wound was tended to.

As they waited they could see an array of dead bodies lying side by side and their banter stopped. Blacks, whites, and Cubans had been laid in separate rows but the shrouds that covered them were color blind. Robert went over to draw a picture of the scene when he noticed that the body of Tutt Phillips was lying there. Further down the row Pablo, their young friend and guide, was lying there among other Cuban soldiers, his head barely visible.

"It looks as if he took a direct hit," Robert said, kneeling down. "He was too young to die. His sister and brothers will be devastated,"

"All these men were too young to die," Stuart said.

"What are you gentlemen writing?"

It was Colonel Roosevelt. His arm was bandaged and his glasses were still caked with mud as he walked by, returning from having his wound examined.

"I'm Robert Williams, sir. Stephen Carmody and I are covering the war for Mr. Hearst's newspapers. He's been badly injured and the doctors are taking care of him. Actually, Colonel, we've met before. My father was Thaddeus Williams. He was an aide to Senator Blanche Bruce."

"Thaddeus, of course. How is your father?"

"He died several months ago as did my brother, Noah. He and I had left Washington to teach at Tuskegee Institute and he died in an unfortunate altercation."

"I'm sorry for all your personal losses but you're young and you seem to have found a worthy outlet for your feelings. Here you are trekking around this Caribbean Island like the rest of us. Good show! When this is all over, come see me in Washington. I could use a resourceful man like you, especially if you are like your father. Good luck with your friend. We have some good doctors here. Now, excuse me, we have a war to win. And you, Sergeant Fineman, look after that arm. We need to get on with this battle."

Roosevelt strode off, stopping frequently to shake hands with enlisted men and officers, white and black alike.

He turned back, laughed, and said, "And you tell your Mr. Willy Hearst that I'm grateful for his persistence in starting this nice little war."

"Yes, sir. I can understand why that man is considered such a formidable force," Robert said, half to himself.

Stephen was able to leave the small field hospital a few days later. He had needed two pints of blood and required fifteen crudely patched stitches across his chest, but no vital organs had been damaged. Weak, unstable, and heavily medicated, they headed off for some food and a little time to relax.

"Tutt Phillips is dead. I thought you'd want to know," Robert said.

"I'm going to send my reports to Pulitzer and say they're from him. We owe it to him."

"Pablo is also dead." Robert stood, set down his cup of coffee, and walked off. "I need to get word to Maria. His brothers should be around here somewhere. I'll find you later,"

"We're going to outlast them, men. The Spanish forces are trapped. We're on the land side and U.S. Navy ships have them blocked by sea. I don't want to lose any more men so settle down. This may take a while," Roosevelt told his officers.

But, even with a lull in the fighting his Rough Riders continued to fall. Yellow fever and malaria had spread through the camp. The American commanders across the island prepared to send the inflicted men home but the military leaders in Washington were afraid of bringing the illnesses to the mainland. There was a stalemate. No one was moved.

Stuart's wound got infected and he was returned to the infirmary where his leg was rebandaged. Then, as his leg improved, he contracted malaria. He lay next to dozens of other men, taking heavy doses of quinine, wanting to go home and get away from the island's stifling heat, mosquitoes and oppressive humidity.

Weeks elapsed before Stuart, Roosevelt, and the Rough Riders were given permission to board a transport ship, the Miami. There were still many men sick and bedridden but as they traveled up the eastern seaboard within sight of the Carolina's outer banks, the men began singing and sharing the beer that their Colonel had allowed them to sneak on board. They arrived at a new base, Camp Wikoff at Montauk Point, on the tip of Long Island. Both white and black troops disembarked and were sent to well-separated barrack areas. Wikoff, however, had never been finished, and it lacked an adequate number of latrines or even enough food.

"This place is shit," Solinski remarked their first night.

"Maybe, but at least the Spanish aren't shooting at us," Stuart commented, still weak and fever ridden.

Chapter Sixteen

Bess was finding it more and more difficult to focus. The two men she loved were fifteen hundred miles away playing soldier. Samantha was a 'running amok' toddler, impossible to keep track of. And, overseeing the cotton harvest, the gin mills, and Moss Grove's main house couldn't all be done by one person even if the day had another dozen hours. Eli Fineman was increasingly frail. Sometimes he was able to get himself together to join her for dinner but as soon as the meal was finished he would excuse himself, kiss his daughter-in-law on the cheek, and say good night. On those evenings Bess would continue to sit, sipping her coffee, happy for the quiet of the early evening. Missy B would bring Sam in from her bath, still smelling of the lavender that had been sprinkled in with the warm water.

Without any plan, Missy had become Samantha's nanny. The young black girl was just one of the house maids, cleaning, doing laundry, and helping out in the kitchen. Then she and Sam found one another and now there was no separating them. They played together, ran together, and even napped together.

Bess carried Sam upstairs for their evening of quiet time when she would tell her daughter stories about kings and princes. These make-believe heroes were always fashioned after her mother, Amy, and her father, John. She'd also weave Stephen, Josiah and Stuart into the tales, regaling her husband as the bravest of them all.

Eli Fineman took great pleasure in his granddaughter. He would have enjoyed seeing his grandson, Samuel, more often, but Rachel was expecting another child and he didn't have the energy for a trip to New Orleans to see them. He was anxious for his son, Stuart, to return home from his ridiculous adventure but all he knew was that the war was over and the Rough Riders were at some post on Long Island. If Bess knew any more she wasn't saying anything.

The gin mill was operating these days from first light to sunset but the share croppers weren't complaining. This newly installed equipment was far superior to the older models, removing more thistles faster than the old cotton ginning process and with less manual labor. Bess had appointed Big Fred to be her overseer. She realized early on that her workers would prefer to take orders from a man. Big Fred wasn't any better than some of the other men but he was Edgar's father and somehow she felt an emotional connection. Deep inside her, without really knowing, she felt that Josiah had caused Edgar's death. Whatever happened, Big Fred's son had been killed by the Klan and Bess felt an obligation. The man wasn't the brightest share cropper at Moss Grove but he made up for it by working harder than any of the men he had picking and baling.

Cotton prices remained strong although they were sure to settle back now that the war was winding down. There was certain to be less demand for uniforms and bedding, general clothing, and all the other products that seemed to be needed each day. She certainly couldn't complain. The war had gotten the country out of its economic woes and people, once again, shared a new optimism.

Moss Grove and the other nearby plantations hadn't been troubled by night riders or the Klan in almost a year but she knew from neighbors, and the Negro's share cropper pipeline that they were causing trouble further south around Baton Rouge. She'd have to be on the lookout and made it a point to warn Fred to be aware.

Every evening Bess brought the newspapers to her room and looked for Stephen's articles. It was her only way to keep abreast of what was happening. Stuart was able to communicate infrequently. From his brief letters she knew that he had been injured and then contracted malaria. She decided to keep that news to herself. Her husband hadn't made it clear how serious his wounds or illness was. If Eli was stronger she would have taken the train immediately to New York to be with him but she was conflicted. In another time she might have enlisted Josiah and Rachel but there was too much bad blood between him and Eli.

Eli was dead. He was found motionless in his room one morning, having passed quietly during the night. He had had a heart attack or a stroke or something, no one was quite sure. Bess just stopped everything she was doing and cried. She felt so alone, so much pressure, and with her husband gone, no one with whom to share it. She sat alone in her room for an hour, crying and trying to gather her thoughts. It was a long hour, but it was all she would allow herself. She stood, took a deep breath, wiped the tears from her eyes, tied a green ribbon in her red hair, and went downstairs.

One servant was sent to get the Rabbi from Baton Rouge. Missy B was told to keep Sam away from her grandfather's room. Mirrors were ordered covered and funeral plans made. There would be no reason to let Stuart know, he was too weak to travel, he couldn't get to Moss Grove in time, and it would just upset him when he needed to get his strength back. Rachel intended to come but she was due at any time and neither Josiah nor her doctor thought it advisable.

Two days later Eli Fineman was interred next to his wife, Ruth.

Josiah had established a friendly relationship with Murphy Foster, one of Louisiana's two U.S. Senators. Foster had needed to carry the vote in New Orleans with a wide margin in his hotly contested 1896 election, in order to offset his opponent's strength in Louisiana's northern parishes. Not only had Josiah donated heavily to Foster's campaign, he had also used his position with the Klan to intimidate voters into supporting the local Democratic organization. Now it was payback time. He wanted reciprocity for his largesse.

"Senator Foster, thank you for seeing me," Josiah smiled, extending his hand.

"Mr. Williams! Good to see you again," Murphy Foster smiled. Both men understood the give and take of politics and neither man would hesitate to use these relationships to benefit their cause.

"Well, first, let us both thank the Lord that the fighting in Cuba and Puerto Rico is over and we can bring our brave soldiers home," Josiah said with feigned sincerity.

"I'll say 'amen' to that."

"With the Spanish gone there will be a vacuum in Cuba and they will need capital to become self-sufficient. I would like your help and a letter of recommendation to General Brooke. President McKinley has just appointed him as Cuba's first independent Governor."

"None of that should be a problem, Josiah. Tell me, what is your intention?"

"I'm going to get into the sugar business, Senator, and, if you will pardon a bad pun, I think it can be a sweet thing for both of us."

Robert and Stephen decided to remain in Cuba after the troops they were embedded with boarded ships for their return to the States. They waved at the men with whom they'd shared battles these past months. The soldiers were happy to be heading home, and when their ships lifted anchor, they waved with renewed vigor at those still on the island, many of them dead comrades who would never leave.

Hearst was concerned about his reporter's injury and in an unusual demonstration of gratitude, he granted both Stephen and Robert a four week vacation with pay before pulling up his yacht's anchor in Havana Bay and returning to New York. He grinned like a spoiled young boy who had gotten his way. He was ecstatic with the war's outcome and its effect on his paper's circulation.

For the first time the two men and their friends would be able to enter Havana as victors and not as insurgents. Stephen continued to move slowly, the wound in his chest not fully healed. Maria and her brothers had claimed Pablo's body and buried it in their small village near Camaguey.

Neither she nor her brothers had been to the capitol for many years and they all felt a need to share in their island's victorious release from Spanish aggression. They were optimistic about their new relationship with the United States. After all, hadn't the American Congress passed laws granting Cuban independence?

Cuban and American flags hung side by side as they rode into the city. Rebel forces had not been allowed to enter for fear of violence against the Spaniards who had agreed to remain to assist in governing the country. Throngs of individual Cubans poured into the city, however, by wagon, on foot and on horseback. There was a festive atmosphere. The city had suffered minimal damage. Most of the fighting had been on the outskirts although small craters and bullets still pockmarked stucco'd walls and gave proof that the transition had not been entirely peaceful. At least all of the Spanish troops were gone.

Maria had an uncle who lived in the city and was happy to share his small home with his brave relatives. After a few days of rest Stephen decided to request an interview with the island's new American governor. He explained his relationship with Hearst, showed his press pass, and was granted an immediate interview.

"Thank you for seeing me General Brooke," Stephen smiled, the bandages from his chest wound still showing from the open collar of his shirt.

"I'm sorry for your wound, Mr. Carmody. I guess you saw more action than you wanted."

"Yes, sir. I was with the 10th Cavalry when we went up San Juan Hill."

"Oh, the colored unit. I understand those fellows acquitted themselves quite well. Anyway, most of the American reporters have gone home now that the war is over. What made you decide to stay?"

"Well, a girl....."

"Say no more. Now, what can I tell you? The war is over; most of our troops have returned to the States. All the Spanish military forces have left and now we find ourselves with the more mundane task of resurrecting the government and the economy."

"I was wondering why almost every department in the new government is headed by an American or a left-over Spaniard. Almost none are headed by a Cuban?

"Simple! The Cuban campesinos have never run a government and until we can get them some experience, it wouldn't work. We are trying to avoid a chaotic situation here."

"What will you do to get them ready?"

"We'll set up programs but it will take time and they will need to be patient."

"One other thing, General, every day more American investors are coming in and buying up land. Aren't you concerned that the island will just become an easy way for Americans to make a lot of money on the backs of Cuban natives?"

"Mr. Carmody, I'm not happy with the tone of your questions. Are you sure that your Mr. Hearst will share your views?"

"No, sir! I'm not at all sure, but I just spent a year seeing Cubans die to free their island of an oppressive government and what I'm seeing now that the Spanish have been deposed doesn't bode well for the future of the Cuban people."

"Give it time, Mr. Carmody, give it time. And give my regards to Mr. Hearst. Now, if you'll excuse me."

Three weeks later a passenger boat docked in Havana harbor and Josiah walked down the gangway. A flower bedecked carriage took him to his suite at the Colonia, one of Havana's most luxurious hotels. He was ushered to an elaborate suite with a large balcony that opened onto a magnificent view of the blue Caribbean.

"Please see that this letter gets to General Brooke…quickly," he told the concierge, handing him an American $5 bill.

The next morning, promptly at 9 A.M., attired in the latest fashion, Josiah arrived at the government building that previously housed the Spanish Governor and which the U.S. Army had now appropriated.

"Mr. Williams, how nice to meet you! Things here on the island are still in disarray. You can imagine. Services destroyed by the war, untrained people asked to do new jobs, and a great deal of anger by the Cuban rebels over our country's efforts to establish order. Please…sit. I can use a cup of good Cuban coffee. It's one of the better things they do here. That, and cigars…the best. Here, let me offer you one," he said, opening a small humidor.

Josiah didn't hesitate. He took one, rolled it in his fingers, bit off the end and lit it...a cigar smoker's ritual before lighting and inhaling the sweet pungent aroma.

"I received Senator Foster's letter asking that I make myself available to you. Tell me, how can I be of service?" General Brooke asked. He was not use to being obsequious but the Senator's letter made it clear this man was to be treated with some courtesy. Since, as Governor, he was here at the behest of the President and Congress, he had rearranged his schedule to accommodate his tall, blue-eyed visitor, his blonde hair long and tied with a simple ribbon in back.

"Some investors and I are interested in acquiring land to produce and refine sugar. I would assume that a great deal of the property that had been owned by the Spanish has been confiscated."

"Yes, it was. But the Cubans are making a great deal of noise about that land belonging to them."

"Of course," Josiah agreed. "It is their island. But without investment from Americans the only thing they'll be able to grow are small amounts of food crops. With our investment they'll have jobs and security. Now tell me, what section of the island would you recommend? We are prepared to offer you 5% of our enterprise for your suggestions and help in speeding up whatever paperwork is required to transfer title of the land to our group."

Josiah wanted to make it immediately clear that any sensitivity on land ownership was a political matter in which he had no interest.

"That is most generous but I would have to put my shares in my wife's name to avoid any question of impropriety."

"That wouldn't be a problem, General. I understand," Josiah said, thinking that this bastard would probably have been happy with 2%.

"There are some properties near Camaguey around the center of the island that are most appropriate. There are several Colonos there, small planters. Your group would be the largest and there is a Centrales, a sugar mill, close by, for processing. You've come at the right time. This is Zafra, from November to April, when all the workers are busy. It's the dry season. After that comes rain and hurricanes. The locals call it 'tiempo muerto', dead time, and little gets accomplished on the island during those months."

They shook hands as he left, their eyes conveying a mutuality of interest. The purchase would go smoothly. Having set his plan in motion, Josiah decided to enjoy the pleasures of Havana. With the encouragement of a small financial incentive, the hotel manager arranged a guide, a very special guide.

Alicia Juarez, dark hazel eyes, long, shiny brown hair held off her face with an oversized tortoise comb and wearing a low cut forest green peasant blouse, walked in to the Colonia Hotel with the gait and bearing of a princess. She remained standing, refusing a chair and refusing to acknowledge the stares of every man in the room, while Josiah was beckoned from his room. He hadn't reached the bottom of the landing when their eyes made contact and he smiled lasciviously. It was a smile Alicia had seen often, but for men who paid well, she was comfortable handling it.

"Senor, buenos tarde. My name is Alicia Juarez. Please call me Alicia. I understand you wish to see Havana. I have a comfortable carriage and a driver waiting for us outside. The carriage actually belonged to one of the Spanish ministers, but as you know, they left in a hurry."

"Senorita, I am at your disposal," Josiah said as she led him to the front of the hotel.

For the next few hours they drove around the city. They visited the large fort the Spanish had built to protect the island from attack by pirates and the harbor through which much of the gold the Conquistadors pilfered from Mexico and South America had passed. He found everything far less interesting than his guide. They stopped for lunch at a small café where they watched the fishermen mending their nets. The fresh langoustine and Cuban rum enhanced their senses.

"Where did you learn to speak English so well?" he asked as they sipped dark coffee and relaxed.

"I had an American lover," she admitted, almost as a challenge.

"It must have lasted quite a while, you speak so well."

"As long as was necessary. Do you plan on remaining in Cuba long?"

"As long as is necessary," he said, smiling. He was sure they were beginning to understand one another, although Alicia's emotions remained hidden behind a mask of aloofness.

They cut the tour short and returned to the Colonia. Holding Alicia's hand Josiah climbed the stairs and into his suite. She followed him willingly and just watched as he undressed.

He stood there, naked, seeming to want her to nod her approval, but instead she turned her back to him and began disrobing. It upset him. He was insulted and felt himself start to get flaccid. He'd show her, he thought angrily as he climbed into bed, waiting for her to join him.

They didn't speak but their occasional outbursts gave testimony to their pleasures. He could feel Alicia climax, once, twice, and a third time. He held back as long as he could and then he was inside and the heat rose within him before bursting forth. His body was drenched. He didn't know how much of the sweat was from the sex and how much was from the humidity, but he didn't care. This girl was a keeper, whatever she cost. Cuba was going to turn out to be an intriguing investment.

The next morning, having enjoyed one another a second time, they sat, the outside doors of the suite open to their Caribbean view, drinking dark strong coffee, accentuated with rum and a dollop of cream. Alicia sat with her legs crossed, stray hairs still damp from the evening's gymnastics, not speaking.

"You don't talk much, do you?" Josiah asked.

"No, scnor. Does that bother you?"

"A little. I have a wife who speaks a great deal. And, please, call me Josiah."

"Si, Senor Josiah."

"No, not Senor…just Josiah."

"I will probably be here another two weeks. Will you stay with me?"

"With the same arrangement the manager explained?"

"What, no discount for two weeks?" he teased.

"I don't know what 'discount' means but if you aren't happy with the arrangement...."

"No, the arrangement is fine, but I would like to know if you were satisfied last night."

"You are a good lover, senor....Josiah," she corrected.

"A ringing endorsement, no doubt."

Alicia accompanied Josiah to the abogado, the lawyer, Senor Rudolfo Antonio, who had been hired to complete the property transfer. They would all need to travel to Camaguey to visit the land that had been suggested by General Brooke, and it would take time for the proper papers to be filed.

"Josiah? Josiah! Hey, over here," Stephen shouted and limped across the street, trying to avoid the horses and carriages that crowded one of Havana's busier streets.

"Stephen. What are you doing here? I thought you would have left when the troops did. And why are you bent over? Wait, don't tell me! This is Alicia, my guide, and new friend. Come, we'll go have a drink and you can regale me with tales of the war and what you've been up to."

They sat in the bar, enjoying the coolness of the fans rotating overhead. Stephen knew Josiah well enough to know that Alicia was more than his guide but his friend's total lack of fidelity wasn't his business.

"I took an uninvited piece of Spanish shrapnel in my chest as we approached San Juan Hill, but it's nearly healed. Mr. Hearst gave Robert and me some time off. I'm just wandering around the island while I decide what to do next."

"And Robert, where is he?"

"He has a Cuban girlfriend, Maria. We were with her rebel brothers during the fighting but now that the war is over I imagine they've gone back to their family's farm. What about you?"

"I'm here as an investor, Stephen. Several of us think there is a terrific opportunity to make money investing in Cuba so we're buying land that used to belong to the Spanish and we'll be growing sugar."

"I understand there are a lot of groups like you buying up the land. Some of the Cubans who fought the Spanish are getting very upset."

Alicia listened but said nothing. She made her living off of wealthy men who could afford her and she didn't care whether they were Spanish or American, although this one was, at least, handsome, young, and very good in bed. Most of what she earned she sent to her family in Santiago. She could earn in a week what took them a year. They were embarrassed, knowing what she did to earn each peso, and they donated an excessive amount to the church, as an atonement that Alicia felt was unnecessary. This new one, this Stephen, was even more handsome than Josiah. He had been well-tanned from the Cuban sun and he had a masculine beauty that took her breath away. She was having feelings that she had never experienced.

"There are those who own and those who work, Stephen. It's the American way."

"And you don't care if it isn't the Cuban way?"

"Frankly, no. I don't care one way or the other. Now, will you have dinner with us? Alicia knows of this place that has great Cuban music. I may even bring my trumpet."

Robert was finding it difficult to separate himself from Maria. The fact that he was black and she was Cuban didn't seem to matter to anyone on the island and it was the first time he could ever remember not being self-conscious about the color of his skin.

The farm her family owned was in terrible condition, neglected from three years of fighting the Spanish. There was a great deal of work to do. Robert's American dollars were able to buy seed and repairs for the few pieces of equipment that hadn't rusted from the island's humidity. Slowly, one acre at a time, they made progress. When evening arrived they would all spend an hour making the house more livable. Neighbors came and helped. Maria and her mother cooked for everyone. Someone always brought a guitar and these campesinos, with so little, enjoyed an evening of wine and music.

Stephen got word to him that Josiah was in Havana and would be traveling to Camaguey soon. There would likely be a very striking, young lady accompanying him.

A week later two carriages came along the dirt road from the west. The first carriage carried a comfortably seated Josiah and Alicia. The second was considerably more crowded with Stephen, Senor Antonio, Josiah's lawyer, and several pieces of luggage sharing space.

Robert and Maria stood at the side of the road as the new arrivals came abreast.

"Josiah," Robert smiled. "Welcome to Camaguey. You are a long way from New Orleans."

"And you're a long way from Washington. Nice to see you."

Camaguey had no hotels comparable to the Colonia but rooms at a small inn had been set aside and, following cordial introductions, they all agreed to share dinner together in the inn's small restaurant. Maria had invited the new arrivals to their home but Robert understood his guests would prefer something a little more structured.

That evening, as they sat in the restaurant they found themselves the only guests. Maria was in awe of Alicia. She was so beautiful, so poised. Here she sat, a *campesina*, uncomfortable, and unsure of herself. She desperately wanted to talk privately to this unusually lovely Cuban woman, and when Alicia excused herself after dinner, Maria followed.

"You are so beautiful, Alicia, and I see how Senor Josiah's eyes follow you."

"I am no prettier than you, amiga. I have just had more practice on how to use what I have. I have made it my business," she said, putting a difficult hair in place and squeezing her cheeks. "Tell me, what do you know about Stephen? Is he not handsome?"

"Quite handsome. He and my Robert were side by side with my brothers fighting the Spanish. He is a reporter for an American newspaper. An artillery blast injured him in his chest but he seems better now. I think you like him, no?"

"I'm sure I could, but I would have to be very careful. This Senor Josiah is very possessive."

"Perhaps when his business is done he will leave."

"It is complicated. My head says he should stay awhile since he pays so well, but the heart says he should leave de prisa, very soon, so I see if Stephen might be interested."

"Your life is too complicated for me," Maria laughed.

"Here, let me show you an easy way to make yourself more attractive," Alicia said, as she pulled back Maria's hair on one side and fluffed up the other. Then she pulled her blouse a little more off her shoulders.

"That should work. Now you are twice as lovely."

"You're telling me that you're going to own more than five hundred acres here in Camaguey?" Robert said, his voice rising in astonishment.

"Why not? These people, probably including Maria's family, will have jobs and…"

"Because they'll be like share croppers in their own country. For God's sake, Josiah, don't you see that? Stephen, you understand my point, don't you?"

"I do, Robert, but maybe that's because we've been here more than a year and we understand what these people fought for."

"They fought for their freedom, damn it, and now blood suckers like Josiah here, are rushing in for the spoils."

"Don't be insulting, Robert. I didn't invite you to dinner to be slandered."

"You're right, Josiah, you didn't. Here are enough pesos for what we ate," he said, angrily throwing some bills on the table. My apology, Stephen, and to you, too, Alicia! Come, Maria, we're leaving."

Josiah's blue eyes flashed in an icy fury. Damn nigger! It was something he'd never said about someone he knew, but the effrontery.

"Waiter, another bottle of rum, por favor," Josiah said, breathing deeply and trying to regain his composure as Alicia, Stephen, and Senor Antonio stared uncomfortably at one another.

"Enough for me, senor," his lawyer said. "I am older and I require more sleep and less alcohol. Gracias for a lovely dinner. I will see you in the morning."

"Is what we're doing that bad?" Josiah asked after a long silence.

"Would you care if it was?" Stephen asked frankly.

Josiah didn't answer and the table was silent as four musicians began playing their last set of the evening.

Unexpectedly, Alicia rose from the table and walked over to the musicians. She gave the guitar player a light kiss on the cheek and faced the only two guests remaining. Her voice started softly, too softly to make out the words, but it built, and with it there was a sweetness and innocence so different from the persona she so carefully cultivated. It wasn't a melody from the city but from the farms and the families that worked them. She swayed as she sang. One could feel the waves beating against the shore...the sugar cane fighting against the hurricane's heavy wind...the pungent smell of the tobacco leaves hung for drying...the campesinos struggling and fighting decade after decade to be masters of their own land. Always for the land, always for the land! She was embarrassed by the tear in her eye as she returned to the table to the silent thoughts of the two very different men who stared, entranced.

It took another two days for Josiah and his lawyer to study the mill, the repairs it would need, and to hire people to run the sugar cane plantation. Stephen found himself coming around, more to see Alicia than to see Josiah, but when it was time to return to Havana, Stephen indicated he would stay in Camaguey a little longer. Robert kept his distance. As Josiah's carriage rode off, Stephen's eyes connected with Alicia's and their non-verbal contact spoke volumes. Fortunately, Josiah didn't appear to notice.

A week later as Stephen was working with Robert and Maria's brothers, a lone rider came up the road with a small bedroll tied on the back of a donkey. Stephen knew who it was. He ran toward the road as the figure climbed down and moved toward him. It was Alicia, and without any words being necessary, they embraced, and found one another's lips.

Chapter Seventeen

"How many women did you fuck while you were in Cuba?" Rachel asked, now seven months pregnant, feeling bloated and not particularly attractive.

Josiah had actually returned from Cuba several days earlier but he'd arranged to meet Sisseretta Jones in Miami. It had been nearly a year since they'd seen one another and the hunger they had for one another made no sense. There was nothing either cerebral or emotional in their coupling. It was purely physical...something they both needed...something they both wanted.

The tall black singer never told him she'd missed her period after their last tryst. She hadn't been with anyone else either. She had made an appointment to have an abortion once she was certain she was pregnant. It was with a questionable doctor in Harlem but the rooms were so dirty and the girl who arrived before her was making such guttural screams from the adjoining room that it made her cringe. She ran out and moved in with an aunt who drank too much. Neither Sisseretta's health nor her career returned to what they had been after her daughter was born. She was a little thing, just over five pounds with long tapered fingers and the cutest toes. She named the baby girl Lily. It was the only name that came to her when she had to fill out papers. It was the same name as one of the nurses who was so nice to her and she hoped it would bring her daughter something good later in life. The first nights, alone, Sisseretta's hands shook and she couldn't stop crying. She had certainly messed up her career and her life.

She left her newborn daughter with her aunt, sometimes for weeks on end when she had work. She still didn't understand herself. She didn't like this white boy. He was smug...just full of himself. But the man did know how to satisfy a woman and she knew, if he snapped his fingers, she'd come running.

"Rachel, it's nice to see you, too. You look radiant."

"Josiah, you are one of the most transparent men I've ever known. If you hadn't had a full complement of women while you were gone, you'd be itchy. Would you care to tell me about it?"

"Rachel, you are my wife and I treat you with the utmost respect. You are also the mother of my son and our next child. Don't expect me to be maritally faithful and don't embarrass either of us by asking me."

"I noticed the word 'love' was absent from your diatribe."

"My love for you is endless. I apologize for its omission," he said sarcastically. "Now, the baby...when is it due?"

"The doctor expects it to be early, not go to full term."

"And, other news?" he asked, eager to keep the discussion away from his varied trysts. Alicia, and then Sisseretta, mocha and chocolate... truly a wondrous feast. I wonder what it would be like to bed them both at the same time, he wondered, listening only minimally to his wife.

"My father died, Stuart was in the Army hospital with malaria he contracted in Cuba, and neither he nor I were able to attend the funeral."

"I'm sorry about your father. Once the baby is born we can go to Moss Grove and you can visit his graveside. Meanwhile, I saw Robert and Stephen in Cuba and they send their regards, at least Stephen does. Robert was quite upset to learn that my friends and I are investing in his new Caribbean playground. Now, shall we celebrate my return with energetic sex or dinner at Antoine's?"

"Well, you may have romped with some island trollop but I haven't, so both might be appropriate," she smiled.

Three weeks later, without warning, Rachel's contractions began. The doctor arrived, along with a nurse, shortly after her water broke. Josiah had already arranged for the best medical man in New Orleans to be on call. He had installed a telephone in his home a year earlier and made certain the doctor he chose had one as well.

Josiah waited nervously downstairs, hearing periodic screams from his wife, then silence, and, finally, a baby's cries. He rushed upstairs and into the room.

"You have a daughter, Mr. Williams," the doctor announced somberly.

"Thank you...thank you both," he said as he approached Rachel, her face damp with perspiration, nestling her new born child.

"We have a problem, Josiah," she said.

"Is the baby healthy?"

"The doctor thinks so," she said as she slowly pulled the cover back.

A very attractive infant girl gurgled and moved nervously in her mother's arms. The baby's hands flailed about and a cute heart shaped mouth searched for something to suck. She was lovely, soft and cuddly. She was everything parents would want but....and it was a big 'but'.... it was clear the infant girl wasn't entirely white. Josiah's heritage had come back to haunt him.

He said nothing. He remembered his father's outbursts and accusations when his wife had borne him a colored child. Josiah had been quite young then but he could hear Henry Roger's anger spew venom throughout the entire house. He later understood that was when his father learned that his mother had a small amount of colored blood coursing through her veins and he inherited it. It was a discovery he refused to accept and it eventually killed him.

It was the reason Amy had later taken all of them from Moss Grove to San Francisco, reluctant to raise a mixed race child in the Deep South where such individuals faced perpetual discrimination. Now he had returned to the land of his birth and his heart sank. He understood the dangers to the fragile life he and Rachel had created, the beautiful infant girl Rachel was cuddling. He couldn't deny the tiny baby looked lovely...her mother's eyes...his chin. But...keeping her was impossible.

"You will keep this entirely to yourself," he said to the confused doctor, standing solemnly at Rachel's bed side. "Do you understand?" he said in a voice that was clearly threatening.

The doctor nodded. Josiah paid him double the agreed upon fee and sent him away. It would take time to resolve this conundrum.

Stuart was finally discharged and, with some difficulty, made it back to Moss Grove. He continued to suffer from recurring bouts of malaria. Beads of perspiration would suddenly appear and weakness in his joints made it difficult for him to stand or concentrate for long periods of time. The Army put him and Solinski on a train from Camp Wikoff into New York City where the two Army buddies said their goodbyes, promising to remain in contact. He found himself in the middle of Grand Central Station, tired, damp, and on his own. He sat down and fell into a deep sleep.

"Are you O.K., mister?" a woman asked. "You're soaking wet."

Stuart stirred. "Malaria…Cuba."

Minutes later the woman found a supervisor and Stuart was taken to a small infirmary two levels down and given quinine pills. He didn't awaken until the next morning, his fever down, barely enough energy to continue his trip.

Bess knew her husband was due to return, but she didn't know when and managing the plantation was requiring her full attention. She was in the fields when Stuart arrived, unannounced, in the middle of the day. He found his daughter, Sam, taking her nap in her upstairs room. He lay down beside her, falling asleep immediately. It was near dusk before Bess returned and discovered her husband still sleeping in their daughter's tiny bed. Sam was whisked away by Missy B once she awoke. Now Bess joined the man she loved in Sam's bed.

"Hello, Mrs. Fineman," he whispered, his eyes beginning to open and smiling wanly at his beautiful wife next to him.

"Hello, Mr. Fineman. Welcome home. You were missed."

He would have liked to make love to his wife but he lacked the strength. Besides, this bed was far too small. He stroked her hair, kissed her, and apologized for his absence. Tears began to well up in his eyes.

"I've been a selfish dolt," he said.

"Yes, you were, but I love you, and you're back. Now we need you to get healthy. I'm really tired of running this place."

It took several weeks for Stuart's health to return. Meanwhile he enjoyed playing with his daughter. Samantha had decided to be her father's nurse when Mommy wasn't around, bringing him tea or medicine or whatever, sometimes real, sometimes pretend. He had given up and now called her 'Sam.' In truth, he acknowledged, it suited her better than Samantha. He spent time sitting by his parent's graves, feeling particularly guilty about missing his father's funeral.

"Stuart, I've gotten word that Rachel and Josiah are coming for a visit with Samuel and their new daughter."

"OK," he said unenthusiastically. "Any special reason?"

"To see you, I'm sure, and Rachel was never able to make it here for your father's funeral either."

"And they have a new daughter. That's nice. What did they name her?"

"Funny, but she never said."

The William's ornate carriage arrived a few days later. Sam and her cousin, Samuel, went off to play. Rachel and Josiah's infant, well protected against the chill, was sleeping, and laid gently into Sam's old crib upstairs, while the two couples settled into the living room. Stuart poured glasses of port for all of them. He was glad to see his sister, not as thrilled to see her husband.

"I want to see father's grave," Rachel said. "But that is only one of the reasons we've come."

"We have a problem," Josiah added, in unusually somber tones, "And we need your advice, particularly yours, Bess."

"You sound so mysterious."

"Please don't make this about your children being heirs to Moss Grove," Stuart said, refilling his glass before even sitting down.

"No. That's a discussion for another time," Josiah said, taking a deep breath before continuing.

"My background has come back to haunt me. Our daughter's skin tone makes it obvious that she has some black blood in her."

"Oh, Jesus," Bess shrieked, putting her hand to her mouth. "My mother always said this could happen but you, Stephen, and I always thought she was overreacting."

"We don't know what to do," Rachel confessed. "Josiah has threatened the doctor and nurse, who helped me give birth, to keep their silence, so now it's just the four of us."

"Have you given her a name yet?" Bess asked.

"I want to name her Ruth, after my mother, but we didn't want to upset you, Stuart. We're so confused."

"Call her Ruth, but if we have the Rabbi come and have her blessed, then others will know. You know Mother would have loved her regardless of her color, but you can't raise her, not in this environment."

"I'm sorry, Josiah," Bess said, putting her arms around him. "Your life has been so full since you returned to Louisiana. Samuel is such an energetic and likeable little boy. This has to have thrown you."

They talked for hours but nothing was resolved and everyone was exhausted. Resolving this conundrum wasn't going to be easy.

It was the next morning at breakfast, Josiah and Rachel's eyes red from lack of sleep, when Stuart walked in, smiling. He poured himself a cup of coffee, kissed Bess, and sat down, a satisfied grin never leaving his face.

"I believe I may have an answer that will work," he said, stirring two teaspoons of sugar into the cup. "At least it's worth a try. While I was in Cuba I ran into both Stephen and Robert. Robert had a lovely girlfriend, Maria, a Cuban girl. They might be willing to raise your daughter, particularly with the right financial incentive."

"That's a wonderful idea," Bess agreed.

"Under other circumstances you might be right," Josiah admitted, "But Robert is quite angry with me for making investments in a Cuban sugar cane farm. He thinks Americans are stealing the land that should have gone to the Cuban people once the Spanish were deposed. I'm not opposed to your idea, but I'm not sure he would do anything that he thought might benefit me."

"What makes you think he'd even consider it?" Rachel asked.

"I don't know that he would, but he's one of the few that understands the dynamics of the problem you two are facing."

"I should present it to him," Bess said, after listening quietly. "I'm the right person, especially if Stephen is still there with him."

"Bess, that's crazy. Besides, I've just returned. We've barely had time together."

"You went to Cuba. Now, I'm going. The only question is whether I should take baby Ruth with me. Rachel, what're your thoughts on that?"

Josiah looked at Stuart and broke out laughing.

"Still haven't won an argument, have you?"

"Stay out of this, Josiah," Stuart said angrily. "I don't think I like you any better than Robert does."

"Stop it, you two!" Bess demanded. "Rachel, I should take the baby, otherwise it would be asking them to make a theoretical decision. Josiah, I think you should give me $10,000.00 as an incentive."

"That's a lot of money," he complained.

"Don't be cheap. You want your daughter raised properly. You have the money. There is no better use for it."

A week later Bess and Rachel took a train to Miami. Rachel cried each time she looked at her young infant daughter. She continued to breast feed her and Bess could only sit close by, sadly watching her sister-in-law wrestle with the tragedy of having to give up her daughter…forever.

Rachel insisted on staying with the child until Bess, carrying the baby tightly wrapped in a blanket boarded an overnight boat that would take the two of them to Havana harbor and a new, very different, life. Rachel stood at the dock, alone, huddled, not against the cold, but against the maternal loss she was facing. The boat became smaller and disappeared into the horizon but Rachel still didn't move. Tears continued to fall and dry on her cheek. It was all so unfair.

The sun came up and promised a fresh beginning. Two handsome couples stood watching the boat dock as brown skinned men attached heavy hawsers before lowering a wooden gangplank. It had been a quiet passing. The hurricane season wasn't due for another two months. This was the time of sunshine during the day and moonlit evenings.

Bess came down the walkway slowly, a blanket wrapped package still nestled tightly in her arms. Stephen reached her first and embraced this woman he had loved for so many years.

"When I heard you were coming I couldn't believe it."

"I had no idea you were still here. You look wonderful. I'm so glad you're safe."

"Do you still love me?" he asked.

"You don't ever have to ask. During the war I said a prayer every night that you would be safe. We'll have time to talk later."

Stephen pulled back when he heard cries from within the blanket. He drew the blanket back and his eyes opened wide.

"Bess? Who is this?"

Before she could answer, Alicia stepped forward.

"Here, let me hold the child. I am Alicia, Stephen's friend."

Bess stared at the Cuban beauty standing before her and then looked back at her love, a look of pleading embarrassment on his face. Her smile said she understood and the two of them connected as they'd always been able, in a dimension of their own, apart from the cacophony of boat, crowds, and infant that circled around them.

They had loved one another for so long, so sure they would share their entire lives together and now, here they were, both having moved forward. Their eyes said she understood the duality of his feelings and his need to continue his life, as she had with Stuart, never denying what either of them felt.

Robert and Maria joined them and everyone began speaking at once. They were told Bess was coming but no one had said anything about a newborn baby girl.

"Take me to the hotel and I will explain everything."

Josiah had booked rooms for them all at the Colonia where he had stayed. The hotel held uncomfortable recollections for Alicia. She had spent too many nights there with too many men and she was sure one of the staff would remember her. She had looked attractively made up then, a consort men desired, not the woman of the earth, and in love, as she was now. She regained her calm once they passed through the lobby and no one gave her a second look.

"Rachel and Josiah had their second child, this beautiful little girl they've named Ruth, after Rachel's mother. Their first son, Samuel, is healthy, and to all appearances, he is white. Ruth, who I've brought with me, is obviously mulatto and, like you, Stephen, it is neither safe nor practical for her parents to rear her, particularly in Louisiana. I have a check for $10,000.00, made payable to you, Robert, if you and Maria will agree to raise her as your own."

"You want me to help that son of a bitch," Robert shouted. "Fuck him. Let him solve his own problems."

"I understand your feelings. Josiah explained how upset you were over his plans to invest, but you and Maria were the only ones we could think of and the money is substantial."

Stephen looked at Bess, and then at Alicia. He was trying to gauge the emotional cost of what he was ready to suggest.

"Alicia and I have discussed getting married," he said, ever so softly. "If we were to get married, and if it was acceptable to Alicia, we could raise her. It might offer you another viable option."

Alicia didn't look comfortable with Stephen's suggestion but she kept her silence. She wasn't interested in being a mother at this point and why, Madre Dios, would he want us to raise a mixed child.

"Thank you, Stephen. None of us knew you had a girlfriend when Josiah left Cuba. He did know that Robert and Maria were seriously involved. Now that I'm here, however, you're right. Either of you could raise Ruth as your own." Bess had noticed that Alicia had blanched at the suggestion but then recovered quickly. It was clear being an immediate mother wasn't something she wanted.

"We all need time to think about the ramifications of taking on a child. The money would be useful but raising a daughter is not an easy decision," Stephen said, taking Alicia's hand and grasping it tightly. She forced a tight smile.

They separated, each deep in his own thoughts. Alicia excused herself in the hotel lobby and returned to the suite where Bess was staying.

"You are the woman Stephen has always loved, are you not?" she asked.

The directness of the question surprised Bess. She felt she was facing a woman with animal instincts...feral instincts if her own well-being was ever threatened.

"Yes. Stephen and I have been in love since we were children growing up together."

"Why did you not marry? I think he still loves you."

"For reasons he can explain if he wishes to. I think he loves you as well and he is a wonderful man. I think you are most beautiful and, if you love him, you can share a life together."

"Gracias, Buenos noches." Alicia turned and walked away.

For the next few days they showed Bess the sights of Havana before traveling to Camaguey. The question of Ruth's future hung in the air, unanswered.

"See all that land over there and the men working it with their machetes?" Robert pointed. "That's the property Josiah and his investors purchased. Those men should be working their own land but everywhere you turn you find rich Americans with political connections owning the best land and the sugar mills. They can squeeze out the small farmers anytime they want, and if sugar prices decline, that's just what they'll do."

There was little that Bess could say to defend her friend's actions so she said nothing. If either couple was going to raise Ruth it would have to be a decision they reached on their own. Trying to defend Josiah made little sense.

Another week went by and still no decision was forthcoming. They had all returned to the Hotel Colonia, five adults, and a small infant. Bess was anxious to get home. She missed Sam and Stuart. She had also missed her period although she hadn't said anything to anyone. She knew her friends were spending long hours deciding what to do. She just wished they would hurry.

"We're all going to return to the United States," Robert said.

"I'm not sure I understand," Bess said. "Does that mean that neither of you is going to raise this little girl? Stephen, you know a white couple can't raise a mixed child without serious risk. And Robert, your father was never even told he had sired a child with the white woman he loved, my mother. We've all suffered from this sort of stupidity. I'm sorry you all feel this way. I'm very disappointed but I respect your decision. Ruth and I will be leaving in the morning."

"You should let him finish, Bess," Stephen said. "You are like your mother, ready to leap to conclusions."

"What Stephen means is that Maria and I will adopt and raise Ruth. We'll take Josiah's money, but not to raise his child. We plan on giving it to Maria's brothers to buy their own land and small mill. At least that way some Cubans might be able to support themselves in their own country. I'm returning to Washington. Colonel Roosevelt asked me to look him up when I return and I've had enough of the old Confederacy. Its blindness and stupidity killed my brother. Washington, D.C. will be an acceptable place to raise a daughter."

"And I'm taking Alicia back to the States with me. Wherever Mr. Hearst sends me, I'll have her with me. That's why we can't raise the baby. I'm not sure where my next assignment might take me."

Bess breathed a sigh of relief when Maria took the infant girl in her arms. She and Robert would make wonderful parents.

"Are you happy, Stephen?" Bess asked when she and Stephen had a few moments alone together. "Alicia is lovely and you make a handsome couple."

"I love her, Bess, at least I think I do. It isn't the love that you and I will always have. Alicia's so….so private," he said, struggling to find the right word. "I think she loves me but the words come out of her and they feel hollow. I excuse it as a language difference or a difficult life but what if it's more than that?"

"I'm sure when you both begin your new life together it will all be fine. I'm glad you've found someone."

"We should both be happy that we've moved forward but we aren't, are we?"

His question hung in the air.

Bess postponed her return another week while a hastily arranged double wedding celebration kept them all busy. Let Josiah pay for the parties, she thought, and the Hotel Colonia has the loveliest facilities. Maria's family came en masse and even though Alicia had no family, she was soon adopted by Maria's father and brothers. Nearly eighty people clogged the lobby and banquet room and the ceremony was conducted both in Spanish and in English. The music was loud and enthusiastic and only Bess' new pregnancy kept her from enjoying the heavy Cuban rum whose sweet aroma wafted through the room.

Stephen accompanied Bess to her boat. The two were alone, as they both had wanted.

"It seems our lives have become one of saying 'hellos' and 'goodbyes' with large chasms of time in between," he said sadly.

"Yes, and I cry for days every time we part and fiddle with my hair and clothes for days before you arrive."

"I love you skinny, pregnant, wearing a gown or overalls...and I've seen you in all states."

"Yes, you have. Alicia is beautiful. I'm glad you've found someone to love."

"Sometimes I think she's like a wounded dove, hesitant to allow anyone to know the private person she hides inside."

"She may need time. We all have scars."

"Good luck with the baby. My best to Stuart." Their kiss was not chaste; it needed to last and to carry them into the future.

"I'm not happy that we had to give up our daughter," Rachel said, sitting in a darkened room in their large New Orleans home.

"There was no choice. Allowing her to be raised by a more appropriate couple was the right thing to do. Robert and Maria will take care of her, especially with the money we gave them," Josiah said, bringing the lights up a little.

"They didn't keep the money. Bess explained they gave it to her family. Robert still dislikes you but at least now a few Cuban families have benefitted from your largesse."

"As long as Ruth is taken care of I don't give a damn what he does with the money. You and I need to move on with our lives. Only," he paused, "No more children. Are we agreed?"

Rachel couldn't speak. She nodded her head imperceptibly, sad at the realization that he was right. He could sense her body convulse in the dim light of the room. They both knew that their relationship would never be the same.

Josiah had finally shaken off the lethargy of the events regarding his daughter. Rachel, however, continued to mope around the house, depressed. Samuel's escapades weren't enough to excite her, she left much of his rearing to a nanny and the idea of sex with her husband had become too distasteful to consider. She was glad when Josiah left the house.

"Your friend Pike is dead," Rene Boudreaux told him.

"What do you mean Pike is dead? Albert Pike?"

"Yes! Albert Pike. Your Albert Pike is dead. They pulled him out of the river yesterday, naked as the day he was born."

"My God. What happened? What do the Police say?"

"There are only rumors. My sons are, once again, working the docks and they hear things."

"Don't be coy, man. What are they saying?"

"That Pike had a liking for young boys."

"You're joking. Albert Pike? He was the head of the Klan for much of the South. It's not possible," Josiah said, amazed at what he was being told. He had forgotten about the Klan, and had not held a meeting in nearly three months. With Pike dead the entire organization in his area could unravel, and with it, his position. He sent word to the members that there would be a meeting the following Thursday, but meanwhile he needed to determine what had really happened.

Phillippe Broussard might know more. The man had dealt efficiently and discreetly with the black builders who needed to be put in their place. Josiah knew that Broussard worked for a wholesale meat company and under the pretext of planning the upcoming meeting, waited for him at its gate at the end of the man's workday.

"Phillippe...good to see you again. I'd like to buy you a drink if you have an hour. Perhaps we can discuss the upcoming meeting."

"Monsieur Williams. How did you know where I work?"

"Discreet inquiries, Phillippe! Is there somewhere nearby we can talk?"

They were in a factory district and had to walk several blocks to find a suitable place to talk. Neither man said a word until they were seated. Both ordered beers, anything else would have brought stares.

"I've been out of the country, Phillippe, and I've come back to learn that Albert Pike is dead. What in the hell happened?"

"He is in hell and good riddance," Broussard said, retreating to his Cajun accent, and taking a long sip from his glass.

"You know what happened to him, don't you?"

"Do you remember Alex, one of the men I took with me on your 'little' job?"

"Yes, short...stocky...curly black hair."

"He's the one. Alex wasn't bright but he was a good follower and a good provider for his family. He hated blacks. The Union Army had refused to give him his land back after the war because he wouldn't sign a Loyalty paper. As I said, Alex wasn't very bright. He didn't know what they meant and didn't even understand he could just make his mark."

"What does that have to do with Albert Pike?"

"Alex had a wife and two children, a son and a daughter...same black curly hair. Pretty children, and they adored their father. The son was ten, eleven ...something like that. Pike knew the family. He'd helped Alex find a job after he lost his farm. None of us ever understood why such an important man would stay close to such unimportant people until Alex came home unexpectedly one afternoon and found Pike buggering his son. It had been going on for several months and the boy was afraid to say anything for fear his father would lose the job that Pike had gotten him. Anyway, Alex went crazy, grabbed the closest thing he could find, a shovel, and struck Pike across the head. Killed him instantly and Alex spent the next two hours hugging his son. His wife came and got a few of us. We just waited until nightfall and threw the fat bastard into the river."

Josiah stood there, thunderstruck at the revelation that Albert Pike molested little boys.

"I guess we've all got secrets," Broussard said.

For a moment their eyes connected and he wondered what this white Cajun knew or even suspected. A chill passed through Josiah and the moment passed. He nodded, stood, and walked away.

Chapter Eighteen

The nation was enjoying a surge of prosperity and the Republican ticket of McKinley and Teddy Roosevelt rode easily into a second term in the Presidential election of 1900. 'Four more years of a full dinner pail' and the captivating hero of the Spanish-American war won almost every state except those of the solid Democratic bloc that now marked the old South.

Robert sat in the outer offices of the new Vice-President. He had been sitting there nearly two hours. Teddy Roosevelt had agreed to see him after being reminded that he was Thaddeus William's son and that he and the Colonel had met in Cuba. Growing impatient, Robert was having second thoughts on whether the man's offer had been genuine.

He and Maria had settled in his old apartment in Georgetown. He had so many good memories of growing up there with his parents and Noah. Now he had lost them all and discovered a new life to share with his young wide-eyed wife. He was going to enjoy showing her the sights of the capitol. The two of them were in love with their new daughter and the three of them were exalted with the excitement of their new adventure.

"Mr. Williams? Mr. Robert Williams?"

A handsome, tall, chocolate-colored man had opened the door from the Vice-President's office and extended his hand with a warm smile on his face. His hair was combed flat and parted on one side.

He sported a handsomely trimmed mustache and spoke perfect English with the preciseness of an academic. The man's clear brown eyes sparkled with the curiosity of someone always eager to meet new people and learn new things.

"Mr. Williams, my name is Daniel Murray. I am the Assistant Librarian of the Library of Congress. Mr. Roosevelt and I have been discussing you. Please, follow me. The Colonel, which he prefers to be called, wants to say hello."

They entered a spacious office and the bespectacled man, still sporting his hunting jacket, sprung to his feet and came around his desk.

"Robert, how good of you to come. I regret having made you wait. You've met Daniel here. Splendid! Splendid!" His words came out as rapidly as bullets from a Gatling gun and his face continued to reflect a genuine cherubic warmth.

"Mr. Murray is compiling an array of writings by African American writers. We want to avoid the debacle of the Chicago Exposition that ignored the Black experience in our country. Next year there will be a large Exposition in Paris celebrating the new century and as part of our country's pavilion we want to present the successes of Black Americans. He needs help and we have agreed you would be perfect for the job. You'll accept, of course."

"Mr. Roosevelt…."

"Call me Colonel…."

"Colonel Roosevelt, Mr. Murray….thank you for your confidence…"

"Bully, now go with Mr. Murray and welcome on board."

They shook hands and Roosevelt returned to his desk, picking up the new telephone on his desk. Murray just smiled, put his arm around Robert, and accompanied him out of the office.

"He is a unique gentleman," Murray said as the two men walked down the corridor and across Pennsylvania Avenue toward the new Library of Congress building.

"I understand you and your family have just returned to Washington. Did I tell you I knew your father? I was quite young, working at the Senate restaurant managed by my brother. At that time your father was working as an aide to Senator Bruce of

Massachusetts. We understood that he had grown up as a slave. Is that true?"

"Yes, sir! I'm sorry to say he died a few years ago."

"And you had a brother, I believe."

"Yes, but he's dead as well, some white trash from Mobile."

"We've arrived. Your desk will be here just across from my office. I'd like to hear more about what happened. Perhaps you and your wife would grace my wife, Anna, and me with your company for dinner."

"We would but we would have to find someone for our infant daughter, Ruth."

"Bring her along…we have seven children and they will relish a new young one. Now let me explain more about the task we are undertaking.

"I've begun gathering copies of the writings of Frederick Douglas, Booker T. Washington, Ida Wells…"

"I know a great deal about Mrs. Wells," Robert interrupted.

"In what way?"

"My close relative, Stephen Carmody, reports for the Hearst newspapers and wrote several articles about lynchings in the South. Mrs. Wells was his mentor in developing the stories. He then traveled with her to the Chicago Exposition and worked on the Homer Plessey articles."

"That's wonderful. I'm sure he'll be able to contribute to our collection. Now I want to introduce you to Mr. Herbert Putnam, our boss. He is a wonderful man and the first professional Librarian ever put in charge of the Library of Congress. He is replete with new ideas and I know the two of you will hit it off splendidly."

> *It is 1901 and the automobile is beginning to excite the public's imagination. There are already ten miles of paved roads in the country and speeds have climbed to eight miles an hour. New York is operating the nation's first motorized ambulance service and Boston's horse drawn trolley is being replaced with a twelve passenger electric bus. New car companies like Ford, Oldsmobile, Columbia and Locomobile are raising money to build assembly plants. A loaf of bread costs $.04 and a new car can cost more than $1,000.*

You could hear the loud engine from the edge of Moss Grove, nearly a half-mile from the main house. A lone driver wearing goggles and a dust coat was coming up the dirt road while blacks ran from the nearby fields and homes to see what the ruckus was. He pulled up to the front colonnade and stopped. Bess ran from the house, her daughter, Sam, and Miss B at her side.

"Do you like it?" Stuart asked.

"It's noisy enough. I know it's an automobile but is it always that loud? It certainly does frighten the horses."

"It's called an Olds Runabout. It generates four horsepower. Imagine…an engine that does what it used to take four horses to do. That's progress. The state's even talking about paving the road between New Orleans and Baton Rouge. That would mean no ruts…a smoother ride."

"And you bought this contraption?"

"C'mon Bess…get in…bring Sam. I'll take you for a drive."

"Take Sam…I'll go another time."

Bess was well along in her pregnancy. She had had one miscarriage since Samantha was born and they did want another child. Now she was being extra careful and riding in some mechanical monster was not her idea of caution.

Sam was a mystery to her father. Stuart had grown up with a sister but Rachel preferred fancy dresses and dolls. Pretty was her favorite word. Stuart and Josiah teased her and then they all went outside where they could swim in the lake or hunt for frogs and catfish or watch the gin noisily removing the thorns from the cotton. That female gentility of Moss Grove was now gone. It had died with his mother's death and his sister's departure. Bess was like her mother, Amy, and Sam was following in their footsteps, riding horses, getting dirty, and preferring overalls to dresses. But all that took nothing from her beauty. She had her mother's red hair and green eyes but she had her father's smile and for that he could never deny that she was his daughter. Mother and daughter…he loved them both.

"I'm taking Samuel and going back to Moss Grove," Rachel announced.

It was well past midnight and she was dressed, sitting in her room, a glass of port unfinished but the nearby decanter nearly drained and only a single dim light that helped form odd shaped shadows. Josiah thought he had entered the house quietly but it would have made no difference. Their lives had not gone well since they'd given their daughter away. Rachel had changed and, perhaps, he thought, so had he. They no longer desired one another. There was always that underlying fear that she'd get pregnant and they would be forced to face the same uncertainty again. Neither of them felt strong enough.

Josiah was spending more and more time at Madame Renoir's Gentlemen's Club where he had his own room. When Sisseretta was in town, which wasn't very often, she'd join him, but mostly it was a series of women who spent a few hours and were gone.

"Do you plan on staying there long?" he asked woodenly.

"I don't know. I just don't know. Will you come and visit? The holidays will be here soon."

"I'll try," he said but they both knew they needed to be apart, at least for now, perhaps forever.

Josiah wandered through the rooms of his large, and now empty, home. Most of the help had been dismissed. He hadn't realized how much sound a young boy could make tramping through a house but with Samuel gone the silence was deafening.

The furniture in most of the rooms was covered but he had renewed his long forgotten relationship with his trumpet. It had grown dusty. He thought it might have been as long as a year since he'd played, but truthfully he couldn't remember. He'd taken to sitting in an unlit room, shadows playing against the walls from the sun or moon, lights reflecting from outside, or another room… perhaps, even, from his imagination. He played; his eyes closed, and remembered San Francisco and simpler times. Occasionally he'd stop, relight a cigar, sip his brandy, and begin playing again, sometimes with the exact note where he'd stopped.

There was a new rhythm he enjoyed tinkering with. He heard it described as ragtime. It was fast and energetic and disrespectful…it had syncopation. His favorite melody was something called Maple Street Rag, written by some young black named Scott Joplin. Every piano player in every brothel in New Orleans had learned to play it. In the south only blacks and coloreds would play it but he heard that in places like New York and Paris, white groups had picked up on it and white couples danced as if someone had dropped a new manna from heaven. The colored kid from Renoir's liked to play it. He said the guests tipped more than when he played slow music.

Josiah had held only one Klan meeting after Pike died. It was a strange sullen group that night. The men, about forty of them, clustered in small groups and whispered amongst themselves. There was less drinking than usual and no one seemed in a mood to shout or talk loudly. They all knew what Pike had done, and who had killed him, but no one mentioned it. It was as if the man had never existed. Josiah named Broussard as his second in command but no actions were planned. He adjourned the meeting after just one hour, admonishing them to keep their eyes open. He told them they'd be contacted if any new activities were set in motion. Josiah then turned and walked out of the meeting without a goodbye or the traditional prayer.

He walked the four blocks to Renoir's. He wasn't sure whether he wanted a woman or just company. He followed the music into the other room. The ragtime pianist wasn't there but it was early and the regulars hadn't arrived. The music felt sweet and low. It was melancholy and matched his mood. Josiah pulled his trumpet from the bag and walked into the other room. Madame Renoir had long ago stopped worrying about a white boy playing with her colored and black musicians. This man with the intense blue eyes paid well and if there was to be trouble it would be on his head, not hers.

Four in the morning he was still playing. His eyes were red and his notes were slurred. The other musicians shook their heads, grabbed their instruments and walked off the small stage.

"It's time to stop, Josiah," Madame Renoir said. "Perhaps you want a room, perhaps even company."

"I think I'd enjoy that," he said in an alcoholic haze, exhausted and morose.

He fell onto the bed, the trumpet gripped in his hand. He knew one of the girls was undressing him.

"You aren't Rachel."

"No, sweetheart! Tonight is Rachel's night off," the voice cooed, loosening his fingers and sliding his arm through his shirt sleeve.

"I don't want one of you girls, you stupid bitch....I want my Rachel...my beautiful Rachel," he said, his voice quivering in a disembodied way.

"Don't get nasty with me. I'm just trying to make you comfortable. I do like your trumpet playing. It's really sexy."

"Suck me off!" he demanded as a bile of anger and hatred filled him with rage.

"Sure, Josiah, whatever you want."

Francine was used to alcohol-fueled men. She had worked at Renoir's on and off for nearly two years and had seen all kinds. Some hit you...some cried...some swore at you....nigger....cunt... whore. The names washed over her. She'd go to church tomorrow and put some of Josiah's money in the poor box. She knew that to the minister she was a sinner, but Jesus understood, she was sure of it. And then she felt a blow on the side of her head. Josiah had swung hard, the trumpet still in his hand and the round edge of the bell caught her on the temple. She looked at him, unblinking, his icy blue eyes glazed, and she fell to the floor, a dark red ring dripping down her cheek and onto the black French lingerie she had purchased a week earlier.

There was no scream, no sound at all. The room was still. Most of the upstairs rooms...the exclusive ones, had walls and drapes that cloaked what could have caused embarrassment, and Renoir's was designed to be discreet and private.

When Josiah stirred it was late the next morning and his head felt as if it had collided with an andiron somewhere far out in the Gulf. He blinked his eyes, moved his legs over the side of the bed, and then he saw her, some woman he didn't recognize, lying, unmoving, on the floor.

He sat there, trying to recall the events of the previous evening, but all he could recall was playing his trumpet, drinking, followed by more music and drinking, and even these memories came streaking like cacophonous blasts of light exploding through his brain. He shook his head and knew one thing for certain; he had to get out of there.

There was a small ewer of water in the corner. He poured it over his head and shook his blonde hair trying to will himself to focus. It was too late in the day to expect he would find himself alone. He put on his pants and shoes, and, partially clothed, he opened the door and walked down the stairs, ignoring muffled sounds from nearby rooms. He could only hope that no one would enter the room for awhile.

He had killed the woman and the murder of a prostitute was a crime he could get hung for…think…think. He needed to get out of New Orleans with as much money as he could. The bank….he needed to get to the bank and withdraw cash. Once they discovered the body it wouldn't take them long to come after him. They didn't know his last name; that was good luck. But someone would recognize him, he was sure.

Within hours he ransacked his house for any jewelry that Rachel had left, taken the cash he'd hidden, and converted whatever he had in the bank to bank drafts.

"Rene, good morning," he said, stopping by his construction site. "I'll be gone and I need you to get these buildings finished. If you have any questions contact my wife or her brother, Stuart. They're at Moss Grove, north of Baton Rouge. I've given the bank authorization for you to take charge and told them you are to get ten percent of the proceeds as a bonus."

"Thank you, Monsieur Williams. That is very kind. Do not worry," his Cajun foreman said, knowing that something very strange was happening. This man has gotten himself into trouble and whatever it is, he needs me. This can only be a good thing for the Boudreaux family.

Josiah rode hard to Moss Grove and arrived near sunset. He was sure they would have already discovered the woman's body. He began to perspire as the thought of men on horses with blood hounds chasing him made his hands shake.

"Josiah, what's the matter? You look like the victim of a shipwreck." Stuart said, the first person to confront him. "Come in, we're just sitting down to dinner."

"Rachel...Bess," he nodded. "I'm sorry to interrupt and I can't stay. Rachel, we need to talk."

"Stuart and Bess are family, Josiah. Say what you want. I will only tell them later anyway."

"Damn it, Rachel. You can do what you want after I leave but you are still my wife and what I have to say is between you and me."

Maybe coming here was a mistake, he thought, his eyes still glazed. Maybe I should have just continued to ride and get out of Louisiana.

"Into the den," she said. "We can talk privately. Meanwhile, you look terrible."

"I think I killed a woman," he blurted out once they were alone. He walked over to the ever present decanters of port and poured himself a tall glass. He swallowed it easily before he slammed the glass down and continued.

"I was drunk and I don't remember a thing but when I woke up she was dead on the floor."

Rachel turned pale and her eyes bulged in disbelief. She stared at this man who had shared her bed for nearly a decade. He had become a stranger. All she could feel was relief that she had taken Samuel and left him. Her mind wandered to something she could understand...something less catastrophic. Everything had changed once Ruth was given away. My daughter would be nearly two by this time, she realized. I wonder if Robert would send me a picture of her.

Josiah paced nervously across the carpet. His father used to sit in this room, he remembered. His hopes of regaining Moss Grove were dashed. It would never be his, maybe his sons, but never his.

"I'm going back to San Francisco and taking the Rogers name again. I've taken what money I could and left instructions that you are to receive the proceeds of the property under construction. Stuart can help you sell our home if you want to. I expect the authorities will be looking for me and I suggest you just tell them we're separated and you have no idea where I've gone. Can you do that?"

She nodded. It was all she could do. She had no desire to ask him the details of the event that had brought this down upon them.

Josiah turned and left the room. He nodded at Stuart and Bess as he passed the dining room. Then he turned, walked back, drained Stuart's glass of wine and slammed the door behind him.

Chapter Nineteen

Stephen and Alicia had sailed by ship from Havana harbor direct to New York City and rented a small apartment. The Hearst newspapers continued to build on the circulation successes of the Cuban war adventure. They were now publishing the *American* as a morning paper and the *Journal* as an afternoon paper often rewriting Stephen's articles for both, frequently using different bylines.

He soared with a macho ego he'd never felt before whenever he and Alicia walked the city's bustling streets and every man's head turned to get a second look at his wife. He was in the center of the Universe and walking a foot above the sidewalks as he felt her returning his smile, aloof to the ogling she continued to experience.

The handsome couple was delighted with New York; every block they walked offered another adventure. Their palettes could savor foods from every corner of the globe and they would watch as new buildings reached up to the sky, almost overnight.

"I have to go to Buffalo for a few days," he said looking out the window of their East side apartment. He looked down the three floors at a pleasant neighborhood view and, fortunately, several long blocks from the tenements filled with immigrants and incomprehensible languages. "Will you be alright?"

"*Por supuesto*, of course," she said, reminding herself to speak English. "I am not a child, Stephen. I want to find a job and work."

"Shall we try and make a cousin for little Ruth before I leave?" he smiled.

"*Por supuesto,*" she teased.

Buffalo was a short train ride and it gave Stephen time to relax. He had worried that a light skin colored man and a Cuban woman could mean trouble, even in the mélange in which they lived, but so far everything had gone smoothly. No one seemed to question Stephen's race and Alicia was too pretty for anyone to care.

His assignment was to report on President McKinley's visit to the new Pan American exposition that had been postponed two years because of America's obsession with its war with Spain. The site was reputed to be a new electrical miracle with lights everywhere, powered from newly installed giant generators at Niagara Falls, thirty miles away.

It was a boring assignment. He wanted to bring Alicia and show her the fair, but she was insistent on finding a job, so he'd come alone.

Stephen traveled with a coterie of other reporters while the President visited Niagara Falls. They returned in the afternoon and readied themselves for a public reception that evening. Most of the reporters begged off, preferring the camaraderie of one another, where they wouldn't have to limit their drinking or their behavior. Stephen stayed with his assignment and stood several yards away as the President and his wife arrived, greeting everyone with a smile and a handshake.

Then pandemonium broke out. A crazed anarchist, later identified as Leo Czolgosz, pulled out a pistol from under his jacket, and shot the President twice before those close by wrestled the assassin to the ground.

For days it seemed that McKinley would survive but the bullet remained lodged in his system and his recovery remained in doubt. Reporters and the world hovered in disbelief. Not since Lincoln's death had a President been assassinated. McKinley expired several days later and there would now be a new President, Teddy Roosevelt, a hero, and a man Stephen had met in Cuba.

With Stephen gone, Alicia was determined to find work. She could read about her husband's exploits each day in the newspaper and she was so proud of him but he didn't make much money and even though her life had changed, she was used to nice things. She had money hidden in the house. She'd converted all her *pesos* to American dollars and as much as she loved her husband; experience had taught her that she must always be able to rely on herself to survive.

She dressed herself carefully and took special care with her hair before leaving her apartment that morning. She walked the 'Ladies Mile' near Broadway and 20th. There weren't many job opportunities for women and she had no intention of working in a factory. She stood in front of the large window of Lord & Taylor displaying the latest fashions and watched elegantly dressed women enter the store. She decided this was where she would work. She entered the swank store and walked by a well-dressed man offering to guide her to the proper department. She knew her way around and didn't want any lowly employee distracting her.

She reached the floor where the department managers sat and went immediately to the corner desk where the secretarial matriarch protected the store's owner from unauthorized plebeians.

"I wish to see Senor Taylor," she said as haughtily as she could.

"Do you have an appointment?" the older woman asked, astounded at this beautiful woman's impudence.

"He will see me. I am here from Havana where I was the top model in the country and consort to the Spanish governor. Please tell him I am here." Her eyes flashed in a no-nonsense authority.

When Alicia left an hour later, the young Mr. Taylor, smiling, escorted her to the door and put her in a carriage. She would begin work the following Monday as a model, donning clothes for the store's most exclusive clients.

Josiah had spirited into and out of their lives, leaving them all confused and exhausted. Rachel was very much aware that he hadn't even asked about their son, Samuel, in the brief time he was at Moss Grove. Bess was hurt that this man she'd known all her life hadn't even said a word about her advanced pregnancy.

Stuart was just angry. None of them had any interest in continuing dinner; they'd all lost their appetites.

It was only a matter of time, and nearly two weeks passed, before four men arrived.

"We're looking for Josiah Williams. We understand his wife and son are here."

"May I ask why you're looking for him?" Stuart asked, watching the men dismount.

"A woman in New Orleans was murdered and we think he might have been involved."

"He isn't here. He and his wife separated several months ago and since she had grown up here at Moss Grove, she came back here with her son to live."

"Who are you?"

"I'm Stuart Fineman. I'm the owner of this plantation and Rachel Williams is my sister."

"May we speak with her?"

"She hasn't been well. Perhaps if just one of you came in and the others waited, if you don't mind. We'll get some drinks and refreshments out to you. There are chairs on the veranda where it's shady."

Stuart guided the man into the den where they sat uncomfortably for what seemed an exceptionally long time before Rachel and Bess descended the staircase, following two young children busy chasing one another.

They were an unsightly pair. Rachel, who had always prided herself on her beauty, and the care she took in maintaining her appearance, looked wan. It was clear that she wasn't sleeping or eating properly and didn't care. Bess, meanwhile, was forced to come down the stairs holding tightly to the rail, unable to see her feet as she set both of them on a step before taking another. The baby was due at any time.

"Into the kitchen you two. Missy B will get you a snack," Bess ordered.

"This is my sister, Rachel, and this is my wife, Mrs. Fineman."

"I'm Inspector Fellows with the New Orleans Police Department. I'm sorry to disturb you but we have been looking for your husband, Mrs. Williams, and our inquiries ultimately led us here. Do you know where he is?"

"The last time I saw him was a few months ago when I left our home and came here," she lied convincingly.

"Can you tell me why you separated?"

"Those are personal matters which are of no concern of yours," she said angrily.

"There is a woman dead; your husband's trumpet was found lying next to her covered in blood, and all his money has been withdrawn from his bank. He's obviously run away and it's hard to imagine a man of means, such as your husband, not making some provision for his son. Do you know if he provided for you?"

"I have a feeling you know more than I do, Inspector. Why don't you tell us what you've learned?"

"What we've learned is that he arranged for his foreman to complete construction of the properties and give the proceeds to you. What we've learned is that your house is on the market and that you are trying to sell it. We wonder why you would be doing that if you weren't aware that your husband had taken off somewhere."

There was an uneasy pause in the conversation and the questions hung there, suspended, without an answer.

"I saw Josiah when I went into New Orleans last month to get some things for the new baby," Bess said, putting her hands on her stomach to validate the advanced state of her pregnancy.

"He told me he had no intention of staying in the house he bought when he and Rachel got married. Too many memories, he said. I remember him clearly saying that," she rambled, clearly forming her thoughts in the same instant she was voicing them. "I came back, told Stuart and Rachel, and they contacted someone to sell the property. You remember, don't you, Rachel?"

Her sister in law nodded obediently and whether the Inspector believed them or not, it would be impossible for him to verify.

"Who was the woman who was killed?" Stuart asked.

"A girl who worked at Madame Renoir's...one of the city's more exclusive brothels."

"And you're reasonably certain Josiah Williams killed her."

"Until he comes forward with some logical explanation, he's our primary suspect. Thank you for your time."

As the men rode off, Rachel, Stuart, and Bess breathed deep sighs of relief.

"Quick thinking, my dear wife."

"You'd better send for the doctor, Stuart. The contractions have started. I think your son is on his way."

Stuart grinned. Bess knew how much her husband wanted a son. She was sure it was some biological need that men have to continue their lineage. He wanted to name the baby Eli, after his father, and Bess couldn't even get him to consider names if it was a girl. He would love a second daughter, she knew, but this one was a boy, her husband had willed it.

Eli Fineman was born early the next morning with a full head of black hair, dark lustrous eyes, and the cutest dimple in his right cheek.

"He looks wonderful, darling," Stuart said after Bess rested and combed her hair. Her face was flush, but she was relieved that this birth had gone more easily than she had expected.

"He has all his fingers and toes and he's well hung."

"I'm glad you checked out all the important appendages," she smiled.

"I told you it would be a boy," Stuart said proudly.

"Yes, you did," she agreed and drifted off to sleep, pleased for them both.

> *Theodore Roosevelt, the youngest man to hold the office of the President, swept into power with the same energy he had used to attack San Juan Hill. There were large corporations to dismantle, national parks to be established, and influence to be exerted over the other countries in the hemisphere. He was a devout moralist and wanted a 'square deal' for everyone.*
>
> *America was prospering but not everyone was sharing in its newfound glory and wealth. Unemployment was at 4%. Yosemite National Park had been expanded. Trains now had electric lights and Albert Einstein proposed the Theory of Relativity but few American blacks were able to share in this bounty. A few black activists, led by W.E.B Du Bois, organized The Niagara Movement, named to effect a 'mighty current' of change in race relations, but it was a small voice in the cacophony of white prosperity.*

"The President has invited Booker T. Washington to a dinner at the White House and you and I have been invited along with our wives," Daniel Murray announced to his new protégé.

The dinner was held a week later with various members of Congress in attendance, although not a single Senator nor Congressman from the Southern states accepted the invitation. Daniel and Anna Murray were seated on Robert and Maria's left, directly across from Mr. Washington. The President was at the head of the table.

"How are you Robert?" Washington asked. "I was so sorry to hear about Noah's death at the hands of those scurrilous bullies. You were both great assets to Tuskegee."

"Thank you, Mr. Washington. It's nice of you to remember. This is my wife, Maria. We met while I was in Cuba during the war. That's also where I encountered Colonel Roosevelt. It seems both he and Mr. Murray knew my father."

"I never had that privilege. Mr. President," the guest of honor said, turning toward the head of the table, "I want to thank you for hosting this dinner. I am truly honored, and it is my fervent hope that such a privilege will allow me your indulgence in asking a favor."

"If it is something I can accomplish, I will certainly try."

"I was hoping there might be a way to get a Federal law to stop these lynchings that seem to be happening with increased frequency and with impunity for those responsible."

"Those lynchings are reprehensible," Roosevelt responded, setting down his fork and touching his embossed napkin to his lips, "But you know as well as I do that the Democrats in the South would never allow such a bill to be passed...states rights and all that cow dung. Even my own party insists on avoiding any legislation that serves the interest of Blacks or other non-white groups. It would be political suicide, I'm afraid, and I'm not ready to do that. I have other objectives that, regretfully, must take precedent. Let this dinner be the government's recognition of your accomplishments, and hope that, at least in some parts of this country, it might be considered a first step."

"I have some vacation coming, Alicia. If you can get time off from your burgeoning career, I'd like to show you Moss Grove and introduce you to the rest of the family."

"My career is going to be rather short-lived. I am not happy losing my figure and I'm not sure what kind of a mother I will be. It is very upsetting to my vanity. I will be showing in another month and my pregnancy doesn't exactly make me a favorite model for those who live in the Brownstones. Congratulations, mi amor y mi vida. It was not my choice to have a child at this point in our marriage but it is my present to you."

"Me, a father," he said as he embraced this woman who had so filled his being with happiness. "Now we have to visit the family."

A young boy and girl screamed with joy as the older black girl pushed them in a swing that hung from one of the giant oak trees. The boy would be tall. He was already stretching inches beyond the bottom of his too short pants. He had a full head of blond hair, soft blue eyes, a delicious smile, and a well-defined cleft in his chin. The girl's red hair and freckles were a stark contrast but her clothes said it all. She wore the same overalls as her friend, not the soft, frilly dresses of most girls her age.

"You be careful, Samuel," Missy B shouted as he pushed the girl higher on the swing, while she sat, resting, and out of breath from the day's heat and humidity.

"But I want him to push me higher. Samuel...push me higher," Samantha demanded.

Twenty yards away the adults watched while a tiny baby boy sucked at his mother's nipple.

"I love watching you breast feed Eli," Stuart said. "Makes me horny and it makes your breasts so large. Put him down and let's go upstairs."

"I don't think so, but I'm glad you're still attracted to me," Bess laughed. Having her husband home and her family around her had brought a new fulfillment of her life. "Ouch, Eli bit me."

"See...at least I don't bite."

A wagon pulled up the drive and stopped in front. Stephen stepped down and helped Alicia descend as she gaped at the huge house in front of her.

"*Dios, es gigante,*" she sputtered.

He laughed and grabbed her hand tightly as Stuart came into view.

"You've arrived. Wonderful! Come, Bess is in back where the children are playing. Rachel is upstairs and should be down soon."

Bess hurriedly put her breast back into her dress and set baby Eli into his crib.

"How wonderful that you're here," she extolled. "Alicia, I'm so glad to see you again...and you're expecting. Congratulations to you both."

The smiles that passed between Bess and Stephen reconfirmed their love and those looks weren't lost on either of their spouses. Alicia's anger flared inside her but her icy demeanor revealed nothing. Stuart, on the other hand, visibly pouted.

"Breathe, Bess," he said angrily. "Take a breath and relax for a moment. Alicia, Stephen knows what I mean. My wife can chatter with happy thoughts for hours."

Rachel didn't join them until dinner was nearly over that evening. Missy B had fed and bathed the children, while Stuart and Bess, Stephen and Alicia, enjoyed tiny petit fours with their coffee.

"You have a most lovely home. I believe it is the largest I have ever seen," Alicia said.

"Stephen and I grew up here along with Josiah, who I believe you met in Cuba."

Alicia's eyes dimmed for an instant. Stephen grabbed her hand protectively and smiled thoughtfully. Neither of them had ever discussed her liaison with Josiah. It had been the catalyst for them meeting, but it remained a subject better left silent between them.

"What do you hear from our trumpet playing friend?" Stephen asked. "With Rachel living here I've gotten the impression all isn't going well with the two of them."

Bess and Stuart looked at one another, not wanting to spoil the evening with a full disclosure of Josiah's troubles. They were saved by Rachel's entrance.

"Hello, everyone. My apologies for not joining you for dinner, I've had a great deal on my mind. You must be Alicia. How wonderful to meet you.

"I might as well tell you all that I've reached a decision," she said without a pause. "Samuel and I are leaving Moss Grove. We're going to try and join Josiah in San Francisco."

Everyone could feel the rush of air leave the room. Bess and Stuart's mouths dropped at the outrageous decision voiced so abruptly.

"Rachel, you are my sister, and I love you. I also feel responsible for your well-being, and that of my nephew, but what you intend to do isn't rational. You and your husband are separated. A divorce would not be unreasonable. He's wanted for murder and if they catch him, they'll hang him."

"What are you talking about?" Stephen asked. "What's going on here? Is this our Josiah you're talking about?"

It took a little while for Bess to explain the events of the past several months. Alicia didn't seem to be surprised. She had her own instincts about this brash blond man with the blue eyes and now, meeting his wife, and seeing his son, she was even more disgusted. Her unborn child twisted inside, seeming to sense her discomfort.

"He is my husband and he is in trouble" Rachel insisted. "Perhaps he and I can begin again. I loved him once and he doesn't deserve to be abandoned."

"I know you will do what you feel you must," Bess said, "But don't take Samuel with you, not until you're settled, and you and Josiah agree to try and have a future together.

"Josiah, Stephen, and I were all shuttled around by Amy when we were children and it isn't good. Leave Samuel here with Stuart, Samantha, and me. He will have stability. You don't know what you're going to find. It isn't fair to expose your son to such risk."

"Bess is right, Rachel," Stuart said, noting that this was one of the rare times his wife had called their daughter by her rightful name. "If you can find Josiah and you decide to stay together, I'll personally bring your son to you."

Rachel said a tearful goodbye to her son and her family a few days later. All she knew was that Josiah intended to go back to San Francisco. He could have stopped anywhere along the way.

"I have friends in San Francisco," Stephen said. "I worked on the newspaper there. I'll contact them and ask them to make some inquiries. When you get settled, contact Sam Russell at the *Daily Examiner*. He was my boss. If Josiah is in the city, Sam can help you find him."

"I will never be able to wear designer clothes again, dear husband. I feel like I have swallowed a hundred balloons," Alicia said after dinner, the two of them alone in their room. "In not too many months, a little hijo will call you padre."

"I've always loved to play with balloons," Stephen said playfully. "Come to bed. We can pretend we're at the circus. They always had the best balloons."

"You don't mind making love to me when I'm ugly?"

"You're more beautiful than ever. There is more to love and, perhaps, our unborn child will understand his parents love one another."

There was a comfortable ease between Bess and Alicia and now that it became family knowledge there was a new baby on the way, Bess lavished care and every garment and toy that Eli had outgrown in his first year.

A telegram arrived a week later from Mr. Hearst addressed to Stephen.

> *Bicycle shop owners in Dayton believe they have created a flying machine. Stop. If they are crazy and crash get me 2000 words. Stop. Get pictures. Stop. If they actually fly keep story to 1000 words.*
>
> Hearst

"Alicia, stay here while I take this assignment. I'll feel better knowing you're surrounded by family rather than alone in our New York apartment."

"I love it here, Stephen. Bess and Stuart have been most caring and I am teaching Samuel and Samantha to speak Spanish."

Rachel reached San Francisco a few weeks later. Stuart had made her a reservation at the Palace Hotel on Market Street in the heart of the city and her heart throbbed with excitement and frightened nerves. She had never traveled alone and this was a new city. Someone had always been there to make her decisions....her father, Stuart, and then Josiah. Now she would need to figure things out on her own and she didn't know if she was strong enough. It was easy to be brave sitting in her home at Moss Grove but now, so far away, her bravery was quickly withering.

There was a message waiting for her at the hotel. Sam Russell, Stephen's editor, had died of tuberculosis a few weeks earlier and, although they'd tried, no one else at the paper was able to locate anyone by the name of Josiah Rogers or Josiah Williams.

She didn't know what to do next. This city wasn't anything like New York, but she and Josiah were on their honeymoon in that city and she saw everything through his eyes. Here there was so much energy. There were cars, and people on the move, and tall buildings everywhere. On one side of her hotel was the Crocker building and down the street was the Main Ferry terminal. Fog was drifting over the city and giving it a grey, eerie pallor. One block up she could hear loud bells clanging as the city's cable cars carried hundreds of people across the city's hills. Josiah could be anywhere. Trying to make some type of decision she opted to climb on one of the cable cars. She held on tight, worried that the jostling of the people and the car pulling against its cable would throw her off onto the pavement.

"You'll be fine," a nice gentleman said, noticing her discomfort. "I'd wager it's your first time."

"Yes...yes, it is."

"Happens to everyone! It's exciting and quite unique, but it's safe. Enjoy your visit to the city," he waved as he jumped off the still moving car.

She saw the red and green cable cars of the Washington and Jackson districts come sweeping out of a side street, their bells announcing their arrival. And where the cable cars didn't go, there were electric and horse cars traversing the city. Streets jutted off at odd angles and homes were visible, perched on distant hills, as far as the eye could see. It was all a wonder.

Weeks and months passed quickly. She started out each day with a map in her hand, sometimes hiring a guide to help her, but money was going out and nothing was coming in. She was reluctant to keep asking Stuart to send her additional funds. She had already done that three times and she had no idea how much money she had at her disposal. Everything she and Josiah had owned in New Orleans was gone and because of lawyers, and Rene Boudreaux's shenanigans, they'd gotten far less than everything was worth.

Going out nights was more difficult. A woman visiting night spots was suspect and in the bars and taverns of North Beach, definitely not recommended.

She missed Samuel...she ached for Josiah. She'd lost her daughter, Ruth, and she still vacillated on whether giving up her daughter was the right decision. Should she go back to Moss Grove, she wondered. She'd try another week...another month, to find Josiah so they could bring their son to San Francisco and be a family once more. She wanted that so.

To make ends meet she took a job at a clothing store on Kearny Street. If she was going to find her husband it would have to be at night, she'd decided. He could be living anywhere but if he was working, he'd be back playing his trumpet. She could work days and look for him at night. Perhaps she could find an escort to go with her.

Chapter Twenty

It had been months since either Stuart or Bess had heard from Rachel. She was no longer staying at the San Francisco hotel Stuart had reserved for her and she'd left no forwarding address.

Stephen had returned from North Carolina and the Wright Brothers successful flight at Kitty Hawk to witness his son's birth. Alicia was in labor for nearly fourteen hours but her silent stoic nature took control and she neither slept nor cried out. She simply stared at the ceiling, in an almost spiritual trance, as Bess and others fussed to keep her comfortable. The baby was stunning, with Stephen's blue eyes and Alicia's beauty. They named their son Thaddeus to the delight of everyone who had known his father. The decision wasn't that simple for Stephen. He made the decision to name his son after the birth father he'd barely known in the hopes he could create a relationship with his child that had never existed with the man who sired him.

Stephen and Alicia remained at Moss Grove while Alicia worked to lose the weight she'd gained during her pregnancy. She was perpetually angry and testy at having lost her shape. She exercised voraciously and barely ate. She was committed to regaining her figure before they reached New York and, in her determination, she ignored her husband, her new son, and her surroundings. Everyone gave her a wide swath, but there was also a relief when she and Stephen announced they would be leaving. His newspaper responsibilities awaited him, he said, but he understood they had outworn their welcome.

Life at Moss Grove seemed bucolic. Cotton was planted and harvested. Samuel's ninth birthday came and went; Samantha was nearing eight and Bess wanted to get the family together for a big holiday celebration. She invited Robert and Maria to come for the Christmas holidays. They were all anxious to see the toddler that little Ruth had become and now they discovered she would soon have a sibling. Perhaps Stephen and Alicia would come as well. It would have been nice for Stuart to hear from Rachel. For him it would be a special Chanukah gift.

As the holidays approached the weather turned unseasonably cold. The ground had an icy crust most mornings. Cotton plants were dormant; the hogs had been slaughtered and were being smoked. Whatever fruits that had been harvested were canned and stored. Accounts had been cleared and money the share croppers earned had been paid. Since 1903's crop had been a good one and prices remained high, there was joy throughout most of Louisiana. It was a time to rest, repair equipment and houses, sew another dress, or patch overalls.

The plantation was festive. Homes and businesses in New Orleans were beginning to be lit with electric lights but that new technology hadn't yet reached any of the plantations further north along the Mississippi. Candles and kerosene lamps were in plentiful supply and evenings were no longer a time just for sleep and solitude. Share croppers brought out their fiddles and banjos.

Both Robert and Stephen's families happily trekked to Moss Grove to share the holidays. The weather had to be better than the sleet and snow that blanketed New York and Washington.

Musicians came up from Baton Rouge and everyone was elated to discover that both Maria and Alicia had wonderful voices. They sang songs of Cuba…their island, the struggle of the campesinos to survive the rain and the winds for a good crop, and a man to share their love.

Early in the morning Stephen found Bess enjoying coffee in the dining room. The rest of the family was still asleep.

"Just the two of us," he said. "A rare opportunity! How are you, my darling?" He leaned over, lifted her chin, and they kissed.

"The same as ever…one day after the next. I love when you are here but I worry about being obvious. Does Alicia ever mention our feelings for one another?"

"Alicia has never been a talker but I have no doubt she knows and has a sense of everything around her. As long as she doesn't ask I don't have to deny my love."

"I know our continual feelings nettle Stuart. Neither he nor I ever bring it up either. It's just there and with two children to raise and a plantation to manage, we're rapidly becoming middle age. How I hate that thought."

"I still fantasize being together."

"As do I…as do I."

Under duress Samantha had been forced to take piano lessons. She learned a few of the popular songs of the day which she played to the ever present teasing from Samuel. He was becoming a brat. He missed his parents and was quick to show his anger. Alicia tried to take him under her wing. He had an obvious crush on her which both delighted the older woman and disturbed Stephen.

"Samuel, let's you and us go fishing," Stephen and Stuart suggested. "We'll get us men away from the women for awhile. We'll even try and convince Robert to join us."

The next day the men took horses and rode to the northwest of the plantation. It was back country, wild and unfarmed, heavy with copses of trees. There was a stream that Stuart remembered from when he was a boy and they decided to camp there overnight.

He was showing Samuel how to put bait on his line when three riders rode up. They were white, dirty, and unshaven. Their presence brought a sense of immediate dread to Robert, who remembered the last time he'd confronted a similar trio and lost his brother.

"Anything biting?" one man asked.

"Just got here! Too early to tell," Stuart offered, trying to sound calm.

"Got anything extra to eat," another asked. "We ain't had nuthin' since yesterday."

"We can spare some food," Stuart offered, heading over to his pack horse and hiding a pistol in his jacket at the same time. He handed a small wrapped package to the closest man.

"You always go camping with niggers?" the third man asked.

"We go camping with friends," Stuart said, making certain his body was blocking Samuel's from danger.

"You'd do well to be more selective in how to pick your friends. Thanks for the grub. You folks have a nice day."

The three men rode off as Stuart, Stephen, and Robert watched them disappear into the trees.

"Do you think they'll be back?" Robert asked.

"I don't think so, but you can't be sure. We'll take turns staying awake tonight. Meanwhile, Samuel…got that line baited yet?"

"What did those men mean?" the boy asked as he tried to keep the hook from lodging in his finger.

"They don't like whites and coloreds to be friends," Stephen said, still watching the trees that had absorbed the riders.

"That's silly."

"It sure is."

Harvey Cobb was someone you would never take notice of. He had to stand on his toes to claim being 5'7". His features were plain and the clothes he wore were threadbare and non-descript. He was single and in his late forties. If he found an extra dollar in his pocket he might use it to buy a few hours with one of the hookers he was familiar with. He knew most of them by their real first names, not the more sensuous names they told the Johns who came looking for a few minutes of pleasant distraction.

Stuart had never met the man but through one of Stephen's old friends at the *Examiner* who knew someone who knew someone, Cobb was hired to help Rachel find Josiah. She had finally written, frustrated, sad, and nearly broke. She was no longer convinced Josiah was in San Francisco, but she knew if she left, she would lose all hope of finding him.

Harvey Cobb was hired to help. It was simple. Stuart would send the man $200. He was promised another $500 if he succeeded.

Cobb was to say nothing to Rachel unless he was reasonably sure he'd unearthed the right man.

Months went by and spring was beginning to brighten the San Francisco mornings. You could actually see Alcatraz from Coit Tower.

"Is this Stuart Fineman?" a thin voice said over the long distance telephone line.

"Yes, it is. Who is this?" Telephone calls, especially long distance ones were infrequent, and expensive.

"This is the long distance operator. Will you accept a collect call from San Francisco?"

"Yes," he said as he heard several clicking sounds on the line, assuming it was Rachel.

"This is Harvey Cobb, Mr. Fineman. I think I've found Josiah Rogers but now I can't find his wife and I don't know how to proceed. You promised me $500 to find him and confirm it with your sister. She's no longer at the address you gave me. You never said she would disappear as well."

"I didn't think she would. I guess you'll have to find her as well. It shouldn't be as difficult. Would another $200 be fair?"

"Quite fair. I'll be in touch."

Rachel had moved to a smaller, less expensive, apartment in the Castro. She was still working at a store selling overpriced lingerie to the women of Nob Hill, depressed at what had become of her life. She had found a woman friend who agreed to join her in searching the clubs along Broadway and North Beach every Friday and Saturday evening. She was beginning to believe she would die before she found her husband or returned to her son.

"Mrs. Williams," the male voice said as he knocked on her door. "My name is Harvey Cobb and your brother hired me."

She peeked through the window to see the short man on her front stoop.

"What do you mean my brother hired you?"

"If you let me in I can explain everything. I don't think you want me discussing your business out here in the open where everyone can hear us."

She opened the door and they nodded at one another. He looked around as he entered, removed his hat, and sat down on the frayed couch.

"Does your brother know you live in such pecuniary circumstances?"

"Mr. Cobb, how I live is no concern of yours. Please explain who you are and why my brother hired you."

"I would love a cup of tea and you should have one as well. This may take a little time. Let me just tell you that I believe I have found your husband."

Rachel's hands began to shake and all the emotion of the past year welled up inside her as she collapsed, sobbing, into the closest chair.

The entrance to Enzo's Bar was through an alley. The sign was small and the alley was dirty and badly lit. Cobb and Rachel arrived around eleven. She could hear the music as they approached, three pieces, one of them a trumpet, and her heart leapt. He wasn't playing well but she knew it was him and she dabbed her handkerchief at her eyes. She didn't want him to see her crying.

The lights inside were dim, the floors were dirty, and the stage was small. You had to shoehorn three musicians onto it and they'd have to play from memory. There was no room for music stands. The small crowd ignored the newcomers and the musicians as they nestled their drinks. Two women drifted amongst the tables looking for a score, another served drinks.

Josiah looked terrible. His cheeks were puffy, his clothes, once of the best quality were now old and worn, hanging from a body that had lost all of its tone. His fiery blue eyes were dim. His entire being sagged and Rachel bit down hard on her fingers to keep from crying out to him. She kept a firm grip on Harvey Cobb's hand, afraid that if she let go, she'd fall apart.

They sat until the last set was finished. Josiah stood and began to put his trumpet away.

"Josiah," she said softly.

He turned and stared. Then, not knowing what else to do, he finished putting his instrument in its case.

"Josiah," she repeated. "Aren't you glad to see me?"

He turned again and she could see tears in his eyes.

"I'm sorry you found me. Please go home. It's too late for us."

"Mr. Rogers, my name is Harvey Cobb. Your brother-in-law, Stuart Fineman, hired me to find you. I've been looking for several months. Your wife has also been looking for you."

"I don't give a shit. Please leave me be," he said, walking away.

"Mr. Cobb," Rachel said, gathering herself. "You may leave. My husband will see me home."

"Are you sure? It isn't safe for a woman to be alone in this neighborhood and your husband doesn't seem glad to have been found."

"We'll be fine," she said, grabbing Josiah's arm and holding onto to it firmly.

Rachel hailed a cab, refusing to let go of the reluctant man she continued to cling to, ever so tightly. Josiah was different, very different, and she was pretty sure she knew what it was. He was using opium. His body shook, and his hands were cold and unsteady, but it was his eyes that told the story. In her months looking for him she had discovered the secret world of opium addicts. Most of the men and women she'd encountered in her search had gone through both their money and their self-respect. They were the detritus of the San Francisco bay and the opium dens that supported them flourished in a city tolerant of sin.

Josiah followed her, emotionless, into her small apartment and sat down. He had lost his energy to rebel and somewhere, he thought, she might have some extra money for him. He certainly needed it.

"Your son misses you. You haven't seen him in nearly two years and I haven't seen him in a year. We are really terrible parents."

Josiah remained silent, taking the cup of tea, and holding it tightly in both hands for fear he'd drop it. He only set it down to gobble the sandwich and cakes Rachel put on the table. It had been more than two days since he'd eaten solid food and his stomach was having difficulty absorbing anything more than alcohol or drugs.

"I have to go. Thank you for the refreshments. You look well, Rachel, but you need to go back to Moss Grove and raise our son."

"I'm not leaving without you. I love you and I want to bring Samuel here so we can be a family again."

"It isn't going to happen. You need to let me be."

"I can help you. We were good together once. We can be again."

"I don't think so. I prefer to forget everything that's happened in my life and opium helps me. I'm a bad person, Rachel, just like my father. I don't deserve the life you and I had...it wasn't real. Let me go. You need to start again," he pleaded.

"Never," she vowed.

Josiah stood, kissed her gently on the lips, embraced her briefly, turned and walked out the door.

Harvey Cobb related the entire story to Stuart, including the fact that Josiah Rogers was addicted to opium and was living almost full time in one of the dens in Chinatown.

"No one is hopeless," Bess said, as she sat, listening as Stuart described the plight of Rachel and her husband.

"I asked Cobb if people could overcome their addiction and he said it happens rarely, but it does happen. There are no drugs, you just have to force the person to stop using and keep them away from the stuff until whatever they've taken, passes through their system. That can take weeks and their bodies go through terrible withdrawal."

"OK," Bess said. "How do we get that done?"

"I would imagine we would need to find someone who knows that culture, how to find which place Josiah inhabits, and kidnap him."

"Remember Mr. Liu? He would know. The Chinese are a very tight community and you're his adopted son for saving him."

The only decision remaining was who would go to San Francisco. It was a difficult time for Stuart to leave. It was planting season. But either he or Bess were the right choice since they knew Mr. Liu and Josiah better than the others. Stephen might have gone but he was getting ready to leave on another assignment. Bess was sure she was the only person who could accomplish what needed to be done and once again her arguments held sway over the others.

Bess arrived in San Francisco and went directly to Rachel's apartment.

"Rachel, you look dreadful," Bess said, stunned at the wraith-like appearance of her once gorgeous sister-in-law.

"I know...I know, please don't lecture me."

"I'm sorry. It was rude of me to blurt out such things. I know what you've been going through."

"How is Samuel? Does he miss me? Does he even remember me anymore?

"Of course, he does," she said, although in truth, she wasn't sure what her nephew still recalled. Nearly two years in the life of a young child was like forever.

"When can we see your Mr. Liu? Do you think he'll help us? I know Josiah is just lost somewhere and wants to come back," Rachel pleaded.

"We'll go tomorrow. Now, let's have a nice dinner and work on getting you to look like your old self. That alone may be enough to convince Josiah to come home."

They decided to visit Mr. Liu in the late afternoon, after his lunch rush was over.

"Miss Bess! We have missed you. We thought you didn't like my wife's won-tons anymore."

"Mr. Liu....it has been a long time and I have often thought of you and your wife. So much has happened since we left San Francisco. Do you have time to sit and share a cup of tea? Perhaps even some of those delectable won-tons you mentioned. We have a problem and we need your help," Bess said.

He seated the two women in a corner and, once introductions had been made, Bess explained their plight.

"I remember young Josiah fondly, him with the blonde hair and bright blue eyes...and always with his trumpet. Now you tell me he is likely living in one of our opium dens."

"Can you help us find him?" Rachel begged. "He needs help."

"Perhaps! There are more than three hundred such dens in Chinatown but few American addicts, most of the derelicts who live there are Chinese. I will make some inquiries. But are you sure you can convince him to leave? These dens are terrible places but those who have fallen under the spell of the drug find it impossible to stop and as demanding as their right arm. They find a reverie… dreams and stupefaction from the magic of the pipe. They smoke one, and then another, and the problems they faced in life vanish with the smoke."

"Mr. Liu, if you can find him, we will get him out," Bess said defiantly.

It was more than a week later before the Chinese restaurant owner sent word that Josiah had been found. Rachel and Bess breathed a collective sigh of relief. It took another two days to make safe arrangements for him to lead the women there.

"We must be very careful," Mr. Liu warned. "These dens are all controlled by Tongs, Chinese crime bosses. They will be angry that we are invading one of their dens to remove a patron but they know we are coming to remove a white man. They prefer to not have white patrons. It makes them susceptible to police raids. But we must be discrete …there must be no violence."

Harvey Cobb had one final assignment. He hired two of the biggest dockworkers he could find. Their job would be to grab Josiah and forcibly carry him to Rachel's apartment. A doctor would be waiting who would examine him and prescribe a treatment. The dockworkers would take turns staying at the apartment in case Josiah got violent. Bess and Rachel would take turns as well, one always being awake while the four of them struggled to purge the drugs from Josiah's system.

Luke and Bret had worked the gold fields for nearly two years. They were brothers, two years apart, and spoke little. They never hit it rich and eventually they found steady work at the docks to be more lucrative. Harvey had used them on two other assignments that required their brawn but it was nothing like this.

The very short Harvey Cobb looked like a toothpick when he stood next to the brothers. He was used to it and ignored the wisecracks. He had a job to do and, without extraneous conversation, he led the two brothers into a basement that reeked of a sweet pungent odor. There was very little light. At the foot of the narrow stairwell the room opened to one dimly lit room, approximately 10' x 15', lined with beds. There was one woman in a corner bed, barely clothed, her eyes glazed. Seven other beds were filled with Chinese men, most awake, smoking from a pipe, inhaling deeply. Cobb thought they were in the wrong place when a man's blonde hair, dirty and crusted, caught his eye.

"That's him. Don't even talk to him. Put the bag over his head; knock him out if you need to."

"Another pipe...get me another pipe...what are you doing?"

It was the only words he could utter. He struggled but the opium use had sapped his strength. He was thin and frail and his resistance was minimal.

The doctor was waiting at the apartment when they returned but Josiah continued to thrash at his abductors.

"Josiah, it's me, Rachel. Bess is here and we're going to help you."

"Leave me the fuck alone. I need another pipe. Don't you understand? We're done. Leave me be."

He tried to sit up but every time he did Luke pushed him back. Perspiration dripped down Josiah's face and he began to tremble.

"I'm freezing. Isn't there any heat in this house?"

"I'll get you another blanket, Josiah," Bess offered, knowing his chills had nothing to do with the warmth of the room.

"Can you take a little broth?" Rachel asked.

"Please, I'm begging you. Get me a pipe or let me go back to where you found me."

"Eat something first, then we'll talk."

He managed to swallow a few spoonfuls before vomiting all over the bedcovers. His body began to spasm and his pupils became tiny dots. He cried...deep sobs as his body convulsed.

"Why won't you let me be?" was the last thing he mumbled before collapsing into unconsciousness.

Two weeks later the ugliness of withdrawal had ebbed slightly. Josiah could sleep for two or three hours. When he woke his words were slurred. Bess tried to shave him but his body would jerk uncontrollably and his face would get another nick.

Luke, Bret, Rachel and Bess became close. Harvey Cobb was gone, on to other unsavory tasks. Rachel and Bess chatted about Moss Grove and their children. Luke and Bret told about growing up on a poor farm in Missouri, the eldest of seven children. Their parents were glad when the boys decided to leave. It meant fewer mouths to feed.

Josiah's tremors eased but it was still difficult for him to hold down food. The doctor came less often now that his patient's vital signs were more stable and his eyes a little more focused.

"Rachel," Josiah said softly. It was the middle of the night and there were few sounds from the nearby street. It would be another two hours before they might hear the sound of milk bottles clanking as they were delivered.

"Yes, my dear. Can I get you anything?"

"I think I'm hungry."

"I'll make some tea," Bret offered, stirring from his chair.

"Who is that man?" he asked.

"One of two brothers we hired to help us recover you."

"Why did you bother?"

"Samuel and I miss you."

"Rachel, I killed a woman, or have you forgotten."

"That was a drunk, forlorn man, and it was New Orleans in a different lifetime. This is San Francisco. You're no longer drunk and hopefully no longer addicted."

Josiah collapsed on the bed and fell into a deep sleep. It was late afternoon before he stirred. Bess was sitting on a chair across from him, smiling.

"Good afternoon. How are you feeling?"

"Like I fell down an enormous hole and I didn't know the way back."

"Hungry?"

"I could eat my trumpet," he smiled for the first time in nearly two years.

A few nights later Josiah's pallor began to improve and Bess took them all to dinner. Rachel was looking better. The two women had gone on a shopping spree at the upscale stores surrounding the

St. Francis Hotel. Bess had even insisted Rachel get her hair done. She also convinced Luke and Brett to do the same with Josiah. By the time they met for dinner near the wharf, they were a splendidly attired quintet and they looked at one another with admiration. The two brothers were paid and sent off with kisses and hugs and invitations to visit Moss Grove, if they ever got to Louisiana.

"I want to see my son," Josiah said, as he, Rachel, and Bess walked along the bluffs overlooking the harbor. It was a breezy day and they could see young boys trying to control their kites as the wind flicked them, first one way, and then another.

"Samuel must be near that age by now. It should be me down there with him doing things fathers and sons do together."

"I can return to Moss Grove, pick him up, and bring him back," Bess offered.

"I want us all to go," Josiah said. He could see the women's immediate reaction…danger.

"Look, I know there is a risk but if I dye my hair, grow a mustache and do whatever, I won't look anything like the man that ran away. I'll use a different name. We won't stay long, and I won't leave the plantation, but I need to go back. It's important," he pleaded.

It took more than a full day of discussions for the women to relent and get themselves energized for Josiah's transformation.

"I will be Frederick Smith for the duration, Freddie Smith of San Francisco."

"Leave your trumpet at home, Mr. Smith," Bess advised. "It's one less connection to who you were."

Josiah's eyes filled with tears as he smelled the hibiscus and lilac that were so familiar to him. He wiped them and kept them closed, letting the sounds and the aromas bring him home.

Bess jumped out, almost before the car came to a halt, running to Stuart and Samantha. Their daughter had even deigned to put on a dress for the occasion, an acknowledgment to her mother that she was no longer a child. Bess grinned.

"Very pretty," she said as the three of them hugged one another in joyous reunion as little Eli waddled toward them followed closely by Miss B.

Samuel stood off to one side, tentative, until he saw his mother with a strange, dark haired man, who he didn't recognize.

It was difficult for the boy to keep his composure. He wanted to be big and brave but he'd been without either parent for so long he was sure they were never coming back. After all, they'd given away his baby sister. Now he was sure they'd decided to abandon him. At least his mother was back. But his father…where was his father?

"Samuel," Josiah said tentatively. "It's me…your father."

The boy moved away from the strange man, closer to his mother, refusing to let go of her.

"It is your father, Samuel. He just looks different. Let's the three of us walk down to the lake and I'll explain."

"You know, you can't remain here," Stuart said.

"I do understand that. My brain and body are still messed up. I want opium more often than I'd like to admit, but I know that if I give in, it's all over. Your sister gave up so much to bring me back from the precipice. And looking like this scared the crap out of Samuel. He still doesn't fully understand, and Samantha avoids me as if I had the plague."

"We're all glad you've rejoined the land of the living. Have you thought about what your future looks like?"

"I want you to buy me out of my share of Moss Grove…or rather Rachel's share. We'll go back to San Francisco and try being a decent family. Whatever you give us will be our beginning, and we'll go from there, grateful for each day. There is a lot going on in California and we can make a good life for Samuel now that he'll have two parents."

"Do you ever think about that girl you killed?" Stuart asked solemnly.

"Every day! I can't remember any of the details. I just remember waking up in a haze and seeing her body. That horrific sight will be with me forever."

"Sam, my parents are taking me to San Francisco," the young boy said to his best friend.

"I'll miss you. Will you write?"

"Of course, and I want you to write to me as well," he said as he grabbed her hands.

Samuel and Samantha were cousins, best friends and confidantes, bound by Moss Grove, similar names, and deep affection. They stayed together until it was time to leave.

Robert and Maria returned to Washington with their young daughter, Ruth, and their own infant son, born at Moss Grove. As Robert had promised, they'd named the boy Noah, Jr. after his younger brother, killed for no reason back in Alabama when they'd escaped for a weekend from their work at Tuskegee.

Robert's efforts to gather writings by black authors for the Paris Exposition was well received and he had garnered a much better understanding of the black experience by reading the material he was given.

Their life was comfortable and routine and Robert couldn't ever remember being happier. Occasionally some of Maria's family would visit from Cuba and there was no better city in the United States to visit and show off to foreign guests.

Stephen, Alicia, and their new son, Thaddeus, returned to New York. After a month of exhausting workouts, she was back to 112 lbs. and she returned to her position modeling at Lord & Taylor, more radiant than ever. Stephen succeeded in getting frequent assignments reporting on national events. He and his son, who was now walking and chatting and asking a constant barrage of questions, would take the train to Washington while Alicia worked. The young toddler enjoyed playing with his cousin, Noah, Jr. but the two boys were the source of constant attacks by Ruth, who preferred pestering them to playing with her dolls. Both the children and their parents displayed a panoply of varied skin tones and while people might often take a second glance, this was Washington D.C., familiar with entertaining visitors from the seven continents. As long as the families remained in their own enclave, they rarely faced the daily racial divisiveness that characterized much of the country.

Chapter Twenty-One

Frederick Smith vanished as quickly as he'd appeared and the blonde blue-eyed Josiah Rogers smiled once again, albeit a little less cocky. Since he intended to remain in San Francisco the rest of his life, the subterfuge Josiah Williams had assumed, could vanish as well. He felt resurrected. Josiah Williams had killed that girl, not Josiah Rogers. He stood taller and walked the streets of the city with his lovely wife and handsome son. Samuel loved the hills of San Francisco and the fog that seemed to make it disappear and become visible again like part of a fairy tale. What he loved even more though was having his mother and father together, laughing, and holding hands.

They rented a large apartment just off Geary. Samuel started school, Rachel took a part time job, and Josiah walked the city, searching for an opportunity that caught his eye. He began carrying his trumpet again, the small bag as common a sight as his coat and hat. He'd played it a few times. He knew his lip wasn't what it used to be, but then, he thought, neither was he. He had never been a daytime sort of a man, more a night owl. He squinted at the bright sun, took a ferry boat to Oakland and back again. He gulped big swallows of damp air and laughed. He had seen the fires of hell. He had no desire to return.

He and Rachel returned to an aggressive sex life but neither had regained the explosive hunger that marked their earlier bouts. It was quieter, more controlled, as if each of them was afraid to awaken the earlier lust that had sent them down a disastrous path.

"Mr. Liu, remember me?" Josiah said, entering his Chinese friend's small restaurant.

"Yes, of course. I am so glad you have recovered. Now you look like the young man who used to visit us with your friends. May I get you something?"

"I want to thank you for all the help you gave my wife. I will be evermore grateful for a second chance. Meanwhile, a bowl of your Wor Won-ton soup would be wonderful. Do you have time to chat?"

"I will bring your soup and we can talk."

He walked back a few minutes later with a large steaming bowl of soup exuding aromas Josiah remembered from earlier years when Amy had first brought the three of them here.

"As delicious as I remember. Mr. Liu, why don't you enlarge your restaurant? You're always busy."

"There is never enough money for such a project. I would have bought my own building for such a restaurant but the laws do not allow me to own property."

"I know, but I could own the land and the building, and together we could make a grand place that everyone in the city would be eager to visit for a special dining experience. I have been looking to make an investment in something now that I'm back in San Francisco and over my drug addiction. You are as responsible as my wife for helping me recover from my addiction, so investing in you would be both a way of saying thank you, and a sound investment."

"I would need to speak to my wife and think about where we would locate such a place."

"I've thought a little about it. There is an empty corner building on the edge of Chinatown that would be perfect. It is close enough to be considered part of Chinatown and far enough away to attract all the 'whiteys' in the city. Rachel thinks it's a grand idea."

The House of Flying Dragons opened three months later, draped in oriental reds and gold leaf dragons. It was crowded to capacity every night.

"I've bought tickets for us to celebrate the success of the restaurant," Josiah smiled. "We're going to the Grand Opera House tomorrow night to see Enrico Caruso and the Metropolitan Opera."

"How splendid," Rachel smiled. "It is so good to have you well and smiling again, dear husband."

"And you to look so ravishing. I now get erections regularly just thinking about you."

"Just keep it in your pants or I'll cut it off," she chided.

"You Jews….always thinking of cutting off a man's pecker."

"Only when it loses its way and asks another woman for directions."

"Ah, yes. Fidelity! A woman's concept."

They both laughed and hugged.

"Where's Samuel?" Josiah asked, pressing his body against Rachel's.

"He won't be home for another hour," she grinned.

Josiah needed no further encouragement. Moments later, giggling, they jumped into their bed and buried themselves in blankets and one another.

They enjoyed dinner at the Palace Hotel and walked the few blocks to the Opera House. It was a balmy Tuesday evening. The stars were out and a three-quarter moon hung like a lantern behind Coit Tower. You could breathe the salt air…warm and musty. The crowd in front of the opera complex was well-dressed and filled with the anticipation of listening to the world's most famous tenor. The men were all bedecked in tuxedos and the women sported only the most current fashions. Dresses touched the ground with a flounce around the hem of the skirt. Waists were held in tight by corsets, and feathered hats matched each ensemble in color and style. The women of San Francisco would not be outdone by their number in Paris or New York.

The highlight of the evening was Caruso's solo 'M'Appari from Flotow's opera Martha. It was a stunning performance and the audience exited the Opera House humming the familiar arias, more than satisfied. Rachel and Josiah moved through the throng holding hands. A chauffeured touring car was waiting for them.

They returned to the Palace for a nightcap. The sommelier uncorked a bottle of 1897 French champagne and they toasted the resurrection of their lives. They didn't arrive home until nearly 4 AM.

They fell into a deep, deep, sleep until an hour later. At 5:18 A.M. they felt a shaking. Josiah's first reaction was that someone was knocking at the door but it was still dark out. Who could it be? The rattling continued. A Chinese vase, a gift from Mr. and Mrs. Liu, fell from the fireplace and broke into pieces. The bedroom window pane shattered and sprayed glass across the room.

"Rachel! Rachel," Josiah shouted. "Wake up. Wake up NOW! I'm going to check on Samuel. Get dressed. Something is terribly wrong."

Across the city buildings lurched and collapsed. The first shock lasted 23 seconds, and for no more than a celestial moment, citizens breathed a sigh of relief. Fathers looked around. Mothers eased the tense grip on the young frightened children they held. But it was a false respite. The next shock, the 'big' one, lasted 42 seconds and hell on earth erupted. From the Stanford mansion atop Nob Hill the family could view flattened structures as far as the eye could see. Near that same citadel of the city only the Flood mansion survived, its Connecticut brick shaking, but holding. The light from the widespread fires blended with the first rays of the morning sun, casting the sky in a bright red and orange hue.

As the eternal hope of a new morning faded, every building along Stockton Street, looking east from Market Street, had fallen and been replaced by a tangle of concrete, wood and bent metal. The fog horns of the early morning ferry boats were replaced by screams, as the bodies of loved ones and strangers lay among the morass of ruptured pipes and buildings.

Gas mains erupted, launching new conflagrations and consuming buildings that had survived the tremors. Fire fighters, attempting to create firebreaks, spread blazes that might have been contained. Broken water pipes drained the pressure necessary to douse the blazes. Half of the city's population of 400,000 souls was homeless within the first hours.

The waters across the Bay, and in the nearby Pacific, roiled in anger. Ships were tossed like matchsticks as they broke loose of their moorings. San Francisco's entire fishing fleet cascaded on top of one another onto the rocks. Nothing was immune. Dennis Sullivan, the city's Fire Chief, died in the initial shock. The Palace Hotel, where Josiah and Rachel had dined the night before, was crumbled and its English bone China and crystal goblets lay shattered amidst tables, beds, and marble columns. Enrico Caruso barely escaped when he ran from his hotel room. All the costumes and props of his opera company were destroyed along with most of the Opera House which had been filled to capacity the previous evening. He never returned to the city again.

Within hours of the news Hearst sent a telegram ordering Stephen to get back to San Francisco as quickly as possible to report on the disaster. Most of the newspaper magnate's presses in both Oakland and in the city were destroyed. He wanted copy and pictures and he wanted them yesterday. When Stephen arrived, days later, the fires were still burning. People were being pulled from the detritus of collapsed homes, sometimes alive, more often dead. Most of the survivors had fashioned homemade masks around their face to avoid breathing the dust and ashes that floated in the air. And, just when the city could have used its oft touted rain, it refused to come. But the afternoon breezes off the Bay continued to whirl, carrying the scent of decay from San Jose to Marin County. Tents were set up wherever there was flat ground, and hopefully, fresh water.

At the point where Market Street intersects with both Kearny and Geary, a large pillared water fountain had been donated to the city years earlier, by the actress Lotta Crabtree. Now Lotta's fountain became a meeting place where hundreds thronged, looking for loved ones separated in the melee of the earthquake.

As Stephen crossed Stockton he heard the cries of a young child. A dozen men working in the area, trying to clear the street, stopped as if in a frieze until they heard another sound. As one, they moved to the spot and Stephen joined them, tossing wood and bricks to one side. Their work continued for hours. They stopped only long enough to be reassured the sounds were continuing. Late in the afternoon, a small baby girl was pulled from the rubble, barely alive, but alive never the less. The men cried. Together they had worked to save her.

General Funston of the U.S. Army's base in the Presidio took control. Soldiers from all around the state were mobilized to fight the fires and provide food and shelter to the thousands who had been displaced.

"Mayor Schmitz, I'm a reporter from the *Daily Examiner*," Stephen shouted as the mayor huddled with Funston and a group of Army officers. "What would you like to tell our readers across the country?"

"Thank goodness for the Army. Tell them the city is down but we'll rebuild. We're an obstinate bunch."

"Are you worried about more earthquakes?"

"We'll handle whatever the good Lord sends our way. If this is his way of testing us, we will prove ourselves to be more than resilient."

It was good copy. It was bull shit, Stephen knew, but it was good copy. With his story written for the next edition he set out to find Rachel, Josiah and Samuel. He knew they lived off Geary and would have been asleep at that time of the morning. The first problem was that there no longer any street signs. Half the city no longer even had definable streets. Buildings had collapsed and fallen light stanchions blocked the way. He began at Lotta's Fountain and headed up the hill.

There were a few people around, their glazed eyes filled with tears, as they bent over, sorting through the shattered remains of their lives, searching for a picture, a ribbon, maybe a relic of the prior week when their lives were bucolic.

"I'm looking for the home where the Rogers lived," Stephen asked, embarrassed to intrude on their grief. "They had a young boy, blond hair, named Samuel."

"They're dead, up there, third house on the left if you can figure out where one heap looks different from the one next to it. Everything looks pretty much the same now, doesn't it?"

"I'm sorry for your loss. Is your family safe?"

The man shook his head and looked away. Stephen stood there, uncertain what one could say in a time like this. It was so much worse than Cuba and the war. He walked up toward the house where his friends had worked so hard to rebuild their lives. It looked pretty much untouched since the quake. The Army had more urgent problems than clearing residential streets.

It didn't look as if anyone had been there since the quake although looters were everywhere. The Army was authorized to shoot anyone caught stealing. The problem was that some of those caught stealing were the very soldiers patrolling the streets.

"They found two bodies, a man and a woman." The man who'd lost his family stood next to him. "They took them away, same group that took my wife. That's how I know. I watched them drive away. They wouldn't even let me make arrangements for a decent burial. They're afraid of disease with all the dead lying around waiting. I hear it could be more than 3,000."

"What about their young boy? They had a son, almost ten years old."

"I don't know. He might still be buried in all that rubble but if he survived he would have been taken to one of the temporary camps near the Presidio."

Stephen thanked him and began to run. Autos and carriages were nowhere to be seen, every available vehicle had been pressed into use to help victims but he waved down an army ambulance heading in his direction, showed his press pass, and stood on the bumper the entire way.

What he saw boggled his mind, tens of thousands of people with nothing but the clothes on their back, often wrapped in an olive army blanket, huddled around makeshift campfires. Some of the men and women still wore hats, a small attempt to protect their pride.

"Where are the children being housed?" he asked a medical orderly.

"Those without parents, or a relative to take them in, are over on that knoll, behind that small enclosure."

"I'm looking for my nephew, Samuel Rogers," he said to one of the nurses that seemed to be in charge of paperwork. "I'm told he might be here. He's nearly ten, blond, blue eyes, and tall for his age."

"Oh, yes, we know that young man. He's already taken charge of twenty boys and become their leader. They shout and make trouble demanding better food and their latest demand... school books. He comes up with it and they follow him. Let me get him."

"Uncle Stephen, how did you find me? Are my parents alright? Can you take me to them?"

Whatever Samuel's latent talents or aggressions might be, at that moment he was a frightened young boy who had been forced to fend for himself, no longer sheltered by parents who had overcome so many obstacles to reunite them all.

"Your parents are dead, Samuel. I'm sorry that I have to be the one to tell you but they were likely crushed in the collapse of your home. It's a miracle you survived. I think you should come with me until we can straighten things out and decide what's best for you."

Stephen couldn't leave the city, not yet. He left Samuel with a family recommended by an old friend he knew from his days at the *Examiner*. Meanwhile there were dimensions to the tragedy being revealed every day and he wanted to tell those stories. Fires were being set by homeowners told that their home losses could be covered if lost in a fire, but not as a result of an earthquake. Buildings that had collapsed from faulty construction were being blamed on corrupt city inspectors. Wealthy families abandoned their mansions atop Nob Hill and moved west toward Pacific Heights. Entire neighborhoods and cultures were torn asunder.

In Chinatown the devastation was the most widespread. The fragile buildings sitting on top of one another, and housing entire families in a single room, collapsed like an enormous pancake. The House of the Flying Dragons lay in a heap, the large brass dragon sign dormant and bent. Neither Mr. nor Mrs. Liu had survived. They and nearly a thousand Chinese perished, most of the rest were homeless. Forgotten for a moment was the racial hatred that had created their Asian ghetto.

Samuel would be returning to Moss Grove. Stuart had gone to San Francisco to help Stephen, get his nephew, and find the remains of Rachel and Josiah. The young boy was still traumatized. Stephen had been to see him once or twice but the boy still couldn't comprehend what had happened to his parents. He sat quietly, holding his nephew, trying to assure him that the boy wasn't alone. They stayed three weeks, trying vainly to find the bodies of his parents. In the end all he and Stuart could do was arrange for a headstone to mark their passing.

They stood in the mist overlooking the Pacific. Funerals had become the most active business in the city. Grieving families needed to pay for a casket even if there were no bodies to bury. Stephen, Stuart and Samuel stood there next to a Rabbi who had been found to say prayers for the dead.

"Maybe Josiah can now rest in peace," Stephen said. "Their life together was so volcanic."

"My sister stood by him. I think they loved one another far more than any of us ever understood."

It was equally difficult to unravel Josiah's financial affairs. The loss of the restaurant was a financial disaster and trying to collect insurance was an intricate web of legalese. They left the process in the hands of an attorney hired to formalize Stuart and Bess as Samuel's guardians and, hopefully, collect some of the assets Josiah and Rachel might have had.

The train ride back to Moss Grove was soothing for Samuel and as the days passed he grew a little more energized. Stuart was there to wipe the boy's tears and talk to him in a calm and reassuring way. By the time the boy saw Samantha running toward him, he was able to smile. She was a year older and he was all too aware that she was beginning to develop breasts. He teased her but she took it good naturedly. Her mother had warned her a little on how pesky boys of that age could be. You needed to tolerate them, she'd said.

"Was the earthquake very frightening?" Samantha asked as the two friends sat under a large magnolia tree near the water.

It was a quiet, late summer afternoon and they could hear the birds chirping in the nearby trees. This was their favorite spot. The adults didn't come here often. Thaddeus and Amy were both buried nearby and their headstones had this strange way of sharing a single ray from the late afternoon sun. It seemed to peak through the branches of the large magnolia tree that provided their graves a protective canopy.

Samantha knew the story of her grandmother and her love for a mulatto man who was also Samuel's cousin and Stephen's father. It brought them all closer together. Now, one of those branches had fallen from their family tree and Samuel had been orphaned.

"It's strange now when I try to think about what happened. I'd gotten up to get a glass of water. I remember turning on the tap and the water looked brown and dirty, and then everything started to shake. The bathroom mirror cracked and that's when I got frightened. I started to run to my parent's room but the room was moving and I fell. I sat on the floor not knowing what to do. I think I screamed out for my father but the house was creaking. Then everything stopped and that was even more eerie. I waited and stood. I had blood on my arm where some of the glass shards from the mirror had cut me. By this time I was really afraid and I needed to get to my parents.

"Then the room started shaking again...worse than the first time. I fell into the bathtub and a bunch of things fell on top of me. This time I know I screamed. I thought I heard my father's voice calling my name. It could have been my imagination, I don't really know. Something hit me on my head and that's all I remember for awhile. When I awoke I didn't know whether it was day or night or how long I'd been there. I shouted but no one heard me. I drifted off to sleep for a few hours. When I awoke I took turns listening for voices and hoping someone would hear my shouts. I was sure my parents were looking for me. Eventually someone did hear, soldiers who were walking the streets looking for survivors. They dug me out and took me to a small hospital. They said I'd been there nearly three days and I was lucky to be alive. My father had apparently tried to reach me but neither he nor my mother ever made it out of their room. I stayed in the camp with other children until Uncle Stephen found me."

Tears flowed down Sam's cheeks and she took Samuel's hand to keep hers from trembling. Even the sun seemed to sink in despair as he related what he'd suffered.

Chapter Twenty-Two

Robert sat in his office at the Library of Congress scanning various newspapers from around the country. It was one of his jobs. He had to read this particular article more than once; it was so violent and outrageous. He seethed with increasing anger each time he read it, hoping that he hadn't really read it correctly.

In St. Charles, Arkansas, a small hamlet in the southeastern corner of the state, the small local newspaper reported that a race riot had erupted and thirteen blacks were lynched.

> At a point along the White River where people liked to gather, a white man, Jim Searcy, was gambling with a black man named Griffin. They got into an argument that escalated into blows. The Police arrived and attempted to take Griffin into custody, telling him that they were going to hang him. He hit the officer, grabbed the man's gun, and fled.
>
> Griffin went into hiding, but angry white mobs were determined to find him. Men gathered from several nearby counties. They searched the area on horseback accosting any black family they came across. Nearly seventy men, women, and children were gathered like cattle and locked in a warehouse.
>
> The angriest of the whites wanted to torch the building.
>
> 'We need to eliminate all the niggers,' several of the posse shouted.

Cooler heads prevailed, but not entirely. Six random men were dragged from the building, marched to a knoll on the highway. The men were made to stand in a line and were then shot. That was a Thursday. By Saturday Griffin and his brother were found. The two of them and five black strangers who had been caught up in the fury were also lynched. Thirteen men dead, four score more threatened, and all because of a dispute over a game of chance.

They were names he would add to his list, Griffin brothers, Baldwins, father and son, Andrew Hinton, and the rest. But he understood they were more than names. These were men with families, women who loved them, children orphaned. They might have gotten up that morning, eaten a bowl of porridge, and decided which tasks on their small farms were the most urgent. Maybe they'd made love the night before, or that morning. They might have reluctantly taken a strap to a young one who'd acted up.

He knew they could also have been men who drank too much and shirked their responsibilities. But whoever they were, they deserved the protection of the law, not the end of a rope. He had never been asked to keep such a list but ever since Stephen's articles on lynching, he found himself adding names and the list continued to get longer. It was a list of black men and women who had been senselessly lynched, killed without a trial…killed simply because of their color. Someday, someone might want to know, he thought.

"We're leaving after the cotton is in and everything is settled up."

Edgar's father, Harold Stump, had come to the back door of Moss Grove's main house to speak with Stuart. He stood there, his hat in his hand, and waited patiently for the owner of the plantation to acknowledge his presence.

"Why, Harold?" Stuart asked. "You've been the best foreman we've had in years. The men like you, and I'm sure you and the missus have been able to put some money aside. Cotton prices have been pretty stable these past few years."

"You've been more than fair, Mr. Fineman, but we done stayed too long here. We should have left once we knew Edgar was dead but we just didn't have it inside us. Now our daughter, Daisy, Edgar's sister, is grown, and we need to show her more than share croppin'. We're gonna head north toward Chicago or Detroit. Lotsa' factory jobs we hear tell. Maybe I'll get a job makin' those new fangled automobiles."

"You'll be missed, Harold. I know Mrs. Fineman will miss your wife as well."

"Can I ask you a question that's always troubled me, seein' as to how we likely won't see one another again once we leave?"

"If it's a letter telling someone who might hire you what kind of a person and worker you are, I'm happy to give you one."

"That's gracious of you and I guess it would be good to have such a letter but that weren't the question. What I need to know is if Mr. Josiah was the one who shot my son? I know he and your sister got killed in that terrible thing that happened in California so it don't make no difference anymore, but it would help my wife and me put some closure on our son being gone."

"Come, Harold, sit with me a spell. I'll have one of the girls bring us some drinks," Stuart sighed, knowing this man was entitled to the truth.

The two men sat silently, not speaking for a long while. It was the hottest hour of the day and it felt good to be sitting here in the shade. Stuart's brow was furrowed. His hair was now peppered with white and he knew he was no longer the brash young man who had found his way to Cuba nearly a decade earlier. He and Harold, whose lives were so different, had both seen a lot of the ugliness that life could throw at you.

"Moss Grove is a good place, isn't it?" Stuart mused. "Sometimes it's even been a sort of sanctuary from all the hatred that absorbs much of the south."

"Your family been here a long time, ain't it?" Harold asked, getting a rare look into the way a white person thinks.

"Pretty much. I remember coming to Louisiana in a wagon during the war. My father was a Union Army officer. We lived in Baton Rouge for awhile and then events conspired to bring us here. Been here ever since."

"You the only Jewish folks I ever known," Harold said, speaking more openly than he was generally inclined to. "We grow up hearin' stories 'bout horns and killin' our Lord, but your family has always been good to us, and to all the share cropper families."

"People make things up from ignorance, Harold. They say things about blacks also but those things aren't true either. People are just people. They want to raise their families, earn a little respect, and smile when the sun shines on their face. They want to see their children grow up and do well. And, yes, the answer to your earlier question is that we are pretty sure Josiah shot Edgar."

"Why he do that, Mr. Fineman?"

"Josiah was a very troubled man. It was everything that happened before you and your family arrived. His mother died when he was a young boy and his father, Henry, another troubled soul, sent him away. I was pretty young when Henry got shot. Louisiana, like the rest of the Confederacy, was pretty unstable after the war. No one, including my father, knew how we'd all survive and grow cotton. Where are your kin from?"

"Small town outside of New Orleans, near Houma. We just kept heading north after the war, looking for work. Probably God directed our feet here and it was all good until Edgar got shot. He was such a nice boy. He didn't deserve no killin'."

"No, he didn't. And now with Josiah dead, I'm afraid we'll never understand what really happened.

"What would Daisy like to do with her life?" Stuart asked after several moments of silence, and eager to change the subject.

"She'd like to be a nurse, care for folks."

They talked awhile longer and shook hands before they parted, their eyes making contact as equals.

It was another month before Stephen arrived at Moss Grove. San Francisco would have a long difficult journey back from its devastation and there wasn't much to report that hadn't been written and rewritten. People around the country had finally exhausted themselves reading stories about fallen buildings. No new bodies had been found for two weeks. The papers had even used some of Stephen's photographs that he'd taken with the $1 Kodak Brownie camera he kept with him. They weren't the quality the newspaper preferred but when nothing else was available, they offered much more than words to express the emotion of the moment.

"Samuel, I have a small present for you," Stephen said, handing a wrapped package to the young boy. He was haggard from his experience and it showed in his bent shoulders and wrinkled forehead. Bess watched quietly as this man she continued to love presented a wrapped package to his young, very damaged, nephew.

The tall, now serious, young man tore off the loosely tied string and brown wrapping paper. Inside was a trumpet, a small dent near the bell, but otherwise intact.

"It was your father's. I found it digging through the rubble. I also found a few pieces of your mother's jewelry and a nice picture of the three of you. They're all yours."

Tears welled in Samuel's eyes as he nestled the brass instrument, dull and tarnished from the weather.

"He used to play it sometimes. He even wrote one song he called 'Samuel,' after me, he said. I can still hear the melody in my head. It's about all I have left."

"Remember the good times. When you lose loved ones they're still alive if you remember good things about them. Your parents worked hard to bring the three of you together, even though it wasn't for very long."

Samuel nodded and walked away slowly, putting the instrument to his lips and blowing softly.

Alicia hated being alone. She had a nanny for Thaddeus. She was sure she loved her young son, but she detested doing motherly things. Her husband was a much better parent than she was. It was an awareness she was willing to accept. She preferred being admired for her beauty, knowing that men were staring at her with unfettered lust, while the women simply stared in envy.

Stephen was still gone. He called when he could, but long distance telephone calls were terribly expensive. She still had her job modeling clothes at Lord & Taylor. She enjoyed wearing the expensive designer dresses, but the evenings and weekends were lonely. She went to the nickelodeon on Saturdays and, if the weather was temperate, she'd take Thaddeus for a stroll through Central Park on Sundays and write her weekly letters to Stephen and her friends in Cuba.

Charlie Taylor, the scion of the Lord & Taylor's small empire, was entranced by this tall, striking, Cuban model. She knew he'd often stand in the corner of the show room, watching. At first Alicia thought he was just monitoring how the clients were being treated. These wealthy women from Park Avenue were the bread and butter of the store's success. But at some point she knew, as all beautiful women instinctively know, that his presence was due to her and not the middle age and over-processed matrons who sat and chattered and knew they would never look as good in the dresses being shown as the enchanting model parading before them.

"I understand your husband is still in San Francisco, reporting on the earthquake. I have two tickets to the new Hippodrome Theater for Saturday evening and since we're both alone I thought you'd do me the honor of going with me," Charlie Taylor asked, as casually as he could. Her Cuban accent excited him… every word offering its own melody.

Alicia was conflicted. She'd heard about the amazing new theatre. It was the largest in the world, they said. She was sure that she and Stephen could go once he returned but his last letter said he might have to be there at least another two weeks and he wanted to stop by Moss Grove before returning to New York. It seems he wasn't only reporting but trying to help Stuart see if Rachel and Josiah had some assets that their son might inherit. And now, here was this gentle, handsome, and obviously, wealthy man, asking her out.

"I can't, Mr. Taylor. It wouldn't be proper. I'm married and you are my boss. That's two very good reasons."

"You're right, of course. What if I get a third ticket and we'll bring my sister, Jenna? I know she isn't doing anything. She's just gotten a divorce and spends most of her time moping around. And, with another woman along, your reputation will be quite safe. We'll pick you up at 8:00 for the show and then have a late dinner. It'll be fun," he said, departing quickly before she could utter any objection.

She stood there following his retreating form. She'd been a consort to enough men to know when they were in heat and this male was displaying all of the obvious traits. He was attractive. She definitely wouldn't let his sister out of her sight.

The show was overwhelming. The program said there were five hundred chorus girls singing and dancing but they moved so gracefully and quickly it was impossible to count.

"Diving horses…circus lions and tigers," Alicia gushed. "My eyes couldn't capture everything if I saw the show a dozen times. Thank you, Charlie. Thank you so much."

Charlie Taylor had arranged for Alicia to wear one of the store's designer gowns and adorn it with whatever accessories she chose. She selected a radiant green silk dress with brocade trimming and rhinestones studded along the neck. Her hair was up in a French chignon, adorned with a pearl comb. She felt herself floating as she walked.

Jenna Taylor French eyed her brother's date suspiciously at first. After all, she was only an L & T employee. Jenna was two years younger than her brother but she had none of his panache. Her ex-husband's infidelity had destroyed more than their marriage. It destroyed her self-confidence as well. Her brown hair was mousy and the dress she wore was a little too large, as if the weight she'd lost was not only from her body but from her soul as well. She retained her aristocratic bearing but the divorce had been a very untidy affair filled with the sordid details of Mr. French's peccadilloes splashed across the city's tabloids. Now she found herself as a third wheel and it was depressing being with her brother and his too gorgeous date. She knew that Alicia was married but that trivial consideration hadn't stopped Jenna's husband from straying. She now had firsthand experience that men were unfaithful and it was a very small leap to believe that wives could stray as easily as husbands.

They dined in the rooftop garden of the Sherry, an exclusive restaurant that was decorated as an Italian garden. Branches of wisteria covered an arbor where the evening summer sky could peak through. This night the stars above New York's tall buildings were more than cooperative.

Jenna's opinion of Alicia soon became tempered by the Cuban girl's apparent innocence. Was it really innocence, she wondered. It was obvious that the woman knew she attracted the attention of men and women but she seemed able to hold herself apart. Maybe it wasn't innocence…maybe it was cunning.

She could see how easily Charlie could be attracted, but in ways that were entirely new, she found herself sexually attracted to Alicia as well.

Jenna had had a single brief experience with a roommate in college. They were in their dorms at the College of New Rochelle. It was a warm summer evening, much like this one. Both girls wore only bra and panties in an effort to stay cool. A harmless pillow toss became something more, and neither girl mentioned it again. Now, years later, Jenna continued to think of it with lascivious pleasure, a sin she'd enjoyed, mixing uncomfortably with guilt.

The soft sounds of a violin quartet filled the starlit sky with the sounds of Chopin. Alicia had been treated well by the Spanish governor with whom she was intimate for months until he was deposed, but the finest restaurants in Havana were no match for this. She breathed deep trying to absorb the essence of the experience. She didn't notice the stares of her two escorts.

"Oh, I'm so sorry," Jenna said as she accidentally tipped over Alicia's glass, sending a small spray of wine onto the green silk dress. "Come, let's go to the Powder room. I'm sure they have something that will get that stain off before it sets."

Jenna stood quickly, taking Alicia's arm and bringing her to her feet before she could object. Charlie stood courteously as the two women hurried from the room, his focus temporarily broken.

"Sit here," Jenna ordered as they entered the elaborately decorated Ladies Room. Two other women were there fixing their make-up.

"Can I help you?" a Negro maid asked.

"Just get me a damp cloth. We'll be fine."

Jenna stood directly over Alicia, the damp cloth in her hand, her eyes gripped on the dark brown eyes and high cheek bones of the young model. Her hand began to shake. Alicia looked straight into the woman's eyes, not shying away, fully aware of the heat building between them. Without a pause, Alicia pulled Jenna down, her hand, warm and firm, on the back of the woman's neck and kissed her fully on the lips. The emotion was palpable and the kiss hung there for an eon.

Alicia released her grip and stood, taking the cloth, and patting her dress. She checked her makeup and then turned and left the room, never glancing back at the other woman, who remained, unmoving, petrified at what had just happened.

"Where is Jenna?" Charlie asked as Alicia returned to the table.

"She'll be along. Why don't you ask me to dance?"

The dance floor was small and Charlie was thrilled to be holding Alicia and whirling her effortlessly around the floor. He would have liked to hold her closer but that would have to wait for later. When they returned to the table Jenna still hadn't returned.

"It's quite late, Charlie. Would you mind taking me home?"

"Not too late for a nightcap. I thought we might stop by the Waldorf. I wonder what could have taken Jenna to disappear like that."

"She did mention that she wasn't feeling terribly well. Perhaps she caught a Hansom and went home. I should go home as well. I have to be at work early tomorrow and my boss is a stickler for punctuality," she smiled.

"I'm sure he'd be forgiving but I'll acquiesce and take you home on the promise you'll go out with me again...soon."

"You are a delight, Charlie but we'll have to see."

Charlie saw her to the front door where she evaded his embrace with a small grateful kiss on the cheek, a smile, and a gloved hand on her beau's cheek. Ten minutes later, as she poured two glasses of white wine, there was a soft tap on her front door. She opened it and smiled.

"Come in, Jenna. I've poured wine for us."

Stephen was finally able to return to Alicia and New York. It was the longest they'd been apart since she'd come to him riding all the way from Havana to Camaguey on an old mule. She seemed so young and fragile then, not the Fifth Avenue model and beauty that she'd become. His love for her had changed through the years but it had never diminished. He loved her now as much as he did then, and together they had created Thaddeus. His heart swelled at all he had in life.

Their love making was savage that first night he returned. He was a parched soul, finally reaching an oasis. They spread their bodies on the fur rug in front of the fire place, listening to the dry logs crackle. They finished a bottle of expensive French Cabernet, a male admirer had sent to her as a gift, thanking her for changing his plain wife into a fashion doyen.

"Those marks on your neck, Alicia. They resemble love bites. Have you been with another man in my absence?" His voice was filled with pain. He'd always felt certain her love for him was as consuming as his was for her.

"They are nothing, Stephen. They are an irritation from one of the recent dresses I modeled. Hold me close. It is cold this morning, is it not?"

Alicia knew the marks on her neck were from Jenna's overly enthusiastic lovemaking. Even makeup wouldn't hide the tiny love bites. She and her new friend continued to see one another; most recently last evening, hours before Stephen returned. She knew it was going to be a problem juggling both relationships but the conflict gave her an extra thrill...an emotional high.

"I need to get up and get to the office," he said, the morning sun peeking through the curtains. "I'm finally due to meet Mr. Hearst in person. I've worked for him for more than a decade but our paths have never crossed."

"I'm very proud of you Stephen," Alicia said, meaning it, but looking forward to some time to think through her conundrum.

She knew that Charlie Taylor would have fired her a month ago for her failure to see him again, but Jenna stepped in and threatened him.

"Why, Jenna, you've found romance," he laughed.

"Not at all what I would have expected from either of you. All of Alicia's beauty wasted on another woman. Obviously, like your ex-husband, Stephen Carmody must be a wimp. I could have changed her attitude if she'd let me but I am unwilling to compete with my sister for the affections of a trollop, no matter how striking," he said as he walked away, continuing to laugh.

William Randolph Hearst assembled his editorial team as soon as the morning edition had gone to press.

"Gentlemen, many of you know Stephen Carmody here. He has worked for many of my newspapers across the country for more than a dozen years and you've read his work. He wrote a searing and emotional series of articles about lynching. He covered the Spanish-American war with distinction, even got himself captured by the Spanish. Most recently he's returned from covering the San Francisco earthquake. I'm very proud of him and I think you all should be as well. He's one of the reasons the circulation figures for the Hearst papers around the country have continued to climb."

Hearst put his arm around Stephen's shoulder and the room burst into applause. It was hard not to blush. Moments later he followed the famous newspaper magnate into the private office he'd commandeered for his brief time in New York.

"Stephen, again, I want to privately thank you for all the fine work you've done." The publisher sat back in his chair, took a large cigar from a silver case, bit off the stub and, with a matching silver lighter, lit up. "These are made special for me. "Now, what were you saying?"

"I just wanted to thank you, again, Mr. Hearst. I hope to continue doing the kind of reporting you like."

"It won't happen, Stephen. You're fired! As of this moment you no longer work for the Hearst newspapers."

It was said so matter-of-factly that Stephen wasn't even sure he'd heard it clearly.

"I'm sorry?" he said, blinking.

"You're fired," the heavy set man said, unbuttoning his jacket and vest as he continued to focus on the cigar smoke whirling around him.

"Why? You just commended me in front of your entire editorial staff."

"We had never met before. I took one look at you and I knew you were coloured. You've been lying to us the entire time you've worked here."

"I never lied. It never came up. I just did my work and it was pretty good work, you have to admit."

"Great work. You're one of the best reporters I have but there isn't any way I'm going to employ a 'nigger' reporter. Pulitzer and the other publishers would make me a laughing stock if it became public, and the rest of my staff would walk out. None of them want to work with a coloured. That's just the way it is."

"This is bizarre," Stephen said, collapsing into a chair. "My entire career...all the work I've done, redefined because I have a few drops of Negro blood coursing through my veins."

"I'm not a sociologist, boy, I'm a newspaper man and that's the way things are in this business, in this country, at this time. I'm sure a black newspaper will be happy to hire a man with your experience."

Hearst returned to shuffling papers on his desk, willing himself to ignore the dejected man standing before him. Stephen stood; shoulders slumped, and left the room. He avoided eye contact with the staff, still eager to shake the hands of the young man Mr. Hearst had lauded so extensively.

Stephen's return to their apartment was hours earlier than expected. He assumed Alicia would be at work, and Thaddeus would likely be at school, but there were noises coming from the bedroom.

He opened the door to find a strange woman lifting her head from his pillow and staring at him in disbelief.

"Who are you?" he asked. "Where is Alicia?"

The satin comforter rustled and a figure that had been nestled in the lower portion of the bed emerged.

"Stephen, this is rather unexpected," Alicia said, slightly nonplussed.

"It seems so. Would you care to introduce me to your friend?"

"Jenna Taylor...Stephen Carmody, my husband!"

The smaller brown haired woman buried her head in the covers, refusing to face the embarrassment of being discovered.

Stephen shook his head and closed the door behind him. Minutes later Alicia, having donned a lace-accented chiffon robe, joined him.

"I now understand the marks on your neck. Am I supposed to be grateful you haven't been with other men? Or are your choices indiscriminate?"

"It is what I am, what I've always been. I have a beauty that seems to attract those of both sexes. I have used it to my advantage since I was fourteen and hungry in Cuba. I make no apologies. Even you desired me."

"Yes, but I loved you. I thought you loved me as well."

"You brought me to America. You showed me a new life and I am fond of you. You cannot feel cheated. I even gave you a son. It almost destroyed my body but you wanted a child and I was the vessel you needed. Now, tell me, why are you home so early?" she said, walking into the kitchen and pouring each of them a cup of coffee.

"I've been fired," Stephen said.

"Fired? Why, for goodness sakes? I thought they were pleased with all the stories you've written. They certainly kept you busy."

"Mr. Hearst fired me because I'm coloured and he doesn't want to have a 'nigger' reporter."

"I'm sorry, Stephen. I don't understand," Alicia said. "What do you mean 'coloured'?"

"I have a small amount of Negro blood in me. Thaddeus, my father, was half-black. You knew that."

"Actually, I didn't know. You never said anything. I have been living with a coloured man all these years," she said to herself, her hands beginning to gesture wildly, her eyes glazed in confusion.

"When we met, you had been in the sun for long months. Many men in Cuba carry skin tanned by the sun. I thought nothing of it…we even have a child, a mud child…a colored child. How could you not tell me?"

She began crying…shouting…tearing at her clothing while Jenna remained hidden in the bedroom. "I am ashamed. I am embarrassed. I feel so dirty. You must leave and take the child with you. I could take a hundred baths and never feel clean again. What will people say when they find out?"

Alicia rushed from the room, slamming the door. She locked herself in the bedroom, threw herself down on the bed, and began sobbing hysterically. Jenna, confused, never the less, found the return of her girlfriend sexually exciting.

Stephen was overwhelmed by the depth of his wife's outburst. How could she have not known, he wondered? She had come to him and they loved one another, he thought. They had never discussed her life before they met nor had she ever shown any interest in his.

This day that had begun with such hope and joy was ending in a complete collapse of his life, not unlike what he had witnessed in San Francisco.

As he continued to sit in the dark, each breath more labored, he heard the front door slam. Alicia had stormed from their home, Jenna following close behind, leaving him alone, out of work, no longer accepted as white, and with a son to rear.

"Where's Mommy?" Thaddeus asked, nudging his father's sleeping form, still draped on the chair from which he hadn't moved.

Stephen rubbed his eyes, red and blurry from a combination of alcohol and tears. He swung his son onto his lap and held him.

"I think we may be on our own," he said softly.

Chapter Twenty-Three

"Welcome to my world," Robert said.

After a week of sitting alone in a darkened apartment all day after sending Thaddeus off each morning to school, Stephen packed two suitcases, took his confused son by the hand, and left the apartment. He felt certain a part of his life was closing behind him

He was bitter, he was despondent, and he was angry. In just a few years he had lost all the women in his life he'd ever cared for. First Amy died, and then he loses Beth. Now he has not only lost his beautiful wife, he has also lost his career. Being a reporter for Hearst newspapers carried a panache...a status that made him walk a little taller. He had mingled with important people and told the country what was happening. And he lost it all because his skin carried a subtle hue that was socially unacceptable. Insane... just plain insanity! But he wouldn't give in...he couldn't give up. Thaddeus needed him to be strong...to move forward.

Alicia hadn't returned nor made any attempt to contact him. Stephen decided the closest temporary haven would be Robert and Maria. For Thaddeus, the train ride was an adventure and the boy alternated between staring out the window and running through the aisles making choo-choo noises to the mixed glee and frustration of the other passengers.

"How could she just walk out on us?" Stephen asked.

"Didn't you two ever discuss the fact that you had some black blood in you?"

"No, it wasn't a subject that ever came up with Alicia or at work. Most days it wasn't even a thought that passed through my brain. One of the rare times it arose was when I did those lynching stories and the woman I worked with, Ida Wells, asked."

"Forgive me if I laugh, dear cousin, but being a little black in this country is like being a little pregnant."

"I've lost my job, I find my wife in bed with a woman, and she leaves me."

"Yes, that is a trifecta, isn't it?"

"Have you given any thought to what you'll do next?" Maria asked, bringing in a tray of snacks, and glasses of milk for Thaddeus, Ruth, and Noah, playing noisily in an adjoining room.

"I know I'll need to find a job, but from what Mr. Hearst told me, it won't likely be with a white newspaper. As soon as they discover why he fired me, I'll be a pariah. I also need to take care of Thaddeus. Being a reporter generally means travel and that can get unwieldy when you have a son."

"Do you think Alicia will reconsider?"

"No, I'm absolutely certain she won't. She'll find a way to get a quiet divorce. She made it clear the thought of me makes her feel dirty. A public divorce could also bring out sordid tales of her sexual proclivities."

"Maria, did you and Alicia ever....?" Robert said, half-smiling, half-concerned.

"No, my darling husband! That is something for which you need not worry. I am true to you, but I do find your cousin quite attractive," she teased.

Stephen blushed and raised his hands in mock surrender.

"I think I'd better swear off sex for awhile. In my most extreme dreams I never imagined women doing what I'm pretty sure Alicia and her friend were doing, and in our bed."

"There are magazines...quite popular ones, I'm told, that can educate you. Only if you're interested, of course."

Robert smiled as Maria planted a kiss on his cheek and went to check on the children.

Ruth was busy taking charge of Thaddeus and her younger brother.

"Mother, the boys won't do what I tell them and I'm older than they are. It isn't fair."

Maria smiled as she picked up some of the debris spread around the room.

"It's a lesson you might as well learn early. Boys and men will often not respond to orders from girls and women. It is in their nature to be contrary."

"Well then," Ruth wondered. "How do we get them to do things…even things that are good for them?"

"Be patient. In a few years it will all become clearer."

"Come to work with me tomorrow. I want you to meet my boss, Daniel Murray. He's the Assistant head of the Library of Congress and one of the highest ranking Negroes in the government. Besides, we get copies of most of the newspapers around the country, including the black newspapers. It could be a good way for you to begin your job hunting."

"Stephen, it is a pleasure to meet you. I've read many of the articles you have written through the years and Robert explained that you have suddenly become unemployed."

Daniel Murray rose from his desk and extended his hand, his dark brown eyes crinkled warmly at the edges. His black hair had pomade that made it glisten everywhere except the part on the right side. His mustache was neatly trimmed and his suit and tie were de rigeur for government managers.

"Please…sit. Robert explained a little of your history but I'd like to hear more, if you'd be willing to share it. I've cancelled all obligations for the morning."

For the next two hours Stephen spoke.

"It began with a hidden love affair between my white mother and a mulatto man who was also Robert's father. The man, Thaddeus Williams, was never told he and my mother had a child together. I only learned the truth a few years ago and it was quite a revelation. I'd always thought my parents were a mulatto couple who were close family friends. As a result I accepted that I was a light-colored mulatto. They were slain in a Klan raid that became a killing field.

"My aunt trekked us all to San Francisco and when I was old enough I got a job at the newspaper. No one asked about my background. Things are a little less tense in California unless you're Mexican or Chinese. Brown and yellow people seem to bring out the worst in the whites out there, particularly the miners and the sailors. Anyway, my life went along. Robert and I went to Cuba during the Spanish-American war as reporters. That's where I met my wife. My life was idyllic until last week when it suddenly imploded. Now I am without wife or career. Thankfully, I still have my son, Thaddeus."

"Your father was well-known around Washington. I'd heard the story of his rise from being a slave to fighting in the Civil War to ultimately becoming an aid to a United States Senator. It's difficult to imagine this other aspect of his earlier life that you've been describing…obviously a remarkable man. I'm sure he would have been quite proud of you."

A secretary brought a tray of coffee and left quietly. Murray was intrigued by his guest. The young man was handsome for a man of any race. His blue eyes captured your attention and held you in their grip. Murray was certain that if Stephen had been white he could have risen to any pinnacle he chose to climb. Our Negro community can certainly use the talents of such a man, he silently told himself.

Murray cancelled his afternoon appointments and Robert joined them for lunch and a relaxing walk around the Mall and along the Potomac.

"They're talking about building some sort of Memorial to Abraham Lincoln around here somewhere. If the Southern Senators have anything to do with it, they'll either never support it, or they'll make certain that it's adorned with Confederate flags." Stephen wasn't sure whether Daniel Murray was teasing or serious.

"I've wanted to do a project for more than two years but I never quite figured out how to get it done. I think you may be the right instrument. A little less than two years ago, September in '06, there was a riot in Atlanta. A lot of people got killed but because of the enormity of the earthquake in San Francisco, that you were busy covering, it never got much publicity. Would you consider going to Atlanta and writing some articles on what happened and how those events still continue to alter that city years later?"

"You're right. I never even knew about it. Would I be able to get paid? I'm sorry, but without a job, it's a question I have to ask."

"Of course! I don't have funds here at the Library of Congress but we are always in close contact with some of the larger black owned newspapers around the country. There are three, in particular, that I'm thinking of. I'm sure I can get them to share your salary and travel expenses in exchange for giving them your stories."

"Then, I'm ready. Robert's wife, Maria, has offered to take care of Thaddeus while I'm gone. I'm excited. Where can I get background information?"

"I'm sure Robert has it in his files. Meanwhile I will explain the project to Robert Abbott at the *Chicago Defender*, Louis Palladium in St. Louis and Edwin Harleston at the *Pittsburgh Courier*. Each of them has the energy and foresight to participate."

Atlanta Riots of 1906 Have Changed the City
By Stephen Carmody

Nearly two years ago, September 1906, Atlanta, Georgia, one of the largest cities in the South, was the scene of an unparalleled rampage. What had been a racial truce for decades was broken by violence and citywide melees that lasted four days. At the end, an estimated forty Negros were killed along with two whites. Scores were injured and property damage was inestimable. This is the first of a series of articles that will strive to explain how it began and what has happened since.

In the twenty years that preceded the turn of the century, the Negro population of Atlanta nearly quadrupled, to the consternation of its white majority. Negro families opened businesses and created their own communities. The elder generation of Negros, many ex-slaves, remembered the decade after the Civil War when they could vote without fear, and take an active role in the affairs of the city.

The total population of Atlanta nearly doubled in the most recent decade, putting pressure on city services such as fire and police, sanitation and medical care. There was competition for jobs and Negros were willing to work for less.

In early fall 1906 two white candidates for Governor, both newspaper publishers, used their voices to frighten white voters by repeated cries of a need to 'keep the niggers in their place.'

'Expand the Poll tax!" cried one. 'Stop assaults on white women!' headlined another.

On a warm September afternoon four assaults on white women were reported, none substantiated. Young news boys fanned through the city shouting the headlines. White crowds began to gather. Mob mentality exploded and an estimated ten thousand white men and boys flooded down Decatur and Pryor, throwing rocks through the windows of black businesses. Men were pulled from their stores and beaten; passengers were pulled off trolleys and pummeled.

By midnight, the crowd still growing, the Militia was called and quelled the riot, assisted by a heavy rain. An uneasy quiet remained for days.

For the next several months Negros and whites who had always had a collegial relationship looked at one another with caution.

Next week's report is 'How Atlanta has Changed.'

"That's a wonderful story, Stephen. The three publishers are impressed and they have authorized me to offer you something more permanent. They will each pay you a salary equal to 20% of what you earned working for Mr. Hearst. It is their hope that you can get other newspapers to join them in syndicating your stories. They will expect at least one story of national importance each week. Are you interested?"

"Of course, Mr. Murray. You've done a lot already but can you help me find additional newspapers for the articles? I doubt I could survive on 60% of my previous salary. Mr. Hearst was never known for paying extravagant salaries."

Harold Stump and his wife, Cecily, had mixed feelings about leaving Moss Grove; he had been there more than ten years. He had met Cecily a few months after he'd arrived, fallen in love, and a year later Edgar was born. Sharecroppin' was hard work but if you got a fair accountin' from the plantation owner, and if the price of cotton wasn't real low, you could provide a decent living for your family. Harold felt lucky. Cecily could sew real good and made nice things that she could sell. She also baked better pies than anyone at Moss Grove and the big house bought them on a regular basis…pumpkin, pecan, and sweet potato. It didn't make no difference, she could do it all. Her crust was like sweet butter in the mouth. And love makin'! Now, in that field, she was even better than her pies. Yes, Harold Stump was a lucky man except for the terrible killin' of his son.

He gave some thought to killin' Josiah Roger's son, Samuel, as revenge. But Samuel's father was already dead, punished by God. No, it was just time for him and Cecily to find a new life.

They found housing near Eight Mile Road on the edge of Detroit. It wasn't much, but they weren't used to very much. He had been given one name, Robert Pelham. Pelham was an influential Negro building contractor who helped black folks arriving from the south get a job.

"Do you know your numbers, Mr. Stump?" Pelham asked.

"A little. My wife reads real good and she taught me some."

"Good. You look healthy. I can probably get you a job working on the docks. Would that be acceptable?"

"Oh, yes sir, whatever you can find, I'd be much appreciative."

"I have to warn you that the immigrants…the Irish and Germans, are not happy working with Negroes and they have started to cause some problems. You'll need to watch out for yourself."

Bess and Stuart rode their horses quietly along the banks of the Mississippi north of their small dock. They could still see the large paddle steamer tied up, loading their cotton for the trip down to New Orleans.

"I always get a kick out of watching those bales of cotton being loaded," Stuart said. "It's the successful end of another year of worry."

"The years have been good overall but we need to talk about the children who soon won't be children any longer. We need to send both Samantha and Samuel off to school. Moss Grove will be lonely without them, but it's time."

"Maybe we'll travel," Stuart said, more thinking out loud than with any conviction.

"I also worry that our daughter needs to meet people beyond Louisiana."

"You've already decided, haven't you?" he laughed, as he got down from his horse. Bess had already gotten down and was sitting on a nearby log. "You've been doing this to me our entire married life," he said lovingly.

"Well, you usually haven't minded," she teased, kissing him on the cheek.

Stuart took the invitation seriously and turned his head to hold and kiss this woman he'd always loved with emotion and tenderness. Bess responded instantly and the two remembered how it felt the first time they'd embraced. The years vanished and they held one another, the only sound the splashing of the water as boats moved along the river.

"Both schools we should consider are in New York. The first is Hunter College, and the other is Barnard. I was distressed to learn how many wouldn't accept a Jewish girl. Of the two I think Barnard would be best, it's affiliated with Columbia University, and I'm hoping we can get Samuel accepted to Columbia."

"And what do you want them to study, where do you want them to work, and who should they marry?" Stuart laughed. Any thought of winning an argument from his wife had long since disappeared.

"They can live their own lives, and I won't interfere, but only after they get a good education."

"And you won't push them a little to a particular direction?" he smiled.

"Well, maybe a slight nudge," she admitted.

Samantha and Samuel would be going off to school and it was time to celebrate. Families from nearby plantations, from Baton Rouge's Jewish congregation, and long time friends from New

Orleans congregated to wish the two of them success and bon voyage.

"Imagine, Samantha, the Army is letting out a contract to purchase airplanes for the first time in its history and Glenn Curtiss' plane has already proven it can out fly the new Wright brothers plane. Isn't this all impossibly exciting?"

David Anthony was a year older than Samantha, tall and lanky with a cowlick that had its own mind. He, his sister, and their parents had driven up from Baton Rouge in a new Oldsmobile motor car with its novel curved dash. It made so much noise it scared some of the horses off the road. It wasn't much of a road north of Baton Rouge and it was almost impossible for these new cars to traverse once the rains started. "Come With Me in my Merry Oldsmobile" was a hit song with lyrics everyone could sing easily.

The Anthonys were part of a small coterie of Jewish families who had known Ruth and Eli Fineman since the Civil War days. Many of them had been present at Stuart's Bar Mitzvah years earlier and the families continued to share in one another's joys and sorrows.

The elder Anthonys had always hoped for a marriage between their son and Samantha, but living fifty miles apart, there was little they could do unless an opportunity presented itself. The Anthonys knew their son was a little gawky and uncomfortable around girls. His brown hair seemed to move in every direction at the same time and he didn't quite fit in his body, but he was sweet, and bright, and exuded a constant energy when he spoke. One would have never guessed him to be Jewish except for a more than prominent nose.

"I don't know anything about airplanes, David. Have you ever gone flying?" Samantha asked.

"No, not many people have, but if the Army is going to buy airplanes and they'll be looking for people to fly them. I hope to be one of the men they select."

"There aren't many Jews in the Army, David," Samuel said, joining the couple with glasses of punch for everyone.

"I'd lie if I had to," he admitted.

"Make sure you don't get into the shower with the other men. I doubt any of them have been circumcised," Samuel laughed, and Samantha blushed.

"Actually, I never thought of that," David admitted. "I guess I'll have to learn to fly some other way. I understand you'll be going to Barnard, Samantha, and Samuel, you're heading for Columbia."

"Yes, we're fleeing the Moss Grove coop."

"New York is amazing," David said. "I saw more people on the streets of the city than live in all of Baton Rouge. It's even bigger than New Orleans and everyone is rushing pell-mell, speaking languages I'd never heard before."

"We had a relative who lived there but now I understand he's moved to Washington so we won't know anyone there," Samantha admitted.

"You'll both make friends in a jiffy, and I'm nearby in New Jersey at Yale. I get to the city about once a month. Maybe we can see one another?" he asked this unusual girl, hopefully.

"Of course," she answered.

"I think I'll leave you two and find a conversation where I'm not a third wheel," Samuel said, bowing unnecessarily.

"Bess, I think I'm going to open a cotton mill," Stuart said, sitting at his desk piled high with papers.

The party had ended and both Sam and Samuel were well on their way to New York and the next phase of their lives.

"What happened to the quiet house…travel…just you and me?" Bess asked, not surprised at Stuart's continued restlessness.

"Listen, we produce the cotton, sometimes we get a good price, sometimes we don't. If we sent the cotton to our own mill we could make a lot more money. That's what a lot of the plantations over in Mississippi are doing. There's still good labor around. What do you think?"

"Frankly, dear husband, I worry about the risk of starting a new business that we know nothing about. It will also mean more pressure here at Moss Grove once you have to divide your attention."

"Look, there is a large mill in New Orleans owned by a man named Charles Maginnis. He owns all sorts of businesses in the city. Let's you and I take a few days, enjoy the city, and see if we can get a walk through. Then we can decide."

Stuart and Bess decided to drive. It wouldn't be any faster but he wanted to show that he was a modern sort of a man. He had a flashy Ford Model K with its unique white tires and polished brass headlights. He was sure he could go as fast as ten miles an hour if he found a decent stretch of road.

When Maginnis learned that some of the cotton he was using came from Moss Grove he was eager to meet the planter. Perhaps there were ways to improve the growing or baling process that could make his mill run better.

"Mr. Fineman, how nice to meet you. Mrs. Fineman, I didn't know you'd be here. Perhaps you'd like to wait for us in my office rather than tramp through a large dirty factory? I can have refreshments brought."

"Not at all, Mr. Maginnis. My husband and I share the management of Moss Grove. I even ran the plantation when he went off to war."

"Alright then," he said, a little nonplussed. "Let us proceed."

Once they left the large yard where the bales were received, the air was fetid and the wooden floors were oil soaked from lubricants.

"We need to unpack and clean the cotton we get from you and the other planters. We fluff it the best we can and put it into this vacuum tube where it gets to our lappers. Those are the workers who feed it into other machines that will convert the cotton bolls into a loosely compacted rope coil."

"Those people you have are pretty young to be working such machines," Bess shouted over the factory noise.

"We have some young and some old, Mrs. Fineman. We don't care about their age as long as they're good workers. Let's continue."

Stuart smiled and grabbed his wife's hand. He'd already realized that opening a cotton mill was not something he'd consider after seeing what was involved but he was entranced by Bess's seriousness. The large number of children working in the factory breathing the cotton fibers was upsetting her.

"Over here we continue to force the fibers into longer and stronger threads where they can eventually be put onto large bobbins."

They continued to walk, finding children of all ages, moving slowly. They were all dirty, some barefoot, most underfed.

"Over here we have the weave room where we run some of the yarn lengthwise. That's called the warp. We interlace these threads with other threads running crosswise. Those are called the weft. At the end we have fabric," he smiled, as if conducting a class.

"What's that overhead?" Stuart asked.

"Those are yarns that we pass through a bath of hot starch and oil. Then we dry them over steam heated drums before being put on looms. We can make sheeting, or more complex patterns, depending on how we set up the loom but that's basically it. It isn't complicated, really, but our people need to pay a lot of attention to detail."

Bess went off on her own, away from the men and Maginnis' glare.

"Hello," she said to a young girl pulling loose threads from the loom. "Isn't that dangerous, getting so close to all those moving parts?"

The girl nodded, embarrassed to be talking with the pretty, well-dressed woman.

"Please, Mrs. Fineman," Maginnis said, frustrated with his guest's wife. "I'd appreciate it if you didn't disturb the workers."

They exited the factory and the din of the machines subsided.

"Thanks, Mr. Maginnis. We appreciate the tour."

"My pleasure…"

"Why is it necessary to have so many children? They are so young." Bess interrupted. "It has to be dangerous, breathing that air and the loud noises can make them deaf."

"We don't do anything different from other mills. There isn't much margin for profit. We do what we do to keep our costs down. Parents bring in their children to work. We don't ask them. They need the children's wages to support their families. Now, if you'll excuse me, I have other obligations. Thank you again for coming. My manager will show you out."

Maginnis turned and walked away, fuming at being questioned in his own factory.

"The effrontery of that woman," he mumbled.

Bess and Stuart drove to a small café and relaxed at an outdoor table.

"I don't think we'll be invited back," Stuart laughed. "You riled him up pretty good.

"Stuart, how would you like Samantha working in a place like that when she was a child? I saw one young girl with a crutch and another with only one arm. There's danger in those machines for the soft bones of children."

"OK, we won't open a cotton mill. Are you happy now?"

"Did you notice that none of the blacks were working on the machines? All the blacks were either lifting the bales or stoking the fires... the lowest paying jobs."

"It makes working at Moss Grove look pretty good, doesn't it?"

"Yes, it does. Now, we have time until dinner. Why don't you take me back to the hotel and ravish me?"

"You don't need to ask me twice," Stuart said, standing, and throwing some bills on the table.

Chapter Twenty-Four

Samantha and Samuel stared, their mouths agape, at the huge ceiling and clock in Grand Central Station. Two porters trailed behind them with their luggage.

"My God, Samuel, have you ever seen anything so enormous?"

"Let's get rid of all these suitcases, get settled in, and meet tomorrow for lunch. What do you think?" he asked.

Samantha and her several bags stored in all niches of a taxi, headed toward Morningside Heights, along the upper Hudson River toward Barnard, while Samuel took another taxi with his two smaller valises and followed the same route toward the adjoining Columbia University campus.

There was a vibrancy that one felt walking the streets and avenues of New York City. The bustling metropolis with new tall buildings going up every week mirrored most of the country. It was 1910 and the United States was rapidly closing in on a population of 100 million. The Federal Government had declared war on large corporate monopolies, such as U.S. Steel and Standard Oil, using the Sherman Anti-Trust law to break them up. New inventions were changing everyday life… the telephone, the phonograph, street lights, and movie theatres. Professional athletic teams provided a new form of entertainment. Gas powered engines were making automobiles practical, and signaling the death knell of

*transportation by horse and carriage. Immigrants poured
through Ellis Island and crowded the tenements around
Mulberry Street. Nearly all had wept openly as they sailed
into New York harbor past the Statue of Liberty.*

"Where shall we go first?" Samantha asked, a scarf around her
neck, her cheeks flushed, and her red hair tucked under a green
bonnet. It was early autumn and there was a crispness and a chill
in the air that they'd never felt at Moss Grove.

"Let's go through the park and walk down Fifth Avenue. If
we're hungry there are plenty of cafes. C'mon, dear cousin. It is a
bright autumn Sunday. Let's you and I introduce ourselves to New
York," Samuel said, grabbing her gloved hand.

Samuel loved his red-haired cousin. He imagined that he
always had, and always would. It was a damn fool notion that
cousins couldn't marry but the taboo was so fixed in his family's
mind that all he could do was love her chastely.

Couples criss-crossed the paths as they walked. The grass was
still heavy with morning dampness. Dogs yelped as their owners
threw sticks for them to chase. Baby buggies were as common
as the sound of birds chirping overhead. Occasionally a gaggle
of geese, heading south, flew overhead, their broad white wings
silhouetted against the blue sky.

The cheery couple exited the park near the Plaza. Most of the
stores were closed but their windows shouted new fashions and
products that every home needed. They bought hot chocolate from
a street vendor and smelled the roasting chestnuts. A few blocks
away they could hear drums and shouting.

"Let's go see what the fuss is," Sam shouted, jumping in glee.
"It sounds like a parade."

"Or a demonstration," Samuel warned. "I don't want us around
any lunatic anarchists. There's always violence when those crazies
show up."

"Well, if we don't go, we won't know," she insisted.

As they reached 57th Street they saw a group of about fifty
women marching, keeping step with a huge bass drum in their
midst. Most of them carried signs, 'Women Have the Right to

Vote,' said one. 'Give Our Mother the Vote' with a picture of young children, said another.

They stopped to watch. On the sidewalks men shouted insults, some crude.

"Go home, lady. Your husband has a hard-on and needs you."

"Your husbands' brings home the family's money. He's entitled to vote."

"But I work," one of the women shouted back. "I work in a sweat shop, with no rights. Why is that fair?"

"Let's go," Samuel said. "These women are just trouble-makers."

Samantha put her hands on her hips and stared at him.

"How can you say that? My mother ran Moss Grove by herself when my father went off to Cuba. And her mother held the entire family together. She faced Indians in Kansas and dragged three children off to California."

"OK," he conceded. "We'll give you and your mother the vote but most women just cook and iron and raise their children. They have little knowledge, and less interest, in what is important in an election."

"And the men who sip beer all day in the tavern, are they aware of your 'issues'?"

"Do you want to continue walking along 5th Avenue or stand here and debate?" he asked.

"Let's meet in Little Italy at Tony's. I want to talk to some of these women," she said, kissing her friend on the cheek and scurrying off before he could object.

"Stay out of trouble," he shouted. He remembered Stuart complaining that he'd never won an argument with his wife and it was clear their daughter was just as headstrong.

"Excuse me," Sam shouted as she joined the throng of women marching to the west side along 57th. "I've just arrived in the city. I'm enrolled at Barnard College and I might want to enlist in your cause."

"Welcome, Miss....?"

"My name is Samantha Fineman. I'm from Louisiana. My friends call me Sam."

"Well, then I'll just call you Sam. I'm Harriot Stanton Blatch and that woman leading our tiny parade is Alice Stone Blackwell. Come, march with us, it's only a few more blocks. Then I'll introduce you to some of the ladies and we'll have something warm to drink."

Sam was handed a placard and moved along, getting smiles from a number of the other women who ranged in age from teenage girls to grey-haired grandmothers. They ignored the jeers and acknowledged the cheers of the crowds that lined the street. Sam noticed that many men supported the right of women to vote and as many women were opposed to it. The latter confused her. There weren't many Negroes on the sidewalks and those she did see seemed to remain mute, reluctant to voice either their support or disdain.

"Barnard is a fine college. What do you intend to study?" Alice Blackwell asked.

"I'd like to study medicine, maybe become a doctor." It was the first time Sam had actually verbalized her thoughts, and hearing her say it aloud added a conviction she wasn't certain she'd actually felt.

"Alice's mother was the first woman to graduate from a college in Massachusetts."

"And my aunt was the first woman in the country to graduate from a medical school," the middle age Blackwell announced. She was a stern looking woman, her hair parted in the middle and pulled tight on each side, held in place by large pins. She had a prominent nose and, had it not been for her piercing dark eyes, and stern brows, she might have been dismissed as insignificant. But, no one who met Alice Stone Blackwell ever accused her of being insignificant."

"And Harriot, why does your name sound so familiar?" Sam asked, feeling the warmth of the coffee dim the chill of the morning's walk.

"You probably heard of my mother, Elizabeth Cady Stanton. She was one of our movement's early voices, back before the Civil War. She taught me that women have equal rights with men and I've never retreated from that position. I'm proud to say I organized the Equality League of Self-Supporting Woman that became the

Women's Political Movement. We have more than twenty thousand members, mostly from the lower east side, girls who work in the sewing trade or in laundries…terrible sweat shop conditions. We hold our parades here and in other cities at least once a month."

"What can I do? I don't know how much time I'll have with all my studies, but I am willing." Sam said, convinced she had found a cause worth supporting.

"We can certainly use more Barnard students to march with us. We have a few from Hunter College but any woman with enough gumption to attend college certainly deserves the right to vote, don't you think?" Harriot Blatch offered.

In any other setting Harriot Stanton Blatch would be mistaken for a middle-class matron. She wore a thin veil over her hat and shoulders. She was heavy and only walked short distances during the parade, preferring to ride in her open four seat roadster.

"I didn't see any black women marching," Sam said. "Don't you have support among the Negros?"

"We do, substantial support, but they get nervous marching. Every time they tried marching in Mississippi the Klan came out and the women got beaten up and thrown in jail."

"We have nothing like this in Louisiana, even in New Orleans."

"Negro civil rights is as big a struggle as Women's Rights," Alice Blackwell acknowledged, "but it is naïve to believe we can combine them without losing both battles. White southern women are just awakening to their rights. Our goals here in the north and out west must remain focused.

"Sam, I want to introduce you to Carrie Catt. She is one of our very talented group who knows how to mobilize support here in New York. She can give you help at Barnard."

"You're going to be a suffragette?" Samuel laughed. "You are one crazy woman, but your mother and grandmother would be proud of your lunacy. You have years of college ahead of you. Why waste your time now on a cause that doesn't help you?"

"You wouldn't understand. You're a man. You get born with all these special privileges just because you have a penis and hair on your chest. More and more women have to work to support their families, so lighten up, and get some of your new friends at Columbia to help us."

Stephen and Thaddeus were playing catch in the park. The trees around them had dropped most of their leaves and covered the ground with a blanket of crisp brown that crunched when you walked. With the trees bare it was easy to see the Capitol building and the White House across the Potomac. There was a fresh bite in the air that foretold that winter was around the corner.

"Hey, not so hard," Stephen shouted as he shook his hand, trying to shake off the sting from the hard baseball he'd just caught.

"Don't be a sissy, Dad," Thaddeus laughed. "That isn't even my fastball."

"Keep it up and we'll get you a tryout with one of the professional teams."

"Negro leagues, maybe," Thaddeus nodded. "A lot of their players are better than the men who play for the Phillies or the Giants."

"I'd rather have you thinking about school than baseball as a career," he said, throwing the ball back. "Let's sit for awhile. My hand is still stinging from 'it isn't your fastball.'"

"Is it hard to be surrounded by mostly black friends when your friends in New York were mostly white?" Stephen asked as they rested on a park bench. They could begin to see their breaths condense into small clouds. The temperature was continuing to drop.

"It's different, I admit. The kids here are a little nicer, actually. They aren't so pretentious...not so worried about what they're wearing. But mostly the boys are trying to figure out the girls and the girls are trying to understand the boys...that and our studies, of course."

"Of course," Stephen laughed.

"Dad, are you ever going to tell me what happened with mother? I mean, I miss her. She was there in the morning when I left for school and when I got home she was gone."

"I'm not sure I've really processed it either. I began that same day as a successful reporter for the largest group of newspapers in the country. I had a beautiful wife and a wonderful son. By the time the sun set that evening I still had you but the other two were gone. It was really in the blink of the eye. And I don't want to say bad things about your mother. I loved her and I know she loved us. I have wonderful memories of the three of us when you were younger."

"But what happened?" Thaddeus insisted. "There had to be a reason."

"I met your mother during the war in Cuba. I was covering the war as a reporter. Your Uncle Robert was with me. He's quite dark-skinned. I'm not. We never discussed race or skin color. I was an American reporter, not bad looking, and your mother and I fell in love.

"Then everything collapsed. Mr. Hearst, my boss, met me for the first time and immediately knew I had some Negro blood in me. I'd never hidden it. I guess I can pass as white and maybe, in some hidden recess, I knew I was living a lie. Anyway, when I explained to your mother what happened, she went a little crazy. She claimed I'd lied to her all these years and she didn't want anything to do with someone who had black blood in their veins. Since you do as well, she left. She just wasn't able to deal with it."

"Do you think she'll ever miss us enough to come back?"

"Thaddeus, I'd love nothing more than to say 'yes,' but I'm not sure."

"Are all adults hung up about skin color?"

"In this country it's all too common. You know that. They fought a civil war over slavery. Your great grandfather, Henry Rogers, was killed for pretending to be white after it was discovered he had a small amount of black blood coursing through his veins. It was a long time ago...just after the Civil War and the Southern whites were pretty unsettled about losing their slave labor. I'm afraid you're classified as colored, not Negro, and not White. Another name for people like us is mulatto, but whatever it is, you need to grow up to be you with no apologies and no shame. Only ignorant people measure a person by the color of their skin. Now, enough lessons, let's go have a hot chocolate. I'm still cold and my hand still stings from your 'it wasn't a fast ball.'"

"Did you see the *New York Post*?" Robert asked, handing a copy of the two day old paper to Stephen.

"No. I try not to read newspapers that don't have articles I've written prominently displayed."

"Then you probably don't read a lot of newspapers," Robert teased. "I get them all at the Library of Congress and I scan them. That's how I found the small paragraph on page seven."

Charles Taylor Marries Fashion Model

Charles Taylor, Vice-President of Lord & Taylor, announced his marriage to Alicia Hernandez, formerly Alicia Carmody. Mr. Taylor is scion and heir apparent to the successful retail chain. Mrs. Carmody, recently divorced, was a successful model in Havana, Cuba, before migrating to the United States. The couple will be honeymooning in Bermuda, accompanied by the groom's sister, Mrs. Jenna Taylor French.

"Did you know Alicia had divorced you?" Robert asked as Stephen read and reread the newspaper clipping.

"Not really. And Thaddeus asked if there was any chance of his mother returning to us. I guess this answers it."

"So, is Alicia with Charlie or Jenna, would you imagine?"

"It could be either or both. It's an attribute of my ex-wife I'd never imagined."

David Anthony left his Yale campus as quickly as he could most Fridays to meet Samantha in New York City. He had never met anyone else quite like her growing up among Baton Rouge's small Jewish enclave. She had an energy and determination missing from every one of the other girls he'd known. Those girls had all made it clear as soon as they reached their sixteenth birthday that they were husband hunting, and their sexual fondling and fumbling was limited to encouraging some boy barely out of his teens to propose marriage for the sole purpose of having sex. Not me, David thought to himself. And then, along came Samantha, bright red hair, green eyes, and a smile that wilted flowers just beginning to bloom. She didn't want marriage, at least not yet. His friends told him he was smitten. Maybe he was. He wanted to share his passion for flying and airplanes. He wasn't sure which was more exhilarating, Sam or wandering through the clouds.

"There are things I want to do and places I want to see before I concern myself with a husband and having children," she stated with absolute, no room for margin, conviction.

"Well, I don't want to get married yet either," David agreed. "I want to fly airplanes. Imagine, Sam, the air rushing by you, dancing in and out of the clouds, with only the sound of your engine interrupting the silence. I'm going to Nova Scotia in a few months. I got accepted to work with a small group that Alexander Graham Bell is financing to build flying machines. I'll get to work with Glenn Curtiss and two talented engineering graduates from the University of Toronto, named McCurdy and Baldwin. It's really exciting."

"I thought the Wright brothers were the only ones making flying machines."

"Apparently Wilbur and Orville are very secretive. They don't want to work with anyone else, so Dr. Bell and these people organized a group called the Aerial Experiment Association."

"I admire your passion, David, but there are things I want to do closer to the ground. I intend to become a doctor."

"Is that before or after you secure the vote for women?" he teased.

"Don't get me started. You sound like Samuel. And speaking of my cousin, where is he?"

"Samuel has a date. He wouldn't tell me more," David said.

"Well, I'm happy for him. Now, where are we going?"

"We're going to have dinner and then we're going to see the new Ziegfeld show with Bert Williams. I want to celebrate my going to Canada and I want to share it with you," David said with a tenderness in his voice that made Sam smile.

Samuel really didn't have a date. Without telling Sam or any of his new friends from Columbia, he had been learning to play the trumpet that Stephen had saved from the earthquake and brought him from San Francisco. It was his last, and only, remaining connection to his father. He could almost feel the man's presence whenever he pressed the keys and pressed his lips to the mouthpiece. It was as if he was channeling his father through the music.

Harlem had become his destination. There were strings of small clubs around 125th Street. More than once he'd walked in, st in a corner, just listening, and when the band took a break, ask if he could join them for a set.

"You white," they'd always start with. "Why you want to play in a black club?"

"White groups don't play the music I like. My father always played in black clubs in San Francisco and New Orleans. He'd come home and tell me about the music and the rhythms. That's all I ever heard...all I want to play."

"Well, if you can blow that thing, we can always use more brass."

At the beginning, he was always a half-beat late coming in and the Negro piano player would smile condescendingly.

"Pick it up, kid, pick it up!" he'd tease.

Eventually he got it right and he'd blow through all his anger.

I lost my father, he thought, suddenly dropping an entire octave. Then my mother found him and we were all reunited and happy. This happier memory got him back to the proper note. Then I lost both my parents in the fucking earthquake and I was almost killed, buried in the debris. Samuel felt his heartbeat speed up and struggled to keep his mind on the right key. What a miserable way to remember your childhood, he concluded.

Clarence Temple, the piano player at Bessie's, became his friend and mentor. They'd go have coffee once the clubs wound down. Clarence walked with a noticeable limp, a gift from a club swung with a vengeance when he was thirteen and helping to pick up books a white girl dropped.

"Where'd you learn to play piano?" Samuel asked. The streets were drenched from a heavy rainfall that was in its third straight day. Even slow moving automobiles splashed rain onto people crowding the sidewalk. All the subways and trains were running late, and the crowd, especially for a Saturday night, had been light.

Clarence was as black as the night and as shiny as the street lights reflecting off the wet, tarred pavement.

"Jackson, Mississippi, a black hell hole of a town. Those white assholes think they won the Civil War, and all blacks are 'niggers' that should still be the property of their white masters. I caught the first train out of there when I was twelve, got a job in a brothel in Chicago and, with a little help, learned how to play. Got married, had a son. When he was six he was trampled by a runaway horse. He'd be about your age right now. He had your smile and your love for music."

"And your wife? What happened to her?"

"Took to drinkin' after our boy died. Eventually it killed her but I was gone by then."

Samuel had already shared the story of how he'd lost his parents. He wanted to tell Clarence that he, too, had a strain of black blood in him but the words wouldn't come out. They just gagged in his throat.

At first there was just smoke, and then you could see flames exploding inside through the dirty windows. Onlookers stood at the corner of Green Street and Washington Square as the upper floors of the Asch Building burned. The Triangle Shirt Factory occupied the 8th, 9th, and 10th floors. They manufactured women's blouses. The normal work week was nine hours, Monday through Friday and seven hours on Saturday.

It was a cold and blustery Saturday afternoon in March and the streets were littered with shoppers bundled against the chill, while the workday for the mostly immigrant women in the building was just ending.

A small fire erupted in a trash bin under one of the cutting tables on the 8th floor. Probably one of the fabric cutters sneaking a cigarette, but no one would ever be sure. There were plenty of exits, a fire escape, freight elevators and stairways, but they were quickly filled with smoke and flames, preventing those on the 9th and 10th floors from descending.

One hundred forty six men and women died from the fire. Some leapt to their deaths, others died of asphyxiation.

Stephen had taken the train to New York to report on the tragedy. He doubted there were more than a few of the dead who were colored, but this was a national story and, black or white, he wanted to cover it.

He wanted to interview Rose Schneiderman, head of the ILGWU, the International Ladies Garment Worker's Union. He was in the audience when she spoke to a huge gathering about the fire:

> 'This is not the first time girls have been burned alive in the city. Every week I must learn of the untimely death of one of my sister workers. Every year thousands of us are maimed. The life of men and women is so cheap and property is so sacred. There are so many of us for one job it matters little if 146 of us are burned to death.
>
> We have tried you citizens; we are trying you now, and you have a couple of dollars for the sorrowing mothers, brothers and sisters by way of a charity gift. But every time the workers come out in the only way they know to protest against conditions which are unbearable the strong hand of the law is allowed to press down heavily upon us.'

"Stephen, is that you?" a pretty pink-faced girl shouted at him, pushing her way through the crowd.

"Samantha, my God, what are you doing here?" he asked, hugging his young niece protectively.

"I could ask you the same thing. All of us girls who support the right of women to vote have united with the union. The fire was a terrible tragedy but it has brought a new awareness to the working conditions of women."

"Well, I'm proud of you. I'll make sure that point gets into my story."

"The last I'd heard you and Alicia were separated and you'd taken Thaddeus down to Washington."

"How about I fill you in over dinner? I have another interview with Rose Schneiderman and some other women after this gathering. You're welcome to join me."

"Wonderful, I'd love that and it will give you a chance to see my friend, David."

"Serious?"

Samantha just smiled and a dimple in her right cheek flashed brightly.

Sam sat quietly to one side as Rose and two other women focused their attention on Stephen. He was as handsome as ever and women of all ages were attracted to him.

"It isn't just the Triangle fire that upsets us," Rose said. She had a stern face, rarely smiling. Her stringy brown hair was pulled back in a bun and it was clear that this was a no-nonsense woman who would take no prisoners in support of her cause.

"Twenty-five women were killed in a similar fire in Newark last month and more will be killed next month, and the month after that, if we don't change the mindset of these factory owners and politicians."

"Rose, this is Samantha Fineman. She's my niece from Louisiana. She's enrolled at Barnard."

"Another female Jewish college student! Good! How do you do, Miss Fineman? Are you for women's suffrage?"

"Of course. I'm working with Carrie Catt. Harriot Blatch put us together to encourage support at the college."

"Then I welcome you to our struggle. It will be a lengthy battle, I'm afraid. We're trying to overcome two thousand years of entrenched belief that men are superior in all things. And I'm afraid us women have encouraged that falsehood. We'll need to change that mindset as well."

Stephen, Samantha, and David met for dinner at a small bistro, Ricky's, in Greenwich Village.

"Are you still interested in airplanes?" Stephen asked.

"More than ever! I even changed my major at Yale to engineering, although they don't have any books or professors who even have the slightest interest in anything that isn't bolted to the ground. They're more into building bridges or tunnels. When I tell them I'd rather build a machine to fly over them they just scoff at me."

"I think it's very exciting. How does one go about learning to fly or build a machine that will fly? Except for the Wright brothers in Dayton, has anyone else accomplished the feat? I saw their flight, if you can call it that. It was on some sand dunes in North Carolina back in 1903. I'm sure it was an amazing accomplishment but since then I've heard very little."

"Oh, there has been a great deal of progress. It might seem like a lot of small steps but now both the Wrights and a group supported by Dr. Bell and his wife have flown more than twenty miles...twenty miles in a machine that's heavier than air," he repeated, his eyes agleam with excitement. "Now that's progress. His plane is called the Silver Dart. Their aeroplane took off from a frozen lake up in Nova Scotia...they even carried a passenger. He designed something called ailerons that help the plane turn and fly level. There are a number of groups in France and elsewhere in Europe all making constant improvements. I tell you, Stephen, flying is the future."

"I'm sorry you aren't enthusiastic," Stephen teased. "Perhaps I'll go with you and see for myself. I'm sure it will make an interesting story for my papers."

"So," Samantha interjected, "You got fired from your job because they found out you're colored?"

"Apparently Mr. Hearst was embarrassed to find out one of his star reporters was less than lily-white."

"I assume he doesn't employ any Jews either," David added.

"I'm sure he doesn't."

"Anyway, I met Robert's boss at the Library of Congress and he organized several Negro newspapers around the country to support my salary and travel, so now I write for them. Their readers in St. Louis or Pittsburgh are supposed to be impressed that their local paper has a national correspondent."

"And Thaddeus? How is he coping without his mother? I would have thought Alicia would want to keep him even though you and she separated."

"Sam, it was the strangest thing. First, I find her in bed with her boss's sister doing things I've never imagined women doing. Then she goes on a rant that she never knew I had some Negro blood, and walks out shouting she wants nothing to do with either Thaddeus or me."

"I'm so sorry," she said, putting her hand on her Uncle's, distraught at hearing of his recent traumas.

"Thaddeus seems to be handling it well. Maria, Ruth, and Noah are there so he has sort of inherited a new family to be with when I travel. Now, let's eat, I'm starved."

"The food's good," Samantha said, having put away a half side of baby back ribs. "These ribs remind me of Moss Grove. My father was always particular about the smoke house, always experimenting with different wood smells. His favorite was maple. How did you manage to select this particular restaurant?"

"You'll see in a few minutes," Stephen said mysteriously.

A piano began tickling out a simple ragtime number. He was joined by a quick-fingered drummer and a bass. It was good music...happy music, with a lively beat, and then a trumpet player entered, and filled what was the last remaining two feet of the small stage. Sam put down her cup and gaped. Her gape turned into a wide grin, and she met Stephen's smile. It was Samuel and he was playing as if he had entered another dimension. The three diners, forks in midair, stopped eating and listened, entranced. None of them had ever heard Sam play. They knew his father, Josiah, was an avid musician, but this was a surprise, a very pleasant one.

When the set ended, Samuel joined them, grinning from New Jersey to Long Island.

"Sam," Samantha stood and hugged this handsome man she would have been happy to love if it had been permitted. "Why have you kept this a secret? You're really talented."

Everyone nodded and the four of them sat together, thrilled at this unplanned reunion.

"I didn't want anyone to know," Samuel admitted. "I never thought I was very good. Mostly I've been sitting in with groups in Harlem, small Negro combos. I met this amazing piano player, Clarence Temple, and he's been showing me how to do some tricky things with my breath. It's made a big difference. I ran into Stephen one night and he got me this gig."

"Are you still taking your classes at Columbia?" David asked.

"I am, although my grades are terrible. Instead of studying in the evenings I wander until I can find some group to sit in with. I know it isn't smart but playing has become really important to me."

Chapter Twenty-Five

Stephen decided to join David's adventure in Nova Scotia. Maria and Robert continued to have Thaddeus share their home and the three children got along famously, particularly Noah, who was glad to have another boy to help shelter him against the aggressions of his older sister. It was easy to see that he would soon be bigger and stronger, but Ruth's charm and obstinacy always seemed to assure her getting her way.

They agreed that David would leave Yale and meet Stephen at New York's Grand Central Station so they could travel the rest of the way together. David had arranged a formal interview with Glenn Curtiss for a job making improvements to the Silver Dart flying machine.

It wouldn't be easy to reach Beinn Bhreagh. The very tiny village was located on a peninsula in Nova Scotia where Dr. Bell and his wife were also building an experimental hydrofoil boat. They had discovered the area on a sailing vacation a decade earlier and bought land there. For more than a hundred years prior to that it had been a sleepy fishing village with less than twenty families calling it home.

Stephen was hoping to get an interview and a few pictures. If he was lucky he might even be able to meet Dr. Alexander Bell. The famous man wasn't camera shy, but he was known to be unwilling to discuss any new inventions. Three days and four trains later, the two men climbed down onto a wooden platform and found themselves at a tiny railroad siding. A car and driver were waiting. Thank goodness for telegraph service since Dr. Bell's new telephones hadn't yet reached this outpost.

"How do you do, Mr. Curtiss? I'm David Anthony. I sent you a letter offering my services. I'm an engineering student at Yale and I want to fly."

"Yes, Mr. Anthony. I'm glad you've arrived. We have a great deal of work to do this summer. But I didn't expect you to bring anyone with you."

"I'm Stephen Carmody, Mr. Curtiss. I'm a reporter for a series of newspapers, and a friend of David. I was hoping to spend some time, and, hopefully, get an interview with you. You've become quite the celebrity now that you are now the permanent holder of the Scientific America Trophy. Your 135 mile flight, your experimental bombing run, and your other exploits have made you an American hero. The public is interested in anything else in which you might be involved."

"Well, Mr. Carmody," Curtiss laughed. "I was prepared to send you right back to the States, but seeing as how you've done so much homework, and impressed me with how much I've impressed you, I must reconsider. I am insistent, however, that you release no story without my permission. It isn't ego but a great deal of what we do here in quite confidential. We have many other groups chasing the same goals, and there are patent and international concerns we are forced to consider."

"You have my promise, sir!"

"David, this is Eugene Ely, one of my test pilots. Eugene, see if you can teach this young man to fly."

Ely had worked for a man that bought an early Curtiss flying machine and proceeded to crash it. It had taken long months to repair it but once airborne, the young pilot didn't look back and headed for the Midwest and Curtiss' small factory, getting himself a job as a test pilot. He received the 17th license to fly issued by the federal government.

"Have you ever flown before?" Ely asked.

"No, but I've done a lot of studying on the subject."

"Well, keep your head about you when you're in the air. Always know where you'd land if you lose your engine."

"We're doing a lot of work for the U.S. Navy," Curtiss said, nodding agreement. "They're far more interested in aviation than the Army and they're excited enough to fund some of our programs. They were quite impressed when we landed a plane on a ship in San Francisco Bay a few months ago.

"With Dr. Bell's money we established the Aerial Experiment Association with only one goal…to get into the air. Our big effort was with the Silver Dart," Curtiss told Stephen, sitting in his small office. He had taken off his shoes and put his feet up on the desk while balancing a cup of coffee. He was tall with an aggressive receding hairline and a large unkempt bushy mustache.

"We crashed that first plane in '09 but then we built a bi-wing made up of steel tubes and bamboo held together by friction tape. We covered the wings with Japanese silk. Its canard…its elevator, was in front, and we carved the propeller from a single block of wood.

"Pull back on the stick…more, more," Ely shouted. "Use your feet to keep the wings straight. Good! Good! Not too much…you're overcompensating."

David struggled to focus and listen to the shouting coming at him as he taxied the plane along the rough, pebbled ground.

"OK, take it up…get enough speed to let the plane go airborne… back on the stick some more….."

Ely's voice faded in the distance and he appeared to shrink in size as the plane lifted 100, 200, 300 feet into the air. David saw trees in the distance and made a mental calculation on whether he was climbing at enough of an angle to pass over them.

Flying was everything he'd hoped it would be. He was one with the sky and the birds and the heavens. He threw his head back, laughed, and let out a scream that he was sure they could hear on the ground.

He could see Stephen and Curtiss exit the building and join Ely and others. They were waving. Did he dare tip his wings to acknowledge them? Better not. Less than twenty minutes later he skidded to a stop near the hangar.

"You can see the entire peninsula," he grinned. "What a feeling. I knew this is what I was meant to do."

"Nice job. Looks as if we have another test pilot for you, Mr. Curtiss."

"I guess you buy drinks tonight, David."

"My pleasure!"

Four weeks later, in the air again for the fifth time, David was not quite so fortunate. The air was heavy. Rain was forecast for the next day but, ahead of its arrival, the sky had turned dark and the humidity had risen ominously. David struggled to keep his wings level but he could hear the engine sputter, struggling to keep going. His engine died when he was still one hundred feet above the ground on his final approach. The plane had no brakes and he could only hope that he could control his landing by keeping his wings level and allowing the plane to run out. It wasn't to be. His wheels touched and his right tire caught the edge of the runway. The plane spun and flipped over. He sat strapped, upside down, as other members of the team rushed toward him. The danger was fire from fuel leaking from the engine upon impact. David could smell the gasoline and tried to pull himself free, but he was trapped. If anything ignited, he'd be burned alive in minutes.

Stephen and Ely ran full out toward him once they understood the danger. They pulled him out as the plane burst into flames. David could feel his feet burning but he was alive. His right leg was broken in two places. The closest hospital was hours away but the roads were clear and the ambulance made good time.

"My son," David's mother shrieked. "You and your fahr-schtunken flying. Why couldn't you stay on the ground like God intended?"

David's parents had traveled from Baton Rouge when they learned their son had crashed and broken a leg.

"Flying is for goys," his father intoned.

Eugene Ely was sitting quietly in a corner of the room with Stephen when the Anthonys arrived.

"I'm fine. My leg will be as good as new in another month. You didn't have to come all this way. Meanwhile, Mom...Dad...this is my flight instructor, Eugene Ely, and you probably remember Stephen, Aunt Bess' half brother."

"He's a good pilot, Mr. Anthony, and he'll be fine to fly again, if he chooses," Ely half-smiled before standing and saying his good-byes.

"Nothing is going to keep me out of the air. It's magic up there. Dad, would you like me to take you flying? I'm sure I can arrange it when I get released."

"No, thank you. I've lived fifty-five years on the ground and I find it quite sufficient."

David's parents stayed four days and left. Stephen had gotten them a tour of the small enclave where the planes were being built and tested, Mostly the two elderly people just shook their heads in disbelief.

A week later David was discharged and, walking with a slight limp, headed back to Glenn Curtiss' office. He was sitting quietly with the white bearded Alexander Graham Bell across from him.

"Welcome back, Mr. Anthony. You see, Glenn, only the young heal so quickly."

"Dr. Bell, this is an honor. I am a big fan of your accomplishments."

There was a tap on the door and Stephen entered. He and David exchanged smiles.

"Nice to see you vertical, David," he grinned. "Dr. Bell, Mr. Curtiss, nice to see you both. Am I intruding? I can wait outside."

"No," Curtiss said seriously. "I think this concerns the four of us. Please be seated. It's a little cramped. This office was never intended for large meetings. I'll get right to the point.

"David, are you Jewish?"

"Yes, sir!"

"And did you not think to tell us?"

"I never thought it was a consideration."

Curtiss and Bell exchanged glances.

"David, I'm afraid it is a consideration, a very significant consideration," Dr. Bell said, his hand moving instinctively up and down his long beard, his forehead wrinkled in concern.

"Our future depends on the U.S. Navy funding our program. They aren't going to do it if they find out that Jews are involved. The American navy is a white Christian man's organization, as is most of the government. Jews, Negros, even Italians and Germans, are all pretty much excluded."

"But I'm a good pilot," David protested.

"You're a very good pilot," Curtiss agreed. "Ely has nothing but praise for your performance. You handled that plane well in a difficult landing. A lesser man might have ended up dead."

"I won't give up flying," David insisted. "If I can't do it with you, I'll find some place that will accept me."

"And you, Mr. Carmody," Glenn Curtiss said, turning to Stephen. "Are you Jewish, too?"

"No, I'm not," Stephen replied, fearing what might come next.

"But you aren't white, are you?"

"I'm mixed. My mother was white; my father was a mulatto."

"And you write for newspapers around the country?"

"Yes, I believe the current number of newspapers that print my articles is nine."

"And, are any of them white newspapers?" Dr. Bell asked softly.

"I don't really know," Stephen admitted. "Initially three Negro newspapers contracted with me but now there are newspapers in San Diego, Wichita and Portland, and I know nothing about their publishers or their readers."

"Stephen, you are a nice young man and a very good reporter. I had lunch with Mr. Pulitzer last week. I asked him about you and recommended he hire you. He almost choked on his salad before he informed me that you had worked for Mr. Hearst for more than a decade until he met you and discovered you were colored."

"Yes, Mr. Hearst mentioned that Mr. Pulitzer could embarrass him in public for using a reporter that wasn't all white."

"I'm afraid you share David's problem. America isn't ready for either of you. We are glad you've both been with us, but we are forced to move forward without your assistance. Good luck to you both."

The changes of train and the ride back to New York began with both men silent, lost in their individual thoughts, and angry at the senseless bigotry. By the second day, however, they each separately realized that stupidity was an integral part of the human condition. They needed to ignore it and move forward. It was time for their moods to change.

"Fuck 'em," David said. "I got to learn to fly this summer and Jewish or not they can't take that away from me. Stephen, that was the greatest experience of my life. Leaving the ground is breathtaking and it's going to be my life."

"And I got stories that no white reporter got. Black, white, or chartreuse, I let the public know how important flying will be. So, I imagine you'll go back to Yale and get your degree. I'll go back to Washington and regale my young son with tales of flying. For now, let's go to the Pullman car and have a drink...my treat."

The world was moving faster. The winds of change were everywhere. New discoveries...new inventions... innovative ideas! No one seemed satisfied with the way things had been. Progressives and Reformists were overthrowing traditional political bosses. Tammany Hall in New York was weakened by the selection of Franklin Delano Roosevelt as a candidate for the senate. Woodrow Wilson's reforms in New Jersey catapulted him to national prominence. Robert La Follette founded the Progressive Republican Party in Wisconsin. Rockefeller's Standard Oil monopoly was broken up. In Europe, war clouds were beginning to form. Turkey and Italy fought briefly over control of Libya, using airplanes as a weapon of war for the first time. China was in upheaval and Russia was ready to explode.

But in America the old hatreds of those who were different remained. The Italians and Germans, who had immigrated two decades earlier and fought for acceptance, now disparaged the Eastern European Jews and others who poured through Ellis Island. Continual distrust of the Chinese and Japanese existed. Meanwhile Negros and coloreds spread across the country, eager to find acceptance and a better life.

"Thaddeus, you've grown two more inches since I left. Look how short your pants are. We need to buy you new ones."

"I got taller and Ruth now has boobies. Noah and I love to tease her. And I may be getting taller but Noah keeps getting bigger. We can't even trade clothes anymore."

Robert and Maria stood to the side, laughing, as they watched Stephen hurl his son into the air.

It was good to be home, Stephen realized.

"I've brought you airplane model kits. You can each build a different type of airplane. We can work on them together. I watched airplanes fly and you'd never think those lumbering things would take off but their engine roars, the plane slides along a level path, called a runway, and pretty soon its wheels aren't on the ground anymore, its tires are spinning in space."

"Is flying only for boys, Uncle Stephen?" Ruth asked. The girl was growing into a stunner.

He looked at her and thought of Rachel, the girl's birth mother. She had the same dark hair, which curled long down her neck and her shoulders. She had an unusually athletic body for a girl, but it seemed to do nothing to diminish her femininity. She had soft tapered fingers and she was beginning to develop curves and the breasts that Thaddeus had teased about. Her dark brown eyes shined brightly with curiosity about everything, except boys, which she knew were alien creatures. There was a café au lait tinge to her skin that made her seem erotic, even in her teen years. She was much lighter than her dark skinned father, her half brother, or the Cuban woman she believed to be her mother. Together they formed an exciting pallet.

"At this point it's pretty dangerous. Even David, Samantha's friend, crashed and nearly killed himself. Maybe someday."

"That's what adults say when they don't want you to do or try something…someday. It's supposed to end the discussion," she said, turning to her brother, Noah, who nodded in child-like agreement.

"What do you plan to do now?" Robert asked.

"Getting to know my son again is my first priority. Then I'm thinking of going to Chicago. I'd like to meet Robert Abbott who publishes the *Chicago Defender*. He's contacted me several times about my articles."

"Does he like them?"

"Not always. He wants more interracial stories. He wants my stories to help end discrimination in the country. That's not always an easy thing to accomplish when you are trying to write objectively. Anyway, first, how about I take all three kids to the zoo this weekend?"

The svelte, middle age black woman, trademark red feather in her hair, stood just off the stage, watching the musicians play. That white trumpet player has a style that seemed so familiar, she thought...the way he crooked his small finger, the way his eyebrows rose on a particularly complicated chord, but most of all the ice blue eyes that stared through the music. She wondered what they were seeing.

Sisseretta Jones had aged. She was no longer the star attraction, the diva of black shows. Now she was a faint shadow that the older customers remembered and the younger ones never knew. She waited for the first set to end. Her vocals weren't due until the second set.

"You're new, aren't you, white boy...and young?"

"I've heard of you Miss Jones, but I thought you were much younger," he retorted sarcastically.

"I deserved that," she laughed. "I'm Sisseretta Jones. And you are?"

"Sam Rogers!"

"And where are you from, Sam Rogers?"

"Here, there, and a few stops in between," he said, picking up his trumpet and blowing out a few drops of saliva that had gathered.

"I'll be nice if you'll be nice, especially since we'll be working together. Let's try again. Where are you from?"

"Born in New Orleans...."

"I knew it," she interrupted. "I think I knew your father. But his name was Williams...Josiah Williams. He also played the trumpet...and he had the same blue eyes as you, eyes that cut through to your soul."

"My name is Rogers, not Williams," Samuel said, knowing that his father had called himself Josiah Williams when they'd lived in New Orleans. He was very young then and never quite understood why his father had changed their name.

"And you think you knew my father how?" Sam asked suspiciously. His father was wealthy and proper and loved his mother.

Sisseretta stopped. She could see distrust in the young man's eyes and if she continued it wouldn't do either of them any good. This boy had a half-sister, Lily, who was almost the same age. That Josiah had been one rutting bull, that was for sure. What do I do now, she asked herself.

"He came to see my show in New Orleans. It looked as if he was entertaining some business gentlemen," she lied. "They came backstage to commend me for a wonderful performance. We had sold out the theatre for better part of a week. My dressing room was so filled with flowers I barely had room to sit. I remembered him because of those magic eyes of his."

"But you called him by his first name, and…" he added. "You knew that he played the trumpet. All that couldn't have happened in your dressing room."

"No, I met him again at a brothel where I performed. He was there playing the trumpet. He liked to sit in, not unlike what you're doing tonight."

Samuel wanted to ask if there was more, but he wasn't sure he wanted to know.

"Let's start. Give me an intro to Alexander's Ragtime Band. That should get their attention and we'll see how good a trumpet you can blow." She smiled. Best to leave some things in the past, tossed on the trash heap of what was. Leave it for what it was, a memory of something that should never have been more than an incident.

"I'm going to the Democratic convention in Baltimore," Stuart announced as he and Bess got ready for bed. The house was quiet with the grown children off to college…sometimes too quiet.

"Am I supposed to be impressed?" Bess teased, actually quite impressed.

"Remember Champ Clark? He's that Congressman who is also Speaker of the House. He stopped by Moss Grove for a night last year. He was heading south to Baton Rouge and New Orleans, trying to gauge his popularity to run for President. He even met with the Jewish congregation in Baton Rouge. It was the first time any candidate running for state office had done that. The members donated a substantial amount to his campaign and, in gratitude; a few of us were named as delegates. Yours truly, I am pleased to say, is one of them." Stuart stripped off his shirt and rippled his chest to his wife's good natured laughter.

"Not bad for a more than middle age Jewish planter," she admitted. "You can definitely be my delegate. Delegate yourself over here, mister."

"Want to come with me? You can leave Eli with Missy B, he'll be fine," he asked as they nestled under the heavy goose down comforter. "Baltimore is close to both Washington and New York. We haven't been away for awhile."

"Convince me," she whispered, moving her fingers lightly between her husband's legs.

Chapter Twenty-Six

It was nice to be together again. Bess and Stuart had arrived from Moss Grove and were enjoying a casual dinner with Robert, Maria and Stephen. Four of them, telling stories of their time in Cuba and the war, embellished more with the rust of memory, than the less enchanting events as they had occurred while Bess enjoyed stoking the conversation with questions about Stuart's obvious bravery and Maria's immediate preference for Robert instead of Stephen.

"Stephen, what really happened between you and Alicia?" Bess asked. "You two were such a handsome couple!"

Robert and Stephen looked at one another and broke into laughter. Obviously the story hadn't made it to Moss Grove. The story gained zest in the retelling.

"I can entertain you with the salacious details," Stephen began, "but the crux of the matter is that I found her in bed with a woman, having some sort of sex with the sister of the man she was working for and she ultimately remarried. It was the same day Hearst fired me and instead of apologizing for her indiscretions she went bonkers when I explained that he'd fired me when he so belatedly realized I was colored. She was married to someone who wasn't 100% white and, therefore, she felt that she had given birth to a spoiled child…Thaddeus. She ran out of our apartment in disgust, her girlfriend, embarrassed, following her in tow. It all made for one hell of a morning."

"What do you mean? You were together for several years. In all that time you never discussed race?" Bess asked in amazement.

"No, we never did. There was never any reason to. When we met, during the war, she was satisfied that I was this handsome reporter who could take her to the States and I was definitely a lot whiter than Robert. I assume that she thought my skin color was from the sun."

"Even the parts that don't see the sun?" Stuart asked, a lascivious grin on his face, and smiles from the others at the table.

"The lights were generally out on those occasions. What can I say? I thought she loved me, but as the fog cleared I realized she was in love with the idea of who I was, and that wasn't enough. Having her reject Thaddeus, that was really difficult. I didn't think mothers could reject their children that easily."

"I'm sure it isn't common, but don't forget that my sister was forced to give up Ruth when she was born with less than lily white skin, and Josiah didn't want to keep her. And, given your limited experiences, perhaps you also never realized women could have sex with other women," Stuart laughed, as the mood lifted.

"Of course they can," Bess chimed in.

"Really," Stuart smiled. "You say that with such conviction. Can you enlighten us from your own experience?"

Bess blushed, and smacked her husband on his arm.

"Of course! You went off to exercise your testosterone so I enjoyed the pleasures of a litany of interesting men and women...a lascivious cornucopia. But it's been a while. Perhaps we should try it. Maria, what do you think? Now that we've had children, we really don't need these men. They're such a bother most of the time."

"We give you our love, we provide you a home, we even dispense our essence," Stuart laughed.

"Ah, yes...your precious essence...your life force...how could I forget?" Bess laughed.

"I think we'd better change the subject. We don't want the two of you running off to rut somewhere when we've just arrived," Robert warned. Only a close family that had been tested by adversity could jest so openly.

"Tell us about the convention, Stuart," Stephen asked. "Is there a story there?"

"More than one, I'm sure. Champ Clark, the Speaker of the House, is the clear leader. He stands a good chance of winning the nomination on the first ballot."

"Don't forget the Democrats have that crazy two-thirds rule," Stephen cautioned. "A candidate can't win with a simple majority and Woodrow Wilson is pretty popular here in the east."

"We'll see. Will you be covering the story?"

"Absolutely. If you like, we can drive up together and Bess can stay here."

"I'd love that. Ruth might like to go shopping. She's so attractive. She reminds me of Rachel sometimes. What does she know about her birth?"

"We've never told her anything. I suppose we should, but it never seemed the right time, and we were always afraid it would shatter her self-confidence."

"At some point it's only fair that she knows. I probably knew Josiah better than anyone, we grew up together. I know how frightened he was confronting his demons. If you'd like me to be present, I'd be happy to be there holding both your and Ruth's hands."

Nervously Maria and Bess entered Ruth's room.

"We have something it's time you know," Maria said, her nervousness evident in a return of her Cuban accent.

It took several minutes for the two older women to explain the facts of Ruth's birth and her parent's inability, or unwillingness, to risk keeping her. The young, dark haired girl sat, almost rigid, feeling the sands of truth erode everything she had always believed about who she was. There was no way she could accept these new revelations calmly. Her eyes filled with tears and her shoulders drooped.

Maria tried to comfort her but Ruth moved away and cowered in the corner of her bed, folding herself into a small ball and sobbed. She didn't understand why she was crying. Nothing she had just been told changed her life. She always thought of herself as a 'mongrel,' not really part of any single race. Sometimes she bragged that she had the best of both the Black and Cuban cultures with no idea why she thought so. Now it seemed she was 90% white and even half-Jewish. But it wasn't the skin color thing. Her parents had lied to her. She was nearly fifteen and she'd never been told the truth. What else might they be withholding from her, she wondered?

"Tell me about my father, Aunt Bess," Ruth said that evening, finally coming out of her room, her eyes still red...her hair in disarray.

"We'd been together since childhood, your birth father, Josiah, Stephen, and me. Aunt Amy held us together, first at Moss Grove, and later in San Francisco. Your grandfather, Henry, had a mulatto mother he had always understood was a white French creole woman. He and his wife, who was Amy's sister, had two children, your father, and a sister who was born much darker. That baby was given away and died in a fire that engulfed the orphanage where she'd been taken. Your father wasn't told about any of this until much later and he became a very troubled soul. Even knowing he had colored blood, he was once an active member of the Ku Klux Klan, as if denying his heritage would make him all white and his demons would disappear.

"When you were born the issue arose again, and neither he nor your mother was prepared to raise a mixed race daughter. Rather than just abandon you to some orphanage, they came to Moss Grove in the hope of finding a solution. The best possibility was the hope that Robert and Maria could give you the love and home you deserved...and they certainly have. Your mother, Rachel, kept in contact through the years. In 1906 both your parents were killed in the San Francisco earthquake but their son, your older brother, Samuel, survived."

"Samuel is my brother? I thought Noah was my brother."

"Noah is your mother and father's natural son; you are their adopted daughter whom they love very much."

"Does Samuel know he has a younger sister?"

"No, he was never told either."

"My God, when you people decide to keep secrets, you really keep them," the young girl said angrily.

Stephen was one of the first reporters on the scene at the convention and filed an early story.

> *Baltimore is a scene of chaos. Delegates from around the country have descended by automobile, train and carriage. People, long used to walking around horse droppings from carriages in every street, now complain about the noise of automobiles. There is a feeling of elation that the Democrats haven't felt in years. The Republican Party is divided and will field two candidates. The lifelong friendship of William Howard Taft and Teddy Roosevelt is over and has been replaced with acrimony. Colonel Roosevelt has formed his own Bull Moose Party. The Democrats are confident they can win this election, and Champ Clark is the man they believe should lead the charge.*

Stephen and Stuart elbowed their way through the crowd. They weren't staying at the same hotel but Stephen's Press pass, and his light skin color, got him into places that most blacks were restricted from in this 'border' city. The Negro reporters were able to get interviews only with northern or western candidates where blacks were more likely to vote. With Stuart's help, and avoiding the question of race, Stephen succeeded in getting a personal interview with Clark. Being from Missouri, Clark would never have consented to sitting down with a reporter tinged even slightly with Negro blood.

Clark took a majority of the delegate's votes on the first ballot and with only a little bit of pressure, he'd be well over the two-thirds he needed. But it didn't happen. Back room meetings, concessions worked out over brandy and cigars, elbow twisting... whatever it took. Finally the New York delegation, controlled by the Tammany hall bosses agreed to support Champ Clark. It would soon be over.

"Our man's going to win now, for sure," Stuart gloated. "With New York's votes we'll get to that damned two-thirds."

Several reporters bolted from the room, ready to relay their story over the telephone to waiting editors, holding presses for the convention's outcome.

William Jennings Bryan, the party's perennial candidate, would not let it be. If Tammany wanted Clark, he and his supporters wanted none of it. They threw their support to Woodrow Wilson, and on the 46th ballot the New Jersey professor secured the nomination. Only Stephen's headline got it right. He'd waited uncomfortably, to be sure, while 'Clark secures Democratic Nod' newspapers were trashed in New York, Chicago, and elsewhere.

"Waste of time," Stuart said, as he and Stephen drove back to Washington. It was a muggy, summer day, and even with the windows down, clothing clung to the skin.

"I thought Louisiana got humid this time of year. I feel like I'm bathing in my clothes."

"Not my favorite time, either," Stephen added. "Is that your total reaction to our democratic process…a waste of time?"

"Once Champ Clark got the money from our Jewish congregation, he ignored us. Except for that meeting he reluctantly agreed to give you, we were invisible. And, he only gave in on that interview because I told him you were syndicated across the country."

"And you didn't explain those were mostly black newspapers, did you?"

"Of course not. Anyway, Wilson should win the election easily although it's unusual to have a Republican like Teddy Roosevelt being more liberal than his Democratic opponent. It's all very topsy-turvy."

Bess and Stuart said their goodbyes and prepared to head for New York. Ruth insisted on taking a week off from school and joining them. She wanted to get to know Samuel better. The limited time they'd spent together had been years earlier. It was time they both shared the truth about their relationship.

"Ruth, you and I will go shopping in New York, and next summer you can come to Moss Grove and see where your parents spent much of their life. Be happy about your life and your future. You've been raised by people who love you. Don't dwell on a past that might have been but never was…it's gone and no longer matters."

They arrived at the recently opened Penn Station, a new sprawling structure with domed ceilings and well-shined brass fixtures.

"Mom, Dad," Samantha shouted as she and Samuel ran down the platform to meet them. They didn't recognize the blossoming beautiful girl with them.

"This is the biggest thing I've ever seen," Bess said. "How did you ever find us?"

"We just looked for the person with the most luggage," Sam teased. "Aren't you going to introduce us?"

"This is Ruth, Maria and Robert's daughter. We thought it was time she saw New York," Bess said. Penn Station was no place to break the news. That could wait until a quieter time when they weren't standing in the midst of ten thousand souls.

"Ruth? Oh, my gosh," Samuel stammered. "You were a little brat the last time we saw one another. We better start over. Let me introduce ourselves. I'm Sam, actually Samuel...and this noisy suffragette next to me is Sam, actually Samantha. C'mon, let's get a taxi and get you to the Waldorf and settled. I made us dinner reservations at a place I know in the Village. Ruth, you stay close to me," he said, a wide grin on his face as he grabbed Ruth's hand, her small case and headed off.

It was afternoon teatime at the Waldorf and young girls in white starched aprons, mostly Irish girls recently off the boat from Dublin and Cork, curtsied and poured as Bess slowly explained to Samuel that he had a half-sister he had never been told about.

"We have one fucked up family," he said, angrily shaking his head. "Every time I begin to get comfortable with my history something else is revealed. Is there more, Bess? If there is, please tell me now. I'd hate to feel another shoe will drop a year from now."

"I'm sorry, Sam. This certainly isn't Ruth's fault. She had never been told either. Your father, Josiah, led a complicated and tormented life but he loved you and your mother very much. At another time, they would have raised Ruth as well. They didn't give her away from a lack of love but because raising her would have destroyed all of your lives."

"I'm not angry, Samuel," Ruth said. "I was upset when they told me but I'm getting used to it. I don't want you to be upset either. I'm thrilled to find out I have another brother."

Ricky's was just beginning to get crowded.

"Where's Samuel?" Ruth asked. She was already looking for the handsome young man who had already found a place in her heart.

"Yes, Samantha, where is he?" Stuart asked. "He is planning on having dinner with us, isn't he?"

"Don't worry...he'll definitely be here," the young conspirator said. "Let's order some wine. Be patient!"

They looked up as the music began and returned to their chatting about Sam's busy life dividing her time between getting women the right to vote and her college studies. Bess wanted to know whether her daughter and David were any more serious.

"If I were an airplane I'm sure he'd be more interested," she laughed. "We're just friends at this point. He was very hurt when they didn't let him continue working with Dr. Bell and Glenn Curtiss simply because he's Jewish."

"Ohhhhhh," Ruth screamed. "That's Samuel up there on the stage, playing the trumpet."

Bess and Stuart's faces turned from shock to smiles as they heard the music and saw the utter contentment on Samuel's face. The small combo was playing W.C. Handy's 'Memphis Blues.' Samantha just sat, smug and satisfied, at having pulled off the surprise.

After the song, accentuated by a nifty trumpet solo, a mulatto girl, tall, with soft delicate features and unusual dark blue eyes, accented with blue eye shadow began to sing softly. She wore a black dress adorned with small silver leaves and her voice was a blend of sultriness and animal energy. The audience held its collective breath while she sang 'After All I've Been to You'.

"Miss Lily Jones," Samuel announced when she was finished. "Give her another round of applause."

Lily sang two more songs and then announced the group would take a ten minute break. Samuel grabbed the young vocalist's hand and the two walked over to their gawking friends.

"Hi, family. Lily, this is Aunt Bess, Uncle Stuart, my sort of sister, Samantha, and my newly discovered sister, Ruth. She and I have known one another…anyway, it's a long story I'll explain some time."

"When did you start playing the trumpet?" Bess asked. "You certainly kept it a secret."

"Stephen brought me my father's trumpet he'd found in the earthquake rubble that had been our house. I didn't do anything with it for a long while. My father always let me sit in the room when he played. He showed me the fingering but I was pretty young and it was hard to hold such a large instrument. I began to play seriously after I arrived in New York. I can see the sounds in my head. I mean, not just hear them…I can see them. Weird, I know, but I love it."

"Well, you play wonderfully," Stuart agreed. "Are you still at Columbia and taking classes?"

"Technically, yes, but the only classes I'm doing well in are Musical Composition and I play in the Orchestra."

"Lily, you have a marvelous voice, and you look absolutely stunning up there. Have you been singing long? You look so young," Bess smiled.

"I'm only sixteen, but I have to tell everyone I'm eighteen or they won't hire me. This is my first professional job. My mother is a singer. She used to be famous, she says, and she still looks good. I auditioned here when she left town for some work in Chicago. I have no idea what she'll say once she returns."

"You have a great voice but don't you think you should finish high school?" Stuart asked.

"That's traditional Jewish Louisiana thinking, Lily. Finish school…get an education!" Samuel laughed. "Stuart, with her body and her voice, she can make more money and achieve a lot more success singing than learning about the history of Europe or how to dissect frogs. C'mon, Lily, time for the next set."

Samuel stood, smiled at everyone, kissed Bess on the cheek and, holding on to Lily's hand, they returned to the stage.

The second set went as smoothly as the first. Ricky's was crowded. Customers lined the long bar but as the band played the intro for their last number, there was a commotion back stage.

Samuel replayed the intro, trying to stretch the time, hoping Lily would appear but moments later he got a sign from the owner that she wouldn't be coming back on stage.

Stuart, Bess, Ruth, and Samantha were still seated, expecting Samuel to join them for a late meal once the last set ended. They assumed Lily would join them. Instead, Sam rushed off stage and raised voices could be heard.

Sisseretta Jones had returned. She was no longer a star. She took whatever jobs were offered and the only gigs available this trip had been singing in small clubs in the expanding Negro neighborhoods around Chicago or Detroit. She had no idea her teenage daughter had auditioned for a spot at Ricky's and been hired immediately. The girl's connection with the handsome white trumpet player had evolved even more rapidly.

Sisseretta watched the first set and a tear formed in the corner of her eyes. Lily was her whole life. The girl had a voice as clear as a crystal goblet. She had hoped to keep her daughter away from clubs, away from the life that had become so tawdry but with that voice, the girl wouldn't be able to stay away. Sisseretta was still wearing her heavy coat, her arm bandaged, and in a sling, from a fall on a too dark stage. She just stood there, an angry look on her face.

"You do this when I'm gone," she said. "Behind my back you audition…you lie about your age."

"I'm ready, Mama. You know I am. And Sam, here, thinks I'm terrific. He thinks maybe we could do an act together."

Sisseretta stopped and stared at the trumpet player standing to one side.

"You, white boy…you planning on running off with a sixteen year old girl."

"She's got your talent, Sisseretta. You know she does. And I'm fond of her."

The black singer flushed. All she could see was that plush bed and the white skin of that blonde haired blue-eyed dazzler naked, next to her. He was something, she remembered that. So many years ago…a different time, a different life. She had been a star and desirable to men wherever she sang. Then the bastard got her pregnant and her life changed forever. She loved her daughter, not like most mothers. This was God giving her a second chance to do things right...something good coming out of something bad.

"I'm glad you're fond of her, Sam, 'cause she's your half-sister. I hoped I could take that part of my life to my grave. I didn't think I'd ever have to admit it. So you ain't runnin' off with her, not now, not ever. You understand me?"

Lily and Sam looked at Sisseretta in stunned silence.

"I had a long fling with your white Daddy. I knew it the minute I heard you play that damned trumpet of yours. Sounded like he returned from the dead just to taunt me."

"When? Where?" Sam stuttered.

"Mostly New Orleans, but another time in Miami. That's when our fuckin' got me pregnant. All that ruttin'...my luck ran out."

"How can you be so sure it was my father?"

"Can't be too many Josiah Williams, blond hair and icy blue eyes...same eyes as you. No, it was your Daddy."

"I think we'd all better sit down," Samuel said, his heart beating faster. His sense of who his father had been was going to suffer once more, sometimes Williams, sometimes Rogers...same man, different lies. Sam's trumpet and blue eyes had linked him happily with the man who had taken him riding as a young boy and walked hills with him in San Francisco. But this same man had killed a woman, become an opium addict, and had probably sired enough children to populate a small town.

"My family is going to want to hear this.

"Listen everybody!" Samuel said as he walked over to the table, the two women close behind. "This is Miss Sisseretta Jones. She's a singer, quite a show stopper when she was younger. Lily here is her daughter. She's just told us something you need to hear."

The five of them sat rapt as the black, middle-age, ex-beauty told about her frequent encounters at the brothel in New Orleans and elsewhere with this handsome white man with the icy blue eyes. The story went on for several minutes in embarrassing detail before she got to the point.

"Lily and Samuel are kin. They both share the same daddy. I went to have an abortion once I missed my period, but I got frightened by the blood, and the young girls screaming and carrying on. I ran from the building and moved in with my aunt 'til Lily was born.

"She was a beautiful little girl from the first time I laid eyes on her. I cared for her myself. She grew up in dressing rooms. What schooling she had, I give her. But the girl can sing and remember every song after hearing it once. We were both fine until this white boy came into our life. Didn't leave me no choice but to tell 'em they couldn't get no closer to one another than holding hands."

Stuart swallowed the rest of his drink in one gulp. What a shit his brother-in-law had been. The bastard had never been faithful to his sister. Rachel was probably turning over in her grave. It wasn't nice to speak ill of the dead but this time he thought it was alright to make an exception.

Bess was the first to react. She got up, went over to Lily and embraced her.

"Your father was very special to me. He wasn't always the nicest person. He struggled with his own private demons. But now that we understand, we want you to know you are part of our family. You, too, Sisseretta."

The older woman was perplexed. None of this was making any sense.

"You sure you in your right mind, girlie? We's colored. You is white. We ain't family. Your white kin loved black pussy and Lily got born. Lots of mixed children like that in this country. New Orleans is full of them...mulattos, quadroons, octoroons. They got all kind of names for them but none of those names is 'whitey'."

"Sisseretta, Josiah had a strain of black blood in him as well. So do Stephen, and Samuel and Ruth. Not much, but enough to keep them from being considered eligible for certain jobs and certain schools."

"Well, don't that beat all. Josiah...colored! And I remember him acting so white and superior."

"Remind me to not ask if there are any more revelations," Samuel stuttered, still trying to redefine his father's legacy. "Two new sisters in a single day is a hell of a lot to absorb. We never really know our parents, do we? Mine has turned out to be either the most evil roué or the horniest man in Louisiana."

"Probably both," Stuart agreed, as the women sat silently.

Ruth and Lily just stared at one another. They were nearly the same age. Ruth's skin color was much lighter but together they formed a most attractive combination of latte hues. They were half-sisters. Each, separately, had always dreamed of having a sister to share clothes and stories. Ruth smiled first. It was a tentative smile but when Lily grinned in return, they both stood and embraced. A tear formed in Sisseretta's eye as it did in Bess' and the two older women clasped hands.

The conversation went on another hour until they were prodded to leave by a staff more than anxious to lock up and go home. Stuart and Bess had limited their stories about Josiah to those parts that were positive. There was no need for his surviving children, which had grown from a single son to three young adults in less than a day, to hear about his Klan membership, or being charged with murder. He had married Rachel. Samuel was born, named after his grandfather. Ruth was born, named after her mother. They ultimately settled in San Francisco where they met an untimely death in the earthquake.

The group, now an interconnected family, found it difficult to separate, even standing outside the darkened nightclub, as the night chill settled in. There was so much more everyone wanted to know, so many questions needing answers. And so many questions that might never be answered.

Samuel, Ruth, and Lily agreed to meet the next morning. There was a small café near Washington Square where they could sit and get to know one another. The sexual tension that had initially existed between Ruth and Samuel was gone, as were the embryonic feelings between Samuel and Lily.

"A week ago I was the only child of parents who were dead and now I have two gorgeous siblings. How lucky can a guy get? You shake a family tree around me and you never know what might drop out." It was intended to be a light hearted comment but there was a rancor…a bitterness that was apparent to them all.

The two young girls understood his feelings. They looked at one another and both knew there was nothing they could say to ameliorate his disappointment.

"Did you both always know you had some Negro blood in you?" Lily asked.

"I thought I knew early on," Ruth said easily. "My father, the wonderful man who I always believed was my father, is dark as night and my mother…the woman I believed was my birth mother, is Cuban. They met during the war. My father was a photographer working with my Uncle Stephen, who was a reporter for American newspapers. Of course, now I know they only agreed to raise me when my real parents decided they couldn't. It seems so wrong that parents could be embarrassed by a new born child. Babies aren't the shading of their skin. They're innocent and pure until we teach them evil thoughts."

"I never knew until last year," Samuel said. "My father's side of the family was, apparently, always in denial, protected by the fiction that our blue eyes meant we were all white. As the family history tells it, my grandfather had two children. My father was born white but a daughter, a few years later, was born colored. That's when he learned his mother had Negro blood. That daughter was given away the same way my parents gave Ruth to someone else to rear. Neither set of parents had any idea how to raise such a child when they'd always lived in a white environment. So, what do we do now that we know?"

"I guess we continue to lead our lives," Ruth said. "I'll go back to Washington, Lily can continue with her career, and you can decide whether Columbia or the trumpet is more important. But we should definitely stay connected. I feel so much more complete knowing I have you both, and how I came to be me."

The three nodded and clasped hands.

"To Josiah," Samuel said, raising his cup in a toast, "he spread his sperm indiscriminately, but we have finally found one another. Here's to finding no more siblings."

The girls laughed and joined him.

Chapter Twenty-Seven

Stephen's articles on the Presidential campaign were well received as he moved between both the Roosevelt and Wilson campaigns, often traveling to two cities in the same day. The Wilson supporters knew that he represented mostly Negro newspapers and gave him short shrift. After all, in the south, few Negros were able to vote and in the more populated Midwest and east, being too attentive to Black enclaves could have a backlash among white groups. Colonel Roosevelt, on the other hand, remembered him kindly from their meeting in Cuba with a vigorous hand shake and a classic Teddy cherubic grin.

The campaign for the Presidency in 1912
is one of the most energetic in American history

By Stephen Carmody

'This reporter has been traveling with Teddy Roosevelt as he campaigns across the state of Wisconsin. Yesterday, at a gathering outside Milwaukee, he was shot by an irate saloonkeeper named John Schrank. The candidate wasn't injured. The bullet lodged in his chest after penetrating both his eyeglass case and passing through a copy of the speech he was carrying in the breast pocket of his jacket. The bullet passed no further. Mr. Roosevelt remarked that campaigning was becoming as dangerous as rushing up San Juan Hill. The deranged shooter was hauled off to jail

midst cheers and applause as Mr. Roosevelt proceeded to continue his speech.

'Liberals and conservatives are both making a strong case for their position but it is Eugene Deb's Progressive Socialist party that is getting the most attention. The bald, energetic Mr. Debs, looking happy, but tired, spoke before a crowd of 15,000 supporters in New York City. Without funds to finance his efforts, pundits doubt he can affect the outcome of the election.

'William Howard Taft, the incumbent President and Republican nominee, has also been campaigning, but without enthusiasm. Roosevelt's ebullience and popularity captivate crowds but having two candidates vying for the Republican vote have left them both wanting. Woodrow Wilson's calm professorial demeanor, and the solid support of the southern states have carried him to victory, winning forty states and 42% of the popular vote. He will be only the second Democratic president elected since the Civil War.'

David returned to his classes at Yale, but he was restless. He wouldn't be happy until he returned to the air, flying through the clouds, and defying the rules of gravity. He persuaded two other students to join him in purchasing a used pusher-powered biplane. The young enthusiasts convinced a local farmer to plow a long narrow stretch of land that was lying fallow for use as a runway, in exchange for taking the man flying. The farmer was so frightened on his first flight he refused to look down at the ground disappearing beneath him. He never asked to fly again.

Every weekend the young men weren't studying for their final exams, they could be found pushing, prodding, and taking turns flying short flights around the countryside, frightening horses and cows with the plane's noisy engines and whirling propeller sounds. Each take off was an adventure, each landing a risk. Theirs was a shared exhilaration and they returned to New Jersey Sunday evenings with their faces wind-chapped, wearing perpetual grins.

"Did you know some engineer in Russia developed a plane with four hundred horsepower engines? That's nearly three times anything we've accomplished in this country," David told

Samantha on a Saturday afternoon, as they sat on a bench near Columbus Circle. It was a pleasant spring day and the two friends planned to walk a good stretch of Manhattan.

It had been nearly three months since they'd seen one another. Sam looked at her friend. David seemed to have grown another inch or two, and added twenty pounds to his frame. The last vestiges of his teenage angst were fast disappearing. Samantha, who had always been confident, now radiated a new maturity, and her body displayed her femininity. To David's mind...and loins, his love of flying and his feelings for Sam had become the yin and yang of his life.

"What would you do with a plane so large?" she asked in genuine interest.

"It would be very useful for the military," he said, forcing himself to refocus on the conversation. "Imagine the people they could carry...and freight...even bombs, if they needed to. And, it will lead to bigger planes. We're so backward in this country. Our government doesn't see the potential. I'm thinking of going to France this summer. They have a lot of airplane development programs. I'm sure with my experience I can latch on to one group or another. What about you? Care to come with me and see Paris? We could make love on the left bank of the Seine and drink cheap wine," he said in mock tones that made it difficult to know how serious his proposal was. In truth, he wasn't sure himself.

"I'd love to see Paris but I've already committed to join other women campaigning to get the vote. We're going to take to the roads and trains to speak on behalf of women's suffrage around the country. A lot more states are beginning to take the subject seriously. With luck, I'll skip out and visit my parents at Moss Grove. I haven't seen them for awhile."

A thousand miles to the west of Samantha and David's meeting, a wet and chilly spring continued to blanket the Mississippi River valley. Stuart was nervous. He hated this type of weather, and for reasons he couldn't identify, his intuition told him there were problems brewing. The cotton plants hadn't yet blossomed. They had survived a few nights of frost earlier in the year but it would take another two months before the hibiscus blossoms popped open to yield their unique harvest.

Still sleeping, nestled in the boll, were thousands of beetles who had begun to call the fields of Moss Grove their home. Thousands of other colonies inhabited nearby plantations until the total numbered in the millions. Each female weevil hatched two hundred eggs and left their small bite marks on the leaves. The eggs that hatched a few days later would feed on the interior of the boll and through three week cycles in early summer, the young blossoms would be consumed, and another generation of weevils would be born. Boll weevil infestations were a unpredictable menace that could produce a financial catastrophe in just months.

Moss Grove might lose as much as one-third of its entire crop. There was no known way to eradicate the infestation. Each plantation tried its own brews of vinegars or mixed herbs. Both Stuart and Bess toiled long hours, side by side with the share croppers and the house staff. No one was exempt. Everyone understood. A lost crop was certain to change everyone's lives.

Two thousand miles in the other direction, across the Atlantic and into the unsettled bowels of Central Europe, a pimple-faced, frail looking, teenage boy, Gavrilo Princip, had just been rejected by the Serbian guerilla forces.

"He is too small and too weak to be of use," their leaders declared.

Two years earlier, the young boy, shorter than others his age, lived with his parents, Peter and Marija, on their farm in Obljaj, a poor rural part of Bosnia. Peter earned a small wage as a postman but it was barely enough to sustain his family. Gavrilo would hurry through his studies and meet with his friends each afternoon, but his life, and the lives of more than a million others around the world, would soon change.

"Gavrilo," his father began. "We cannot continue to feed you and your younger brothers and sisters. I just don't earn enough. I've arranged for you to live with your older brother in Zagreb."

The reluctant teen traveled to the teeming city. He enrolled in school but within the first week he was expelled for participating in a protest demonstration against the national authorities in

Sarajevo. He grew a mustache in an attempt to look older but his height and narrow shoulders couldn't conceal his scrawny body. Gavrilo moved again, this time to Belgrade, where he failed an entrance examination that would have assured him a secondary education. He became increasingly depressed and angry. His new family became other disenchanted young men. Together they joined the Union of Death, a group of young Serbs, Bosnians, and Croats demanding independence for Southern Serbian peoples from the Ottoman Empire that had ruled his part of the world for nearly four centuries. Similar groups formed across the country and seethed with an anger that eventually had to explode. The country was abuzz with mobilization toward what would soon be the First Balkan War.

In Constantinople, the leaders of the Ottoman Empire were unwilling to cede any of their long held territory. Gavrilo and his friends didn't care what these Turkish despots did. They wanted independence, and they would fight to attain it. In less than a year the Serb rebels succeeded in pushing the Turks from much of their territory. Gavrilo celebrated and tried to return to school.

Stephen and Robert were sharing cool glasses of lemonade on the porch of Robert and Maria's small Georgetown home. Noises from Thaddeus and Noah could be heard nearby as the boys tossed a baseball from one to the other. Ruth was in the kitchen with Maria, putting the finishing touches on dinner.

"Ruth is a young lady. Any plans for her?" Stephen asked.

"We need to do something. I'm getting tired of shooing the teenage boys away."

"Well, she's a beauty. If you remember, so was her mother."

"And all it got her was Josiah, and lots of trouble. Where are you off to next?"

"Several of my newspaper clients have asked me to consider going down to Mexico. Our friends south of the border have become very revolutionary-minded. Pancho Villa, their hero, has returned. They see an American democratic government to the north that's prospering and they want the same type of life. I hear rumors that a lot of adventurous 'gringos' are sending arms and planning to join the fracas. But, after the excitement you and I shared in Cuba, it all seems rather tame. What do you think? What do you hear?"

"Our government is keeping hands off. Villa controls most of northern Mexico with the support of a lot of Americans who see him as a cross between Daniel Boone and George Washington. The problem is that most everyone doubts he can run a country."

"It doesn't sound like the type of war you and I covered."

"It isn't. Our war had Teddy Roosevelt and Hearst and well-defined bad guys, the Spanish."

"Well, I need to find something exciting or I'll lose my income."

"There certainly are a lot of exciting changes going on across the country; any one of them might make a good series. Wilson's new administration! Democrats in control for the first time in more than thirty years supporting new programs! There's also the instability in Europe with all the Balkan countries trying to bring down the Austro-Hungary Empire

"In Russia, groups on the left want to overthrow Tsar Nicholas, and redistribute the country's wealth. Their prophets, Marx and Engels, have already riled up people in England and Europe. The 'have-nots' are frustrated with the inequalities in society. Another young man we keep hearing about, Vladimir Lenin, is gaining support. He's educated… a powerful speaker, and a true zealot.

"A lot of people in Washington think the same discontent could become a major movement in this country. Debs, and his Socialists, are demanding major changes. You might find it interesting to interview him, find out what he thinks."

"Dinner is ready," Maria said, pulling Robert from his chair.

Stephen opted to delay heading out to find his next stories. He decided, instead, to visit Moss Grove once Thaddeus' school was out for the summer. Two things interested him. The first was the boll weevil plague that looked as if it would ruin the economy of several states. And the second was the exodus of thousands of southern Negroes to the north and west. He didn't know if the two situations were related but since most of his newspapers were black owned, he was sure he could piece together more than one interesting story. Besides, it would be a chance to spend time with his son, who was growing like a weed, and speaking with an ever-deepening voice.

Ruth wanted to go to New York. She would stay with Samantha, even travel with her. Maria was more convinced that her daughter really wanted to seek out Samuel who was continuing to divide his attention between Columbia and Harlem. Related or not, there was definitely an uneasy connection between them. Sooner or later those Rogers genes mean problems for people, especially young women.

Stephen and Thaddeus headed west in his recently purchased Olds and although America now spanned three thousand miles from east to west and had forty-five stars in its flag, there were still less than a hundred miles of paved roads in the entire

Stephen intended for them to stay as far north as possible to avoid any encounters with white men angry that a colored person might own a new fangled automobile. Lynchings were still all too common. More than five dozen black men had been strung up each of the past five years for reasons more imagined than real. A half-century had passed since the Emancipation Proclamation, he mused, as they passed into Ohio, and yet so much remains the same. Even the Federal Government has begun creating separate rest rooms, work places, and lunch rooms. Until now it had always been just the southern states. We are more and more isolated, he mused, and he wondered what sort of life his son would grow into.

Thaddeus was enjoying himself, staring out the window, mooing at cows grazing lazily in grass pastures alongside the road. He waved and smiled as they passed wagons pulled by old horses. Each sight was a new adventure.

They passed into Illinois in early afternoon and spotted a car at the side of the road, its right front tire buried in a ditch. A young woman paced up and down, her blond hair askew, while a boy about Thaddeus' age, curly black hair and wearing knickers, sat on the running board watching her.

"We should see what's wrong," Thaddeus said as Stephen slowed his car.

"Can I help you?" Stephen asked, coming to a stop alongside.

"It would be a blessing," the woman said, with the hint of an Irish brogue. "My car just stopped, like a dumb mule. At least I could kick the mule and it might respond."

"I don't know a lot about automobiles but let me take a look. My name is Stephen Carmody and this is my son, Thaddeus."

"My name is April Donovan and this is my son, Terry."

Stephen moved some wires and looked at the tires but it was all foreign to him.

"I think the best thing might be to just tie a rope to your bumper and tow you into the nearest garage."

With Stephen and the boys pushing, they got the car back on the road. April sat in the front car next to Stephen, tired but relieved, while the boys enjoyed themselves, being slowly towed.

"That was sweet of you to stop and help. We only saw a few cars and none of them stopped."

"Lady in distress, and all that," Stephen smiled, fascinated with the lilt in her voice and the dimples that became more pronounced when she smiled.

"Are you colored?" Terry asked, pretending to drive the towed car and trying hard to keep the dust from the road out of his mouth.

"Yes," Thaddeus responded. "Is that a problem?"

"Not for me. There just weren't many blacks or coloreds in the area around the coal mines where we lived...except those so covered with coal dust they looked like niggers, no offense meant."

"None taken. You Irish?"

"Yes! Is that a problem?"

"Not to me. I lived in New York for awhile. Lot of Irish people there. I've gotta ask...is anyone left in Ireland? Seems they musta' all come here." Both boys laughed and sat back, each glad they had someone their own age to talk to.

The two cars passed slowly through the countryside. Each time April and Stephen caught one another's eye they both smiled, beginning to relax in one another's company. Five miles and an hour later they reached a small town and found a repair shop that worked mostly on farm equipment.

"It'll take me a while to see if I can fix it," the mechanic at Harkin's Garage said. "Why don't you folks get a bite to eat and come back in an hour or so?"

Stephen and Thaddeus sat across from April and her son. Stephen couldn't stop staring at this blond, hazel-eyed woman in front of him. Nervously, she tried to fix her hair, still unsettled by this interruption to her plans but fascinated by this ecru gorgeous man who had come to her rescue.

"Can I help you?" the waitress asked, looking warily at the unusual foursome sitting at her table. It wasn't often, even in Illinois, that one saw a white person at a table chatting with a handsome man who piqued her curiosity. The man wasn't a Negro, she knew, but he wasn't exactly white either.

The food was bland but if Stephen was asked what he was eating, he wouldn't have known. Thaddeus and Terry got restless and asked to be excused. Without waiting for permission they scampered from the table and ran outside.

"You keep staring," April said.

"I guess I was. It's hard for me to take my eyes off you. Has anyone told you how pretty you are?"

"That's Irish blarney and I don't think you're Irish."

"What...you never heard of the Black Irish?" he laughed and she shared his laughter, her dimples deepening. "So, what are you and your son doing driving alone across the desolate farms of Illinois?"

"I'm leaving my past and heading west hoping for a new life for me and my boy."

Stephen's forehead wrinkled with questions he wanted to ask. He waited quietly, sipped his coffee, and hoped she'd continue.

"My husband, John, died in a coal mine accident. There were fourteen men...fifteen families destroyed. They were working on a vein a hundred feet underground when a tunnel collapsed. They were trapped with nothing but methane gas to breathe. They probably died within minutes but it took nearly a week to bring their bodies to the surface. After burying him and getting a check for $100 from the mine company there was nothing left there for me. John never saved us any money. He drank his paycheck ever Saturday night...he and his cronies.

"My father died from alcohol and a fall into an open drain one night when he was besotted. My mother died in childbirth. I grew up with the name April hearing my kin tell how my parents had wanted two more daughters to name May and June. Maybe losing my mother, and his wife, is what made my father drink so much. I don't know. All I know is coal mines never meant anything to me but grief."

Tears formed in April's eyes and she wiped them gently before tossing her hair to the side, lifting her chin and smiling.

"And you, my Lochinvar, who pulled me from the despair of a broken automobile, who are you, where are you going, and how do you come to have a nice colored boy with you?"

"I am a reporter, traveling with my son to visit family north of Baton Rouge. I have a strain of Negro blood in me and my son's mother was Cuban. If either of those facts upsets you, I'll understand," he admitted, hoping against hope that this woman might not care.

They gathered the boys and walked back to the garage.

"Broken axle," Andy Harkin said, wiping his hands. "Probably a week before I can get a replacement and then it'll cost you close to fifty dollars, labor and all."

"Fifty dollars is about all I've got in this world," April said somberly.

"What if you sell the car and come with Thaddeus and me? When you're tired of us I can put you on a train. Incidentally, you never told me where you were heading."

"Los Angeles! Have you been to the nickelodeon? All those movies...a lot of them are being made in Los Angeles, I thought I might find a job."

"Well, you're certainly pretty enough."

Andy Harkin watched their exchange and looked at the car again.

"I'll give you fifty dollars for the car as is, if you want to leave it," he said.

"Make it eighty dollars and you've got a deal," April said, confidently, having made up her mind to take the fifty. She was intrigued with this tall, handsome, latte-colored man and his son.

"Seventy...best I can do," Harkin said, frowning.

"You've got a deal, Mr. Harkin, and thank you."

Bess, Stuart, and the entire staff of Moss Grove continued to focus on the infestation to the cotton crop but they were eager to take a respite when guests appeared unexpectedly. Stephen introduced April and Terry. They settled on the veranda and relaxed over pitchers of lemonade and plates of sandwiches.

"I've never seen a plantation before," April said. "It's so large. I read a book once about the Civil War and places like this but I didn't know such homes still existed. It's all so different from the black dust where I grew up."

Stuart explained their boll weevil nightmare and excused himself. He mounted his horse and rode off again, hoping to salvage another section of the field.

"More lemonade?" Bess asked. She'd aged. Her hands were raw from working around the thistles, sometimes killing the adult aphids by squeezing them, sometimes dowsing the plant with an herb and vinegar mixture that burned the fingers that had been scratched by the hibiscus's sharp thorns.

The next day Stephen, Thaddeus, and Terry joined them, learning as they went. The boys had become friends with an ease only the young achieve. Bess was exhausted and stayed behind, inviting April to keep her company. Missy B helped by bringing water and sandwiches to the workers. It was no longer a white and black task. There would be no income for either the plantation, or the sharecropper families, if the crop wasn't salvaged.

It was Sunday before everyone rested. The four adults sat at the dining room table, enjoying a late breakfast. The boys had grabbed a roll earlier and run off somewhere. The voices of the workers singing spirituals from the Moss Grove chapel nearby wafted through the quiet air.

"We join the families in church sometimes and they seem happy to have us there. But today I'm too exhausted from working in the fields. God will just have to excuse me since this weevil infestation must be another one of His periodic plagues," Bess said.

"On another subject," Stephen said, sipping his coffee. "Are a lot of your people leaving the south?"

"In droves! Not just Moss Grove, we've lost less than most, but a lot of the neighboring plantations have seen a third of their families just up and leave overnight, not even bothering to settle their accounts."

"Why? Haven't these families grown up around here? Don't they have roots?"

"I could try and explain it to you from my perspective but you'd do better having them explain what's going on. As close as we are with our 'croppers,' they still think of us as white strangers that they prefer to keep at a respectful distance."

Once another day of fighting aphids had passed, and a respectful time for dinner was allowed, Bess and Stephen walked over to one of the sharecropper cabins.

"Charlie, this is Stephen, a close family friend. Would you explain to him why you and your wife, Judy, have decided to leave Moss Grove and head north?"

"Won't you both come in and sit a spell?" Charlie Culpepper asked. He had washed his hands and face but the smell of weevil fighting sprays still seeped through the entire small hovel that was his home.

Apart from the pervasive acrid odor, the small cabin was clean. There were curtains hanging from the two windows and furniture that had clearly seen several generations of use.

"I've put on water for tea," Judy Culpepper said, smiling, as she peeked out from their small cook stove area. "We don't have guests very often. Please sit."

"Stephen is a reporter. His parents both lived at Moss Grove before the war. He writes for several newspapers around the country. Most of them cater to black readers and he wants to do a story on why so many Negroes, mostly share cropping families, are leaving the south. Since I understood that you're going to leave Moss Grove next month, I hoped you'd speak with him."

"Newspapers that cater to black readers? Can't be too many of them," Charlie offered.

"More than you realize," Stephen smiled. "Most of them are in the larger cities and a few are out west. About a dozen of them subscribe to what I write. They tell me that nearly fifty thousand people might see my stories. I know it's hard to believe but we've become a big country."

"You going to use my name?" Charlie asked, his eyes lighting up.

"If you want. I'd be sure and spell your name correctly."

"I'd like that…my wife's name, too. She's Judith, but we all call her Judy. I call her Precious, but that's when we're alone." Charlie grinned, his mouth wide, showing several teeth missing.

"I won't tell my readers that," Stephen laughed.

"Sharecroppin' is just too hard and too uncertain," Charlie began. "We lost one child, a baby girl, a few years ago to the croup…her lungs filled up with somethin' bad. Now these aphid things goin' to take more from us. Got to be something better for me and my missus.

"I got a cousin in Pittsburgh. He works in one of those steel mills. I can get a job starting at $.20 an hour, that's $2.00 a day, and more than $10 a week. Me and Judy…Judith, here, can have a decent life up there knowin' the money is gonna' come in week after week. We might even be able to save a little."

"You'll be missed, Charlie," Bess said softly.

"We like it here, Miss Bess. You and Mr. Stuart good people. You ain't never cheated anyone. We know lots of folks at other places always looking over their shoulder for someone taking advantage of the fact most of us can't read or write or do numbers."

"Are most of your friends heading north to work in factories?" Stephen asked, sitting and taking notes.

"Quite a few! But some head west. A lot depends on whether they got kinfolk that can get them started. Everyone's always nervous about settling some place where there's a lot of white folks that hates black folk. I'd die before I settled in Mississippi. Them folks still fighting the war, waving their damned flag."

"Charlie…don't cuss!" Judy said, frowning.

"That's OK, Mrs. Culpepper. Stuart swears a lot more than that," Bess said.

Tea was served with a little honey to sweeten the bitter herbs. A small plate of crackers was set between the guests. Bess knew these had probably been saved for a special occasion and she felt guilty. She decided she would send the Culpeppers off with canned jams and salted pork to comfort them on their trip.

It was dinner the third night and the children were off playing somewhere. Stuart, April, Bess, and Stephen sipped their coffee. Stuart smoked a tiny cigar and the three watched the glass fly catchers on the table send forth their sweet scent to attract the pests that had come into the dining room attracted by the lights and odors.

"Can we talk about Eli?" Stephen asked. "I've been hesitant to ask."

Bess looked over at her husband and tears filled the corner of her eyes.

"He died a little over a year ago," Stuart said softly. "He contracted a mild case of Yellow Fever that he should have survived easily…only he didn't."

"I'm so sorry. All we heard is that he became ill and died. We weren't aware of any of the details."

"There were two other children at Moss Grove that died from the same infection," Stuart said, exhaling a deep sigh. "They were the youngsters of two of our sharecropper families…a boy and a girl about Eli's age. They could have been infected at the small school where they all played together. We really don't know."

"And I'm too old to have another child," Bess said weakly.

"But you have Samantha and she's a wonderful young woman."

"Yes, but she's grown up and on her own. We get letters and she's all involved with the women's right to vote. We'd hoped that her relationship with David would mature and they'd settle down near here and get us some grandchildren we could spoil. But it hasn't turned out the way we wanted. His head is in the air, literally. All he can think about is airplanes."

"I spent time with him in Nova Scotia last year. He's very bright and a nice young man. He was disappointed when he got bounced from their airplane development program.

"Stuart, I'm especially sorry that you lost your son," Stephen continued. "You won't have someone to carry on your name and that must have made the loss even more difficult."

Stuart could only nod. He excused himself and left the room to uncomfortable silence.

"I'm sorry, Stephen, but you're right. Eli was named after Stuart's father so it was losing that connection as well. He spends a lot more time now at the Jewish Congregation in Baton Rouge. He needs a certain type of solace that I can't give him."

April enjoyed meandering near the river. She found being alone a new experience and the smells and sounds exuded a serenity that made her feel quite special.

"I could put you and Terry on a train," Stephen said, coming up quietly. But I'd prefer to drive you to Los Angeles. I've never been there even though I grew up in San Francisco."

"I'd like that," she said softly. They were alone, watching the moon's reflection ripple across the water. Stuart and Bess had gone to bed early. Not far away they noticed the adjoining headstones of Thaddeus and Amy.

"These are my parents. They'd loved one another since they were Terry and Thaddeus' age. He was colored and my mother was white. There was no way in those days they could share their love openly. My son is named after him."

"Perhaps God has joined them in eternity," she said. "Us Catholics believe He is a caring God."

"You need to know I'm feeling deeper about you each day but I don't know if our future together would be any easier than what my parents faced."

"Perhaps we'll find a place," she said, tilting her head. He kissed her and felt the heat from her lips meet his. They embraced, as the cicadas and boat whistles played a soft orchestral accompaniment.

"I hope you don't mind my spending part of my summer with you," Ruth said, unpacking her small valise in a corner of Samantha's apartment.

"No, it will be fun. My roommate left as soon as the semester was over. She went home to Philadelphia. Her father is a furrier and he promised her that if she got good grades, he'd make her a fox stole. I think they're hideous but I'm told that they're quite fashionable."

"All the wealthier older ladies in Washington wear them, but the idea of wearing a dead animal around my neck isn't terribly appealing," Ruth agreed.

"It worked for my roommate. She suddenly became terribly motivated."

"I need to ask you something up front," Ruth said, eager to change the subject.

"OK, but you needn't look so serious."

"Sam, you're Jewish, but you look like everyone else so no one thinks anything about it. I clearly have colored blood in me and anyone who sees me will have an immediate reaction...a few of them may be non-committal but a lot of others may react pretty negatively. I've never spent time in an all white world. What do I do? What do you do? Aren't you worried?"

"Look, I've been pretty focused on helping women get the vote...all women, not just white ones. You'll travel with us, hand out pamphlets, and ignore all the idiot men that usually line up on the sidewalks and tell us to go home and breast feed our babies. Some of their remarks are a lot more lewd than that."

"But you know your groups haven't been active in the South. Your women don't want to mix voting rights with civil rights. You admitted that to me yourself."

"They don't. They'd like to, but I can't disagree with their conclusions. They believe they can do a better job changing attitudes on race in this country once women can vote. I'm sure some of the women, though, are as racist as their husbands. Look, let's try it. I can't guarantee what will happen but I promise that if anything embarrassing happens, I'll leave the marches and we'll both go somewhere together. Maybe we'll visit Moss Grove. I would love to see my parents. Does that sound O.K.?"

Ruth nodded and smiled.

"In that case let's go have some dinner. How about we go down to the Village, have something to eat, and see if we can connect with Samuel? I think he's still playing at Rick's."

At the mention of Samuel's name the young girl blushed before throwing the rest of her clothes in the drawer.

They could hear the sounds of the trumpet before they even entered the cafe. It was a trill that climbed and lifted your spirits with it. The club was filled with a lot of young college students swaying with the music.

"That's as good as anything I heard in Harlem," one boy announced to his girl friend, who nodded in agreement.

Sam could tell the song was 'You Made Me Love You,' but Samuel was playing it in a style she'd never heard before. The piano plunked out the melody, the drum and bass players kept the rhythm, but Samuel played around them, surrounding the song, teasing it, often playing at a double beat. The back-up men were laughing as they tried to follow what he was doing. They seemed to feed off one another's energy. For the next half hour, Ruth and Samantha just stood near the entrance, watching the crowd energized by the music. The band took a break and the crowd thinned. A table opened on the side and the two girls rushed to the chairs.

"Can you give this to the trumpet player?" Sam asked the waiter.

"I can, lady, but he gets a dozen of these every evening."

"Tell him to read this one...I'm his sister."

"Sure, but other women have tried that also...doesn't work," he laughed.

"OK, then just tell him Moss Grove is waiting for him. He'll understand."

"Well, my two favorite ladies," Samuel said as he came over, passing several outstretched hands on his way from the small stage. "Are you slumming?"

"Of course," Samantha teased. "It looks as if you've been crowned king of the college set...coeds by the dozen."

"And they're much nicer than your friends at Barnard...these girls have more on their minds than books. They also have bigger breasts."

"They only look bigger," she laughed.

"And Ruth, you are looking very nice. When did you arrive?"

"Just today. I'm staying with Sam," she said, struggling to keep her cheeks from getting flush again.

"Have you given up Columbia all together?" Sam asked him bluntly.

"You sound like my mother...and my father," he jibed, avoiding a direct answer.

"Well, have you? I keep assuming that as your trumpet playing gets better your school grades get worse."

"That's probably a good assumption," he said, motioning to one of the waiters for something to drink. "Actually, I finished the semester with two C's and a C minus. I managed to scrape by my Chemistry class through hard study and some fortunate mentoring by the smartest girl in my class...and, now that I think of it, the only girl in my class."

"Did she teach you biology as well?" Samantha teased.

"Cute, very cute," he smiled. "Where's David? Aren't you two inseparable?"

"We're just friends. Maybe a little more," she admitted. "He has so much passion about flying and that might always mean more to him than I will. Anyway, he's off to Paris tomorrow morning to get involved with airplanes. He says that France is far ahead of our country developing what he calls 'aeroplanes.'"

"Are the French any more tolerant than Dr. Bell was?"

"I have no idea but I suspect he'll find out eventually."

"So," he asked Ruth, "What do you ladies have planned for the next two months? Are you going to hand out pamphlets as well?"

"I'm with Sam for the summer. It's good to be away from my parents and my father's constant worry. If that means pamphlets and marches, I'll do it enthusiastically. And, what about you? Have you seen Lily recently?"

"We'll be together tomorrow. There's a small band concert at a park in Harlem and she'll be singing. Why don't you both come?"

"Sam, how about it?" Ruth asked hopefully.

"We're going to see David off in the morning but the afternoon is free and it will be nice to see how Lily is doing."

It took Ruth and Samantha nearly an hour to find the pier from where David would be sailing. He wasn't traveling on any of the normal passenger liners. He was going on a twenty year old cargo ship named Le Monde, a rusty scow that looked as if it would have difficulty leaving New York Harbor, much less crossing the cold waters of the Atlantic Ocean. David was standing at the gangplank, shifting his weight from one foot to the other, looking anxiously for a friendly face. He smiled when he saw the two women hurry toward him.

"You made it," he grinned, dropping his bags, and putting a more than friendly embrace on Sam.

"We had trouble finding you. This is a cargo ship. Are they even allowed to carry passengers?" she asked.

"I didn't ask. All I know is they have six cabins and the fare is one-third what the other ships cost. At twenty knot speed I'll travel the three thousand nautical miles across the Atlantic and reach Le Havre in six and one-half days. I can tolerate anything for that time as long as I don't have to swab the deck."

"Are you excited?" Ruth asked. "Imagine! Paris! Men are so lucky being able to go anywhere they want?"

"Come with me," he teased, "Both of you; either of you."

"You go and have a good time. Do lots of flying and come home safely," Sam said with an unexpected sincerity. She heard herself acknowledge for the first time that she had feelings for David other than simple friendship.

A similar recognition seemed to come upon David and they held one another more intensely in a way that was clearly more than fraternal friends. Ruth discreetly moved away to give them their last few minutes alone. The couple sealed their goodbyes with a deep kiss and a promise to explore their future together more seriously at the end of the summer when David was due to return. He turned and headed up the gangplank, a suitcase in each hand. As he reached the main deck, he dropped both cases, smiled, and blew a kiss.

The girls waited until the tug boat began pulling the ship through the harbor. Sam took a deep breath, trying to regain her emotions, put her arm around Ruth and walked back to catch a taxi.

The mostly black crowd found seats where they could, as five musicians set their stands up on the tiny makeshift stage. Many of the women wore elaborate outfits replete with hat and gloves. They had just come from church and felt ready to get in a party mood.

Off to one the side of the stage Lily clasped her hands nervously.

"I've never sung in front of an audience this size," she said, taking in deep breaths.

"You'll be fine."

"Easy for you to say, you're white."

"Is that your answer to everything?" Samuel laughed. "Can't white trumpet players be nervous as well...even if they aren't all white?"

"Is that your response to everything?" she said, relaxing a little.

They grasped one another's hand, their eyes smiling, and he led her to the microphone in the center of the stage as light clapping grew in hopeful anxiety.

Lily's first number, 'Smile and The World Smiles With You,' brought enthusiastic applause from the crowd. Her young voice had matured and the band added a resonance that kept her on key and on beat. Sam was careful to not overplay, letting her shine, and shine she did.

Samantha and Ruth arrived in the middle of her song and stood in the back of the few hundred people, now overflowing the seats onto the lawn. The growing throng, including a large number of Columbia students, liked the music. A few, standing on the grass, began to dance. The entertainment went on for nearly an hour when loud shouts could be heard from the other side of the park and a few bottles came, hurtling through the air. A group of young hooligans,

Poles, Italians, and German immigrants from the lower East side, had decided to cause trouble. Most had downed a few beers before heading up town and within minutes a melee erupted

"Niggers!"

"Wops!"

"Kikes!"

Epithets came from every direction as people scampered to get away from the clubs beginning to flail against any body that was close enough to be struck.

Samuel grabbed Lily by the arm and headed for a safe sanctuary. Samantha saw the direction in which they headed and pulled Ruth along in the same direction, barely missing an arm swinging toward Ruth. She stopped and punched the boy, dropping him in his tracks. Ruth stared at her friend in disbelief.

"You swing a wicked blow, Sam," she said appreciatively.

"When you grow up with boys, you learn to hold your own. Let's get out of here and find Samuel."

Samuel gathered the three women and headed for his dormitory at Columbia. They could hear police bells heading toward the park. The building was near empty when they arrived. School was in it's off season and those students enrolled for the summer were out enjoying the weekend.

"Does this happen often in New York?" Ruth said, exhausted from the rush.

"Oh, sure," Samuel said, putting some water to boil on his small stove. "That's what keeps us all fit and alert. We have riots at least once a month."

"I'm serious. If that's New York, I'll go back to Washington."

"It's not," Samantha said. "He's teasing you."

"Actually, I'm not. The roughnecks who live near the bottom of Manhattan get frustrated every so often and look for some group to blame for their miserable lives. Today it was Negroes. Last month it was Union workers against the Plutocrats on Park Avenue, or the wealthy families in their brownstones. It only takes a spark to set off someone's anger. Samantha's suffragettes are often targets of men who are out of work, or those who feel their masculinity threatened. It's a thing a lot of men seem to worry about."

"Are you threatened?" Ruth asked, her eyes taking on a mischievous glint.

"No," he laughed. "My manhood is quite intact."

As David's ship rolled across the choppy waters of the Atlantic, Gavrilo Princip found himself a foot soldier battling a surprise attack from the Bulgarian army, their ally only month's earlier. He had difficulty understanding why friends were now enemies and enemies were now friends. The treaty signed in London had done nothing to ameliorate the territorial ambitions of the Turks, the Greeks, the Macedonians, the Serbs, and the other tribal combatants. Small armies from Romania, Greece, and Turkey now confronted Gavrilo and his friends huddled together in shallow trenches. Central Europe was ablaze.

Gavrilo, his brother, and other members of his guerilla group were spread five yards apart staring into the darkness on the Serbian border near the Bregalnica river. It was June and it didn't get dark until past 9 P.M. They were all hungry and Gavrilo had drank too much coffee. He wanted nothing more than to go to the rear and empty his bladder but he knew his friends would think it was another sign of his weakness. If something didn't happen soon, he'd end up wetting his pants.

An hour later the sky was lit with artillery shells cascading over them and around them. An occasional scream erupted behind him. They were told to begin shooting although they had no idea who was shooting at them and even less who they were supposed to be killing.

Gavrilo and his group were ordered to retreat; an hour later they were ordered to move forward again. In those few moments he was at least able to empty his bladder against a bush. He jumped in fright when he suddenly realized he was urinating on the uniform of a dead Serb soldier. His stream ended abruptly.

It was more than a week before the Bulgarians retreated for good. Gavrilo's brother had been shot in the arm. Without decent medical attention it had turned gangrenous and had to be removed above the elbow. Another friend had been killed by shrapnel. Gavrilo Principe, barely sixteen, wished he was back in the safety of his parent's home. He was frightened, alone, and devoid of optimism for the future.

David arrived at Le Havre and immediately took a taxi to the Deperdussin Company on the outskirts of the city. It was an hour ride on a much potted, muddy road, with his driver wary about pushing his small car above ten miles an hour. Approaching the factory David looked up and saw a small biplane cruising overhead at less than a thousand feet.

He entered the building, watching a Monocoques taxi slowly toward the runway. This sleek, single wing plane had won the famed Gordon Bennett trophy in the United States the previous year, the first airplane built that could exceed 200 mph. Yes, David felt, he was definitely in the right place.

"I'm sorry, Mr. Anthony, you are not in the right place," Monsieur Bernard, the factory manager explained. "We build airplanes here but we need very few pilots. You need to go to Laon, in the north. We have a larger facility there and they are busy training many pilots. Since you already know how to fly, they will likely hire you. I will send a telegraph to Monsieur Bleriot telling him you are on your way."

Louis Bleriot was a French entrepreneur and international success story. He had amassed a fortune perfecting acetylene headlamps for newly popular automobiles and amazed the world with his flight across the English Channel, landing on the white cliffs of Dover. He had traversed the twenty-two miles from French soil in thirty-seven minutes. It was the first time anything heavier than a balloon had succeeded making such a flight and the prize provided him the additional capital he needed to begin building new airplanes in earnest. His long waxed mustache, coiffed hair, and intense eyes hid a brilliant mind.

"Mr. Anthony, welcome to Bleriot," he said, extending his hand.

"I understand you already know how to fly. How does one so young come to achieve this skill?"

"I've been flying for more than three years. Friends and I purchased a pusher bi-plane from some chaps in Massachusetts. I also managed to fly a Silver Dart."

"Well, we'll give you a chance to try one of mine. You can find rooms in the town nearby. Come back the day after tomorrow and I will see what you can do. If you are what you say, I can offer you a job."

David wandered the small town of Laon the following day, beginning with a glass of Bordeaux at a small cafe that overlooked the town square. The city was a thousand years old and sat in the north of France, at the crossroads of a hundred battles during the Middle Ages. The air smelled different and he found himself constantly looking skyward whenever he thought he heard an engine.

Across the square a large dark church dominated his view. He finished his wine and walked over. It was dark inside but down the long nave the light seemed to shine with iridescence from the stain glass windows.

What's a nice Jewish boy doing in a Catholic church, he mused. He had been vague on how he'd learned to fly the Silver Dart for fear Monsieur Bleriot would learn why Dr. Bell and Glenn Curtiss had fired a trained pilot from their program. He had no idea whether a French Catholic had similar aversions to hiring a Jew.

There was a chill in the air the following morning as Bleriot greeted David and the two walked toward a long, low building. Workers dressed in coveralls were rolling out a fragile looking single wing airplane.

"This is a Bleriot XI. It is similar to the plane I flew across the channel. Do you think you can fly it?"

"Yes, sir, I do. But may I run it along the ground for a few minutes to make sure I have a sense of the controls?" David responded.

"Of course. You may not have flown a plane like this. It has a horizontal stabilizer and I made some major improvements on the landing gear. I think you'll like what I did."

David remained on the ground less than five minutes before taking the plane to the far end of the runway where he could take off into the wind. He waved to Bleriot and others as he flew past them. He tried a roll and then banked the plane sharply in the opposite direction. The propeller sputtered for a moment and then grabbed hold again. David felt comfortable and if he wasn't trying to make a good impression, he would have stayed in the air much longer.

"Impressive," Bleriot said. "You start tomorrow. Between testing new modifications, I would like you to help train new pilots."

David smiled. He had traveled half way around the world but he would now be doing what he loved. It would have been wonderful if Samantha was here to share this with him.

Chapter Twenty-Eight

All quality, No Premium
Turkish and Domestic tobaccos, when expertly blended, produce a smoke more pleasing than either kind smoked alone. That's what you'll find in Camel Cigarettes, the world's first packaged cigarette.

New products were being announced daily as 1913 came to a restless end and 1914 lay ahead, so full of promise. Henry Ford's assembly line was altering manufacturing concepts. He would soon introduce the 8-hour, $5.00 workday. More people were learning to drive and horses were being pushed from cities. Eyes moved to the sky and necks craned as new tall buildings were erected and airplanes passed overhead. The first ship had traversed the Panama Canal in October, reducing the trip from San Francisco to New York by 7,800 nautical miles. It seemed that there was nothing man could conceive of, that couldn't be achieved.

'One day all Serbs will be united under one flag,' Danilo Ilić wrote as he finished editing Sarajevo's only Serbian language newspaper. "Gavrilo, take these articles to the printing room."

Danilo, older than Gavrilo Principe by several years, was a senior member of the Black Hand, and a leader in the Serbian freedom movement. The Austro-Hungary Empire had been weakened by the two Balkan wars, but Serbs seemed no better off, and they were becoming restless. It was easy to recruit young men to their cause.

The April rains passed and the flowers of Sarajevo blossomed into a cacophony of bright colors. Spring was everywhere but in the hearts of angry Serbs.

"I have selected you because I sense that you are all patriots," Danilo told the seven young men sitting rapt before him. "The Archduke Franz Ferdinand and his morganatic wife, Sophie, the Duchess of Hohenberg, will be visiting Sarajevo in two weeks. Killing them will serve notice of our conviction to not rest until all Serbs are independent. I am sending you to Serbian Military Intelligence for training."

Gavrilo, who had never handled more than a club, squirmed the first time he fired a pistol and experienced its backfire. His friends laughed at his clumsiness but he just smiled and held his anger in check.

Franz Ferdinand, nephew of Franz Joseph I, Emperor of all Austro-Hungry and heir apparent to that throne, the most powerful empire in the world, and his wife had come to Sarajevo on a visit of state. They rode through the city in their 1911 Graf & Stift open touring car on a warm spring day in June. Earlier someone had thrown a grenade at their car but it had been deflected by Ferdinand, and exploded harmlessly behind their car.

Now, minutes later, from out of the sizeable crowd that gathered to see the royal couple, seven men broke through the cordon of uniformed guards marching alongside their car. Gavrilo reached the car on the narrow bridge that passed over the river and, using a small Browning pistol, fired, point blank, hitting both the Archduke and his wife. The Archduke's last words to his wife were 'Don't die darling, live for our children.' But it was too late. Neither survived the barrage, and before any medical attention could reach them, they both lay dead. Panic ensued and the assassins rushed away into the safe houses they'd been provided.

Within the month all the conspirators were caught. Those over twenty-one were quickly executed. The younger assassins, such as Gavrilo, were sentenced to long prison terms. Their fate was irrelevant. The damage was done... the fuse was lit.

A few weeks later, as retribution, Austro-Hungary declared war on Serbia. A secret treaty, dating back more than twenty years, now required France and Russia to mobilize if either Austro-Hungary, Germany, or Italy went to war. Italy restrained itself, but England's mutual defense treaty with France demanded that it and other members of the British Commonwealth enter the fray. Sides were chosen and the armies of Europe mobilized to attack one another.

Stephen and April had just passed into California when they heard the news that most of the countries of Europe were at war. He wondered whether the United States would become involved and whether he'd have to watch men die in battle again.

They found a small apartment to rent for $50 per month on Willoughby just west of Hollywood and close to where the boys could go to school. The city had a renewed buoyancy since the Los Angeles Aqueduct had begun flowing fresh water into the burgeoning desert community several months earlier. The City of Angels, once no more than a pueblo, was small compared to what Stephen remembered of San Francisco, but its climate was more temperate, and there was plenty of cheap land for everyone.

The Irish widow and the light colored reporter had become a couple. April understood, reluctantly, that Stephen would need to leave soon. That was how he earned his living. Her first husband hadn't traveled more than a quarter mile from home his entire life, but that was deep in the ground and it killed him. That's what men do, she mused, they leave their home to work. I'll just have to love him enough to make sure he wants to come home.

Stephen read the reports in the *Examiner*...Wilson was for neutrality. The United States had no foreign alliances and with large immigrant populations from all combatants, involvement was impractical. The United States would not go to war. He sighed in relief.

But he realized there was no question our country will get involved. Maybe not in the actual fighting, but there were now one hundred million people living in this country and most of them feel strongly about one side or the other. My readers particularly will want to know whether American black folks will be affected. To find that out I'll need to return to Washington.

"You know I've fallen in love with you," Stephen said. The morning sun strained through the thin window shade. He had his arm around April, both of them lying there nude, blankets askew. It was still early and the silence around them meant the boys hadn't yet woken up. He stroked April's hair and moved his fingers down to the dimples in her cheek.

"I love you as well," she said. "You have turned my life around and the fact that Thaddeus and Terry have become such good friends is a bonus. I worried that I was ruining his life by taking him away from where he was born. I just knew I had to get away from a life of black coal. I had no one to share my concerns, but then I met you and now we have the boys to share as well."

"I understand. I've had the same concerns since Thaddeus' mother left us."

"And for another woman, you said. I don't think I've ever known someone like that. The men in the mines used to tease about sissies and the like...but women...my goodness!"

Stephen moved his arm and sat on the edge of the bed as the mood in the room changed suddenly.

"We have a decision to make...a difficult one."

"I know. I'm not naive. I'm Catholic and you're not."

"That's not what I meant and you know it."

"Oh," she said in mock surprise. "I'm Irish and you aren't."

"Funny...you're very funny this morning. Perhaps I should ravage you once again, fair maiden, and then you might take me seriously."

"Ravaging is good. I know what you mean, my love, but that's something that's never bothered me."

"People will always look at us because of the difference in our skin color. They may not say anything but it will be there. As light skinned as I am, it cost me my job with the Hearst newspapers and my stories about Dr. Bell's airplane developments. I worry about whether I'm being cautious enough when stories take me into the South. And, Thaddeus is the same shade as I am. That can cause problems for both he and Terry."

"I love you, Stephen. I love Thaddeus. We aren't in the South with their evil Confederate flags and white hooded thugs. It's better here in Los Angeles. It isn't perfect, but nothing is perfect. We'll make it work."

Three days later they walked into City Hall and married, their sons standing proudly as their witnesses. They were a family.

Cotton prices soared with the news of war. The infestation of boll weevils had abated for the time being and the biggest problem now was finding enough workers. Plantations competed with factories for cheap labor, and the lure of cities and jobs attracted blacks in droves.

Stuart could no longer gallop through the fields. His old wound from fighting with the Rough Riders in Cuba bothered him and, as he told Bess with increasing anger and frustration, 'I'm just getting too damn old.'

"Don't worry, my darling, just having you hold me is enough love at this point," she said as her husband rolled off in frustration.

"Sorry, Bess. The damned thing won't respond. I hate feeling this way, the aches when I go to bed and when I wake up, and worst of all, a penis that doesn't work the way it used to, and when it's supposed to stream, it just trickles."

"Stuart...we're both getting older. My breasts sag, I have weight and inches that never existed before, and wrinkles...when I look in the mirror sometimes, I see a map of Louisiana."

"OK, you win. We're both over the hill but we're not ready to be planted in the ground, not by a long shot."

"Then get yourself up and join me for breakfast. We do need to decide how Moss Grove is going to be run as we get older. Either Samantha needs to come home and get married to someone who can help her, or we need to hire someone who's more than a foreman."

"If Eli had lived, he would be here to help us," Stuart sighed. Bess grabbed his hand and they embraced, each lost in his own emotions. The loss of their only son, who had died so young, brought feelings of melancholy that never left either of them.

"The Boch have massed several divisions along the Rhine. They intend to strike with enough force to push all the way to Paris. We must stop them," General Armond said. He was old, white-haired and wore a chest full of honors from a career filled with French ventures around the globe. "Can your aeroplanes help us?"

Louis Bleriot had brought David to the meeting. The French inventor tried to explain what his flying machines could, and could not do until he got enough funds to build new models. The only airplanes available to them were eight squadrons of the Bleriot XI that carried no armaments. At a speed of sixty-six mph and a maximum altitude of thirty-two hundred feet, all it could do was to scout enemy positions and harass troops on the ground with grenades. David Anthony had joined the small French Air Corps and, because he was more experienced than the other pilots, he was selected as one of the flight leaders. He was tall, knowledgeable, and American. Bleriot hoped his presence at today's meeting would impress the French generals.

David and his squadron could follow the forward progress of the German divisions and send back information by dropping weighted notes to the French artillery commanders. Their planes were safe from the enemy cannon fire directed at opposing troops but their slow speed made them targets for German sharpshooters. The wings of David's Bleriot often returned peppered with bullet holes.

Germany was equally limited in the air. They flew a limited number of Taubes, a bi-plane designed with oversized dove-shaped wings. Airplanes had become a tool but they had not yet become a weapon.

French and German pilots would often circle one another in a friendly camaraderie as neither had more than pistols to attack one another. A few of the pilots from both sides fired their pistols, but the jerking motion of the planes made hitting one's target random luck.

David was popular with the French pilots but he was careful to never appear naked. He'd join them in church most Sundays when they weren't flying. He had no intention of being 'washed out' because he was Jewish. The Dreyfus affair was no longer headline news in the country, and there were Jews in the French army… but only a few, and always looked upon with suspicion. David just didn't want to take the chance.

Ruth wasn't comfortable staying with Samantha. There was too great an age difference and Sam's friends were either masculine women whose only interest was getting women the right to vote, or college girls more interested in finding a husband than finishing their studies. And, the two girls had vastly different temperaments. Samantha always seemed to be rushing somewhere. She had boundless energy, waking early and ready to conquer the world. Ruth preferred hanging with Lily. They hadn't a lot of time together but it was clear from those occasions that they fit better. She didn't want to alienate Sam, who was supposed to watch over her and she found it difficult to explain her feelings.

"Sam, do you mind if I spend a few days with Lily?" Ruth asked, not sure how the simple question might be received.

"I'm not terribly comfortable with the idea," Samantha admitted. "If you two want to spend time together, go ahead, but please come back here to sleep so I'll know you're alright. I promised your parents I'd be responsible. Can you live with that?"

"I suppose so," Ruth pouted. At least she and her half-sister could have some fun together.

"Robert, you need to come to New York," Samantha shouted into the telephone. "Ruth is dead and Lily is in a coma at the hospital. Please come…now!"

"What happened for God's sake?" Robert's disembodied voice screamed across the miles.

"No one knows for sure. The two girls spent the evening together. Ruth was due back here by midnight but she never arrived. I called Samuel. I thought if anyone knew where the girls were, he would. He'd seen them earlier in the evening at Rick's but by the time the first set ended, they were gone. A few hours later the police found Ruth and Lily in an alley. Lily was barely alive. Ruth was dead. Please…please come. I'm frightened."

"I'll leave Noah with Maria. I'll be there as soon as I can."

Samuel was pacing the halls at the hospital when Samantha arrived. They could see Lily lying comatose, tubes and cords covering her body.

"Do we know anything more?" she asked.

"Not really. A police detective was here. Apparently the girls had been drinking with some unknown men at a club in Harlem. Some time later they were both found raped and left in the alley. Whoever was with Ruth was bigger or rougher. She must have tried to fight him off and he hit her pretty severely."

"Do we know anything about the men who did this?"

"No, but the police are showing a picture of the two girls around the clubs in the area to see if they can find out anything."

"We may not know anything until Lily regains consciousness."

By the next morning Sisseretta and Robert joined them at the hospital where Samantha and Samuel had fallen asleep in chairs set up near Lily's room.

"You shouldn't have let Ruth out of your sight," Robert said. "Maria and I shouldn't have let her come to New York."

"Don't blame Samantha, Robert," Samuel intervened.

"I suppose you all want to blame Lily for leading your girl astray," the tall black singer, said, through tears and a choked voice. "It could have been the other way around, you know."

"It is my fault," Samantha said, crying. "I knew Ruth was bored with what I was doing. My friends are all older..."

"And white," Sisseretta interrupted.

"Mostly," Sam admitted. "Lily was more her age..."

"And color," Sisseretta interrupted again.

"Samantha may have made an error in judgment," Robert spoke up, "But no one can accuse her of being prejudiced. Our entire family has grown up in mixed relationships, Samantha included. I'm sorry if I appeared to blame you, Sam. I know this wasn't your fault. But I've lost my daughter, and I'm probably not thinking straight."

He pulled her to her feet and they embraced.

"I am so sorry, Robert. I loved her. She was full of so much energy and promise," Sam whispered through her tears.

"Your daughter will be fine," the doctor said as he pulled down his mask and faced the small group waiting expectantly, not really knowing who Lily's mother was.

"I'm her mother, doctor," Sissereta said, her voice cracking in emotion. "Thank you. When can I see her?"

"The police are in there now. I think you should wait until they're finished asking their questions. She's still sedated and confused, but she's trying to explain to them what happened."

The two detectives exited the room twenty minutes later and immediately faced a small cordon of visitors demanding to know what they'd learned.

"According to Lily, both she and Ruth were raped and beaten" the older detective said, referring to his notes, "They met these two men at a place in Harlem called Happy Feet where they'd gone to hear some music. The two men bought them drinks. Everything seemed fine. The four of them left and went to a second place. The girls wanted to go home at that point and they thought the men were escorting them outside to find a cab, but instead they were forced into a nearby alley and that's where it happened. The girls tried to fight them off but these fellas were big."

"Did you learn anything about the men?" Robert asked.

"They were white, probably college boys," the second detective said. "One was named Homer, the other Clancy, but they called themselves Salt and Pepper. The story they told the girls is that they'd been friends since childhood and one was light, the other dark, so the nicknames stuck. She thinks they mentioned a hotel on Lexington, the Roger Smith. We'll let you know if we find anything."

"Thanks, detectives," Samuel said.

Sisseretta entered the room alone, asking that the others give her time with her daughter.

There was much discussion on whether Ruth should be buried in Washington where she was raised or Moss Grove where she was born.

"I think it's time she came home," Samantha said.

"I don't think so," Robert decided. "Her birth parents aren't there. They were buried in San Francisco when they were killed in the earthquake. Ruth was our daughter. Maria and I raised her from infancy. She has a brother who is going to miss her as well. We are all in agreement that our daughter needs to be buried close to her home."

It took two weeks for everyone to gather at the small cemetery outside Georgetown. Stephen came from California, leaving the boys with April. Stuart and Bess had come from Moss Grove. Samantha and Samuel had taken the train from New York but Sisseretta refused to allow Lily to come. She wanted no more of either Harlem, or show business, or these people. She had kin outside Chicago. It was time to settle down, give Lily time to heal, and get to know her daughter better.

The police had learned a great deal in the interim. The men's names were Homer Draper and Clancy Andrews. They were seniors at the University of Virginia and played football. They had come to New York for the weekend to blow off steam and after they raped the girls, they'd rushed back to the hotel in a panic, grabbed their stuff, and took the first train back to Richmond.

The authorities were trying to get the boys back to New York but they were facing plenty of legal resistance.

Stephen decided that this was an important story and went to Richmond to see if he could interview the two men. He talked to the editors of the *Richmond Planet* who would occasionally print his articles but, while they said they might be interested in running the story, they wouldn't get involved.

"You colored?" Homer Draper asked, facing Stephen. The coach of the football team had agreed to allow his two players to meet with a reporter. He had initially refused, but under pressure from college officials, he had reluctantly acceded.

Homer Draper was the bigger of the two students by at least ten pounds.

"Yes, I am," Stephen replied, refusing to be cowed by this young bull. "If it's a problem, let me know. I'm a reporter and I'm here to get your side of the story."

"We can talk to him, Homer," Clancy Andrews smirked. "It's nice to find a nigger who knows how to write."

"Sure, we'll tell you what happened. We didn't rape those girls. We admit we went to New York to get laid, and brown pussy is our favorite, know what we mean?" he asked salaciously.

Stephen said nothing. He would have loved to pulverize these two, but for now he needed them talking.

"We met them, we bought them drinks, and they said they were willing to give us blow jobs. If that went OK they'd even come back to our hotel with us for more fun. They said the blow job would be $5.00 and anything more would be another $10. It was then we realized they were prostitutes, not the innocent looking girls we thought we'd been spending time with," Homer continued.

"Anyway, we agreed, went into the alley, and that's when they demanded double. You're a man, you know that ain't right."

"It's like he says," Clancy added. "Here we were with our pants down and our peckers out, and they want to renegotiate. That's when we got in an argument and things got out of hand. What happened was an accident, nothing more."

"And that's your story...that they were prostitutes and tried to scam you?"

"Yes, and that's what you should say in your story."

"You men know that what you're telling me are lies. You know it and I know it," Stephen said.

Both boys grinned, their lips tightly closed, in what Stephen thought was pure evil.

"The truth is what we say it is, and our lawyer says they won't never get us back to New York where a God-fearin' white man could never be certain of getting a fair trial."

The men were right. Stephen's story inflamed the black communities in both Richmond and New York but in the end Virginia refused to extradite Clancy and Homer to New York to stand trial. 'Insufficient evidence' they said. The anger died, and Ruth's death, and the attack and rape of Lily, went without anyone being punished.

Samantha returned to Barnard and sat in her room. She refused offers to join the suffragettes. She had lost her zest. She continued to feel responsible for Ruth's death and she missed David terribly. She knew he was flying airplanes in France and enjoying the thrill and danger of war. Why men would enjoy killing one another so much was something she'd never understand.

One week went by, then another. Her roommate returned for the fall semester.

"You look terrible," the girl said. Lauren Townsend was from Philadelphia, nothing less than the Main Line, wealthy parents and private schools all her life. She was thin, with a hawkish nose and eyebrows that seemed to lie flat on an elongated forehead. Her primary concerns were finding a husband, finding a husband, and finding a husband. Classes were definitely secondary.

Samantha made an instant decision. She was going to skip the fall semester and return to Moss Grove. She wanted to spend more time with her parents and she wanted to visit David's mother and father in Baton Rouge.

"Are you feeling any better?" Bess asked her daughter.

"I still think about Ruth and what I should have done."

"You're going through what I went through when you left for New York…terrible worries that something would happen to you and it would be my fault. That's what caring people do…they worry about what ifs. Ruth's death wasn't your fault. There are terrible people in the world and they cause pain and suffering for the rest of us. On a happier note, what do you hear from David?"

"He's in the war, flying with the French, and happy to be doing what's he's always enjoyed. I think I love him. It took me a while to come to that conclusion."

"That's wonderful. Do his parents know?"

"I'm not sure. I want to visit them while I'm here."

"Samantha, you need to know your father isn't doing well. He's getting severe pains in his stomach, and the doctors aren't sure what's causing them. We're also both getting old. If this were just a business I'm sure he'd sell it, but Moss Grove has been so much of our life, it would be like lopping off an arm. Stay extra close to him."

It felt good to be home. Missy B had died the previous year just as a change in the weather stemmed the boll weevil infestation. Sam visited her grave and sat for awhile, remembering the woman who had reared her.

She could see the pain in her father's eyes whenever he moved suddenly. She loved sitting with him in the early morning and the late afternoons. Sometimes he would doze off, then wake with a start and smile at her. He'd ask her a question, forgetting it was the same one he had already asked, and she'd answered, minutes earlier.

Samantha was returning from her visit to the Anthonys when she noticed an unfamiliar automobile. It gave her an uncomfortable premonition. Her mother was standing at the foot of the stairs, leaning unsteadily on the newel.

"Mother, what is it?"

"It's your father. He had a major stroke early this morning. This is Dr. Osborne. He arrived too late, I'm afraid."

"Father...gone?"

"He's gone, Sam," Bess nodded, her cheeks damp with tears. "The silly, funny man who made me laugh. The boy who insisted on going off to war. The strong, decisive man who ran Moss Grove during good times and bad. Your father...gone."

With those final words Bess' body began to wrack and the tears flowed. The doctor helped her into the family room and motioned one of the servants to bring some hot tea. Samantha cuddled her, joining in the tears, and sharing the loss she, too, felt.

Stephen and Samuel both made it to Moss Grove for the funeral. The Anthonys drove up, along with several other families from the Jewish congregation in Baton Rouge. And, when the mourners left, there were echoes of quiet. No one wanted to speak. Even the servants and sharecroppers walked with a lighter step, not wanting to intrude on the family's sorrow.

"What happens now?" Samuel asked. "Who runs the plantation with Stuart gone?"

"He had been trying to find someone these past months but he'd had no success at all," Stephen said. "Those who seemed interested either didn't understand how to grow cotton, or how to manage this type of business."

"I'm going to stay and help mother," Samantha said. She had been nearly silent since the funeral and her mood had been taken as one of grief.

"I've thought a lot about it. I'm the only one who knows what to do and what I don't know, my mother can teach me. Moss Grove needs to stay in the family."

"It isn't the kind of life you had planned," Bess remarked. "What happens with college, with women's suffrage, and all those things?"

"By all those things, do you mean David?"

"All right, what about David?"

"When he's through flying, if he loves me, I'm hoping we'll marry and share Moss Grove together."

Samuel decided to spend some time in New Orleans. Standing at Stuart's graveside, he understood that the farce of remaining in college was a waste of time and energy. He knew he had changed. He was somber and there didn't seem to be anything in the world that held his interest...his trumpet maybe, certainly nothing else. The loss of Ruth and now Stuart affected him deeply. All those people killing one another in Europe bothered him.

He said goodbye and hitchhiked to New Orleans. He checked into a dingy hotel and spent long days alone watching children come and go. He walked the city. He felt as if he'd lost his soul and when he returned to his small room, he just lay on the bed, staring at the ceiling, sometimes crying himself to sleep. Clarence Temple, his piano playing mentor, had given him the name of some musicians who were playing something called jazz and they might be looking for a good trumpet player. Samuel finally picked up his trumpet, took a long deep breath, and left his room in search of a new life.

Stephen wanted to return home. Traveling to new places no longer held the same excitement now that he had a family waiting for him, a family he loved very much. In a different time he and Bess might have renewed their love for one another. They continued to love one another but they both understood it was a love filled with memories of yesterday. They had each been forced to take different paths.

The winter of 1914 saw an expansion of the fighting

in Europe. German forces moved forward against Russia. Turkey entered the war on the side of Germany and immediately launched an attack against Sevastopol on the Black Sea. German submarines hounded the British fleet, sinking several destroyers and cargo ships. The French regrouped and halted the enemy advance. Trench warfare in Europe began with neither army able to move very far against the other...

Early in 1915 800,000 Russian troops, the bulk of their Army, began to push German forces from their territory. Great Britain sank Germany's most formidable battleship. Nearly four million men were in uniform in the four corners of the globe, fighting and dying.

"I've received a letter from David," Samantha said to her mother. "He's been sent to England. It seems the English are far behind the French in airplane design and production. Their government got angry when two German aircraft flew over the southern part of their country at Christmas time. The British planes couldn't fly high enough or fast enough to reach them. They've now committed a lot more money to get themselves up to speed and they want someone to train pilots."

"Well, that makes him a little closer...and a lot safer."

"I'd love to visit him. I haven't seen him in more than a year."

"I received a letter as well," Bess said. "It arrived yesterday addressed to Moss Grove, north of Baton Rouge, no address.

"Who was it from?"

"Here, read it."

Hello, I'm writing to tell you my mother, Sisseretta Jones, died just after Christmas. The doctor said it was from too much smoking. She coughed herself to death. I wouldn't ask but I had to borrow money to give her a decent burial and I hoped you'd see your way clear to sending me $100 before the loan people do me harm. I work in a factory but there isn't any way I can earn that extra money and they threatened that if I didn't pay them by the end of the month they'd make me work for them in

*one of their sex houses. I think I'd kill myself before I'd
let myself be handled like that again.*

                                                            Lily

"I sent her $200 and told her to use the rest to come here
and stay with us. I don't know if she will, but she'd certainly be
welcome," Bess said, sad that this woman who had carried and
raised Josiah's child, died so alone and so impoverished.

Stephen could sense the warmth as his train passed through
San Bernardino on its final leg into Los Angeles. The sky was clear
and the tension in his body began to dissipate.

"Dad," Thaddeus waved as he and Terry rushed through the
crowd moving along the platform. Red caps, nattily attired, carried
the suitcases of arriving passengers. He could see April smiling. The
boys reached him first but the familiar hug he'd always received
had been replaced by warm handshakes and deep-voiced greetings.
They both now carried themselves as young, confident men.

"You guys have grown another two inches. Have you started
shaving yet?" he asked teasingly, as they walked three abreast,
happy to be together."

"Every week or so. Mom objects. She says if we shave this early,
our hair will just grow faster. Is that true?" Terry asked. His black
hair had remained curly and his brows had thickened. He was a
handsome man and Stephen was quite sure the girls had already
discovered him. The thought made him reevaluate Thaddeus. In
his mind his son was still a boy, but now he was no longer sure.

Stephen never had a chance to answer. He and April reached
one another and embraced, their lips pressed tight, their bodies'
one. The boys stood close by, smiles on their faces. They, too, felt
the unity of a loving family.

"Can we go get an ice cream?" Thaddeus asked. Stephen
reached into his pocket and took out a coin as he and April basked
in the sun on the clean white sand beach at Santa Monica. The two
teens scampered across the hot sand toward the vendor on the
nearby boardwalk.

The small waves came near them in a steady rhythm and the cool air blew against the warm California day. The beach wasn't crowded midweek. Stephen and April had allowed the boys to play hookey from school on this first day they were all together.

"I love you, April Donovan," he said, lying on his back, squinting into the sun.

"That's April Donovan Carmody, if you please. And I love you, Stephen Carmody," she responded, turning her body toward him, sand sifting through her fingers along his chest and belly.

"Excuse me, folks," a man's voice broke their solitude. When they looked up they were facing a uniformed policeman with Terry and Thaddeus standing next to him.

"You look like nice people," he said apologetically, "But you aren't allowed on this here beach."

"I'm sorry?" Stephen asked, sitting up and brushing the sand off.

"Blacks ain't allowed on this beach. They've got their own beach, at Pico, about a half mile to the south. Now I know you ain't exactly Black but you ain't exactly white either, so I'm just going to assume you didn't know the rules."

"Officer, we aren't bothering anyone," Stephen said.

"I don't make the rules but I do get paid to enforce them, so please leave or I'll have to arrest you."

The four of them were silent as they drove back to their apartment.

"Why do they have those stupid laws?" Terry asked.

"People are blind and ignorant sometimes," April added.

Stephen seethed. He had hoped California would be different, and in many ways it was, but when it came to race it was much the same. The people who had moved into the state had arrived from somewhere else and brought their attitudes with them.

April put her hand on her husbands' and smiled.

"Forget the beach, let's go to the movies."

"Sure," Thaddeus said. "In the dark of the movie theater we're all the same color."

Their lovemaking that night was more intense, as if each of them was trying harder to demonstrate that their feelings were all that mattered. They had waited to make sure the boys were asleep after returning from the enthusiasm of the Charlie Chaplin movie they'd seen. Now, in the dark, April was silhouetted against the street light outside and he could see the shape of her breasts and hips as she undressed. The sight of her never failed to arouse him. He could feel his penis harden as he undressed. He thought of Alicia for a moment, remembering that in all their encounters, he'd never felt the total commitment of his mind and body the way he felt with April.

She stood over the bed, looked down, and smiled.

"All that…just for me."

"Just for you," he whispered, raising his arms. She fell into them and they embraced, closing out the world. It was just the two of them, in love, caressing, not sure where one body ended and the other began.

She took him into her mouth and moved slowly as his hips rose to meet her. She stopped and let her fingers play on the hairs along his chest as he moved between her legs and breathed in her essence.

When they both climaxed they laughed and lay on their backs, holding hands and hearing the sounds of the street outside for the first time.

"I'm so angry at what happened today," Stephen said.

"Don't be. We all recovered pretty well, even the boys."

"Especially the boys! I thought I'd break a gut laughing at Thaddeus' comment about everyone being the same color in the movies."

"Neither he nor Terry get terribly bothered by it. Every so often an incident arises at their school but they deal with it."

"You never told me," Stephen said, sitting up.

"There was no reason. You were traveling."

"White bullies, I imagine."

"Actually, one of the incidents was with black boys. Seems Thaddeus and one of the Negro girls were talking together. One of the black boys, a little older, got jealous. Stephen, this happens in life. When I lived in Pittsburgh the Polish boys and the Irish boys were always getting into it. Sometimes a few German kids would join in. It's what boys do when they have too much testosterone and nothing to do except play with themselves."

"You seem to know a lot about it."

"I had brothers. Half the time I could hear noises in the bathroom. Now, if you feel up to it, this Irish lass feels ready for another romp."

Chapter Twenty-Nine

Violence around the world had become endemic by 1915. Germany pushed into Poland; Turks slaughtered Armenians and a combined force of French and British soldiers attacked enemy forces in Greece. Poison gas was used against men on both sides. Simple tear gas gave way to mustard gas and that, in turn, was replaced by phosgene and chlorine. Chemical weapons now killed rather than incapacitated. Gas filled cylinders were launched as artillery shells, exploding over a wide swath of trenches. As long as the wind didn't shift and the troops weren't protected with masks and protective clothing, they could be sure of a large body count.

The United States struggled to maintain its neutrality but in May two torpedoes from a German submarine sank the British passenger liner, Lusitania, and 123 Americans were killed. President Wilson demanded that the 'rights of neutrals be respected.' For many Americans the drumbeat of war began to sound more loudly.

"Welcome, errant traveler," Robert said, as he picked up Stephen at the Washington train station.

"It was difficult to leave April…and the boys… and the warm sun. I arrive here and I'm damp from the humidity even before I get off the train."

"Complain, complain! C'mon, Maria and Noah are looking forward to seeing you."

Noah had grown into a young man, easily as tall as Thaddeus, although considerably darker. He was well-built, with muscles that could have only come from long workouts. But with it, he had his mother's smile and a softness around his eyes that belied the firmness of his body.

"How long did it take you to get those muscles?" Stephen asked.

"I like to work out. I usually do about fifteen minutes a day if I'm in school, a little more on weekends."

"Noah was ill a few years ago. The doctors thought it was a mild case of tuberculosis, and part of the regimen when he got better was to get his body in shape. Now I'm afraid to discipline him," Robert laughed.

"That's what he says. If there's a problem, he just has my mother talk to me. How's Thaddeus? He must have gotten pretty big," Noah asked, crushing Stephen's hand in a grip that made him wince.

"He's nearly as tall as I am but he's not as hefty as you."

"And Dad tells me he has an Irish brother...they get along OK?"

"And how is April?" Maria injected, coming in from the kitchen.

"She got a job. She's an extra in the movies. If you looked really quick, you'd see her in front of a crowd in one of the Perils of Pauline serials. I think it's exciting but she says it's terribly boring. They just shoot the same scene over and over again. But the boys get excited. She had a chance to let them watch the movie being filmed one day near the downtown train tracks...and yes, the boys get along wonderfully."

"Tell me what's exciting in Washington these days," Stephen asked as they sat over dinner that evening.

"The sinking of the Lusitania pretty well eliminated any popular thought about supporting Germany. There is still a majority of people who want us to stay out of 'Europe's war.' It's not our war, they shout. And, there are a lot of Americans getting very rich supplying both sides. That's one of the reasons German submarines cruise the Atlantic. They want to stop supplies from getting to England and France."

"I'm not sure there's a story for my readers in all that, at least not at this point. They can get those stories from the Hearst papers. I was thinking about writing about that D.W. Griffith movie, Birth of a Nation. It's stirring up a lot of racial divisiveness between Negros and whites, even in laid back California."

"I don't know much about it," Robert said. "I thought nickelodeons were the Keystone Kops and silliness."

"Griffith changed that. This is a three hour film, longest ever made, and it's about the Civil war. Every black they show is either evil or stupid or both. Imagine a sequence of a Negro man attacking a defenseless white girl. Bigots think it's real because it's up there on the screen. It validates everything they always believed. They showed the movie in Mobile, Alabama and several whites went on a rampage smashing black businesses. The same thing happened in two or three other southern cities. I worry that people can make more hate movies against Jews or Irish or short people or fat people and the audience will believe what they see."

"Are people really that gullible?" Maria asked.

Robert and Stephen looked at one another and nodded. Their lives were testimony to ignorance and bigotry.

"I think the big story is the movement of Negros from the South. It's got the politicians very unsettled. Take the south side of Chicago, for example. It's now the largest black enclave in the country, and that's going to increase the number of Illinois Congressmen, and reduce the number from Mississippi, Louisiana, and the other southern states. Over the past decade nearly two million people have up and moved out of the south.

"I met one family, Clarence and Judy Culpepper, who moved from Moss Grove. They felt they could get better jobs and raise their children somewhere they didn't feel like second class citizens. I think they settled in the Chicago area. Maybe I'll go see how their new life is working out."

"Your old friend, Ida Wells, lives there as well. She married someone named Barnett and they own *The Conservator*. I get letters from her every so often complaining the government isn't doing enough for Negroes."

"*The Conservator*? That's one of the newspapers that print my articles. I didn't know she was involved. Then it's settled, Chicago will be my next destination. Interested in joining me?"

Robert looked over at his wife. He loved this woman but he had this urge that he needed to travel somewhere. It was the same wanderlust that had taken him to Cuba with Stephen seventeen years earlier.

"You go!" she said. "I have family coming from Cuba. Take Noah. He needs to see more of the country."

Robert smiled. He remembered why he loved this woman.

Samuel walked the crowded streets of the French Quarter. Since he had decided to move on with his life his sole companion was his trumpet but nothing had presented itself for the two of them. There was heavy dampness in the air that foretold wet weather on the way. He pulled up his collar to keep out the chill. Couples of all hues walked arm in arm without incident. White men of substance escorted lavishly dressed mulatto women into haute d' cuisine restaurants, where they sat in velvet curtained booths. Samuel knew these women lived separate lives during the day. If they ever entered one of the mansions on Esplanade, it would be through the rear door.

He carried a small bag with his trumpet and he moved from one side of the street to the other in a zigzag pattern, hoping to catch the sounds of the right sort of music wafting through the air. He wasn't sure what the 'right' sort was but he knew he'd recognize it when he heard it. He had tried to find Renoir's where his father had met Sisseretta Jones and begun his downward spiral, but that building was no longer a brothel. It had been converted to small apartments.

He wandered near the railway station where a sign greeted him:

Welcome to Storyville
By Order of the Garter: Honi Soit Qui Mal Y Pense
(Shame to Him Who Evil Thinks)

By accident he had wandered into the city's red-light district. New Orleans had finally joined the practice of European seaports and legalized prostitution. And, from what he could hear as he walked, the quality of the music was much improved.

He stopped in front of a large mansion with an onion-shaped dome. A small sign announced it as The Mahogany and inside the sweetest music he'd ever heard caught his ears.

"Can I help you?" a short, way too heavy woman with pendulous breasts asked. "My name is Lulu White and I welcome you to Mahogany Hall, the finest bordello on Basin Street. All my girls are octoroons, and I have forty young lovelies at your disposal. They are also clean and very skilled," she added with twinkling eyes.

"It's actually your music that attracted me. We can talk about the girls later. Who's that playing?"

"His name is Sidney Bechet...best horn player in Louisiana."

Samuel entered and found an unoccupied upholstered settee where he could watch the musicians. He sat and listened until the set was over. The black man on the stage could clearly play.

"Mr. Bechet, my name is Samuel Rogers," he said once the set was over and the musicians took their break. "I play the trumpet and I thought I was pretty good but you're something. How do you play those arpeggios with such speed and such clarity?"

"I'll show you. Let me hear you play."

Samuel pulled his trumpet from the bag, cleared the valves and began to play, slow and soft at first. Several of Bechet's musicians came over to listen and nodded appreciatively.

"You've got pretty good chops for a white boy. Here, try this," Bechet said, playing several chords rapidly.

Samuel followed and the band came in behind them. By the time they were playing Jelly Roll Blues the audience had gotten into it, clapping loudly. Lulu White stood nearby, smiling.

"You're free to sit in anytime, Sam; you've got talent but keep that lower lip firm," Bechet said, extending his hand.

"Thanks…now we can talk about one of your girls, Lulu," Samuel said. He'd found what he was looking for.

Samuel vacated his hotel and rented a small apartment on the far side of Bourbon Street. During the day he enjoyed nothing more than walking along the quay watching the paddle boats arrive from up river. Some would have passed by Moss Grove, he realized.

Most nights he sat in with Bechet and the others at the Mahogany but news of his playing soon got around, and he found he could sit in at other houses as well. The curiosity of a white horn player was always an attraction. His life felt better for the first time in years.

It had been raining the past two days and the waters coming up from the Gulf were roiling. Ships were bouncing against their anchors. Cafes had closed and boarded themselves up against the uncertain weather. There was only a small crowd at the Mahogany when he arrived.

"I suspect the rain will keep a lot of the customers away. That and the fact not many ships choose to dock in this type of weather. A lot of the Captains prefer to ride out these storms at sea."

"In that case, we'll play for ourselves," Sidney Bechet announced. He pulled out his coronet, motioned to Samuel, and they began dueling with one another, as the drummer laughed, pounding his sticks in beat.

Within an hour, they heard windows crash and the girls began to rush downstairs.

"It's a hurricane, sure as I'm standin' here," Lulu shouted. "Cover everything you can. Put up the shutters before we're flooded."

Two of the girls slipped on the wet carpet as they came down the stairs.

"Annabelle, be careful. Mary, put on more practical shoes," Lulu hollered over the storm's noise.

"Annabelle, come with me," Samuel shouted above the din of the heavy rains now drenching the city. Samuel had enjoyed Annabelle's company his first night. They flirted with one another after that, adding extra flourishes to a few notes whenever she passed with another customer.

They found a dry corner in the kitchen and lit candles for light while the heavy rain pounded the roof and lightening punctuated the night.

"We should be safe here," he said, throwing a table cloth over Annabelle's shoulders to keep her dry.

She was lovely, even soaked through, he thought.

"Annabelle is a lovely name," he said, finding a half open bottle of port and pouring a glass for each of them. "We may be here for awhile. Tell me about yourself. I don't even know your last name."

"White! Lulu is my mother. I have no idea who my father is. I suspect he was just one of Lulu's customers. She's been in this business a long time."

"And you're alright with that?" he asked, trying to get his mind around the matter of fact way she accepted her origins.

"It's been a decent life. My mother sent me to school but by the seventh grade I began getting my period and developing breasts. Schooling didn't seem important and we needed the money, so here I am. What about you? Most white boys come, spend a night, and move on."

He hesitated. It was always uncomfortable to explain that he wasn't technically white in the southern sense of the word. Such an admission could always have serious consequences.

"I just love playing trumpet and New Orleans has the best musicians in the country."

It was all he wanted to say at this point. Instead, he embraced her more closely, turned her head toward him slowly, and kissed her... a slow, languid kiss. She responded willingly. He moved his hand to her breasts and felt himself get hard as he bent his head and began moving his tongue slowly, finding a dark brown nipple. He was prepared to continue when they were interrupted.

"Annabelle, are you down there?" Lulu called from the doorway.

"I am Lulu. I'm here with Samuel. We're just trying to stay dry."

"Everything is fine for now. You two come out." She eyed the white trumpet player suspiciously as they entered the main lounge and Annabelle struggled to rearrange her dress.

"Did she tell you that she's my daughter?" Lulu asked later as servants continued to dry the floors from the pouring rain that continued to leak in.

"Yes. Don't worry, Lulu, I'm very fond of her," Samuel said, using a towel to help dry the music stands.

"She's not healthy. She has epilepsy and can have a fit come on her without notice.

"How long has she had it?"

"The first seizure I can remember was at her school when she was no more than seven or eight. She fell on the floor and began flailing. They said her eyes disappeared into the top of her head and the other children got very frightened. They contacted me and immediately wanted her put in an institution. They were afraid she might infect the other children. I assured them I would care for her at home and I've kept her close ever since."

"Has she ever had something happen when she was with..." he hesitated. "A customer?"

"Once," she laughed. "The man thought he was so special that he'd caused it. He was so proud of himself he left a fifty dollar tip and bragged about his prowess all over town. Still, it can be serious, and I don't want her hurt. You understand me?"

"You don't know me very well, Lulu, but I'm a nice person. I'd never want to hurt Annabelle."

She looked into his deep icy blue eyes and smiled.

"Help me dry some of this rain."

The south side of Chicago was nothing like Stephen suspected. He'd passed through it when he'd been at the International Exposition in 1893, but that was a long time ago, more than twenty years now that he thought of it. In those days most of the white faces along State Street had been European immigrants. Now those faces were black and colored, and the stores and businesses catered to their new clientele.

Noah's eyes were wide with discovery. Robert walked next to him, his arm around his son's shoulder. Even the train ride had been a voyage of discovery. The three men had shared a single compartment and the all Negro Pullman porters smiled openly at their infrequent colored passengers.

They took the elevated train into the city. Noah was nervous looking down on the people passing below, many driving automobiles, some even in horse-drawn wagons. They got off and began walking, facing a brisk wind off Lake Michigan that pulled them along.

"There's a big parade tomorrow," Robert said, "The Fourth of July and all that. We should take Noah to see fireworks."

"I'd like that. I'll bet they light them over Lake Michigan."

"Settled! We'll get checked into our hotel. I want to call Ida Wells and see if she remembers me," Stephen said.

"Stephen Carmody, how could I forget you? You and I were together in Tennessee fighting all those losing battles. You should come over to dinner, right now," she said, shouting into the black and walnut wall-mounted telephone.

"Ida, I'd love to but my brother, Robert, and his son, Noah, are with me."

He paused, laughed, and nodded his head realizing Ida wouldn't take no for an answer.

"I see you are as decisive as I remember. Yes, thank you. We'll see you in an hour."

"You look wonderful, Ida," Stephen said, as they entered the large brick home.

"And you are still too handsome for this old woman to dally with. Stephen, this is my husband, Ferdinand Barnett. I've told him about the series we did on lynching and passing out pamphlets at the Exposition. God, that was eons ago."

"Mr. Carmody, you are a fine writer. I'm pleased that your articles appear in my newspaper."

Dinner was casual. The Barnett's Negro cook served lamb stew and enough side dishes for Noah to pick and choose.

"Did you have enough to eat, Noah?" Ida asked as they enjoyed their after dinner coffee.

"Yes, ma'am. I don't usually eat that much but I was really hungry."

"And you, Stephen, what brings you to Chicago...besides seeing me, I mean?" she laughed.

"I met a family at Moss Grove that was leaving share cropping to come to Chicago and work in a factory. It seemed to me that a lot of black folks were doing that and I want to write about how their decision has turned out for them."

"The colored population in Chicago has nearly quadrupled, the same in Detroit and other cities here in the Midwest. Some people think it's a good thing, lots of people don't like it at all," Ferdinand Barnett said, his voice baritone, his words as carefully enunciated as if he were trying one of his court cases.

"Tell me more," Stephen said, pulling out his notebook.

"The first generation of blacks and coloreds that came up north was pretty illiterate. A lot of them hadn't even worn a pair of shoes until they were grown men. They didn't bathe regularly. I confess they were a real embarrassment. Those of us who were already here, and more established, tried to help. We funded church programs, got teachers to volunteer their time, and taught the women basic sanitation. Some programs worked, some didn't. One problem we faced was that families were coming in faster than we could absorb them and what had once been comfortable neighborhoods were beginning to resemble overcrowded rabbit warrens.

"One good thing, though! They could get jobs, they were willing to work, and they worked hard. But when the economy stalled and there were fewer jobs, there was trouble. They had been taking jobs away from the Germans, Poles, and the other immigrants who had gotten here first and thought they were at the head of the line. It caused a great deal of racial tension and some rioting. Each ethnic group felt safer in their own neighborhood and the city settled into ghettos.

"Now the children of that first wave are doing better. The problem is, most aren't interested in helping new families that arrive. They think they did it all on their own, so everyone else should."

Robert and Stephen sat quietly, absorbing what they'd just heard, Noah spread himself on the floor and turned the pages of *Motoring Magazine* and its color illustrations of new automobiles.

"Hello Charlie...Judy! Thanks for seeing me."

"Mr. Carmody, are you here all the way from Moss Grove?" Charlie Culpepper asked. He was still wearing his overalls from his work at the stockyards and the odor from cattle manure reeked from his clothing.

Judith Culpepper poked her head out from their small kitchen and smiled.

"Can I fix you of plate of something? You still lookin' awfully skinny."

"No, thank you, Mrs. Culpepper," Stephen smiled, his cheeks working hard to ignore the scent of manure.

"Charlie, get out of those clothes. You smell of cow shit and we got company."

"Yes, Precious," he laughed. "Give me just a minute and I'll be back."

Stephen used the time to stand in the kitchen doorway.

"Are you happier here than share cropping, Mrs. Culpepper?"

"Does my husband smell of dung, Stephen? I certainly am, manure and all and, please, call me Judy."

"How about Charlie, is he happier?"

"You see how straight he walkin'? We was afraid his back would be permanently bent from pickin' cotton. I think that's why niggers in the south always seem to be humble in front of white folks. They weren't bein' humble, their backs was sore from totin' those heavy eight foot long bags of cotton."

"I thought Charlie wanted to work in a factory that made automobiles?"

"I did," Charlie said, walking back in, smelling of lilac soap, his hands and face scrubbed. "But so did a lot of other men and the factory bosses preferred men who knew their numbers. All those immigrant fellows didn't speak much English but they knew their a,b,c's and how to add. Best I could do was the stockyards. Ain't too bad. I still get my paycheck every Saturday and them cows always need feedin', waterin', and slaughtering. We can never keep up. I smell bad most times but Precious here loves me enough to tolerate it."

"Says you!"

"You know I is your superman, that's what you said last night."

"That's enough, Charlie. We got company...mind your manners."

"So you're glad you came?" Stephen asked.

"It ain't just the work. In Chicago we live amongst our own kind, we shop at stores owned by black folks, and there's no one around who wants to chat about what it was to be a slave. We got music, and movie shows, and friends. It's hard for most of us, particularly the younger families with children but I suspect it's just as hard for Eye-talians who are trying to raise their young-uns."

"I'm glad you're happy," Stephen said, closing his notebook, and getting ready to leave.

"You give our best to the Finemans. They was decent folks to all of us."

"Stuart Fineman died last year. Their daughter Samantha is helping Bess Fineman manage the plantation."

"We'll say a prayer for them in church this Sunday."

It took a while to locate Lily Jones. There were a large number of Jones' in Chicago but thanks to the staff at *The Conservator* and the gentle prodding of Ida Wells-Barnett, they found her living in a small walk-up. She was not the Lily who had sung so beautifully. She had healed from the rape and beating but something inside her had been destroyed.

"Stephen...Robert," she said weakly after opening the door.

They walked in slowly, stepping carefully over trash and clothes lying everywhere. Robert walked to the window and pulled up the shade.

"Too bright," she complained.

"How long have you been living like this?" Stephen said softly.

"I don't know. What month is it?"

"Not a good answer. Put some decent clothes on and wash your face. We're taking you out of here and getting you a good meal."

"I'm not hungry," she said, sitting on the one decent chair and pulling up her legs.

"We are. Come, you'll keep us company."

Lily brightened a little over a platter of eggs, bacon, and multiple cups of coffee. Robert and Stephen sat quietly, giving her time to collect herself. She was no longer the ingénue singing torch songs while Samuel played his trumpet. This girl had seen the depths of hell and she didn't seem sure there was a way back.

"I was still recovering from the rape and beating when my mother died," Lily said, more coherent now that she'd eaten. "We were living with my aunt but my mother was the only one bringing in any money. She said it was from singing but the way she looked when I woke in the morning, I think it was more.

"Bess and Stuart sent me some money to pay for the funeral and get clean with the loan sharks but then my aunt died and I'm still afraid to go out at night. Now, tell me, what are you doing in Chicago?"

"Stephen came to do a story on black families that have moved here from the south so I decided to join him and bring Noah with me."

"Noah must be a young man by now. And, how is Samuel? Do you stay in contact?"

"A little. Last we heard he was playing trumpet at a brothel in New Orleans."

"That sounds like him. I don't think college was ever his thing."

"I want you to come with us tomorrow to meet a friend. I'm sure she can get you a job and a place you'll feel safe."

They all celebrated together that evening watching fireworks reach the sky from a barge in Lake Michigan.

"They're alright," Noah said, "But the ones they have in Washington are better."

Ida Wells and her husband took charge of Lily. They even moved her into a spare bedroom.

"You can't leave, Stephen. There has been a terrible accident on the Chicago River. Noah can stay here with Lily. The rest of us have to leave...now."

There was chaos and confusion at the dock as Ida, Stephen and Robert arrived. People were screaming, ambulances were gathering the few survivors, soaked and shaking, and sending them to the hospital. But the cold waters of the river had refused to give up many of the passengers who had already sunk to the bottom of the river. Stephen's story told the horrifying events.

> *It was to be a fun day for the employees of the Western Electric Company picnicking on the lawns of Michigan City, Indiana, just across the lake from downtown Chicago. Families arrived early and began boarding the boat, the S.S. Eastland, children shouting, people hailing their coworkers. Women and children outnumbered the men nearly four to one. Most of the fun-seekers huddled on the port side where they could watch the boat leave the dock.*
>
> *The weight of so many people on one side of the boat brought catastrophe as the ship began to list heavily. Water poured in and people were trapped on, and below, deck.*
>
> *The Mayor's statement that "Somebody made a big mistake" seemed inadequate in light of the enormity of the tragedy. More than nine hundred bodies have been recovered and hundreds more are still missing and feared dead. Divers continue to comb the bottom of the river but the strong current had likely moved most of the remaining bodies out of their reach.*

Chapter Thirty

Bess was busy writing checks and examining invoices. Samantha stood behind her, peering down at the stack of papers.

"There is certainly a lot more paperwork than I would have believed."

"Moss Grove isn't just our home, Sam, it's our livelihood. When your father was alive he did most of this work. I'm having to learn as I do it and if you're going to run things, you've got to learn it as well."

Bess sat back and looked at her daughter, still not sure she really knew this mature woman who was once a stubborn child. Stuart and I conceived this person. Now he's gone and I've gotten old. Moss Grove needs to hear the screams of young children again.

"Excuse me!" A tall, elderly black servant knocked gently on the open door and brought Bess out of her reverie.

"Yes, George?" Bess asked, giving a shake of her shoulders to bring her back to the present.

"There is a man in a uniform downstairs askin' to see the ladies of the house."

"What kind of uniform?" Sam asked.

"Don't rightly know but it got medals and stripes and things."

"David, it must be David," Sam shouted and ran through the door and downstairs.

David stood at the bottom of the stairs, smiling up, and the two collided in an embrace.

"Oh, Sam, how I've missed you? Marry me, this instant."

"Yes, oh yes, I love you, I love you, I...."

He interrupted her with a kiss that consumed them both, a kiss that defined the depth of the love they had both been unsure of for so long. The world disappeared, Moss Grove disappeared, the war in Europe disappeared, and they stood, in each other's arms, squeezing out the months they had been apart.

"If you'll stop for just a moment, I'd love to say hello to our returning hero," Bess laughed, waiting at the landing, wondering, finally, if the sounds of young children would now return to her home.

"Mrs. Fineman, great to see you again," David said, breaking his embrace, but continuing to keep Sam wrapped within one arm. "You look wonderful. I'm sorry that Mr. Fineman is gone..."

"Breathe, David! Breathe!" Bess laughed. "Do your parents know you're back?"

"No," he said, a little chagrined, "I wanted to see Sam first. Do we have your permission to marry?"

"I think Samantha would be very upset if I said 'let me think about it', so, of course, with my blessings. And I'm sure Stuart would have given his as well. Now, let's sit and have something to eat and tell us what's happening."

"The war has become pretty stale-mated," David said, between huge bites of the sandwiches that that been placed in front of him.

"The Germans take some land and then the French and the British take it back. Both sides are making bigger, faster airplanes. They even have some now with machine guns that shoot bullets between the blades of the propeller, really ingenious, but it makes flying a lot more dangerous. A lot of the aeroplanes on both sides are being shot down and good men are dying. It also makes them short of pilots and they won't give me enough time to train them. Those with only a few hours of practice don't have much of a chance to survive...it takes its toll. I've taken a leave of absence for a month and then I've told them I'll return."

"A month? That's not very long to plan a big wedding here at Moss Grove," Bess said.

"David doesn't want a big wedding, mother, and neither do I. We talked about it in our letters. We thought we'd have a small wedding at the Jewish temple in Baton Rouge and enjoy a brief honeymoon in New Orleans."

"You already knew David was going to propose and you never told me?" Bess asked, a stunned tone in her voice.

"I never actually proposed in my letters," David interjected, his mouth full of ham and bread. "I just said I had something important to ask her."

"But.....," Bess started to protest.

"Mother, David and I haven't been together for nearly a year. Would you mind if we had some private time together?"

Sam stood, grabbed David's hand, and the two hurried from the room, Bess's mouth agape, her stunned eyes finally turning to a smile.

Two weeks later David stood, in his neatly pressed uniform, watching Samantha Fineman, his bride to be, come slowly down the short aisle to the strains of Lohengrin. David's family sat in the front row, happy at the mitzvah of the day, but visibly uncomfortable. They wanted the wedding to be at their temple, surrounded by their friends, not a place like this.

The Mahogany was closed to the public. Samuel had convinced David and Samantha that it would be the perfect setting for their wedding and now, his trumpet set aside, he was walking this woman he'd always loved, down the aisle to give her to another man. It was sad...it was sweet. It was a lot of feelings kaleidoscoping inside him but it definitely wasn't easy.

The girls who worked in this upscale brothel were ecstatic. Each had selected her prettiest dress and helped one another put on less garish makeup. They smiled and giggled. Lulu helped, giving special attention to her daughter, Annabelle. Sidney Bechet and his musicians added a violin player for an extra touch and played music that was more sedate and a little less jazzier than they were used to. Samuel had even found the men matching jackets.

Samantha was a picture to behold. She wore the same white, lace dress her mother had worn when she married Stuart, and her grandmother, Amy, had worn when she'd married John Shipley, a Union army officer. And now, two generations later, she was also marrying a man in uniform.

Bess' eyes glistened as she watched her daughter come down the aisle. She was finding it difficult to breathe from the blend of all the emotions she was feeling. She looked at Stephen. She loved him and always thought the two of them would marry, that is, until she was told they were half-siblings. But Stuart was a wonderful husband and made this day possible.

Samantha smiled as she approached her husband-to-be and the make-shift chuppah, probably the first and only time a New Orleans brothel had hosted a Jewish wedding. Tall, handsome David smiled back at her.

The dinner was catered by Simone's, one of New Orleans top restaurants. Simone Carpentier, the owner, was one of Lulu's regular customers and the two very different entrepreneurs had apparently worked out a unique barter arrangement.

"Sam and David, I want you to meet Annabelle," Samuel said, introducing the girl to the new bride and groom and holding her hand tightly…

"You look positively gorgeous, Samantha," Annabelle gushed. "And David, you are so handsome in your uniform. I swear, I've never seen a more handsome couple in any of the magazines I look at, and I look at a lot of them."

Samantha looked at Annabelle and smiled. Then she looked at Samuel. He was fond of this girl, she could tell that. But it was more. There was something very protective in the way he held her. It would be nice if he found someone to love.

"I'm through traveling and reporting," Stephen said to Robert. "I watch you and Noah. I see how alone Lily became once she lost her mother. I have a lovely wife and two growing sons waiting for me in Los Angeles. I don't want to be away chasing stories half the year."

"What will you do to earn a living?" Robert asked. They were sitting on Moss Grove's veranda, enjoying their coffee after having returned there after the wedding. Robert and Noah were leaving the next day for Washington.

"I'm going to publish a newspaper. I mean, why not? I know the business. As a matter of fact it's the only work I've ever done."

"Where are you going to get the money to get started?"

"Actually, I was thinking of asking Mr. Hearst."

"Mr. Hearst?" Robert repeated, aghast, trying to keep himself from laughing.

"You mean the Mr. Hearst who fired you for being colored... that Mr. Hearst?"

"His firing me doesn't mean he didn't like me. All he can do is throw me out of his office again."

Stephen's train ride home was uneventful. He slept soundly to the clickity-clack of the iron wheels against the rails and he stared out the windows during the sunny days of summer as he passed through Iowa into Nebraska and onto Utah. He was getting closer to April, Thaddeus and Terry. He now thought of both boys as his sons. He was sure April thought of them the same way and he was pretty sure the two boys thought of themselves as brothers. They were a family and they needed their father around. It wasn't fair to have April shoulder the entire parenting burden by herself. He'd find a way to raise the money to start a newspaper. He'd even found a name for his paper...*The Banner*. He hoped he could create some type of memorable motto, such as 'We intend to wave equally on Americans of all races.' He'd run it by Mr. Hearst, if he got the chance.

He took a taxi to the apartment on Willoughby and walked in unannounced to a vacated set of rooms. No one was there. The furniture was gone and the closets were empty. His mind flew back to the last time he'd entered his residence unannounced and found his model wife in bed with another woman. He wondered if this was déjà vu. He walked out to the manager's office.

"Gordon, do you have any idea where my family moved to?" Stephen asked.

"Hey, Stephen, welcome back. Sure, I have their address. April said she'd found a house on Croft, near La Cienega. Didn't you know?"

"No idea, but I haven't spoken to her in a week or so. When did all this happen?"

"Late last week. She said she had to act quickly or lose it."

Stephen's cab ride this time was short, and he laughed as it pulled up in front of the small Spanish-style bungalow. The entire front yard was covered with boxes. April and the boys were struggling, trying to lift one carton that was clearly too heavy and bring it inside. They stared at the yellow taxi and screamed when they saw Stephen.

"About time you got here," April smiled.

"You are full of surprises," Stephen said, picking up one end of the carton.

"C'mon, Dad, lift it higher," Terry laughed.

"Maybe's he's getting too old," Thaddeus chided.

"Wow, nice house," Stephen said, depositing the box on the wood floor, and wandering around, to the satisfied glances from his family.

"Only sixty-five dollars a month with an option to buy it for $3,500.00. What do you think?"

"I like….I like. Can we afford it?"

"Between your income and mine, we should be just fine," she smiled. "I've been getting pretty steady work. Two studios, Jesse Lasky and Famous Players came together to form a new studio, Paramount, and they're making lots of movies. The casting manager likes me."

"How does he like you?"

"Don't be silly. He's sixty with a pot belly and a wife and five children."

"That doesn't mean he still doesn't get that urge," Stephen smiled, half serious.

"Don't talk that way in front of the boys."

"They certainly don't look like boys any more. They're both taller than I am. Anyway, you better be making good money. I've quit my reporting."

April dropped the box she was carrying and the crack of something glass within said that whatever it was, would no longer be of any use.

It took the balance of the evening beginning with hot dogs and beans to give everyone time to describe what they'd been doing since Stephen had gone to Washington more than a month earlier.

"Your own newspaper...that's wonderful," April gushed. "We'll teach both boys to set type and we'll all go find interesting stories that need telling."

"I knew I loved you. I was worried you wouldn't want me to take the leap. I'm so happy I think you and I should retire so I can make ravenous love to you."

"Don't talk that way in front of the boys."

"Thaddeus, who is she referring to? We haven't been 'boys' in years. Does she know we've been shaving for nearly two years and we graduate next year?"

"Parents...they can be so difficult to raise."

"Fine! Then give your old doddering parents a little time to themselves."

"Mr. Hearst, thank you for seeing me."

"Stephen Carmody! I wondered what ever happened to you. I heard you've been writing for some Negro newspapers. You're looking well. And, why wouldn't I see you? You were a good reporter for me. I just couldn't employ you."

"Yes, I remember that's what you told me."

"So, how can I help you?"

"I've been writing syndicated stories for nearly a dozen papers since I left your organization but I'm tired of traveling. I want to be closer to my family. I intend to start my own newspaper in Los Angeles."

"You'll be competing with my *Examiner*."

"I'm sure I won't be much competition. With of my experience and contacts I intend to focus on Negroes and other racial minority readers. Now that Los Angeles has plenty of water I expect it to grow. I want you to invest. I'm calling the paper *The Banner*."

"And why would I invest in a newspaper that caters to blacks?"

"Because you're a good businessman and you know it's a growing segment of the population."

"How do you propose to get ads?"

"The same way I'm going to convince you to invest...to show businesses that it makes sense."

"I knew I liked you, Carmody. Too bad you aren't all white."

"Too bad you don't have a little color blindness, Mr. Hearst, and then we'd both be better off."

"Touche! Alright, I'll invest but only if I get editorial say-so."

"Sorry. I can't do that. I need independence in that area."

"Spoken like a true newsman. OK...but don't disappoint me."

Leaving his new bride wasn't easy. It felt so good and so right to be with one another, David thought.

"I'll be back as soon as I can," he said, as they sat on the mossy bank near the river. Large white gulls flew overhead and wispy clouds moved lazily. A few ships passed north and south hailing one another with blasts from their steam horns.

"Robert has asked me to return to London via Washington. He wants me to meet with someone in the military. He was very secretive and I have no idea what it's all about, but it will be nice to see Robert and Maria before I return to England."

"Noah must be a young man by now," Samantha added, not happy that her new husband was going off to war and danger.

David had been told a reservation awaited him at the Hay-Adams hotel, a short taxi ride from the train station.

"David Anthony," he told the desk clerk. "I'm told you have a room for me."

"Yes, Mr. Anthony. Please sign this form and take the last elevator on the right. Your room is on the 3d floor."

David entered the elevator and pressed '3' but when the doors closed the elevator began to descend. He hit other buttons but nothing happened and a few moments later it stopped and the doors opened. A tall stern man faced him, the man's badge and side arm in clear view.

"Your name, sir," the man asked, unsmiling.

"David Anthony. What's going on here?"

"Please follow me, sir. It will all be clear shortly."

David followed the man at a steady pace for nearly a hundred yards. They were probably in a tunnel under one of Washington's streets. His guide knocked on a door at the other end. It opened and a familiar face greeted him.

"Hello, David," Glenn Curtiss said. "It's been a few years. You're looking well."

"Mr. Curtiss? What is going on here?"

"Come in. I want to introduce you to Mr. Robert Lansing. He's just been appointed as the new Secretary of State."

"Hello, Mr. Anthony. I'm glad we could arrange this meeting. Please sit and be comfortable. I'm sorry for all this secrecy but we thought it necessary. You have unique knowledge of what all the powers in Europe are doing in developing airplanes and how they are being used in battle. We want to pick your brain for a few hours. Our country is committed to neutrality. We want to stay out of Europe's wars but we may not be able to do so. We need to better understand what we might face. Glenn says you worked for him as a test pilot and since then you've flown in both France and England. We want to have you talk to some of our people. Will you do that?"

Robert Lansing was every inch the patrician, pin stripe suit, salt and pepper hair and neatly trimmed mustache. He was acknowledged as quite bright and carrying the full confidence of the President in his new assignment as a Cabinet officer.

David was stunned. He could only nod.

Sandwiches and drinks were brought in. Several men entered, including three in uniform. None wore insignias that David could identify. There were no introductions. Four men with large notepads formed an arc around David and began asking questions.

What is the fastest plane being used? How does the machine gun synchronize its firing between propeller blades without hitting them? Do the guns jam often? How fast? How high? Who has the best pilots? Why? What is Bleriot developing? DeHavilland? Fokker? How do you elude a pilot coming up behind you? From above you?

David fielded the questions as well as he could. His answers always came back to a few basics...more airplanes, better trained pilots. Faster...higher altitudes...more armament and...something he hadn't thought of for awhile.

"You need to put some form of communication in the planes. Pilots need to be able to talk to the ground and with other pilots. Waving and signaling doesn't work, it's too cumbersome."

Glenn Curtiss and Robert Lansing sat in the corner, just listening. The meeting lasted three hours. The men nodded to David, stood, and exited without thanks or farewells. David stood and stretched. He was exhausted.

"Thank you, Mr. Anthony. Glenn was right. You were very helpful. I wish you a safe voyage to England." Lansing shook his hand and exited through the same door as David's inquisitors.

"Come, David," Curtiss said. "I'll walk back to the hotel with you. I understand you're due to have dinner with family members. Please try and limit what you tell them about this meeting. Washington has very big ears and a dangerous tendency to take things out of context."

"Glenn, I need to ask you a question."

"Of course. After all the questions you've been asked, I'm sure I can answer at least one of yours."

"You never told them I was Jewish, did you?"

"No, I didn't."

"If you and Dr. Bell thought it was relevant enough to dismiss me from your program, why not now?

"That's going to take more than this short walk to explain. Let's sit and have a cup of coffee.

"There is an increasing amount of pressure from wealthy and influential Jewish people around the world to establish a Jewish homeland in Palestine. An end to the Diaspora, they say. People such as the Rothschild families in France and England and various bankers in America have gotten behind a man named Theodor Herzl and his World Zionist Congress urging governments to make a commitment.

"The German government has actively pursued the support of the Jewish community. There are large populations of Jews in Germany and many are being killed by both sides because so many of the battles are being contested in rural civilian areas where they live, such as Galicia, Poland, and Lithuania. 600,000 of your people have been banished from Russia by the Czar. They've been accused of supporting Russia's enemies. The fact that Jews fought for all of the powers on both sides seems to have been forgotten. Jewish businessmen have also been accused of profiteering. Nothing was proven but the accusations remained. They became everyone's scapegoat. They couldn't win.

"I make it a practice to never listen to irrational rumors. I made my own decision. I know what sort of a person you are and I didn't want your knowledge tinged by anyone's bias. And, listening to you, I know I was right. I'm sorry you were dropped from our program. You didn't deserve that treatment."

> *The elections of 1916 were close and bitterly fought. Woodrow Wilson's campaign message was simple... 'he kept us out of the war.' The Republican candidate was the Supreme Court Justice, Charles Evans Hughes. The country's bias had turned in favor of Great Britain and France after frequent stories of German atrocities against civilian populations were printed. Still, Americans opted for neutrality; it was 'Europe's war.'*
>
> *Hughes went to bed election night believing he had won the election but results from the Pacific Coast states hadn't yet come in. After midnight those results showed that Wilson had won California by 3,800 votes out of a million cast. A reporter called Hughes to get a quote and was told that 'The President is asleep.' The reporter replied, 'Tell the President, when he awakes, that he isn't the President.'*

The *Banner* struggled. It was difficult to convince Negro businesses to advertise in a Negro newspaper. The city already had the *New Age Dispatch*, owned by Frederick Roberts, who had migrated to Southern California from Colorado a few earlier. His paper was better established. Roberts would soon run and be elected to the State Assembly. Local businesses were eager to barter advertising in his newspaper for political favors. Stephen needed to make the *Banner* different.

One evening he and Alice went out to dinner and listen to music in the newly energized area around the city's Central Avenue. Restaurants and bars played the new 'jazz' music which Stephen had first heard Samuel play. At the Cadillac Café, Jelly Roll Morton was playing his famous Jelly Roll Blues. His song had become a national sensation. During the break Stephen introduced himself and explained his relationship to Samuel Rogers. Morton remembered him well.

"Good trumpet player that boy. One night after the club closed he, Bechet and I jammed together till morning."

That was the break Stephen needed. Morton introduced him to all the club owners and The Banner suddenly became the city's only paper to report on what was happening musically in the city. Alice convinced several friends at the movie studio to advertise their new movies. Soon if you wanted to know where to eat, what shows to see, and who was doing what, you needed to read The Banner.

> *As the winter months of early 1916 transitioned into spring, the armies of Germany, Russia, and France were all on the move. At Verdun, French casualties were high and had it not been for the use of all their reserve forces, German soldiers would have continued their thrust toward Paris. In the air Germany's Fokker was proving to be devastatingly effective. It outmaneuvered both British and French aircraft. It had speed and moved with facile ease. Their pilots would fly a hundred feet above the ground and strafe the trenches with their guns, sometimes dropping grenades for good measure.*
>
> *Meanwhile, the Allies planned a joint assault along the Somme by British and French forces to be supported by Royal Flying Corps air squadrons.*

David was busy training British pilots for the planned assault using a new plane, the Sopwith Pup, a highly maneuverable biplane with its own synchronized Vickers machine gun.

There was haze the morning of July 12th. David had trained another squadron of pilots for the attack but the team leader took sick and David made a last minute decision to lead twelve planes over the English Channel with the hope of harassing enemy shore positions in northern France. They needed to prevent enemy planes from slowing the advance of the British ground forces.

German artillery had been modified to spray flak, small pieces of metal, at airplanes, and the British planes were meeting a heavy barrage. A hundred yards off shore, at about 3,000 feet, David's plane was hit and the right fabric wing covering of his Pup was ripped to shreds. He could feel the controls go and the plane dip into a steep dive.

"Dammit!" he shouted out loud, everything he'd learned through the years passing through his consciousness. "Pull back on the stick...work the rudder."

He couldn't gain altitude but he could glide. He cut his engine to reduce pressure on his wings and got the plane into a more gradual descent.

"Thank God there's no fire or I'd be dead for sure. Two thousand feet...one thousand feet...five hundred feet, Channel straight ahead."

Grey water and bouncing white caps were coming up to meet him. He banked slightly hoping to catch the eyes of the fishermen in their boats throwing out their nets. Then he was in the water and grateful for all those times he'd frolicked in the Mississippi with friends. His arm felt funny, it didn't seem to have any strength. The water was cold, and salty, and then arms were lifting him up.

"Monsieur, it is not a good time of the year to go swimming."

"I think I swallowed the entire English Channel," David coughed, his eyes red, his hands shaking.

"Your shoulder...I think it is broken," the fisherman said. "Come, we will get you warm. These days we are pulling out more pilots than fish."

Within days David found himself in the small hospital of the Royal Flying Corps near Manchester.

"You're a very lucky young man, Captain Anthony. We were able to set your broken arm. You'll be fine in a week or two. One of your squadron is here to see you."

"Good morning, Captain," Al Koso, said, smiling broadly.

"Al, how are you? How did the run go? Did we do any damage? Did all the men get back safely?"

Koso was a tall, white haired Eastern European who had also enlisted in the RFC. He was from Philadelphia and had the frame of a small house. He could barely fit into the small cockpits and more than once his British officers tried to get rid of him. But you couldn't help but like the man. He was unassuming and could fly rings around most of the other men. He and David had shared a beer more than once, despite one being an officer.

"The men are fine. We lost Sammy…German machine gun got him, but we knocked down two of their planes. We thought you were gone for sure when that shrapnel tore up your wings. Nice job getting down."

Their shared passion for flying had cemented their friendship from the first time they'd met. David mentioned how he'd only been married a month when he'd been asked to return to England. He described Samantha and Moss Grove and his life in Louisiana.

"Have they figured out yet that you're Jewish?" Al asked casually, before adding, "Don't worry, so am I."

"What gave it away?" David asked.

"What else, your reluctance to shower with the other men. I knew it wasn't because you were an officer."

"Are there other men around us sharing the same secret?"

"Probably! Most of the Brits wouldn't care, but some of their senior officers can be pretty stodgy. I wouldn't trust them further than the ends of their waxed mustaches."

"Well, let's keep it between us," David cautioned. "I need to get out of here and back to my unit."

"Patience, meyna chaver (*my friend*). Give yourself time to heal."

"Hello, Jelly," Samuel said, walking into the Starlight room on Central Avenue.

"My goodness, Sammy Rogers, boy trumpet player. What brings you so far from Storyville?"

"I heard they're banging some good music in these parts so I picked up my new bride and decided to see for myself. My brother lives near Hollywood with his family. It gave me two excuses to get here."

"I met him, Stephen something-or-other. He owns a newspaper. But he's colored and you're white. How'd that come to be or am I being too personal?"

"Actually we're both mixed. I'm beginning to think we've all got strains of milk and chocolate somewhere in our past. Anyway, I hear it's all jazz out here, no ragtime."

"No ragtime. Ragtime's passé. With jazz we get to improvise. The guys like it and the customers really dig it. Want to sit in with us?"

"I wouldn't miss it."

Samuel and Annabelle had stunned Lulu when they told her they wanted to marry. Lulu still felt uncomfortable about the almost white boy and nervous about trusting him with a daughter who had a history of seizures coming on her at unexpected times. The look of sheer adoration on her girl's face told her that there was no way she could refuse, but she fixed Samuel with a steely glare that said, without saying it, he'd better take good care of her. He understood.

Samuel hadn't thought much about falling in love. He had never gotten over his feelings of abandonment. He was sure he'd never bring anything but bad luck to people who got too close. He was orphaned by the loss of his parents in the earthquake and that was after his father and mother seemed to have already forgotten him...then it was Ruth and almost Lily. Life had treated him badly until he'd he met Annabelle. She was damaged as well. Maybe they could care for one another.

The news that they intended to go to California agitated Lulu even more. Losing her daughter to a husband might be acceptable. Losing her to a far away city had come as an unexpected shock. This time the wedding at the Magnolia was a smaller, almost family, affair. The working girls were good to Annabelle, they'd watched her grow up. Each one got her a very personal gift and they all cried tears of happiness.

Annabelle had never been farther from the Magnolia than the shores of the Mississippi. The train ride was an adventure and making love in a bed riding over rails was fun. Having sex with a man who wasn't paying her was magic. Samuel felt both love and caring for this fragile girl. He would touch her, kiss her breasts, and move his hand down between her thighs. But he couldn't clear his mind from the worry that something he might do could cause her to go into a convulsion.

"Sam," she'd said. "Please don't treat me like a porcelain doll. I really won't break, and making love won't bring on my epilepsy. If anything, our feelings are so strong, it might never return."

Stephen and April were wonderful. They showed off their two sons, different in the shade of their skin, but alike in all other ways. They showed off their home and willingly played tour guide.

"We're living in a Garden of Eden," April said, driving by the large homes on Adams Blvd and even larger ones in Pasadena. They strolled on the Ocean Park boardwalk and enjoyed Abbot Kinney's amusement park and Venice-like canals.

Annabelle felt as if she'd died and gone to heaven. No more heaving, sweaty men with liquored breaths and flaccid penises. She had a husband who loved her. She was in a beautiful land with a family that loved Sam, and by extension, loved her as well.

The Starlight Room was crowded. Stephen and April had agreed that Thaddeus and Terry could join them to see Uncle Samuel play with Jelly Roll Morton. The boys listened to a lot of jazz and had their favorite artists, none of whom April recognized.

The band was playing the 'Jelly Roll Blues' as their opening number. They would also close with it. Their second number, 'Beale Street Blues,' was straight from the south and Samuel found himself playing a duet with Morton's quick piano arpeggios. 'Poor Butterfly,' their last number of the set, was a pop tune that allowed Samuel to show how sweetly he could handle the trumpet. His table of fans erupted in applause as the band ended. Annabelle swelled with pride. She knew he was good but this was an audience that understood and appreciated this music and the man she loved.

The Somme River runs east-west from the Bay of Dover to the center of France, well north of Paris. In early July the Allies began a heavy artillery barrage that lasted eight days. On the ninth day 100,000 French and English soldiers left their trenches and attacked German positions along the river. Bayonets met, steel against steel, in bloody hand-to-hand combat. Twenty thousand English soldiers died…the bloodiest day in British history. Another sixty thousand were injured and by November, nearly five months later, there had been no definitive change in their positions. More than one million casualties littered the battlefield.

The Accrington Pals were a British unit of nearly eight hundred friends from the same school and Midlands community, fifty miles north of Manchester. After training, the Pals were designated the 11th Service Battalion of the East Lancashire Regiment. They had volunteered when their country asked for their help. They trained together. Their mothers knitted socks and scarves and traded recipes and stories about their sons. More than half the Pals were killed in the battle of the Somme on the first day…most of the rest were injured and the community never recovered from the loss of so many of their young men.

Robert's responsibilities were expanded as he, and other key staff of the Library of Congress, were temporarily assigned to both the State and War Departments. America was neutral, but it wasn't idle. Trade with Great Britain was increasing and pulling the country into a state of unparalleled prosperity. Germany was becoming increasingly nervous about America's ability to resupply their enemy and their U-boats continuously harassed the increasing number of ships that traversed the Atlantic.

Robert's reassignment, albeit temporary, was uncomfortable for he and other Negro managers who had higher Civil Service ratings than white staffers. Slurs and criticisms, usually unfounded, could be heard as whispered remarks through the building's corridors.

The War Department was trying to update a wide array of instruction manuals on everything from 'How to Drill Infantry Soldiers' to 'How to Transport Troops' to 'Housing for Soldiers with Dependents.' It would not have been proper to go to war with manuals written for the Civil War a half century earlier.

What Robert saw in addition, however, were reports from both the Allied and German military commands. Russia was losing ground every day against the German war machine. The Tsar was unpopular and there were no modern factories in that country capable of producing either guns, artillery, or airplanes. In Europe the war was exhausting both sides. Men and materiel were being used at a rate twice each combatant's ability to replace it.

"The planes the Royal Aircraft Factory are giving us to fight with aren't nearly as good as what the Germans have," David argued, having returned to his assignment in England. "They're too slow and no matter how well I train our pilots, we're going to lose them."

"Anthony, you're an instructor. Our factory people know what they're doing," Major Cochran said, as the two watched several planes take off.

"With all respect, Major, you haven't been in combat the past six months. Baron Richtofen's air group shot down nine of ours in one sortie. Six of those pilots crashed and were killed. I trained those boys. What do I say to their families?"

"It must be your training, Captain. Our planes are top notch."

"Major, you have your head up your ass if you believe that, and if you want to court-martial me for being insubordinate, go ahead. Either get me better planes or I'm going to return to working with the French."

David walked away, furious, leaving his superior speechless. Senior officers in the British military were not spoken to in such a manner. David's resignation was accepted and he returned to Louis Bleriot in France.

"Those people are incompetent," he said, sitting across from the French airplane manufacturer.

"Why are you surprised? They are British. They will always choose the easiest path rather than the best one. You need to try my new SPAD. I think you'll be impressed. Tomorrow, you fly...tonight, dine with me. My favorite chef has opened a new restaurant and promised me Tournedos that will melt in the mouth. He has also set aside an 1895 Cabernet from St. Michel, where I played as a young boy. We will dine together and toast your return."

It felt good to be back with someone he respected. Bleriot had the ear of the top French officials and if he said he could do something, they financed it.

"My SPAD VII will go 120 mph, even in a climb. Don't tell anyone but as soon as I get a bigger engine, it'll do better than 150. It turns on a dime and is the best thing in the air in a dogfight. It runs rings around the German planes. I think you'll be pleased.

"That's amazing. My Sopwith would look as if it was standing still. I wish the American government would realize what aeroplanes can do."

"Eventually they will. Meanwhile, you'd better get organized. I need you to train a great many pilots."

Chapter Thirty-One

Samantha was expecting. She said nothing to her mother when she missed her period. There was just too much work to do. Moss Grove was so much more complex than she'd ever understood. She had to decide how many acres to seed and which ones to let lie fallow or change to alfalfa or corn. Did she have enough share cropping workers? More families were leaving and the ones she found to replace them often had very little experience. How was the equipment and machinery working? Would it last another planting season? What was the forecast for rain? Was the price of cotton likely to go up or down?

Her mother had turned more and more of the plantation's decision-making over to her daughter. Sam knew her mother was still grieving the loss of her husband. Something inside of the younger woman realized sadly that her mother had started marking time until she could be reunited with her deceased husband. Sam's hope now was that her mother would live long enough to see a grandchild born here at the plantation.

Sam needed David to return. She hadn't written to tell him that he'd be a father early in 1917. His frequent letters explained that he was now in France and much happier working with Louis Bleriot than the British with their bloated egos. But she needed him at Moss Grove and there was no way she could ask him to give up his passion for flying. It was what he loved. I can't ask him to come back...not now, she realized.

"Mother, come downstairs and have coffee with me. It's a lovely day and I've an idea I want to discuss with you," Samantha said as she knocked on Bess' door.

"Later, dear. I want to rest a little longer."

"Nonsense! It's the middle of April, the birds are singing, and I feel wonderful. I need to share it with you."

Sam entered her mother's room and dragged Bess from her bed good naturedly, laughing and smiling.

"You're a pest," the older woman growled meekly.

"Of course I am. That's why you love me."

"What are you so worked up about?"

"I'll tell you over coffee."

The two women opted to have coffee and rolls on the veranda where the early spring sun could warm them. The smells of honeysuckle mixed delicately with the fresh chicory-laced coffee and they smiled easily as they watched two hummingbirds nuzzling at the nearby rose bushes.

"It is a beautiful day. Stuart and I used to sit here together in the early mornings when there was almost no sound, just a myriad of scents that we would try to identify," Bess mused.

"Mother, I want to invite Stephen's and Robert's families here for the summer. Thaddeus, Terry, and Noah are men now and they can help me. I think Thaddeus and Terry will graduate from school in June and Noah is only a year behind. It would be wonderful to have everyone back at Moss Grove again, don't you think?"

"That's a lot of people here. Do you think that it might be too much considering that you're pregnant?"

"How did you know?" Sam asked, astonished at her mother's comments.

"I'm your mother and I may be old, but I'm not senile. You're flush, you're breasts are popping out of your dress and you're flitting inches off the floor. I'm sure the entire staff has figured it out."

"Good. Now I don't need to hide throwing up from morning sickness," Sam laughed.

"I think it's a wonderful idea, having everyone here," Bess agreed.

"You are a hulk," Thaddeus said, as he shook Noah's hand. "What happened to the scrawny kid who I helped pester his sister? Oh, I'm sorry," Thaddeus blanched. "That was a terribly insensitive thing for me to say."

"Ruth's been dead for a few years now. I miss her but it's a lot harder on my parents."

"Noah, this is Terry, my other brother," Thaddeus said, eager to change the subject.

"Hi!" Terry smiled. "I heard you were the size of a small house but I didn't believe it. I'm glad we're friends. I don't think I'd ever want to get on your bad side."

"I like to think I don't have a bad side," Noah laughed. "I've been working out since I was really sick a few years ago. Now I just continue with it from habit and it does get me attention from a lot of girls."

The three looked at one another and grinned. Standing next to one another, their brown, beige and white skins told stories that strangers might find difficult to believe.

Neither Robert nor Stephen had been able to make the trip. Robert's work at the War Department had become more intense as the fighting in Europe and the Middle East continued in unabated bloodshed. Stephen's fledgling newspaper was finally making a small profit but it was edgy and he didn't want to risk being absent from the daily crises that frequently and unexpectedly might arise.

Maria was thrilled to be back in Moss Grove. She had wonderful memories of the first time Robert had brought her here. April almost had to cancel her plans to visit. There was a movie scheduled to begin shooting with a terrific part in it for her. The casting director assured her she was a shoo-in, but at the last minute they gave the role to the Director's mistress. Stephen said she'd lost the role to the 'casting couch,' a tawdry, but common, occurrence in young Hollywood.

Bess's energy returned and she felt ten years younger, thrilled at having guests to entertain and feed. The first thing she did was tell everyone about her daughter's pregnancy, much to Sam's instant embarrassment.

"I'm fine. Really, I'm fine. Guys," she asked. "Do you feel like working? I could really use your help. This is the time of year we bring in the cotton."

"Absolutely," they said, all nods and smiles.

"Do we need to ride horses?" Terry asked. "I've never been up on anything other than a small pony at a carnival."

"You can walk or take a car part way but most of the horses at Moss Grove are quite gentle. Your choice," Sam smiled.

Within days the three young men were out early, working the fields' side-by-side with the share croppers. They complained about the sharpness of the thorns that cut their fingers until some of the black workers showed them how to be more careful. Noah lifted the heavy bags filled with cotton as if they were small pillows. He became an immediate favorite of the field hands.

A few days later Thaddeus decided to surprise everyone. He drove out to the section they were working, and set a wind-up Victrola on the hood of the car. Within minutes a new hit, 'Bugle Call Rag,' was playing loudly and everyone nearby stood and stared. To a man, everyone broke out laughing and began clapping to the music, even the foreman. The work seemed to flow much easier after that. Thaddeus assigned one of the younger children to change the record and wind the machine when it was necessary. If the child forgot and the machine wound down, he was instantly reminded by shouts from his parents and others working the field. Harvesting cotton to the sound of lively music seemed to make it less of a chore.

"Thaddeus, that was a wonderful idea," Sam told him that evening.

"He's just strange," Terry said. "He listens to music on our small radio when he does his homework or his chores. I guess he doesn't like silence."

"I have something special to play for you. I've been saving it."

Barely containing himself, Thaddeus ran to his room and pulled a record from his pile, removing the paper sleeve and wiping it gently with his shirt.

'Jelly Roll Blues' came on fast and loud, its toe-tapping rhythms familiar to them all. But this arrangement was different. After the first chorus a trumpet began to play and the other instruments settled into the background.

"That's Uncle Samuel," Thaddeus said proudly. "My father met a record producer and after listening to the band at the Cadillac Café where they were booked, he agreed to press a record. I don't think it sold too many but my parents bought at least a dozen copies. I took this one for myself."

"Play it again," Bess asked, a tear forming in the corner of her eye. She knew it was Samuel. She could hear him, just as she remembered, the sweetness and clarity of each note...the tremolo when he cascaded up and down the scale. She looked over at her daughter. Sam's eyes were also damp and misty. She could sense that the spirits of Josiah and Rachel were there in the house with them as Samuel's notes ricocheted against the walls.

As summer was coming to an end Maria and April decided they needed to return home. The boys opted to remain through the holidays. With Samantha's pregnancy progressing and David unable to get home, the three had huddled together and decided it would be their job to keep Moss Grove going. It was past harvesting time but it would still be necessary to clear the fields, plant a few winter crops, and settle the plantation down for winter.

The three young men had become fast friends but Noah had also cast his eye on a pretty teenage girl who always seemed to appear as he was dropping his filled bag of cotton into the truck. Her name was Felicity...Felicity Adams. She was a tiny girl, not frail, but no more than a stripling when she stood near Noah. Her skin was as black as charcoal with a sheen that emanated a glow reflecting the passing sun. Noah had never seen anyone so lovely and his pulse raced whenever she approached.

Felicity always had a fresh glass of lemonade waiting for him, afraid to speak, but not afraid to smile.

"Ah, brother," Terry teased. "That little brown strumpet has her eye on you, tasty morsel that she is."

"Don't tease him," Thaddeus said. "I mean, really, he's three times her size. He'd squash her. He's Gulliver to her Lilliputian."

Noah smiled but didn't say anything. He did like the girl, although the two of them had never been alone. He'd tried to extricate himself from his brothers on more than one occasion but they seemed to know his intentions and rode him even more. It finally got to be too much.

"Alright, you guys. I like Felicity and I want to spend some time getting to know her. If that's a problem, I'll just have to crack your two heads together."

"I don't want my head cracked," Thaddeus laughed. "Terry... you want your head cracked?"

"No, I don't think so. Enjoy, big brother, but be gentle, she's a fragile little thing."

Samantha and David's son was born in February. They named him Stuart. David's family and much of the small Jewish congregation drove up to Moss Grove for the bris, surrounded by love and shouts of 'Mazel.' Felicity and Noah were now a couple and the teasing had stopped. 1917 was going to be a wonderful year. David was sure to return soon.

Stephen sat in his Los Angeles office surrounded by newspapers from around the country. His mood had improved considerably since April had returned home. He wasn't used to the two of them having the house to themselves but their two boys were already young men and, if they hadn't remained at Moss Grove, they'd probably be off somewhere else. He was proud that they'd decided to remain and help Bess and Samantha.

He thought that the life that he and April had fashioned was near-perfect. The newspaper was in the black, making at least a small profit. And April got just enough small movie roles to satisfy her and supplement their income. They continued draw stares whenever they left their own neighborhood and he'd been shouldered in an ugly way more than once. They had a few white friends but it was easier to relax in black neighborhoods. He was worried that might upset April but if it did, she never showed it.

They'd been invited to a few parties by studio people but showing up with a colored husband wasn't doing April's career any good.

Today all the newspapers shouted the same headline in the largest bold type faces that fit above the fold. The United States had declared war on Germany. It was April 1917 and it should have been just another pleasant spring day. He looked out his window. Cars were moving, children were playing hop-scotch on the sidewalk and the sun was shining. It was a lot like yesterday… only it wasn't. It would never be like yesterday again. Yesterday our country was at peace and today we are going to war and his sons would be at risk. He picked up Hearst's *Examiner*:

U.S. Declares War

President Wilson today, 5 April 1917, received a declaration of war against Germany from Congress. The likelihood of our country's entry into the war has been mounting for more than a year since Germany announced unrestricted warfare against all Atlantic shipping as their response to the effectiveness of the British blockade. The German U-Boats have sunk numerous unarmed vessels crossing the ocean and dozens of American lives have been lost.

In January the German Foreign Secretary Arthur Zimmerman sent a note to his counterpart in Mexico proposing an alliance that would support a Mexican military effort to regain Texas, New Mexico and Arizona territories. When the contents of that communiqué were released, our government felt it had no further option other than to declare war.

Robert's new assignment was a transfer to the Committee on Public Information. The nation had to be unified in favor of Allied forces and America's entry into the war. Their job would be to explain the need for public support and to denounce Germany and the Central Powers that supported her.

Large numbers of men would be enlisted to help the Committee by touring the country and delivering brief, but well-articulated, public messages to clubs, schools, and businesses. Robert was one of only a few Negroes selected after someone belatedly recognized that the black community would be more supportive if they heard the government's clarion call to arms from one of their own. In the same way, prominent Catholics and Jews were also brought into the program.

Meanwhile, Herbert Hoover, a talented engineer, was selected to run the Food Administration. His job was to ensure the well-being of the nation's food supply and expand it to support the ever-growing demand for food from European allies whose own lands had been shredded by war. To save food for export Hoover launched voluntary programs including 'Meatless Tuesday' and 'Wheatless Wednesday.' He urged the planting of 'Victory gardens.' The Fuel Administration, in the same vein, urged 'Heatless Monday' and 'Gasless Sunday.' America was being mobilized with a plethora of '___' less days and patriotism gained a renewed popularity.

April got a job with the government acting in short films that would be shown in the Nickelodeons. She played a housewife urging her husband and children to conserve. She'd wag her finger when they complained about no bread. It's Wednesday, she mouthed, as the words flashed on the screen. Her movie family enthusiastically walked to church on Sunday to avoid using their gas-fueled automobile. The nation was being bombarded on every level and a sense of determination exuded from every city.

Thaddeus, Noah, and Terry drove to the movie house in Baton Rouge just to see April perform. They applauded wildly.

Stephen's editorial a month later said it well:

> 'All these meat-less, wheat-less and other do-without 'isms are good fun and the minor discomforts they impose are all tolerable. But the United States has not yet sent troops into harm's way. No American had yet faced mustard gas or German artillery. No young boy from New York, Chicago, or Baton Rouge has lost an arm or been killed.
>
> Our government's encouragement to disdain everything German…food, music, and literature is inane. Eliminating the music of Wagner and Beethoven from concert repertoires is equally absurd. We are being urged to report any hint of enemy support as if reporting on our neighbors was a good thing. German families, who

may have been in our country for more than a century,
are being harassed simply for being German. The newly
enacted Espionage Act is fine. It makes it illegal to hinder
military recruiting or aid the enemy under penalty of
large fines or prison.

We need to recognize...albeit belatedly, that we need
a modern well-equipped Army. At the end of 1916 our
army, with mostly outdated equipment, numbered little
more than 100,000 men. Much of that equipment was
left over from the Spanish-American War that I had
participated in nearly two decades earlier.'

In May 1917 the Selective Service Act was passed requiring all men to register. Stephen, Samuel, and Robert were too old. Terry, Noah, and Thaddeus were exactly what the country needed to fight the war but the initial call was for unmarried men ages 21-31. There was another problem, only Terry was white. Noah and Thaddeus were colored. The law made no distinction but society and the Army did. Blacks, Coloreds, and Whites would never be permitted to serve together.

"I need you to send a note to people like Glenn Curtiss and other Americans," Bleriot said, sipping a morning coffee across from David.

"Now that the Americans are in this struggle we need them to replace all the war materiel we've been losing. We need at least two thousand aeroplanes a month."

David laughed. "My country hasn't produced half that many in the fourteen years since the Wright brothers first flight."

The French and the British also needed men and arms to replace their depleted manpower...casualties had been high. President Wilson appointed General John 'Black Jack' Pershing to run the Army.

"We're going to need a million men," Pershing shouted to his adjutant. "They tell me I'll be lucky to get a half million by year's end and if young Americans are going to be sent to fight in a European war, they'll damn well do it under American officers."

"Mr. Williams, how do you do? Thank you for coming to my office."

Emmett J. Scott was a bespectacled, erudite looking man, well-dressed, with a serious but affable look on his face. His forehead carried a perpetual wrinkle and he seemed to smile and grimace at the same time. Robert had heard of him but they had never met. Scott had been Booker T. Washington's confidential secretary and was heavily involved with Tuskegee University. Now the man had a new and formidable task ahead of him. And, here I am, Robert mused, sitting across from him, being offered coffee. He wished his father had lived to see this moment.

"I know your experience with Tuskegee was a tragic one. I am truly sorry for the violent loss of your brother, such terrible needless violence."

"It was never the fault of the school, Mr. Scott. It was the bigotry of those around it that caused the death of my brother. It was a long time ago but I still feel his loss."

"I'm sure. I need your help. There are ten million Negroes in this country, slightly more than ten percent of the population. German sympathizers are trying to stoke racial anger between blacks and whites in this country across the Midwest and the south. We need our people to be as patriotic as they always have been. To accomplish this we need to get our message out that an American victory against Germany and her allies will benefit all of us, black and white.

"What we don't want are stories about race riots and lynchings capturing the headlines of our newspapers. We don't want people like Eugene Debs and others dividing us along racial lines."

"And how do you propose to get out this message?" Robert asked.

"Through black-owned newspapers and black speakers at churches and union halls! We'll shout it off roof tops, if necessary," Scott said, warming to his subject.

"I want stories that laud the accomplishments of the 8th & 9th Cavalry Divisions that fought so bravely in the Spanish-American war and will certainly be among the units we send to fight in France. I want your ideas...new ideas. I want to undertake anything that might work. I want you to begin by meeting with Julius

Rosenwald. I think you'll be impressed. He's one of the owners of Sears, Roebuck and he's been appointed as a Member of the President's National Defense Board. He's also on the Board of Tuskegee and he's donated generously to programs that encourage Negro education."

> *French ground forces mutinied and refused to fight. 20,000 men deserted as they faced the onslaught of German artillery. The French Army was in disarray. Commanders were replaced...harsh punishments were meted out, but it all had little effect. France's ability to mount an effective fighting force was gone.*
>
> *The Russian revolution saw similar desertions from the Tsar's army and that country withdrew from the war. This freed up large numbers of German divisions back to the main battles in Europe and put additional pressures on Allied forces.*

"Hello, David," the familiar voice said as David left the cockpit of his Breguet and removed his leather helmet.

"Al...Al Koso. What are you doing in France? The last time I saw you I was in the hospital."

"I remember. Glad to see you'll be out of here soon. I've seen your file. You've doing a lot of flying again...new planes, better tactics. I've been promoted and reassigned as your aide. I'm now a Lieutenant in the U.S. Army Air Corps on temporary assignment to the French Air Corps. You've being reassigned as well, now that we're in the war. Congratulations, Major Anthony. You and I will be working, and maybe, flying together."

"I should be grateful but without new airplanes and more pilots you and I will be as useless as the proverbial 'teats on a boar.'"

"I'm sure it will be awhile. Our War Department is nothing if not snail-paced. Got time for a drink?"

"For more than one. I'll even buy."

They entered a crowded tavern just off base and grabbed a small table. It was noisy, mostly airplane ground crews. A large board over the bar counted French and German losses and changes to it were rarely pleasant events.

"I was happy to get away from the British," David said, sipping a cold, dark French beer. "Their pilots are good fellows but their senior officers are assholes, more worried about protecting their Oxford 'bums' than their men. I like the new Breguet...good reports."

"The Germans have been kicking our butts with their Albatross," Al added. "The Sopwiths just aren't a match. We've been losing two and three times as many planes and pilots as the Krauts. The new SPADs and Breguets are more than a match though if we can get enough of them."

"Yep...better speed and range. I can stay up for nearly four hours, even carry a small bomb load. Soon we'll be able to reach Berlin and rain hell down on the Kaiser."

David and Al could talk airplanes for hours and it was early morning before they returned to their barracks and a few hours sleep.

"Listen, you men are cadets, not pilots," Koso shouted to the group of fifteen uniformed young faces arrayed in front of him. David stood off to the side, smiling at Al's slang and implied threats.

"If you want to survive up there, you need to listen, and listen good. If you ever plan on getting laid again, you'd better listen. Then you need to think. When 'Jerry' comes at you there won't be time to think. You'll need to react and remember what Lt. Al told you. We're going to do it on the ground and then we're going to do it again in the air and no matter what I tell you, some of you are going to get yourselves killed in your first skirmish. Make sure it's the guy sitting next to you...not you."

"I'm thinking of enlisting," Thaddeus said. He, Terry, and Noah, were lounging under the trees nestled along the river banks.

"I've been thinking the same thing," Terry admitted. "I think I'd enjoy going over to France, killing some Germans, and whispering amour to some French girls."

"And which of those thoughts has the highest priority?" Noah laughed.

"It's the girls, definitely the girls. I know Terry and it's definitely girls," Thaddeus grinned. "What about you, Noah? Want to join me and fight for our country?"

"I'm not sure. It seems like the right thing to do but now that I've met Felicity, the idea of leaving her doesn't sound good. Besides, I'm a year younger that you guys. I'm not even sure they'd take me."

Terry and Thaddeus' return to Los Angeles was a happy event until the boys explained their intention to enlist in the Army. April had splurged and bought a large roast at the Farmer's Market on 3d street. It had been several months since they'd all enjoyed a full-sit down dinner together and she wanted it to be memorable. It was Sunday and a quiet day at the newspaper. Their glances and frequent touches made it clear they'd all missed one another.

April stared at her sons as they devoured the meal she'd prepared. They ate like hungry lions. Her sons had changed. They were no longer boys. The summer months working in the fields of Moss Grove had toned them both and they carried themselves with a new assurance in their demeanor. Terry no longer had the pasty white skin of coal miner parents. He would never be as dark as Thaddeus but the rays of the sun had been good to both of them. She struggled to reorient her maternal instincts to this new paradigm.

"I've been in a war before and it isn't the fun and excitement you think it is," Stephen said, his brow furrowing, as he remembered the months he and Robert had spent in the mountains of Cuba. It hadn't been all that bad, he admitted to himself, until he recalled all the men killed, or badly wounded, and having to live the remainder of their lives as less than a man. He hated the idea that one of these two boys, who he loved so much, might meet such a fate.

April sat quietly, unsure of her feelings. Her films and appearances encouraging the public to buy Liberty Bonds had enveloped her. She was full of patriotism and the righteousness of America's young war. But now that it was no longer an abstraction, she wasn't so sure. What if Terry or Thaddeus got shot or even killed? Would she feel the same way? But they were no longer boys and they would make their own decisions. And like all the widows she'd known, like herself, who had lost her first husband in a coal mine cave-in, she'd have to carry her grief and move on.

"You'll need to sign since we're only 17. You know we're capable…" Thaddeus said.

"….and if we have to wait until we're 18 the war might be over," Terry interrupted.

"Would that be so terrible?" Stephen asked, knowing, as he looked at April, that neither of them would win the argument. "You understand they won't let you serve together, he said, hoping to change the direction of the discussion.

"We've talked about that as well," Thaddeus said, glancing at his white brother. "Terry and I have discussed it. If Noah had decided to enlist, I would have gone with him since he's the darkest skinned of the three of us. But I'm pretty close to the same tanned skin color as Terry so we're going to enlist together and not say anything. If they figure it out, I'll deal with it then. The whole skin color thing is all crazy and wrong anyway but nothing says we have to admit it. And, I intend to win more medals than Terry does, so they'll be happy to have me."

Stephen and April looked at one another. The idea of 'passing' was never something they'd spoken about but Stephen had gone through most of his life avoiding the issue so there was no reason to believe Thaddeus couldn't do the same.

"I need to return to Washington," Noah told Felicity. Normally he would have sat with her by one of the small tables that rested outside the plantation church but she had become such a part of Noah's life that Samantha and Bess thought of her as one of their household.

"Why? Why can't you stay here with me? Miss Sam needs you. You're the only man around here who can help her and take charge, especially now that Terry and Thaddeus have run off to the Army."

"I haven't seen my parents for awhile and with a war on everything has changed. I need to have a quiet talk with them. I have a few more months of school and then, depending on how the war goes, I may enlist. But I love you. I will be back if you'll wait for me."

He took her in his arms and nearly engulfed her. When he kissed her it was with a passion that was new to them both.

"I love you, Noah. You need to come back to me. I don't want to think of a life without you."

"You stay away from those other boys or I'll have to break 'em in two," he laughed.

"Robert, I want you to help me write a letter to the President and everyone else we can think of. We need them to establish Negro combat units for this war and not push our people to the side as cooks and servants. General Pershing has made it quite clear that he prefers a white army and we can't allow him to have it. We need this nation to look on our men with the same pride as any other 'doughboy.'"

"We do have the 9th and 10th Cavalry," Robert reminded him.

"Forget it. The 9th is heading for the Philippines and the 10th is slated to head for the Mexican border. If we do nothing they'll be shuttled back to national park duty guarding buffalo after that. The nation will continue to think of blacks as second class citizens. We need a unit that's going to be in the middle of the action."

"Thaddeus and Terry have enlisted, Dad, and I'm thinking of joining up as well," Noah told his father after they had helped Maria with the dishes and all gotten comfortable in their living room.

"You are a year younger. If you'll wait until you're their age, your mother and I will agree. Be patient. We lost your sister; we wouldn't like to lose you. What about Felicity? What does she say?"

"She'd like me to come back to Moss Grove."

"Stay here. Help me. I'm busy trying to get a whole bunch of reluctant Congressmen and Generals committed to put together a black combat division but there is a great deal of resistance. Under pressure from the President they organized one but whenever you ask someone why they haven't been sent overseas to fight, you get excuses.

"Sunday there's going to be a march up Constitution Avenue by a bunch of white bigots and, probably, some Klan people, demanding the entire military be kept white. I understand the officers were given direct orders to not participate or voice their opinions on either side of the issue. It came directly from the White House. They were afraid of starting a race riot right here in the Capitol. That doesn't mean we can't stand along the parade route with our own signs. The NAACP, that they organized a few years ago, has solicited support from around the country."

Noah stood next to his father as a few hundred whites carrying signs or wearing hoods marched along a street crowded with thousands of angry blacks, eager to attack the marchers. Instead, all they could do was heckle.

"Oh, my lord," Robert said, staring at one of the men marching and carrying a 'this is a white man's country'.

"What is it?" Noah asked, staring at the ashen look on his father's face.

"That man...the one with that sign. I know him. That's Homer Draper. He's the boy who raped and murdered your sister, Ruth. Stephen interviewed him just after it happened and showed me his picture. It was a long time ago but I remember that he was on the University of Virginia's football team. He's older now but I'd never forget his face."

Robert left the crowd and sat down on a nearby bench, drained by the memories of how his beautiful daughter's life had been cut short. Noah wandered off, wanting to give his father time for his private sorrow. Robert dropped his head in his hands and cried. A randy white football hero with an ego bigger than his prick had raped and killed her. The crowd began to dissipate but Robert continued to sit.

Noah walked through the crowds that lined the street, never losing sight of Draper. The man was big but he'd gone to seed, wasn't taking care of himself. A few blocks later, the march ended, the men shook hands with one another and moved off in different directions. Draper started walking west, moving slowly, savoring the satisfaction of having touched shoulders with other men who felt the same way he did. Noah thought he might be heading for a streetcar. It was late afternoon. Shops were closing and people were heading home for dinner. Most would stay in, a few might go out to a movie or café.

"Keep walking, and don't turn around. I have a knife in my pocket and I'd love to rip out your guts."

"I don't have much money," Draper said, his voice nervous. "You can have it all. I've got a watch, too."

"Into the alley up ahead," Noah said, keeping himself close.

Homer Draper's hands began to shake.

"Please. Please don't hurt me," he stammered.

Noah put his knife away quietly, raised both his huge hands and came down on Draper's shoulders. The man dropped to the ground, unconscious. Noah understood fully that if Homer Draper could recognize him, he'd call the police immediately. Noah would become an immediate fugitive and he had no intention of ruining his life for this bastard lying prone in this darkened alley.

Noah decided embarrassment would have to be enough. He removed all of Draper's clothing, threw it in a corner and lit a match.

"Fuck you, you white piece of trash," he said, walking away, frustrated that he couldn't punish the man further.

Terry and Thaddeus joined other white recruits at Camp Lewis in Washington for their training. They had passed through the enlistment procedure and brief physical easily, and without incident, as they huddled with other partially-clad men. Their training was scheduled to last six weeks but, standing alongside the other recruits, they were warned that if they didn't do well, they could be kept longer. The balance of that first day was spent getting a uniform that fit and learning the intricacies of organizing their foot locker.

It was 4 A.M. the next morning when a very huge and bulky Sergeant named Buford 'Something' began screaming for them to get their asses up, their uniforms on, and line up outside.

"It's still dark, for Christ's sake, and it's raining," Terry muttered to Thaddeus. "This might have been a really bad idea."

"Since you're all out of shape, I'm only going to run you for two miles this morning, kinda' loosen you up before breakfast. Anyone can't keep up gets to clean the latrine," Buford bellowed.

"Take that bayonet and lunge," Buford shouted. "Pretend that dummy is a nigger coming to fuck your sister."

Thaddeus blanched and felt bile rise in his throat. Terry put a calming arm on his shoulder.

"That should get you angry. Carmody...don't shake its hand; kill the son of a bitch...harder...again. Stowers, you show him how. He's too genteel. Show him how a real soldier kills. Good... good," he shouted as the young Corporal lunged forward and up, wrenching the innards from the straw dummy.

The first American units sent to fight the Germans was designated the First Expeditionary Division, under the command of George Patton. It was constituted in May 1917 and sailed from New York Harbor for Le Havre, France in late June. It was an all-white, regular army unit; at least that's what its records indicated. Terry and Thaddeus had enlisted together, undergone basic military training without incident and were part of that contingent. Privates Thaddeus Carmody and Terry Donovan were Infantrymen and heading toward the type of grand adventure young men have always relished.

Chapter Thirty-Two

The French wanted Patton's Light Tank Brigades integrated into their divisions but Pershing was resolute. The American Expeditionary Force would fight their own battles led by their own officers.

"I feel like shit," Terry said, his face green, his hands holding his stomach. He and three others in his squad had become terribly sea sick crossing the Atlantic.

"If this damn ship doesn't stop rolling I'll barf up my entire guts before we land."

Thaddeus was busy ferrying fresh cold water for Terry and several other putrid-looking soldiers who were throwing up from constant nausea. The fetid air did nothing to improve their condition and the high waves that battered their convoy kept them below deck.

It would have been smoother if the ship slowed but fear of enemy U-Boats meant their ship and its escorts were forced to travel at maximum speed on a direct course.

Still not fully recovered, they disembarked at Le Havre and were shuttled onto Lorries and trains toward Lorraine in the northeast. It was a grueling two day trip with cold food and little sleep. Despite the discomfort and deprivation the men sang and shouted. Spirits were high and they would meet the 'Jerries' soon. After all, they were American 'doughboys.'

"Hear those guns," Thaddeus said. "We're getting close."

"Listen men," Lieutenant Bryan Upshaw began, raw young faces staring up at him. He was a Massachusetts lawyer, who would also be seeing his first military action. Upshaw came from a family of Brahmins north of Boston. Four generations of Upshaws had called Harvard their home but Bryan Upshaw III was the first man in his family to see military service and at 5'6", if he stretched, he barely qualified.

"The picnic is over. We're headed for the front at Nancy, about four miles to the east. The German 8th Division with its heavy artillery is spread in a front about three miles wide. Our French comrades have lost a lot of men and need a rest. You'll be replacing them. You'll be moving into well-fortified trenches but don't get careless…and whatever you do, do not stick your heads up out of curiosity …enemy snipers can shoot out your eye at well over a mile."

Upshaw stood and faced his men.

"Someone should tell him to stand," someone whispered.

"He is…he's just so damn short," another laughed.

"We didn't bring a lot of our armament, men," Upshaw said in a very stentorian voice. "It was either more men and less supplies or the other way around. The brass opted for more men." He tried to smile in an 'I'm one of the boys' style he'd used with juries but his men didn't care. They either wanted to fight, eat, or shit…maybe all three. What they didn't want was conversation.

"You're going to be issued French rifles and gas masks. The Germans have been known to lob artillery shells filled with mustard gas, so keep 'em close. Good luck and keep your heads down."

They moved up at night by squad, twelve men at a time, parallel to the trenches and sidled in twenty yards apart. At mornings first light the artillery barrages began again in earnest. Thaddeus stuffed cotton in his ears to muffle the sound and handed some to Terry.

Freddie Snider, a twenty year old from Toledo, stood on the ledge of the trench and peaked over.

"You can see the flashes from their…" He never finished. He fell back into the trench, his eyes still open, a small red dot on his forehead.

"Shit," Terry said. "Lieutenant…medic…someone. Snider took a bullet."

Upshaw hurried over, bent down and shook his head.

"Damn! He was warned. You were all warned. C'mon, move him to the back, the Graves crew will get him," he said, walking back dejectedly. Snider was the first of his men to get killed.

Light Colonel Billy Mitchell stood in front of his desk, unpacking files from his well worn leather briefcase. He had been in France since April, assigned by the American War Department, to learn everything he could about air combat. It was all new, the planes, the tactics who was who, and what was what.

"Come in," he said, without turning, at the knock on his office door.

"Captain Anthony reporting, sir," David said, standing at crisp attention.

"Yes, Captain…at ease," Mitchell smiled, putting down a stack of papers and extended his hand graciously. "I prefer informality whenever possible. May I call you David?"

"Certainly, sir."

"Please take a chair. I've read your file. Impressive! You've logged a lot of hours in both France and England. You were a test pilot for a brief time with Glenn Curtiss. I want to know as much as possible about the planes you've flown and anything you've learned about tactics."

The two men spoke for more than an hour. Mitchell ignored knocks on the door and phones ringing. He was only interested in air combat. They moved to a large map of Europe where pins marked the location of various Allied and enemy Divisions.

"Where are the airfields? Why are the Germans having so much more success in the air than we are? Is it their planes or their pilots?"

"The Fokker's synchronized machine guns are effective and the German pilots know how to use them. They'll try and get behind you and blast away but they can also come at you from above or below. The Sopwith Triplane is more maneuverable and has a good rate of climb but I prefer the Bristol fighter for all around performance."

"And pilots?"

"We're training them but it takes time. If we put them into combat too soon our losses skyrocket."

"We've started building Jenny's at several factories in the states but the start up is much slower than they promised. Your first six will arrive in early January. We're estimating fifty hours of pilot training and our first combat experience with them by spring. Your new assignment is to make it happen."

Christmas 1917 at Moss Grove was cold and damp. It also had an unpleasant emptiness. Even the cries and laughter of a newborn could only lift spirits briefly. Samantha missed David. Little Stuart and his father still hadn't met one another. Felicity longed for Noah. They wrote one another three times a week and Noah phoned occasionally from Georgetown but she missed burying herself in his big arms, engulfing her, and making her feel safe. At his parent's insistence Noah agreed to finish his last year of school but Felicity was sure his desire to enlist was greater than his desire to marry and settle down and he'd be absent even longer.

Bess wasn't doing well. She was troubled by a constant chill in her bones despite large crackling fires burning in most of the rooms. A heavy wool shawl wrapped around her shoulders was her constant companion. Samantha just wouldn't permit herself to become lethargic. The demands of the plantation wouldn't allow it. She needed to plan for spring planting. Cotton prices should remain high as long as the Army was producing so many uniforms. It didn't take her long to realize what a help Terry, Noah, and Thaddeus had been. It was too bad Stephen or Samuel weren't here, she mused.

In a small apartment on the Avenues, Samuel fussed over Annabelle. San Francisco's fog hung like lace draped over the nearby hills and, in the early morning, it was frequently impossible to see the homes across the street. Annabelle was well-along in her pregnancy but because of her epilepsy the doctors were more than a little worried. They didn't know what to expect but they were certain the two conditions placed extra stress on the young mother's system.

"You men worry too much," Annabelle said, her breathing labored, her brow damp with perspiration. She was in her sixth month and she'd been careful to control her weight gain.

"This baby is going to be fine, you'll see." She smiled at Samuel. The looks of love that passed between them spoke volumes…I love you…I'm really worried…please don't leave me.

April and Stephen had suggested they stay with them in Los Angeles where the weather was warmer, at least through Annabelle's pregnancy, but Samuel had steady work at the clubs in North Beach. What he hadn't been able to explain was his need to return to the city that had given him several happy months with his parents as a family. Even now he found himself walking the street where they'd lived. He recalled, with dampness in his eyes, his father holding his hand as they walked from the cable car to their home. The earthquake ended that part of his life as abruptly as a door slamming in his face.

He was fortunate that their next door neighbor, Harriett Finkle, a widow, was kind enough to keep their adjoining doors open when he was gone, in case Annabelle needed anything.

"It's going to be a wonderful new year, Annabelle," Samuel said. "We'll be a family. Maybe your mother will visit."

In fact Lulu wanted to come the moment she heard her daughter was expecting but leaving her brothel to others was a formula for disaster. Her girls could be talked into leaving for other houses. Customers might not pay and the police could get more aggressive. Besides, the holidays were always the most profitable time of the year. January, she decided…January would be best.

New Year's Eve Samuel and Annabelle lit a fire, pulled a blanket around them, and toasted the New Year. It was 1918.

"Here's to the three of us," Samuel said, raising his glass, staring at the orange and red flames.

The glass dropped and shattered. Annabelle fell to the floor and began having tremors…her entire body was convulsing. Her eyes were glazed, not focusing.

"Annabelle…Annabelle! Mrs. Finkle," he screamed. "Call the doctor…get an ambulance."

By the time daylight arrived, Annabelle had died from a combination of complications of her pregnancy and her epilepsy.

The baby, a frail tiny infant girl with a sparse crown of black curls and the promise of a dimple in her cheeks, arrived more than two months early and was barely clinging to life at five pounds. She had blue eyes and a skin that was newborn pink over the color of sand reflected by the sun. Samuel was distraught, his body wracked with grief, his sobs a torrent of sadness. Annabelle had made his life rational and now he failed her. He had lost another loved one. He began to think of it as 'the Roger's curse.' It was he who had gotten her pregnant and the pregnancy had been more than her body could deal with. The child had been her idea and now she was gone. He had a daughter but it was his wife he wanted.

"You took my wife, damn you. You, who is supposed to be a loving God. Why? She was such a good person," he blustered to unknown entities.

Lulu White arrived a few days later. Stephen and April took the train from Los Angeles for the funeral. Samantha and Bess sent flowers and apologies for not being able to get there in time. The baby was still in the hospital being cared for and the tiny infant, who would never be held by her mother, was still unnamed.

The apartment felt empty. Mrs. Finkle brought in cakes and food but no one was really hungry.

"I want to take the baby back to New Orleans with me," Lulu said. "A father raising a daughter by himself isn't a good thing."

"Neither is raising her in a brothel," Samuel said softly, knowing he was facing a difficult conundrum.

"I want to name her Anna, after her mother," he said, having reached his first decision. "Lulu, are you alright with that?"

The brusque woman, nodded, tears in the corner of her eyes.

"Anna Rogers…welcome to the world. You'll need to be strong," he half-whispered. "You were conceived out of love and that should be a good start. I've also decided to go back to Moss Grove and help Sam. It'll be close to you, Lulu, and Bess and Samantha will be thrilled. Anna and Stuart can keep one another company. It isn't the New Year I'd envisioned but I think I can make it work, and, at least, I need to try." In truth, he wasn't sure. He'd be returning to where the Rogers had first made their mark and where the curse from their strain of black blood brought death to so many loved ones.

In the early months of 1918 the weather across France was cold, wet, and blustery. Arctic winds drifted from the north and troops froze in their trenches. Cases of frostbite were all too common. Food rations were sporadic as supply trucks were unable to move across icy muddy roads.

Thaddeus, Terry, and their entire squad huddled together in shifts. The long boring hours had even softened Lieutenant Upshaw's demeanor. Two more of his men had been killed, one of them from the soldier's own hand grenade that he neglected to throw after he'd pulled the pin.

"We're going to be moving up, men. Private Carmody, take three men and get ready. When night falls I want you up and searching out soft spots in the enemy's fortifications. You'll send one of the men back within two hours with whatever information you've gathered. At 4 A.M. our artillery barrage will begin so make sure the remaining three of you are hunkered down. At first light our division moves forward. Understand?"

"Yes, sir. I'll take Privates Donovan, Jones, and Smedley."

"Good choices. Make sure you have enough ammunition, water, and something to eat, **AND** don't forget your gas masks."

At midnight the four men gathered facing Lt. Upshaw, a map of the area spread on the small makeshift table between them, a small dimly lit lantern casting shadows on the side of the tent. The men had blackened their faces. Terry and Thaddeus smiled at the obvious humor of that situation.

"Two to three hundred yards out you may encounter their forward skirmishers. With luck they won't be too attentive. If they sound the alarm we're all in trouble. You need to surprise and kill them before that can happen. Beyond that you will likely encounter a barbed wire barricade. You'll need to cut it and crawl through. What we need to know is how far away their trenches and concrete bunkers are and how well they're protected. You stay there. Don't go any further. I don't want you killed and more important to all of us, I don't want you discovered."

The moon was hidden behind clouds and they were blessed with almost total darkness. Thaddeus' compass and sense of direction would have to keep them headed toward their objective. The crawling was slow with their rifles nestled in their arms just inches above the slurried terrain.

"Shit," Smedley muttered. "I've already got mud in my crotch."

"No talking," Thaddeus whispered. "Stay close."

Twenty minutes later, they could hear voices ahead and a little to the left. They stopped and listened, barely able to see one another.

"Terry, ten minutes! We'll meet in the middle at the sound of their voices. We're going to need to take them out quickly, before they can warn the others," Thaddeus motioned Terry and Jones to the left. He and Smedley moved to the right.

The men moved silently, their stealth their only protection. They couldn't see their counterparts but Terry knew that Thaddeus would be where he was supposed to be, and as the seconds counted down, the four men moved as one. Two of the German soldiers on duty were relaxing, enjoying a smoke break, carelessly unaware that the lit tip of their cigarette had become a beacon for armed men. A third soldier napped nearby. In seconds the four Americans slid into the enemy trench, their knives poised, penetrating deep into the necks of the German sentries. The three Krauts were dead before being able to fire a warning shot… their first goal had been accomplished.

The four of them huddled together, aware that these were the first men they'd actually killed. Jones was shaking. Killing wasn't the same as thrusting your knife or bayonet into a straw dummy. He'd seen the man's eyes as he'd pushed the blade into his enemy's carotid artery. The German soldier couldn't have been more than sixteen and Jones thought the boy looked strangely like his cousin back in Buffalo.

"Grab something to eat and drink a little water. Settle your nerves. We'll rest for five minutes and then head out again," Thaddeus said softly. They had done well so far. He decided that Jones would be the one he'd send back once they'd passed through the barbed wire.

It was still black as hell. Terry always thought that was a funny metaphor since Hell was supposed to be filled with fires but he often thought about silly things when he didn't want to focus on ugly uncomfortable things, and crawling in the dead of night made him want to think about anything but sloshing his way through French mud during the winter. Southern California and pretty girls at Santa Monica made for much better musing.

They reached the barbed wire and paused. Terry and Jones were twenty yards from Thaddeus and Smedley. Each pair could occasionally hear the click of the wire cutters from their counterparts and everything was going smoothly until Jones, still unsettled from killing a human being, cut himself on the sharp barbs.

"Shit...shit," he moaned.

"Ve gatz?" came a shout from ahead of them as flood lights came on. A German sentry asking 'who was there' had heard the noise and alerted the others.

The spotlight caught Jones kneeling, a glazed look in his eyes, holding his bloodied finger, as the others shrunk themselves and pushed down into the dirt.

"Me, Private Jones," he said, thinking quickly and standing. "I'm alone on Recon but you've caught me."

He put his hands into the air and moved forward but he hadn't taken two paces before rifle fire dropped him to the ground. The German flood lights sprayed back and forth looking for others as their soldiers called out. Thaddeus was sure they'd leave their bunkers and search for anyone else traveling with the man they'd killed, but no one came. They waited for long minutes after everything went quiet again before crawling toward one another.

"Smedley, I want you to go back and report to the Lieutenant that we only got as far as the barbed wire and where it is. Terry and I will move toward that small group of bushes but he'll need to hit this area with artillery. Now go!"

"What do you think about during times like this?" Terry asked as he and Thaddeus lay side by side, covered with as much foliage as they could find without making too much noise. Smedley had been gone about ten minutes. At one point they thought they'd heard a rifle shot. Maybe Smedley was dead or wounded, Thaddeus worried. We're never going to know whether he made it back or not until the artillery barrage begins.

"I don't think I've ever been in times like this. All this killing! Reminds me of the Civil War battles I read about in school. My grandfather was a soldier in that war, first for the south, then the north. All of that killing and all of this bloodshed really makes you wonder if wars ever really settle anything."

"It did bring an end to your grandfather being a slave, didn't it?"

Before dawn, as planned, the French and American artillery barrage began. The French 75's rained shells...fifteen per minute, entire battalions of them. They were overshooting the barbed wire protection but somewhere behind it the German divisions were hunkering down getting ready for the Allied offensive.

"This is shit," Terry said. "We need to move."

Thaddeus nodded and they crawled slowly out from behind the foliage, moving forward, hugging the ground.

"I'll go left, you go right," Thaddeus whispered, nearing the barbed wire that had killed their buddy. They cut the wire and sidled through, hoping the Germans were still deep in their trenches avoiding the artillery.

They each lobbed a grenade into the trenches, then another. They started firing and within seconds gunfire was coming back at them. They slowed their fire, trying to make every shot count. It wouldn't do to run out of ammunition before Upshaw and the rest of their men arrived. And then it was over and the Germans began retreating, slowly at first, then in pandemonium.

"Great job, Terry," Thaddeus shouted as the rest of their unit approached.

"Private Carmody, you were supposed to send one of your men back. We thought you'd all been killed." Upshaw said, his uniform grimy, his face now battle weary.

"Jones was killed but I want to recommend him for a medal. He stood and faced the Krauts trying to divert their attention. We were sure we were goners. I sent Smedley back. Didn't he make it?"

"Never got to us. Where is Private Donovan?"

"He should be....Terry...Terry...are you alright?"

Thaddeus ran toward where Terry had been hunkered down. He was still there, unconscious, fresh blood on his jacket.

"Medic...can we get a medic over here?" Thaddeus shouted, kneeling down.

"Here, let me help you...we can carry him to the medics in less time than it will take for them to get here," Upshaw said.

"Hey, not so rough," Terry said, opening one eye. "I'm damaged government property."

"Thank God you're alive. Relax...we'll get you taken care of."

"It's a big piece of shrapnel," the doctor said. "Impossible to know whether it was from enemy artillery or one of our own but you're lucky it didn't hit any vital parts."

"Does that mean I'm a hero?" Terry teased, smiling at Thaddeus and Upshaw standing nearby.

"You men did well and I'll certainly put you both in for a Field commendation. You'll also get a Purple Heart for being wounded."

"See, Thaddeus, I told you I'd get more medals than you," he said as the morphine helped him slip into unconsciousness.

> *Dear Mother and Father,*
>
> *I'm sorry I couldn't tell you but I was afraid you would continue to pressure me to remain in school. Things in Europe are moving so quickly I decided I needed to volunteer now.*
>
> *You would have laughed if you'd seen me at the recruiting office. There were a bunch of scrawny white and colored boys and when the sergeant saw me his eyes bulged out and he didn't seem to care if I was fourteen or forty. I told him I was nineteen and he passed me right through.*
>
> *I've been sent to Camp Whitman in New York, near Poughkeepsie, and assigned to the 369th Infantry Regiment. They call us the Harlem Hellfighters or the Black Rattlers. They're training us for combat not just cooking or serving...real combat.*
>
> *Please be happy for me. I love you both. I also hope you'll extend your love to Felicity. If she'll have me when this is all over I intend to ask her to marry me.*
>
> *Noah*

His letter to Felicity was shorter but much more difficult. He promised that if they gave him a leave before shipping him to Europe he'd come straight to Moss Grove. He hoped she'd wait for him.

> *Events in early 1918 were moving rapidly. The Germans, eager to end the war before American resources overwhelmed them, launched a major offensive on the Western front with the goal of dividing British and French forces and move toward Paris quickly. Heavy artillery barrages by giant cannon produced at Germany's Krupp Metal Works and carried on flat bed rail cars enabled the Krauts to penetrate all the way to Paris. The Allies found themselves in steady retreat. Without motorized support and with long supply lines, however, the German Army found itself stalled. They could advance no further.*

"I am not going to have a black or colored Combat Division in my Army, Pershing stormed. "I'm not even going to have a Colored Combat Company and I don't give a damn what Congress or the President orders. They'll bolt the first time they face the enemy. There's not enough fighting blood in the black man to fill a good drinking glass and they aren't bright enough to follow orders."

The General huffed and puffed, storming angrily around his office as his Adjutant read him an official letter from President Wilson obliquely demanding the establishment of colored combat units.

"You need to do something to appease them, General. What if we train them and then send them to fight with the British? That might satisfy everyone. They'd see combat but we wouldn't have to tarnish the image of our white soldiers."

"I like the idea but they've made it clear they don't want blacks tarnishing their lily-white Army either. Try the French. They'll be thrilled to get additional men of any color. Make sure it's done. Meanwhile, tell our President we will accommodate his request."

The 369th Regiment started life as the 15th New York Infantry, located in a cigar store in Harlem, the music from a dance hall on the floor above blaring loudly, playing new jazz riffs. Two hundred eager Negro men, many with previous military experience, crowded inside. When war was declared the unit was renamed and sent to Camp Whitman for training.

Noah Williams was promoted to Corporal before they boarded their transport ship for Brest. He had astounded his Sergeants and white officers by his strength and agility. Their boat was set to sail on 17 December but, once on board, with their gear stowed, the Captain refused to sail due to a snow storm. Then the ship began to leak. Noah and his buddies had been given no leave after their basic training. Europe and the Germans were awaiting their arrival.

Colonel William Hayward, their white commanding officer, demanded that the ship sail and, finally, days before New Year's, they left New York harbor.

Their first assignments were the typical Negro 'move this' 'cook that' labor assignments and despite Hayward's requests that they see combat, nothing came of it until March when General Pershing relented and signed an order assigning the 369th to the French. If Coloreds are going to fight, he'd said, let them do it with the French. The men were given French helmets and rifles to supplement their American uniforms and in April they joined the French 16th Division in the trenches.

"You the biggest nigger I've seen around these parts," the friendly soldier said, ambling up to Noah. "My name is Henry Johnson from Albany, New York."

Noah extended his hand. "Noah Williams...Washington, D.C."

"Think we'll ever see combat?" Johnson asked.

"I sure hope so. I didn't come all this way to peel potatoes for the white officer's mess."

Johnson had been a redcap porter on the New York subway system, carrying luggage and moving freight. The work he was forced to accept was boring and demeaning. He wanted more from life. Fighting the Germans had to be better. He enlisted and given a new uniform. A generous smile returned to his face. This was more like it.

"Well, I want to stay close to you," Henry laughed. "I figure you'll block anything that comes my way...sort of like standing behind a tree."

"I'll do what I can," Noah smiled.

Noah became his Company's spokesperson. The little bit of French he'd learned around the Capitol was more than anyone in his unit knew and the French soldiers were equally ignorant of knowing English. Within weeks, Noah's color became irrelevant as the better supplied American doughboys gladly traded cigarettes and chocolate for brandy and brie. But there was no combat. There was ditch digging, ammo unloading, kitchen work, and guard duty. The men got angrier and angrier and Colonel Hayward's pleas became louder and more indignant.

"We got our wish, gentlemen," he said as he faced his troops. "We'll be fighting with French troops. Check your gear, clean your rifles, and take extra socks. The Quartermaster will issue you ammunition. Be ready to go at 0600 tomorrow. Dismissed!"

Shouts rang out everywhere as men clapped one another on the back and rushed off to have their last beer or write their last letter.

Chapter Thirty-Three

"She's beautiful," Samantha said, taking little Anna in her arms. It was clear the tiny girl was colored. She had a light milk chocolate hue that amplified the soft warmth she exuded. She was so glad Samuel had brought his young daughter to Moss Grove and she had no intention of raising this complex issue with this man she had grown up with and adored. That would have to be at another time when he wasn't as emotionally fragile as he was now. She had never seen him look so weak. His eyes were sunken from lack of sleep and he still carried the loss of his wife on his shoulders.

"I'm so glad you and Anna have decided to live with us here at Moss Grove. I need your help. I'm overwhelmed."

"I'll do what I can. I haven't been much more than a trumpet player these past few years but I suppose cotton is in my blood. Look at my descendents."

"I'd rather not," she laughed, as little Stuart crawled over, pulling himself up uncertainly and looking up at this new man.

"Daddy," the toddler chimed.

"No, little man," Samuel said, lifting the boy up. "I'm your Uncle Samuel. Can you say 'Samuel?'

Samuel stared at the row of headstones aligned before him, Samuel Rogers, Jedidiah Rogers, Henry Rogers and their wives, the generations who had built Moss Gross and caused whatever 'Roger's curse' led to him losing so many people for whom he cared. His parents, Josiah and Rachel, were marked by simple marble carvings, their bodies lost in the morass of San Francisco's earthquake. He hadn't been able to rid himself of his depression. If it hadn't been for Anna, he would have been happy to end it all with a single well-placed bullet.

Samantha made no demands on Samuel for the next few weeks. Bess got a resurgence of energy and the warm sun began to heal their bodies. But throughout the main house emotions were still unsettled. There had been no mail from David nor from the other men of their lives. Felicity came over more often and enjoyed spending time with the two young children, wanting to stay close to Noah's kin.

"I'm ready," Samuel said one day, struggling with his demons but determined to move forward. "I don't want to live off your largesse forever. What can I do?

"How about I put you with our foreman, Claude Jefferson? I think if you spend a little time with him you'll get a sense of how we plant cotton these days. It's changed a little...better equipment..."

"...and no slaves!"

"Right...no slaves. It gives our people a better incentive and it's to everyone's interest to produce a good crop."

"You ever work a plantation, Missa' Sam?" Claude Jefferson was a short, stocky, Negro with dark splotches pasted like ink marks across his face. His question was asked with a wary openness he often used with white folks. He had a good thing here at Moss Grove and he didn't want to appear 'uppity' to folks he'd just met, at least not in Louisiana...maybe other places as well.

Claude had been born a slave on a tobacco plantation in South Carolina. He'd been luckier than some but he never knew his pa. When he was seven, his mother died giving birth to her fifth child and she wasn't yet twenty. As soon as they told him he weren't no slave no more, he hightailed it west but when he saw that big river in front of him he figured he'd come far enough. He'd been at Moss Grove now into his third year and it suited him, he mused. The white folks were decent, food was good, and there were some pretty young 'nigra' girls for him to choose from. He'd need to settle on one and get married soon. He was making too many of the share croppin' families nervous. They were keepin' their daughters away from him.

"Look at my hands," Samuel complained. "I doubt I'll ever be able to hold a trumpet again."

"They do look pretty raw," Samantha said, gently holding them and seeing the blisters. "I'll get you a pair of soft leather gloves… you'll still be able to work and they'll protect your fingers."

Samuel went over to where Anna and Stuart were playing and, despite his earlier protests about the condition of his fingers, he took out his trumpet. The children loved to hear him play.

"I wrote a special song for you, Anna. And Stuart…you need to tell me whether you think it's any good."

The first notes were flat and both children laughed. Samuel massaged his scarred and stiff fingers and closed his eyes. He let the seconds pass as he slowed his breathing. His young daughter and nephew stared. It was as if they were watching a fairy tale where a handsome prince suddenly appears. This time when Samuel raised his trumpet and began playing the music was sweet. His eyes remained closed as the strains of a new song, the best of jazz and gospel, floated out the windows and across the newly planted fields.

In his small house, Claude Jefferson left his chair and stood on his porch. He smiled. I can teach that boy about cotton, he thought, but he can teach us all what music means. That's Godly music… it sure is!

Private Terry Donovan, wearing two medals on his chest, and a heavy padded bandage on his side where a large piece of shrapnel had been removed, gripped Thaddeus in a tight embrace.

"You know, I'd have traded these medals for a chance to stay and fight with you," Terry said.

"You did well. It was the luck of the draw that the metal hit you and not me. Give my love to our folks."

Terry waved from the lorry as it drove off. He sat next to the driver while four soldiers on litters crowded in the rear. They would all be going home on a near-empty transport that had recently ferried thousands of troops from the states across the Atlantic Ocean to Europe.

The German offensive stalled and the Kaiser's goal of ending the war with a surgical thrust failed. They hoped that a well-planned attack against Flanders could defeat the British forces ensconced there and launched a diversionary attack along the Marne Rive. They were surprised to meet unexpectedly stiff resistance from Allied troops under Marshall Foch, who was struggling to coordinate troop movements of French, Italian, British and American forces, including the Black 369th, now nicknamed the Harlem Hellfighters, ready to face their first real combat.

Colonel Hayward's Regiments were spread across two miles of trenches facing well-established enemy fortifications. Artillery shells passed one another in steady arcs frightening every living thing with their ear-splitting noises. He thought he might get objections to a Negro unit fighting alongside but the French and British Commanders just seemed pleased to have American military support. One British Captain poised to discuss leading black troops into battle getting a stern look from his superior officer, stopped him up before the suggestion could leave his lips.

"Noah, take your squad and move down the line another fifty yards. We need to spread out. Make sure your men have their gas masks at the ready and wait for my orders before taking any action."

Machine gun fire was intense and the summer heat compounded the tension that nervously soaked through the men's uniforms. There were bugs everywhere. They were enjoying a feast from the fetid wounds of men lying dead between the barren yards that separated the opposing forces.

"Don't get yourself killed, big guy," Henry Johnson said, squatting on his helmet, and looking up at his Squad leader.

"I don't intend to, Henry. My girl back in Louisiana would be mighty upset if I didn't come back."

Before they could continue they heard the rattle of tanks heading toward them, belching smoke from small cannon fire. Behind them troops moved cautiously in their wake.

"Fire…fire…and keep firing," Colonel Hayward shouted through the din and over the tiny Signal Corp telephone he used to reach his Company commanders.

French Howitzers fired, and seconds later, fired again, their crews black with smoke as they moved in unison, load, close the breech, stand back, fire, open the breech, stand aside as the spent red hot shell casing came out the breech. Then start all over again… less than a minute.

On Noah's flank British tanks sought to engage the German tanks, their chain-like treads struggling to gain traction on the uneven terrain. German tanks burst into flame as artillery shells made contact. Others turned and engaged the smaller British tanks, the heavier cannon obliterating their enemy upon making contact. For nearly an hour the battle continued until, out of fuel and ammunition, both sides retired.

"Masks…get your masks on," someone shouted. The Kraut's artillery began launching shells that exploded over the troop formations.

A yellow haze slowly began to descend. Noah checked those around him through the thick lenses of his mask.

"Make sure no one has bare skin showing," he ordered. Then he heard screams a few yards away. A young kid from Ohio, Buddy Turner, was writhing on the ground, blisters beginning to form.

"Help me! I'm choking," he whispered. Turner had failed to don his mask securely and he had yanked it off to wipe his already inflamed eyes.

"Henry, come here," Noah shouted, although the combination of the mask and ongoing artillery barrage made him barely audible. "We need to get Turner out of here and back where he can get some treatment.

Henry Johnson and Noah each grabbed one of Turner's arms and lifted him. As quickly as possible they moved down the trench to the intersection that would take him to a safer area. Once they found some medical help they turned and scurried back to their position.

The British and Americans retaliated with their own barrage of gas canisters and the favorable winds began to disburse its ugly yellow cargo over the German formations. Even through the cacophony of artillery bursts and rifle fire it was impossible not to hear the screams of German troops as their skins began to blister.

When dawn broke a half-quiet pervaded the battlefield. Noah heard the sound of airplanes. He looked up. Two squadrons of Sopwiths were heading over the German lines, dropping grenades and looking for German Fokkers that would be coming at them from the north. He wondered whether David was in one of the planes, Noah thought, as he drifted off for a few minutes of sleep.

"Donovan, we're giving you three weeks leave and then you'll be reassigned," a pink-faced Lieutenant told him. "I'm glad you're wounds are healed. The doctor says you can leave tomorrow once they give you one more going over. I just wanted to give you time to give some thought to what you might do."

Terry Donovan was lucky. The hospital just outside New York City had been set up for a large number of returning wounded but Terry was one of the early ones and he had been solicitously cared for including visits from musicians and show people from the city's theatre district. Once W.C. Field stopped by, another time Al Jolson.

"Thanks, Lieutenant. I think I'll head home to L.A. and see my folks first. Any idea where I might get assigned?"

"No, but we can use men with combat experience in a lot of places. If you think of anything before you leave, let me know and I'll see what strings I can pull."

That evening Terry placed a call home. It would have been expensive, more than a dollar a minute, except the Army provided it as a free for their hospitalized soldiers. After the mandatory 'glad you're safe' and 'when are you coming home' comments as well as the 'I love you' all around, they turned to more specifics.

"Thaddeus is fine. He's a good soldier and the men respect him. No...no hint of problem on his race," Terry responded. "We're all so grimy, we all look alike anyway. Dad, I have a chance to suggest my next posting and I wondered if you had any thoughts on the subject?"

"Well, it would be nice to have you close to home," Stephen said. "I'm sure your mother would be thrilled. She's standing here next to me and nodding. On the other hand it is a chance to see another part of the country."

"That was my thinking also," Terry said. "I thought I'd ask about D.C. I could see Noah."

"Noah enlisted. He's in France with the 369th...the Harlem Hellfighters."

"Wow, I thought he was too young to be accepted."

"He lied about his age. He's so big no one thought to ask."

"I can believe that. Maybe I'll try Washington anyway. They say that's where the action is and Robert and Maria are there. I'll try and come home first. Now, put Mom on so I can say hi. I love you guys."

Terry didn't make it back to Los Angeles. The moment he suggested reassignment to the Capitol, the Lieutenant smiled, picked up the phone and four hours later Terry was on the train heading to the city with connections south to the Capitol.

Bess was playing with Anna and Stuart on the lawn near the river. They were rolling a ball between them when her arm stopped in midair and she fell over. The children tried unsuccessfully to rouse her. Samantha heard shouts and rushed out with Felicity and one of the men hurrying behind her.

"Mother...mother," Sam cried. "Please...please be alright."

Bess was carried to the house and laid on her bed but she was gone. She had passed from this world and joined Stuart, the man she'd loved for most of her life, in the next.

"She was a great lady, Samantha," Samuel said, running in from the field the moment he heard. "And she had a full life. She died enjoying her grandchildren...not a bad way to go." He put his arm around her and let her cry.

Bess was buried next to her husband, Stuart. Lulu had driven up from her place in Storyville and held tightly on to her granddaughter. Anna squirmed. She preferred to stand next to Stuart, her almost-older brother. Samantha tried vainly to not cry but she felt so alone…so overwhelmed by life.

Sam fell asleep the moment they returned to the house and the small coterie of guests stayed only long enough to pay their respects. It was the following afternoon before Sam pulled herself together enough to come downstairs and see the children and confirm that Moss Grove was continuing to function. She knew her mother would never have permitted her to remain lethargic for long.

> Lance Corporal Leonard Skinner was assigned to a British gunnery regiment gathering for action at Etaples, France when he took ill. He was hospitalized with high fever and his illness was diagnosed as viral pneumonia. The problem was that his system wasn't responding to the traditional medical treatment for pneumonia and whatever he had was extremely virulent. Within days another ten cases were reported and patients were quarantined.
>
> "This isn't any pneumonia I'm familiar with," one doctor proclaimed. "And, we're getting reports of other outbreaks from American units as well."
>
> Skinner died four days later and a third of the others who were infected didn't survive the week.
>
> "We have something on our hands we're not familiar with," an American doctor said at a hastily called meeting.
>
> It was the early signs of a pandemic most would call the Spanish flu.

"Corporal Williams, take your men and move up forty yards in front of our lines…be on the lookout for German patrols," Colonel Hayward ordered.

Noah and his depleted squad crawled forward just as dusk was dipping the sun to the west. It cast a burnt orange glow and the feint outline of a quarter moon began to be visible in the nearby sky. The men hadn't gone more than half the intended distance when they encountered a German patrol in front of them. Two dozen well-armed Krauts were arrayed in front of them. Everyone began firing at once and screams attacked the early evening's quiet as Noah's men struggled to battle their way to survival. Within ten minutes both groups had withered to a smaller number of men, vicious and determined to kill the last of their enemy.

"I'm out of ammunition," Henry Johnson shouted.

"Me, too," Private Needham Roberts added, standing next to him.

"We're all low on ammo," Noah hollered. "If we retreat, they'll kill us."

"Then let's attack," Johnson screamed, pulling a large Bolo knife from his pack, and rushing forward.

Noah and his remaining men leapt to their feet and appeared as a wall of dark thunder. They joined Johnson and the eight remaining black soldiers careened forward, screaming epithets and brandishing their weapons as clubs, butt-ends waving over their heads. The Germans froze as one…Black American soldiers, which they'd heard about but never seen, were rushing them like madmen. Moments later, smiles on their faces, Noah's squad surrounded the remaining German soldiers, now disarmed, stunned into inaction by the fierceness of their attackers.

Noah, Johnson and a dozen other Negro soldiers were enjoying their beers at a tavern in a small village near Champagne. The entire 369th had been pulled back for a rest and to await replacement troops for the men they'd lost.

"We damn well deserve this," one of the men observed in a distinctive southern accent.

Noah, now a Sergeant, nodded. Henry Johnson and the entire Regiment were going to be awarded the French Croix de Guerre for exceptional bravery but it was sitting with friends enjoying a cold beer and ogling the cute barmaids…that was even more satisfying.

Across the room were several tables filled with French and American soldiers watching them…not smiling.

The men from recently promoted Major George Patton's Tank Brigades and support troops had also been given a brief respite from the frontlines...their first in nearly two months.

Le Coupe Shoe wasn't the only café in the Village but the family who owned it had three young daughters, and their girlfriends, to serve the visiting soldiers. None of them knew more than a few words of English but their French accents, their smiles, and their peasant blouses were enough to command the attention of all the males present, most of whom hadn't seen a comely woman in months.

Noah sat quietly, deep in his own thoughts, as Pinkham, a young private, dark as a moonless night, cozied up to Louisa. one of the French girls. Her father, standing nearby, wiping a glass with a questionably clean towel, just smiled. The Negro Private put his arm around her. She offered no objection but when she responded gaily to a small kiss he put on her lips as he held her chin in his hand, it was more than a few of the white soldiers watching them could tolerate.

"Get your hands off that white girl, nigger," a blonde skinny soldier shouted from across the room as he stood, fury in his eyes, threats in his voice. The crosscurrents of conversation in the cafe stopped instantly and eyes followed the invisible daggers between the blonde soldier and Pinkham, his arm still around the girl.

Pinkham ignored the taunt and continued to lavish his attention on Louisa. She was the first girl he'd spoken to since he'd left Chicago nearly six months earlier.

Chairs scraped against the floor as three men stood in unison from the back of the room and moved forward toward the bar. Time seemed to stop and an electric charge filled the room. Wordlessly the crowd divided itself into three segments, the watchers who stood off to the side, the Negros, now in a line along the bar, and Patton's white tank soldiers, their eyes glaring at the affront of these coloreds. This type of 'nigger' flirtation with a white girl certainly wouldn't be tolerated anywhere in the South. A good lynching of one of these blacks would have put them all in their place.

As Noah stood to join his men the white soldiers took a step back. It was one thing to mix it up with a skinny kid like Pinkham but this man with three stripes on his arm was the size of Mobile, Alabama.

"You men need to control yourselves," Noah said in a soft but commanding voice. "Private Pinkham, please let the young lady return to her serving duties."

"It's too late, Sergeant whoever-you-are. No nigger is going to take liberties with a white girl while we stand idle…and, if I can count, we outnumber you." The white private with a tank emblem on his arm had become his group's spokesman.

"That's what the Germans thought," Henry Johnson said, pushing himself forward. "And they looked a lot tougher than you."

"Noah…is that you?" a voice rang out from the back of the room, hidden by the row of combative white soldiers who stood ready to pounce. Someone had already run to get the MP's before a melee landed both groups in the brig.

Both groups stopped as a tall white Sergeant pushed himself through the cordon arrayed in front of him.

"Of course it's you," Thaddeus said, laughing at seeing his cousin in front of him, thousands of miles from where they'd last seen one another.

"Thaddeus," Noah laughed, coming forward and grasping him in a bear hug.

Whites and Blacks stared in anger and in disbelief and the issue of Private Pinkham and Louisa faded to irrelevance.

"You know this nigger, Sergeant?" one of Thaddeus' squad asked.

"I do and I don't think you want to tangle with him. Barkeep," he smiled, "Beer and Wine for everyone…Noah and I will figure out who's paying."

Johnson, Roberts, Pinkham and the rest of the black soldiers continued to stare as their Squad leader and this white Sergeant sat at a separate table laughing and smiling. The angry white tank soldiers were confused as well but they retreated from their ready-to-fight stance and returned to nursing their free beers.

Noah explained his enlistment and his unit's recent experience with a large German patrol.

"Did you see the soldier standing next to me, Henry Johnson? He now has a new nickname, 'Black Death.' His bolo knife was a mean weapon against that patrol. He's being awarded a special medal. He was a Red-cap until the war, peaceful as all get-out. You never know, do you?"

"Combat seems to bring out the best and the worst. At least Terry's safe. I don't think his wound is permanent. I'm sure his folks are glad to have him home. You know we barely averted a major scuffle, something neither of us needed."

"I find it amazing how little the French care about skin color and how easily it can inflame ignorant southern 'crackers.'

There was a sudden burst of shouting from just outside the café and, as one, Thaddeus and Noah stood and rushed outside. The white soldiers had waited for Pinkham and his buddies to leave and fists were flying everywhere. Noah and Thaddeus forced themselves into the pile of arms flailing in all directions, the glint from knife blades reflecting off lights from the Café.

"Break it up!" Thaddeus demanded, as Noah picked up men like kindling and hurled them away from the brawl. Whistles in the distance indicated that the Military Police were on their way.

Several of the men broke away before the MP's arrived but in the end, Johnson, Pinkham, and Noah were put into one van while Thaddeus and three of Patton's tank infantry were pushed into a second van.

The following morning Noah and Thaddeus were marched, separately, into a large conference room. Sitting there in a single row, were the serious faces of the Commandant of the make-shift Army base, Colonel Patton's Adjutant, Captain Upshaw, Thaddeus' Commanding Officer and Colonel Hayward, Commanding Officer of the Negro 369th Regiment.

The two young soldiers, standing side by side at attention, managed to look at one another and wink. What had happened wasn't funny and they knew it. The Army was always worried about racial strife. There had been plenty of incidents through the years and, now that blacks had been given guns, many whites feared even further violence.

"Stand at ease, men," the military police Commandant ordered. As senior officer present, he would preside over this hastily called panel.

"You men both have exemplary records and from the reports we've received you know one another and tried to stop this brawl; is that true?"

"The men had just returned from some pretty intense action, sir. They were just letting off a little steam," Thaddeus responded.

"Is that how you see it Sergeant Williams?"

"Yes, sir," Noah said, his voice firm, his eyes forward.

The officers all looked at one another, hoping that their men's simple explanation would put this embarrassment to rest.

"How do you men know one another?" the Commandment continued.

"Our paths crossed at one point or another, probably when we were living in Louisiana," Noah lied, uneasily.

"I see. Is that all of it, Sergeant Carmody?"

Colonel Simmons, the Commandant, was from Florida but he'd been posted to New Orleans. Something instinctively itched at his skin. This Sergeant's skin color wasn't just tanned, it was something else.

Thaddeus felt Simmons staring at him and, besides, he was tired of shading the truth.

"No, sir! Sergeant Williams and I are cousins. Our fathers were half-brothers. They shared the same father, the man I'm proud to be named after."

The soldier, who had escorted Thaddeus and Noah into the room, and had remained, standing guard at the door, dropped his rifle. Every eye turned and then turned back in stunned silence.

"I'm sorry, Sergeant Carmody. You are a decorated member of Colonel Patton's tank corps. That is a white unit, is it not?"

"Yes, sir."

"But you are standing here telling us, I believe, that you are not entirely Caucasian. I mean, you aren't 100% white."

"Yes, sir. I mean, no sir. I am not 100% white."

"You men are dismissed. We will reconvene in two hours to consider this new development. Guard, take these men back to the holding area?

"Which one, sir? The white one or the black one?"

"I don't give a shit. Just get them out of here and someone get me some aspirin."

Noah turned and whispered, "Why did you have to say anything? I'd have covered for you."

Thaddeus just smiled as the Guard led them to a common holding cell.

"Damnedest thing I've ever heard," he said as he exited, locking the door behind him. "But I'll see you get some decent food. I want to see how this all turns out."

The faces of all the officers were stern as the two young men were returned to the Conference room two hours later. It was impossible to tell what had been decided.

"Sergeant Williams, all accounts against you have been dropped. We have decided that you were simply trying to break up the fight. All the men involved from both units have been confined to their quarters for a month and, where possible, they will be reduced one rank. You may go, you are dismissed."

"May I speak, sir?"

"Go ahead, but make it brief. We have a war to fight."

"Sergeant Carmody was the one who stopped the fight inside the bar. Had it not been for him there would have been more violence and considerable property damage. I believe he should be exonerated as well, **SIR**," he emphasized.

The final 'sir' brought a smile to Colonel Hayward's face. He was proud of his Negro regiment and this man in front of him demonstrated both their honor and their hope of achieving parity between the races.

"Thank you, Sergeant, but Sergeant Carmody isn't in trouble because of fighting. Please take a seat. You can remain, if you like.

"Sergeant Carmody!" he continued. "I tell you in all candor that we are perplexed on how to deal with you. You have demonstrated your bravery and your leadership ability but you lied to the U.S. Army and that cannot be condoned."

"I'm sorry, sir, but I never lied. No one ever asked me anything."

"Yes, yes, but you lied by omission. You understood whites and blacks were not allowed to serve together in our Army.

"We've decided that a public court martial is not in the Army's best interest. We don't want anything leaking to the press that we had a Negro hero leading white troops into battle. You will be immediately transferred to the 369th Regiment and stripped of your rank. This meeting is dismissed."

Upshaw and the others left without a glance. An official reprimand would be placed in his military file for failing to recognize that he had a soldier of mixed race serving in his unit. Further it was suggested most strongly that he was not to consider commending that soldier for the heroic action he'd displayed.

The room was empty and most of the heated air had gone with it. Noah just nodded his head and smiled. Colonel Hayward had remained and extended his hand to the latest addition to the 369th.

"Welcome, Private Carmody. Sergeant Williams will show you around. We depart in three days for an area near the Argonne forest."

Chapter Thirty-Four

It started as a short, single column story in Stephen's L.A. Sentinel under the headline: "Negro soldier decorated for bravery while leading white soldiers into battle."

Within weeks the story was picked up and reprinted by the majority of the black newspapers around the country. The white-owned newspapers, under pressure from the government and military officials, refused to reprint the story until the British tabloids got wind of it, to the enjoyment of the British public, and the chagrin of the U.S. Army, particularly General Pershing.

"Who is Thaddeus Carmody?" the General shouted.

"Just a simple doughboy that went through Basic Training as a white soldier…he's very light complexioned. He performed well in battle and everything was fine until a racial incident arose at a café in France where white and black soldiers were relaxing."

"I knew putting Negroes into American uniforms would explode in our faces, damn it."

"Sir, he'll be a brief hero to the Black community when this is all over but for now I suggest we let it die down. He's been reassigned to the 369th Black combat regiment we were forced to organize. By the time the war is over this'll all be forgotten. I think we need to be worried more about this flu illness that seems to be spreading. More than two hundred of our trainees at Fort Riley, Kansas have taken ill and the Italian divisions are being depleted by their soldiers dying from this damn thing, whatever it is."

"Maria, did you see this article in the newspaper?" Our Thaddeus has become a beacon of bravery, it seems," Robert laughed, his shoes off, his feet on the table in front of him.

"It seems that Stephen's newspaper in Los Angeles was the first paper to release the story. Other Negro papers picked it up and now blacks and coloreds all over the country are full of pride. They always knew they could fight as well as any white soldiers. Now one of their own has proven it."

The next morning Robert discussed the article with his boss. Should their encouragement to young black men include this revelation? Would it encourage other colored men to try and pass? They agreed that Robert would discuss the matter with Stephen, who had started the entire fracas. Meanwhile he was looking forward to having Terry over for dinner.

Thaddeus' returned to his barracks to get his things. The other men, with whom he'd served, stood, stopped what they'd been doing and stared. A few voiced slurs under their breath. One, the southerner who had launched the initial tirade against Pinkham, made certain Thaddeus heard him.

"I always knew there was a stench in this place. Couldn't place it 'cause I didn't figure white men could smell so putrid."

"Knock it off, Hiram," another man shouted as he walked toward Thaddeus.

"I'm sorry this happened, Sergeant…sorry about losing those stripes. You were a good squad leader and you don't deserve this treatment."

"Thanks, Paul. I'll be fine but…" he turned to the men watching him. "You are a great bunch of guys and I was proud to serve with you."

With the exception of Hiram and three others, they all came over and shook Thaddeus' hand.

"Welcome to the Harlem Hellfighters," Noah said, his arm around Thaddeus as he walked his cousin through his new assignment, introducing him to the members of the squad on whom he'd be depending.

"Stephen," Robert said, his voice raised, phoning his cousin three thousand miles across the country. "Terry never arrived. We expected him on the late train from Grand Central Station. We waited for that train and the next but no Terry. Maria and I wondered if he'd contacted you."

"We haven't heard from him. Maybe he met a girl. If I hear anything I'll phone you. Until then all we can do is wait."

Three days later Stephen and April got a very different long-distance telephone call. It was from a hospital in Maryland. The Administrators there had finally gotten the information on Private Terry Donovan's next of kin from his military records. As best they could reconstruct what happened, Terry had been with a girl in New York who was already contagious with the Spanish flu and he contracted it. On the train to Washington his fever must have spiked. In Baltimore the Conductor summoned an ambulance and Terry was taken to the hospital. Two days later he died.

Their son was dead. He had survived the war but now he was gone. April had to be sedated. Stephen made arrangements for Robert to retrieve his son's body and make the necessary funeral arrangements. It would take some days for them to travel from Los Angeles but they would do so as quickly as possible. Meanwhile they prayed that their other son would be safe.

The 369th moved up toward the Dormoise River facing well-entrenched German Infantry. The French artillery supporting them was forced to stop frequently to prod their teams of horses to pull the field pieces forward over wet, sticky land, rutted from exploded artillery shells and shredded barbed wire. Bodies from the American 1st Battalion lay strewn around them, dead from enemy fire. It was a chilling sight, crawling through the mud, suddenly touching the extended arm or leg of another soldier who had tried the same approach hours earlier.

Noah's squad was facing steady machine gun bursts coming at them. He had already lost two men. Thaddeus blended in easily with the men in his new unit. At first they were insulted that this man had preferred to pass himself off as white...then they were curious. Within days, however, Thaddeus had fielded their questions, it was all forgotten, and his experience in combat was all that remained. Everyone was happy to have another solid soldier in their squad.

The small hamlet of Sechault lay ahead. The previous two days another black regiment had tried unsuccessfully to take the village. The overwhelming German forces had thrown them back in disarray, scattering the black troops among the French units who had been fighting alongside. Now it would be up to Noah and Thaddeus and the rest of the 369th Hellfighters.

Soldiers from Company D cleared a German machine gun nest hidden in a brick farmhouse as Company C, which included Noah's squad, attempted to cross the Ripont swamp as bullets crackled against the water, setting up small eddies. Fighting was fierce and screams came from all sides intermingled with machine gun fire, shouts and the sounds of artillery. It was an amalgam of terror that lasted three days.

Four more of Noah's squad had died. One, a young boy just turned nineteen from Athens, Georgia, was killed by a grenade that exploded at his feet. The other three survived the fighting only to come down with fevers. Before the doctors understood what ailed them, they were dead, lesions pock marking their bodies, high fevers and chills destroying their immune systems. Being Negro, they had been put into separate hospital tents. The Army was very diligent about keeping their black and white soldiers apart. The three men had died from the ever-increasing epidemic of Spanish flu. The close living conditions, and less than sanitary environment, made it ripe for the spread of the disease. The American medical staff was overwhelmed. French doctors and nurses were brought in to help.

She was sitting on a bench when he noticed her. He could see how exhausted she was. She had taken off her shoes and was alternately rubbing her feet and sipping a cup of tea.

Thaddeus watched for several minutes before getting up enough nerve to join her.

"I've brought you a fresh cup of tea," he said. "You don't look as if that one you've been sipping did the trick."

"Merci," she responded, looking up and seeing a tall, well-tanned, American soldier with the most startling blue eyes.

"My name is Thaddeus, Private Thaddeus Carmody, at your service. May I join you?"

She smiled, and he took that as acceptance.

"I'm afraid I don't speak French," he said, sitting quickly and removing his cap. This girl had dark shiny hair that formed a page boy just above the collar of her nurse's uniform. A few dimples rested charmingly on her high cheekbones, and her almost purple eyes set off sparks inside him. There was a familiarity he didn't understand. It was almost as if they had known one another in a prior life.

"I speak only a little English. My name is Amelia Girard. You are here because you are ill or you are visiting comrades?"

"Some of our squad isn't doing well. Their injuries are quite serious. I thought I'd come by and cheer them up. They're over there in the third tent."

"But that is a tent for your colored soldiers."

"Yes! We're all part of the Army's 369th Regiment. We just returned from the front."

"You are colored? You don't look colored."

"Does that bother you?" he asked, sadness apparent in his voice and in the dejected look on his face.

She paused before answering. She had never felt so immediately connected to a man before. She had never actually conversed with a colored person. There were several black and Indian girls in her nursing classes but this was different and she was having trouble catching her breath at her reaction to him.

"I don't think so," she said, trying to process the idea.

"My mother was Cuban; my father was half and half, black and white, so I guess I'm just a hybrid."

She laughed, and the lilt of her words lit up her entire being. Her exhaustion from having tended sick and wounded casualties for fourteen straight hours seemed to lift.

"You are like a soup of many flavors…a little bit of this and a little bit of that."

"And you? Tell me about you?"

"I am from Marseilles. The Girard family has lived there as long as I can remember. My father is a fisherman. His father was a fisherman and his father before him. My two younger brothers will probably become fisherman when they are old enough. Our house smells of fish all the time. I hate fish…the smell, the taste. Poisson is poison to me. I am sorry, it's a little joke. I'm not very good at jokes.

"Anyway, I left Marseilles, came to Paris, and went to school to become a nurse. And now I am tired of the war, I am tired of the Germans, and the noise, and the Generals who argue while young men die, or sometimes worse, spend the rest of their days in pain and suffering."

"Will you have dinner with me?" he asked softly, caught up in her passion and her beauty. "If not tonight, then soon?"

She stared into his eyes and smiled as if she'd made a decision.

"Oui! Tomorrow…this bench, at six."

Thaddeus sat nursing a glass of Bordeaux and watched the women of the village returning home with their baguette and bags of vegetables. There was only another half hour of sunlight. After that the town got dark quickly. He had waited at the agreed upon bench for nearly an hour but Amelia hadn't shown up. He walked to a nearby café where he could continue to see their meeting place across a small ill-kept park. If she didn't show up soon he'd leave. He needed to be back at his base by ten.

"May I join you?" she said, coming up quietly behind him.

He jumped slightly and stood. There she was, smiling. His heart leapt.

"I am sorry I am late." Her French-accented English was a lilt, but then everything about her was a musical banquet.

"I thought you'd changed your mind."

"No, we were overwhelmed with more wounded men today, nearly thirty men, some came in on trucks, some by ambulance. Thaddeus, it was terrible to see limbs missing, eyes burned from gas…some so young." Tears filled her eyes, the purple in them shining from emotion.

"Here, sip this wine and try not to think about it."

They finished their wine and strolled slowly around the battered streets of the town holding hands. Neither of them had been hungry for dinner. Amelia took Thaddeus' arm and moved closer. Whether she was frightened or tired or feeling some other emotion, he didn't care. Having her walk so close evoked emotions of caring and protection and…he was afraid to say it, feelings of love. He had never felt love before. Oh, sure, he loved his parents, and he loved the rest of his family, but this was different. He breathed deeply of her being and held her more closely.

"I'm tired of training pilots," David complained to Al. "I want to get back to combat."

The Jenny was a bi-plane that America produced easily and the Signal Corps had ordered thousands. New cadets took readily to its smooth controls.

David had submitted more than ten requests up the chain of command. The first nine had been ignored. By summer, however, he had gotten his wish and returned to the cockpit of a SPAD, now equipped with a larger cannon, bigger engine and stronger wings.

"With this plane we can beat the shit out of the Fokker," he bragged. He knew he'd never catch some guy named Eddie Rickenbacker in confirmed 'kills' but he would definitely get his share. He dreamt of facing Von Richtofen, the infamous Red Baron flying his Fokker triplane. The German ace was credited with shooting down more than eighty allied planes and every good British and French pilot wanted a crack at him but the Baron's luck ran out and he was shot down and killed in April. "I hope he roasted all the way down," one British pilot said seriously.

When Colonel Billy Mitchell was directed to plan a combined air attack near St. Mihiel, David got the assignment he wanted. Planes from France, Britain, and the United States would mount a joint air campaign to drive the Germans from the skies.

September came and the rains held off. Half the planes were assigned to support ground troops and move the battle line to the north and east. David was assigned as a squadron leader of twelve SPADs to take out the German aircraft. For the first time since the war began, allied forces would have better planes and a numeric advantage.

The first day David got on the tail of a German pilot who wasn't paying attention. Several bursts from his gun and the Fokker's attempt at eluding him ended. David followed the plane down as it crashed into a hillside and burst into flames. He also saved one of his men who had somehow found himself fighting two German planes at the same time.

The second day was different. On his third sortie David's guns jammed and he was lucky to elude a Fokker pilot who chased him across the sky, machine gun blazing. David climbed straight up toward the sun in an effort to elude his attacker, hoping that the glare of the sun in his adversary's eyes might make it more difficult to remain a target. At maximum altitude for his SPAD, he turned and dove, eluding his enemy. Two miles out, however, he ran out of fuel and barely glided back to his airfield on a dead engine, his wings peppered with bullet holes.

But the Germans had no intention of ceding control of the air easily. By the end of the second day, as the sun was setting, more than 120 planes were strewn across a hundred miles of countryside and half of them were American, French and British. Outnumbered, the enemy had matched Allied losses evenly.

By the third day all his men were exhausted. He had lost two of them to enemy airplanes and a third to an anti-aircraft artillery burst. But the Germans were tired as well and David heard rumors that the Jerrys were beginning to run short of fuel. They would be unable to fight if they couldn't stay in the air.

> *On the ground more than one hundred thousand German soldiers surrendered and were taken prisoner. Their armies had suffered more than six million casualties and were in retreat across the entire front. August became September and American troops were arriving at the rate of ten thousand a day. Bulgaria surrendered, Austria and Hungary followed. In early November as Allied forces poised for a massive assault on German territory, their people revolted and the Kaiser fled. A new republic was established and Germany sued for peace. The guns became silent. The birds regained control of the air from the metal and wood machines that had driven them away. The war was over. Men left their trenches and stood erect, no longer afraid of being killed by an enemy sharpshooter or suffering the effects*

of poison gas. Soldiers cried and hugged one another unabashedly. Ten million people had died; six million of them civilians.

Two million Americans had been in uniform including 380,000 Negro and Colored soldiers. Of those, nearly 50,000 lost their lives from combat in fierce front-line battles.

Noah, Thaddeus, and all the survivors of the 369th Regiment joined in the jubilation when loud speakers in the camp announced the end of hostilities. Stillness filled the air until church bells rang out a new day.

The 369th's famous band, led by Lt. James Reese Europe, played louder than ever. Black and white soldiers...everyone within earshot, applauded at the jazz marches that were particularly American. They would all be going home soon.

"The war is over, Amelia," Thaddeus said. "Where does that leave us?"

"I always thought I would return to my nursing studies in Paris but since we've been together, my heart and my head do not know what I am supposed to do."

They were together in bed, naked under a thin coverlet. Their bodies were damp, Amelia's dark hair askew on Thaddeus' shoulder.

"I love you, you know."

"I know, and I love you. I have never loved anyone before. It is a new...and frightening, feeling but I don't want to imagine being apart from you even in a small way."

"The Atlantic ocean is a lot more than a small way. We have many decisions to make."

Their conversation ended abruptly as Amelia's hand slid down the blanket and began to caress Thaddeus' thigh gently, her fingers gliding, a silly, loving grin lifting her cheek bones. She giggled and tucked her head under the blanket. Thaddeus' body responded... the muscles in his legs tensed and he got hard.

"You French are insatiable," he groaned.

"Oh, really! And how many French girls have you known?"

"Are we saying all of France or just Paris?" he teased.

She squeezed his testicles gently.

"If it is more than two or three, I will squeeze so there will be no more."

"You win…you win…" he said, smiling, twisting to his side and embracing her tightly. Their kiss was deep, their tongues touched and neither wanted to release the moment. Their lips continued to press as he entered her again. She was still moist from their earlier lovemaking and they became as one, their hearts beating faster in a synchronous rhythm. Being separated was not going to be an option.

> *America breathed a collective sigh of relief…her 'doughboys' would be coming home. The wheels of factories that had produced guns and tanks and uniforms slowed and stopped and began thinking about what peacetime would mean. There were better roads and automobiles and people might want to travel or move. There was a new beat to the music. It was livelier…less structured. Movie theatres were showing people in small towns how others lived.*

Across the country, brisk fall winds were beginning to take the leaves from the trees. But in Los Angeles summer hadn't yet exited. Stephen and April drove downtown to share in the celebration of renaming Central Park for General John 'Black Jack' Pershing, the symbol of America's victorious participation in the war to end all wars. It was November and Stephen's newspaper had used its entire front page to shout 'Armistice' in the largest type font he had. He had even hired a photographer to take pictures of the celebrations around the city.

April promised herself she wouldn't cry. Thaddeus was safe but Terry was gone and not even from a damn German bullet. She watched the American flags flutter in the wind, forty-eight stars and she remembered growing up in Pennsylvania when local flag makers would get a burst of business every time a new state was added. She'd buy her son a small flag and he'd run through their neighborhood with the other boys waving it for everyone to see.

"I'm sorry, April. Maybe we shouldn't have come. Too many memories," Stephen said, putting his arm around this woman he loved so much. "We can go home if you want."

"No. We should be here, for both the boys. There are just so many yesterdays to remember. We've been so lucky. The boys got along so well from the first time they met."

"Thank goodness for flat tires," Stephen laughed, "Or we would have driven right by you. C'mon, I want some cotton candy. Let's get sick in honor of Terry and Thaddeus."

Robert returned to his job at the Library of Congress. The nation's first experiment with daylight saving time was over until next spring. The idea of giving rural and factory America an extra hour of daylight to work and grow crops had been a wartime success but now days were getting shorter.

He was glad to be back in these marble corridors he'd come to know so well. George Putnam, the Library's long-time Director, and scion of New York's publishing house, Putnam and Sons, had been busy securing money from Congress to buy more books and manuscripts and provide more services.

"It's nice to have you back, Robert," Putnam said, extending his hand as they both sat. "We have a number of programs I'd like us to consider now that the war is over. We are still a country suffering from vast racial chasms. You and I will never be able to eliminate them but I want us to continue to gather as much relevant factual material as possible. Black regiments had fought extensively in the war. American Negroes are no longer clustered in the South. Every major city has colored neighborhoods as well as Irish, German, and Jewish clusters. I want our Library to be the repository of everything written about this transition. Can you help me?"

Charlie and Precious Culpepper left Chicago in mid-1917. The meat packing companies in Omaha, Nebraska were offering twice what Charlie earned at the Chicago stockyards. They were actually going to pay him white man's wages. He and Precious would no longer have to suffer the cold blustering winters that blew so harshly off Lake Michigan.

They found friends and family in Omaha as well as black restaurants and shops. There were safe schools for their children. They also found a lot of angry white folks. Their men were on strike for an eight hour day and Omaha's nearly ten thousand colored were glad to get the jobs vacated by the mostly Irish Catholic, German, and Eastern Europeans who had worked there for generations.

Stephen wasn't aware that his old acquaintances had moved but the rumblings of an explosive racial situation unnerved him and he decided to see for himself. He didn't travel as much as he had in the past but all his reporters were on other assignments. When he got off the train in Omaha he felt the anger around him. He wired his first story back to Los Angeles the next day:

> *Edward Cudahy, Jr., only son and heir to the Cudahy Meatpacking Company, nine years old, has been kidnapped. Rumors that he was taken by angry union members out of work for nearly two months has sent the police running amok chasing suspects. Experienced black workers have been imported from Chicago and other cities to run the packing lines...class and racial war is simmering in every café and on every street corner.*

The article got reprinted in the local paper. Precious saw the story and Stephen's byline. She tracked him down and, an evening later, the three of them shared dinner together.

"We should have stayed in Chicago," she said.

"Hard to turn down all that extra money though," Charlie said.

"Is it dangerous, Charlie?" Stephen asked. "I mean, do you have to cross picket lines?"

"Oh, yes. Every morning there are near hundreds of white men brandishing clubs and knives shouting at us...Nigger! Scab! And a lot worse I don't like to repeat in front of my wife. A lot of us have weapons hidden...just in case, but we would sure be outnumbered. Two policemen already killed a black kid working as a bellhop last week, no reason we know of."

Stephen wrote two more articles that week, said his goodbyes and returned to Los Angeles. Nothing in Omaha had been resolved...hatred still simmered.

Noah, Thaddeus, and Amelia sat together in one of the cafés that had survived the war. The proprietor had managed to keep his wine cellar intact from both German and French artillery barrages but he was happy to open bottle after bottle for his guests in uniform, particularly the attractive French nurse who reminded him of his daughter.

"Lieutenant Noah Williams, a Negro officer! I toast you. You certainly deserve it."

"Why is it so unusual?" Amelia asked.

"We don't have many black officers in the American army. Black troops have normally been led by white officers. I guess old habits die hard."

"They sure do. I'm still waiting to get my first salute from a white soldier although I nearly got one from a kid from Minnesota until his buddy, who was from Mississippi, gave him a hard nudge in the ribs. I just ignored it. It was either that or knock their heads together."

"Well, you're certainly big enough," Thaddeus jibed.

"I can see the headlines now, 'Black officer sets off race riot.' Forget it. I'm getting out of this man's army and back to Felicity. I'll marry her if she'll have me."

"If I recall you're three times her size. You'll need to be careful you don't crush her. And, after you get married, Moss Grove… Washington?"

"I don't know. What do you think America will be like, better or worse?"

"I'm not optimistic," Thaddeus said, grasping Amelia's hand. "We don't know what to do either. We just know that we intend to face it together."

February 17, 1919 was a cold, blustery day in New York City. The wind whipped through the canyons of buildings but along 5th Avenue crowds, wearing heavy coats, scarves, and gloves… and mostly black and colored, cheered. Their Negro divisions, including the 369th Regiment, were being honored. As their band led the procession, Lt. Noah Williams, Sgt. Thaddeus Carmody, and thousands of others marched sprightly, grinning from ear to ear. Flags waved. W.E.B Du Bois cried. Robert and Maria clapped and pumped their fists as they stood next to Stephen and April. Samantha had reluctantly remained at Moss Grove. She had hoped that David would have returned and together they could bring young Stuart to share in the celebration but her pilot husband was still in France. Amelia was also in France, awaiting a visa.

It was a grand event. The men marched from midtown Manhattan to Harlem. Thousands followed and the music grew in volume every mile, from marches to jazz riffs, glad to be home, proud that they had proven something to themselves and, hopefully, the nation.

That evening they dined at a newly opened restaurant in Harlem, Dixie's Ribs. It was packed, standing room only, but when Dixie Cummings, the owner, saw two soldiers, one black and one she wasn't sure of, standing there, she sat them down at the first open table and announced their dinner would be on the house.

"We have two soldiers, here," she shouted over the din of the restaurant.

"I'm buyin' dinner for them all…who's going to buy them drinks?"

The entire crowd volunteered and enthusiastic men and women came over and shook their hands. Thaddeus and Noah were asked to stand and address the diners. Reluctantly, they stood and smiled at one another.

"A toast to the men of the 369th Harlem Hellfighters," Noah shouted, "Heroes one and all."

"You know, Dad," Thaddeus said, talking softly, "The French wouldn't let us march in their victory parade in Paris. We were pretty sure they were pressured by Pershing's people. Keep the story of blacks in battle on the back page."

"I'll make sure it's on the front page, I promise you that."

Chapter Thirty-Five

1919 should have been a year of optimism in the United States. Pershing's boys had done America proud. In September nearly 100,000 New Yorkers lined the streets from 107th Street to Greenwich Village to cheer 25,000 members of the 1st Division, bedecked in their military uniforms, trench helmets, and carrying full packs.

The bands and parades were unable to disguise more fundamental problems. The Spanish flu was continuing to devastate families from New York to California. Food prices had more than doubled since the war had begun. Labor strikes continued to cripple industries as Unions gained membership and managers were finding it more difficult to act unilaterally.

In Omaha, a twenty-three year old black man, named Will Brown, was accused of raping nineteen year old Agnes Loebeck. Every hatred, latent and overt, gushed forth. 'Niggers have taken white jobs at Cudahy and now they are raping our women' was shouted in newspaper headlines of the *Omaha Bee* and repeated on those new fangled crystal sets people liked to listen to.

Days later, an angry white crowd of thousands vented their anger in front of the police station where Mr. Brown was being held. Within hours the building was overrun, guns were wrested, nearby local businesses were pillaged, and the city exploded. Pandemonium spread. The mob took more than one thousand guns from the police lockers …they were intent on vengeance. The courthouse was set on fire. The mayor of the city was hanged, suspended from the arm of a traffic signal before being cut down. He barely survived. Sixteen hundred soldiers were necessary to quell the riot. Much of their blood lust wasn't satisfied until Will Brown was lynched.

Before the year ended, Clarence Culpepper was killed coming home from his job at Cudahy. Union strikers were suspected but no one was prosecuted. Precious was broken-hearted. She returned to Chicago and moved in with her sister. The light that had been her life was snuffed out and she spent the rest of her days sitting in a chair, gazing out through a dirty window pane, hoping for the day she would join the husband she had shared nearly a half-century with…the only man she had ever loved.

Christmas at Moss Grove would be special. David had finally returned. He had made a down payment on a Jenny with his separation money and flown it from New York to a small field north of Baton Rouge. After a very brief reunion with his parents, he'd borrowed a car and surprised Samantha. They fell into one another's arms. Sam was unable to stop the flow of tears at being held in her husband's arms. She'd had to be strong for so long. She wanted to stop being the responsible one. Thank God David was home and safe. She and David could finally work together, raising Stuart, managing Moss Grove, and just plain loving one another.

They watched Stuart playing with other children. His son had grown so tall in his absence.

"Stuart, come here," his mother shouted. "I have a surprise for you."

The little boy looked up and slowly walked over, not quite sure who the tall man was standing next to his mother.

David bent down so that he and his son were eye-to-eye.

"You probably don't know who I am. I'm your father," he said softly.

"I know," the little boy said. "Mommy showed me your picture. Did you bring me an airplane?"

"I did, a small model just like the one I flew. And, if you want, we can go flying. Would you like that?"

He scooped up the toddler and tears welled up in his eyes. God, it was good to be home.

Amelia's ship docked in New York harbor after a ten day voyage from Le Havre. As she walked down to the dock, nervous and uncertain, into a noisy crowd, she saw Thaddeus waiting for her, an enormous bouquet of gardenias in his arms and her nervousness disappeared. She laughed and threw herself into his arms, the flowers forgotten. Their embrace spoke volumes. Throngs pushed and shoved around them, but they were alone, each certain that they would be safe as long as they held one another.

Thaddeus had arranged rooms at a lavish mid-town hotel. They didn't leave the bed until late afternoon the next day. Their love, their emotions, and their desire coalesced. They were one another's yin and yang, wordlessly getting to know one another's pleasure before exhaustion set in and they suddenly realized how hungry they were.

For the next few days they enjoyed the sights and smells of New York before taking a train from Grand Central for their trip to Louisiana.

"Your country is so big," Amelia said, her nose pressed against the glass of the moving train.

"Does anyone call you Amy?" Thaddeus asked casually, his hand stroking his love's dark hair.

"Oui, my brother. He was always too lazy to say Amelia so he shortened it."

"Did I meet him?"

"No, he was killed early in the war. Both of my brothers were killed. My parents were devastated. My father was sure my brothers would join him as fishermen even though they'd secretly told me that going to war was the best chance they'd ever have to get away from Marseilles."

Thaddeus grew silent and seemed to drift into the past, into stories he'd been told but never really connected to himself. Amelia felt the ambience of their compartment change. She looked at this man she loved, came away from the window and settled herself into the crook of his arm. She loved to hear him speak.

"My grandfather was also named Thaddeus. I was named after him and I inherited my blue eyes from him. The woman he loved all his life," he continued, "my birth mother, was white. They only shared one weekend together, away from public scrutiny, but she had gotten pregnant. Since he was mulatto, close friends convinced her to keep the birth a secret. My father was never told the woman he loved was going to have his child. He was raised by those friends until they were murdered by the Klan.

"My grandmother's name was Amy. It is a little unsettling to realize that we will be married at Moss Grove, sharing the same names, at the same site, where they fell in love. I certainly hope the country is a little more inclined to accept our racial blending than when my grandparents loved one another."

"I am certain that we have their love watching over us."

"I love you my Amelia…my Amy," he said, laughing, pulling her down into the covers, burying his head in her breasts, his hand moving between her legs as the train clacked against the metal tracks.

Noah traveled directly to Moss Grove once he was released from active duty. His superiors energetically tried to convince him that being one of only a few Negro officers in the U.S. Army meant he had a special responsibility. He avoided giving them a direct answer. He and Felicity would need to discuss their future and the only thing on his mind at the moment was holding her.

She met him at the train station in Baton Rouge. Her eyes were damp with tears of joy and once his huge arms enveloped her, it was the present that mattered. Discussions of their future could wait for another day.

Samantha convinced both couples that a double holiday wedding at the plantation would be magic. David laughed every time he heard her rehearse her arguments but it hadn't taken a great deal of effort. Stuart had warned him the first time they'd met that Fineman women were headstrong; he'd never won an argument with Bess, Samantha's mother and David should be prepared for Sam being a similar whirlwind.

Thaddeus and Noah accepted instantly. Stephen and April were now on their way from California and Robert and Maria were on the train from Washington. The extended family would be together for the first time in years. The end of that terrible war in Europe would be another reason to celebrate.

Winter had arrived. Smoke from each shareholder's cabin wafted through the chilled air and blended with the heavy smells of maple and oak coming from the smoke house. It had been a good year for cotton. The crop was sizeable and the entire harvest had been sold early. Prices began to drop once the war ended in anticipation of a decline in a need for uniforms and bedding. Meanwhile a new energy began to pervade the main house. Family and servants all walked with a lighter step, dusting, cooking, and decorating the house for the holidays. The children ran through the house, up the stairs, hiding in closets. Anna hid and Stuart screamed, trying to find her. Felicity's younger sister, Mabel, tried to keep up with them but it was an endless task.

Samuel returned from New Orleans. He found himself increasingly restless, his hands shaking, his eyes bloodshot, his emotions a cauldron of nerves. He was sleeping less than two to three hours a night, and then only with the help of a couple shots of bourbon. He had brought such misfortune to so many people… everyone he'd ever loved was gone and he was certain that if he continued to raise Anna, he'd eventually bring her unhappiness as well.

He loved his daughter. She was so much like her mother… tender and considerate. But she would be happier at Moss Grove with the family. It was impossible to have a little girl share his fucked-up emotions and Moss Grove would never be his heritage. That plantation had belonged to his father, and his grandfather, but the world had moved forward. Cotton, gin mills, and sharecroppers meant nothing to him. He needed to feel the cold emotionless touch of a trumpet's mouthpiece on his lips. He needed to force the instrument to bend to his will, as he caressed the keys, and his tongue blew musical kisses. It was love, and with his Anna gone, the trumpet was his only mistress. Anna needed much more than a trumpet player could provide, and so he said goodbye and returned to the brothels and night clubs of New Orleans. Jazz was the new vernacular and he had learned to speak it as well as anyone.

The day of the wedding began with a light winds blowing a damp mist off the Mississippi, threatening the day. Cumulus clouds gathered overhead. By eleven, however, the weather began to improve and a warm sun promised the newlyweds a blessed day. The original plan had been to have two ministers, one black to sanctify Noah and Felicity's vows and a white minister to make Amelia more comfortable. It wasn't necessary. Both couples were thrilled that an old friend would perform the ceremony. Reverend Jesse Dinsmore had driven up from New Orleans. His father had presided at the weddings of both Thaddeus and his brother, Matthew. The son had followed in his father's footsteps.

Stuart, wearing a rare pair of long pants, the slightly older Anna on his arm, walked down a makeshift aisle strewn with rose petals. Felicity came down on the arm of her father, nattily attired in one of Stuart's old suits and smiling at the elegance he and his wife were sharing. He thought his life had been blessed when Mr. Lincoln freed the slaves. He and his wife never dreamed their daughter would one day be wed in a grand home he'd never been allowed to enter, except once through the cellar door.

Amelia came next, holding on tightly to David's arm, as Thaddeus and Noah stood side by side, next to the minister, smiling.

"Dearly beloved," Reverend Dinsmore began. His words were nearly lost in the auras that surrounded the young couples.

"We are doubly blessed today. Two young men, back from a terrible war, fought far away, are back on American soil. One, to marry the young lady who has waited patiently for him. The other to marry a special young lady from France. They will be starting new lives together, looking forward to their futures with optimism and promise…leaving the evils of the past behind them. In a few short days we will enter a new decade, filled with the promise of peace and, perhaps, a new tolerance."

The celebration continued late into the evening, each couple receiving good wishes for their new beginning. Thaddeus took Amelia's hand and they walked away from the music and partying. They could hear the sounds of the evening as they moved further away from the house, closer to the river. The owls hooted their plaintive dirge, the cicadas blending in, the splashing of the river against the sand banks providing the percussion, punctuated by the croaking of a lovesick toad.

"I need you to see this," Thaddeus said softly, careful not to disturb the sounds around him. A bare sliver of a moon resting lazily on the horizon gave them enough illumination to mark their way.

Rays of the moonlight shined on two headstones, now weathered by decades. Amy Shipley *nee* Williams and Thaddeus Carmody Williams lay next to one another in the shade of an old magnolia tree, along the banks of the Mississippi River. Each headstone bore the same inscription...'Their Stars Were Now Aligned.'

"My grandparents...Thaddeus and Amy."

"It will be easier for us," Amelia said. "We will make it work."

Epilogue

I've been growing cotton on my land more than a hundred years for lotsa' good families and a few that weren't so good. Early folks planted trees, some oak, and some magnolia for shade, and rose bushes to pretty me up. They gave me a name, Moss Grove, and I'd like to think I gave them fair reward for treating me with such respect.

I've watched children born and old folks die. I've seen war that's scarred my ground and blood run into my soil. I've watched the Mississippi River rise and fall and cotton bolls burst from the richness of my brown earth. But most of all, I've watched the smiles and tears of white folks and black folks struggling to understand one another.

Some of those early trees have died. It's the cycle of life, I guess. But one thing's for certain. Those cotton bolls will pop open next summer, and that one magnolia tree that shades the headstones of that white girl and that colored boy who loved one another so much will still be my special place.

Acknowledgements

Winds of Change is my third novel and writing has become a major occupation late in life. It could not have been accomplished without sincere support from friends. I want to especially thank Barbara Kosoff for her cover design, Jon Jackson for his computer acumen, and Linda Martin, Lauren Silinsky, and Barb Arsenault for their thorough editing. A special thanks belongs to John Paul Owles, Joshua Tree Publishing and the entire staff of Valley Village Publishing for their 'hand-holding' throughout the entire publication process.

About the Author

Carole Eglash-Kosoff lives and writes in Valley Village, California. She graduated from UCLA and spent her career in business, teaching, and traveling. She has visited more than seventy countries. An avid student of history, she researched the decades preceding and following the Civil War for nearly two years, including time in Louisiana, the setting for her first historic fiction novel, *When Stars Align*, which has received 5 Star reviews. It is a story of bi-racial love set against war, reconstruction, and racism. Most of all it is a story of hope.

In 2006, following the death of her husband, she volunteered to teach in the black townships of South Africa. Her first book, *The Human Spirit – Apartheid's Unheralded Heroes,* relates the stories of an amazing array of men and women she worked with, people who have devoted their lives during the worst years of apartheid to help the children, the elderly, and the disabled of the townships. These people cared when no one else did and their efforts continue to this day.

She has also established …a better way…a program that offers financial scholarships and mentoring to qualifying high school graduates to assist them during their first and second years of college.

Other books by Carole Eglash-Kosoff:

WHEN STARS ALIGN

ISBN-10: 1456738909
ISBN-13: 978-1456738907
412 Pages 6" x 9"

Also Available: Hard Cover & Kindle

More information is available at:
whenstarsalign-thebook.com

*I am emailing to tell you how much I enjoyed your book, Moss Grove (**When Stars Align**). Somehow the book landed on my desk and I decided it was fate telling me that I should read it. I'm glad I did. The characters were so well developed, the story compelling, and your writing style had me turning page after page. Congratulations on a fabulous book.* **Lonnie Quinn, CBS Television, New York**

***WHEN STARS ALIGN** is beautiful. I felt like I was right there with the people—the rich characters. I could see them, feel the depths of their feelings and appreciate their circumstances. The story flowed and carried my spirit with it, often shaking me to the core. I loved the narrative and voice of the author. The historical references were educational and put everything into context. Addressing such unfortunate hatred, bigotry and man's inhumanity-to-man is courageous. Balancing those atrocities with stories of kindness, humanity, love, unity, family, cooperation, beauty, and mutual respect is genius. I hope there will be a sequel.*
Victoria Dahan, Spain & California

This is an incredibly well written book...a remarkable job capturing universal human emotions and frailties...The dialogue is simply smashing. The characters are realistic and resonate on a soulfully deep level.

June 2011 selection, Pacific Book Review

Synopsis

The love that Thaddeus and Amy feel for one another can get them both killed. He is colored, an ex-slave, and she is white. In 19th century Louisiana mixed race relationships are both illegal and unacceptable.

Moss Grove, a large Mississippi River cotton plantation has thrived from the use of slave labor while its owners lived lives of comfort and privilege. Thaddeus, born more than a decade earlier from the rape of a young field slave by the heir to the plantation, is raised as a Moss Grove house servant. His presence remains a thorn in the side of the man who sired him.

Deepening divisiveness between North and South launches the Civil War and changes Moss Grove in ways no one could have anticipated. With the war swirling we see the battles and carnage through Thaddeus' eyes. The war ends and he returns to Moss Grove and to Amy, hoping to enjoy their newly won freedoms. With the help of Union soldiers, schools are established to educate those who were formerly prohibited from learning to read. Medical clinics are opened and businesses begun. Black legislators are elected and help to pass new laws. Hope flourishes. Perhaps the stars will now finally align for the young lovers.

In 1876, however, the ex-Confederate states barter the selection of President Rutherford B. Hayes for removal of all Union troops from their soil in the most contested election in American history. Within a decade hopes are dashed as Jim Crow laws are passed, the Ku Klux Klan launches new violence, and black progress is crushed.

When Stars Align is a soaring novel of memorable white, Negro, and colored men and women set against actual historic events.

Other books by Carole Eglash-Kosoff:

THE HUMAN SPIRIT
– Apartheid's Unheralded Heroes

ISBN-10: 1452033064
ISBN-13: 978-1452033068

240 Pages 6" x 9"

More information is available at:
thehumanspirit-thebook.com

Reader Comments about **The Human Spirit:**

The more I read, the more I enjoyed it. Helen Lieberman is truly a credit to humanity—if the world had more like her, what a wonderful world it would be! I am now looking forward to reading about the Hayes-Tilden times. Merci pour tout.

Dennis Hill, attorney, Encino, California

Dearest Friend...came home last night after a trying trip to Cape Town and to my surprise I saw a package on our dining room table...from the USA and hastily I opened and WOW!!!!! your book and the cherry on the top is that I am featured in your book.... I am stunned and have no words to express my appreciation and gratitude towards you... i started early morning to read and I am really fascinated by your amazing work...you have outdone yourself and did an absolute great work...i enjoy the book tremendously this far and cannot wait to start read and learn about this amazing people you write about. Thabiso is in Heaven and cannot stop talking about your magnificent writing skill and great humanitarian works...

From your St. Helena Bay Family

Johan and Team

Synopsis

Apartheid in South Africa has now been gone more than fifteen years but the heroes of their struggle to achieve a Black majority-run democracy are still being revealed. Some individuals toiled publicly, but most worked tirelessly in the shadows to improve the welfare of the Black and Coloured populations that had been so neglected. Nelson Mandela was still in prison; clean water and sanitation barely existed; AIDS was beginning to orphan an entire generation.

Meanwhile a white, Jewish, middle class woman, joined with Tutu, Millie, Ivy, Zora and other concerned Black women, respectfully called Mamas, to help those most in need, often being beaten and arrested by white security police.

This book tells the story of these women and others who have spent their adult lives making South Africa a better place for those who were the country's most disadvantaged.

www.ingramcontent.com/pod-product-compliance
Lightning Source LLC
Chambersburg PA
CBHW030537260626
47157CB00006B/2074